THIS DREAMER

THIS DREAMER

The Chronicles of the Marked | Book One

Sara Watterson

This Dreamer

The Chronicles of the Marked | Book One

Paperback
ISBN: 979-8-9857474-1-6

Ebook
ISBN: 979-8-9857474-0-9

Hardback
ISBN: 979-8-9857474-2-3

Published by Inevah Press
Edmond, Oklahoma
www.inevahpress.com

Library of Congress Control Number: 2022903305

For my daughter Lena

The letter in Chapter 48 is for you.

Part I

*I was looking in the visions of my mind
as I lay on my bed, and behold, a watcher,
a messenger, came down…*

Daniel 4:13

1

What a strange feeling, being miraculously knit together, unwoven, and then made whole again.

Evie felt the fiber of her mortal body pull tight in completion as the sudden pressure of solid earth sent her arms wide. She stepped back, but not quickly enough. Her backside thudded to the ground.

Lovely.

Eyes still closed, she reached out and brushed tingling fingers over soft grass and breathed in the fresh-cut smell.

She opened her eyes, dark lashes fluttering in the brilliant light. She sucked in a breath at the heat on her skin. The sun. She'd never felt anything quite like it. Like a gentle caress from the heavens.

This was the moment she'd been waiting for. Today was to be *her* day —a day to celebrate her first time on the ground.

But that was before they snatched her dreams away.

She'd been so angry. So hurt. She'd acted impulsively.

What have I done?

Her breathing shallowed, and she put her head in her hands.

The option to turn back had long passed.

On a slow exhale, she forced her muscles to relax. She'd be back before anyone knew of her absence. Then she raised her head and lifted an arm to expose her palm to the wondrous heat.

Her once-pale hand, now a rich honey tone, glowed in the golden light. Joram had warned she'd look different on the ground, but seeing it was something altogether different.

Even if they hadn't wished it to be, today would be a day of firsts just as she'd planned.

Her first time on the ground.

Her first time in the sun.

Her first time in a mortal body.

A smattering of yellow flowers shivered in the soft breeze. Rustling trees enveloped the meadow, and beyond them, skyscrapers towered in a rectangle like unmoving guardians. A city park, then. A timid smile tugged at her lips.

I'm finally here.

Her boots scraped on a rigid surface where a circular metal disk stood out among the spongy blades. How could the humans not realize a portal peeked from the green here in plain sight? A foreign dot on the otherwise vibrant landscape.

The warm breeze picked up tendrils of her long dark hair, and she closed her eyes to feel it brush her cheeks, her arms—invisible air tickling her skin.

But even as she stood serene, her smile faded. What if they realized she was gone? What would they do? This trip was not authorized, and surely no other Watcher in all of eternity had ever disobeyed so blatantly. She opened her eyes again.

A strange sensation pounded at her ears.

It was coming from *her*. Placing a hand over her heart, Evie let her palm capture the quick rhythmic motion. From her studies, she knew it to be an indication of the blood thrumming through this body. Her smile returned. Oh, how she'd dreamed of this moment—standing on the ground in a mortal body. The beating slowed as she put her crimes out of her mind. She traced a finger down the blue veins at her wrist.

Behind her, Joram cleared his throat. "Are you about done inspecting yourself?" Laughter broke up his warm voice. "Your face looks like you can't decide on an emotion… as usual, I suppose. You'll pass brilliantly as a human."

Evie turned to the travel coordinator, ready to defend her immortal solidity, but forgot his jab as she took in his altered appearance. He cocked his head, amused, a few paces away. Clearly, *he* hadn't fallen flat upon arrival. His skin—normally a flat grayish hue—held a similar golden tone as hers. His hair, several shades darker than usual, shadowed eyes now a light blue. Despite these alterations, his features were much the same, and his build was as tall and familiar as always. He raised an eyebrow at her inspection.

Her cheeks warmed—another new sensation. Ignoring him, she rotated in a slow circle, arms spread wide.

"This is amazing. Exactly as I imagined." And she had imagined it. Many times. "Do I look like myself in the same way you do?"

"Yes, but your skin and hair are darker, like mine. Your eyes, though" —he gestured toward her face—"they're still gold." From his pocket, he produced a pair of dark sunglasses. "You'll need to wear these while we're here. I didn't have time to program you to Sector Five Blue."

She slid them on, her idiotic grin back in place. "How do I look?"

"You look great. Now, let's get going before someone sees you twirling about." He strode down a well-manicured stone path toward a noisy street.

She smirked at his back and jogged to catch up.

"Joram, will they forgive me for this?" she asked, falling into step beside him.

"Probably not."

When she whipped her head toward him, he shrugged. "Oh, I'm kidding. How should I know? It's irrelevant because they're not going to find out. Look, you're here. You wanted this. You might as well enjoy it."

He was right. She should enjoy herself. This sector provided so much to see and do. And she intended to catch a glimpse of one particular mortal—for her research, of course. That's what she always told herself, even at her Control Room desk. This was her chance to see the Dreamer.

Thinking about this impending *research*, she grinned. Curiously, her mortal heart thudded a little faster.

2

Adan sucked in a breath as consciousness plunged him back into reality.

The force of his body's awakening jarred his desk, and his heavy books crashed to the floor. His hand flew to his chest where his heart thundered, unharmed. His breathing came in great heaves as startled faces gawked at him.

Oh no. Not again.

The real fear melted as grins and sneers replaced the student's shocked expressions. Girls giggled, and some guys laughed outright. Others eyed his hand on his chest. He pulled it back under his desk.

Great. Mr. Haywood was making his way over. A flurry of movement erupted as students shuffled their cell phones out of sight. "Adan, were you sleeping in my class again?"

"Yes, sir," he mumbled. "I didn't get much sleep last night."

"That's twice in the last week, and Mrs. Stone said you did the same in her class."

"Sorry. It won't happen again."

"Maybe a call to your parents is in order." Mr. Haywood returned the books to Adan's desk and walked away.

Adan fought the urge to say, "Yeah, well, if you find my parents let me know." He'd drawn enough attention.

His gaze flicked across the room to where Garran dwarfed his tiny desk. Their gazes met, and his lips tightened as if to hold back the same comment. But it would've come out more like, "I'm not sure you'll find them, Mr. Haywood, since Adan's mom left him at a shelter seventeen years ago." But Garran looked away, a muscle in his jaw twitching.

Jealousy didn't sit well on the overgrown man-child. Their Guardian gave Adan what the other boy thought should be his. Never mind that Adan didn't want it.

The bell rang, signaling the end of the day, and he made his way to his locker. The hallways cleared as students rushed off to one party or another. Tonight, people from all over would migrate to the city to celebrate the Festival of Alvar.

As he slammed his locker, someone barreled into his arm. The well-placed blow shot fiery pain through his already raw skin.

"Didn't see you there, *Dreamer*." Garran spat the word like a curse. "How's the arm?"

Probably bleeding now. "What do you want?"

The meathead lumbered closer. "You think you're better than everyone—Uzziah's golden child. I have no idea why he keeps you and your brat little brother around."

Adan bristled at the mention of Ben.

"But I can tell you one thing. You're a Dreamer—whatever that is—but you're marked by a Strength Wielder. You're going to be a disappointment to every person you come across."

Something hot bubbled up inside Adan, but he clamped his mouth shut. Some secrets he had to hold close.

Usually, he'd stand his ground and fight. But no one without the Strength Gift would be foolish enough to square off against a Strength Wielder.

"Hey, what's going on down there?" Both boys jerked toward the voice echoing down the hall. Their principal, Mr. Kelsey, strode toward them, dress shoes clicking on the worn linoleum floor.

A smile widened Garran's irritating mouth. He slung an arm over Adan's shoulder.

Adan hissed at the pressure but kept his expression neutral.

"Oh, nothing," Garran called out. "Just having a discussion."

When the man reached them, he paused to look them over, likely noting Adan didn't share Garran's ease. "Boys, there's no fighting on the school campus."

"Oh no, we weren't fighting. Only a minor disagreement. I'm headed out anyway." With a laugh, Garran extracted his arm from Adan's shoulder. "Did you know Adan fell asleep in English again?" He shook his head and started down the hall.

Great. Here came another lecture. But before Mr. Kelsey could begin, Garran yelled back as he pushed out the double doors. "See you tonight, Adan."

It was a promise.

After Mr. Kelsey's lengthy lecture about respect and getting enough sleep, Adan blinked into the bright afternoon sunlight, free to travel the five blocks to his apartment. Thank goodness for weekends.

The lecture grated. It wasn't as if he wanted to sleep in class! More like, he didn't want to sleep *at all*. Disturbing things played out in his mind while he lay unconscious.

He plunged his hands into his pockets and took to the busier-than-usual sidewalks. Horns blared, brakes squealed, and music pulsed.

Like his classmates, most city dwellers rushed off to begin their holiday weekend. With a population of over 6.2 million, Shura would swell under a stifling press of pedestrians.

After entering his apartment building, he hurried to the elevator and pressed the button for the top level.

He scowled at the mirror lining the back wall, tugged at his rumpled hoodie, and tried to tame his unruly dark hair. He gave up the losing battle as soon as the doors slid open. Adan stepped into the foyer where the Guardian Uzziah and his twelve trainees—including Adan—occupied the entire floor.

Familiar voices drifted down the hall as two of the other trainees, Elias and Chase, bounded toward Adan. Chase, tall and lanky, ran the last few steps and slid in his socks to stop in front of Adan.

"Well?" Holding his hands out, Chase grinned and, with a quick nod, flipped his hair out of his eyes. The kid wore blue from head to toe.

Raising one brow, Adan laughed. "You know white is the festival color, right?"

Elias, who was a bit shorter in both hair and build, shuffled next to Chase, trying not to spill a glass of water.

"Yep." Elias grinned like a five-year-old.

He wore all red. Together, they looked ridiculous.

"Okay. Just checking."

Chase smoothed out the front of his shirt. "We don't want to blend in. We want to stand out."

"The ladies won't be able to look away," Elias added.

"I don't think you have to worry about that. They'll be staring all right."

Both three years younger than Adan, the boys came from wealthy families. How else could one afford to buy an outfit they'd never wear again? They were all right, though.

"Adan, check it out." Elias glared at his water glass. An orb of liquid lifted from it and hovered a hand's width above.

"Don't mess up." Chase poked a finger into the floating blob.

The water fell, most of it splashing to the floor, and they all jumped back.

"Wow." Adan brushed at his jeans. "That was, uh, something."

"Chase messed me up."

"I know. That's why both of you should clean it up."

As the two boys grumbled toward the kitchen, Adan padded down the hall to their bunk room and tossed his backpack onto his bed. Years ago—before Adan and Ben arrived—Uzziah merged the space from two typical bedrooms into a single larger one with enough bunks for ten boys. Though a bit crowded, it was home. For now. The girls were lucky. Only the two of them occupied the third bedroom.

Adan sat on the floor before his wardrobe and rummaged through the bottom drawer. His fingers brushed a crumpled old photograph. He listened to make sure Chase and Elias were on their way out and then grabbed the photo to straighten it against his knee.

In it, his brother, Ben, slept in a rolling cart with a hospital band still circling his tiny ankle. Though the camera focused on the newborn, a dark-haired woman sat in the background on a clinical bed. She stared into the distance, not bothering to glance at the photographer.

Not only was this the single photo they had of Ben before the age of five, but it was also the only image they possessed of their mother. She'd tested positive for some substance or another. So, the day after it was taken, a social worker delivered baby Ben and the photo to the foster home where Adan was living.

He flipped the photo over where, nine years ago, that social worker had jotted an address—their birth mom's last known residence. Someday, he would knock on that door, demand answers, yell, get closure. He snatched a book from his backpack and slid the photo between the pages. Someday.

But what might he find? Would it match the picture he'd formed?

He'd walk up the stone steps to her townhouse and knock. His mother would pause from making dinner to answer. When she opened the door, she would smile, and the garlicky smell of spaghetti and meatballs—his favorite—would waft out. Two dark-haired boys would run forward, clinging to her legs as they peeked out at him. A well-dressed man, just home from work, would ask who was there and come to stand behind them.

Adan shook himself as an ember of anger deep within himself burned brighter the way it always did when he thought about his mom. He fought back the questions it ignited.

Why was I born if she didn't want me? Why am I here?

Returning to the reason he was digging in this drawer, he pulled out his old, white festival half mask. He shoved the dingy thing atop his head, slid the tiny book into his back pocket, and left the room.

Before he could hail the elevator, a muffled thud echoed from the apartment's other end. He followed the sound and pushed through the door to the training room where Uzziah aimed with a throwing knife and hurled it the length of the open space. A blur flew to bury in the center of his intended target, where the force knocked it back several feet. The swirling marks that branded Uzziah as a Guardian glowed on his arms as he released his considerable power. Though his hair was graying, Uzziah had the well-toned body of a much younger man.

He spotted Adan, and the marks faded, as did his unnatural strength.

"I didn't expect anyone home today," he said. "Aren't you going out to celebrate?"

"Yeah, I'm about to meet Ben at the park." Adan walked over, feet squishing on the padded floor. "Is this what you do when you think no one will be home? Hurl knives, wear jeans? What about 'respecting the art'?"

Uzziah's strange golden eyes twinkled. Like all immortals, Uzziah aged at turtle speed here. He told them once that if he returned to the immortal realm—the Control Room—his bodily clock would reset. All the boys speculated on how old Uzziah was, but none dared to ask.

"I'm killing time, if you must know."

"I thought you'd be gone since you couldn't keep Ben company this afternoon."

Uzziah shrugged into a button-up shirt. "I'm here, as you can see."

Adan tested a theory. "Not yet time to meet your visitor?" As Uzziah's head jerked up and amber eyes went wide, Adan hooked his thumbs in his pockets, rocking back on his heels. So, he was right.

"In case you haven't figured it out, you can't keep secrets from the Dreamer. My amazing Gift allows me to know the future with almost five percent accuracy."

Uzziah laughed then, buttoning his shirt. "Those aren't very good odds, are they?"

No. No, they weren't. Adan's Gift was next to useless. The Guardian before him could give the Gift of strength. Some of his bunkmates and friends were Water Movers or Healers. But no, he had the Gift of nightmares—of waking up frightened in front of a class full of his peers. Worse, he didn't know a single other Dreamer. No one had even heard of the Gift—if that's what one could call it—until Uzziah had declared it so.

"You dreamed about my messenger?" Uzziah straightened his collar.

"Yeah, well, I wasn't sure that's what it was. Lots of things happened at once, but I did see two people appear and give you something. I couldn't see their faces, but they glowed like you do in my dreams, so I thought maybe they were like you."

"Interesting." Uzziah rubbed his smooth chin.

"So, are they from the Control Room?"

Uzziah's lessons had included a complete history of the Control Room and the other worlds—sectors, as he called them. But he'd rarely talked about them since that six-week history lesson so long ago. Many humans didn't get such knowledge and likely didn't know such a place existed. That, or when they did hear, they refused to believe.

Uzziah's brow knitted. "Yes, the Control Room. You say there were two? I've never had more than one messenger before. Perhaps your dream was only half right."

"Yeah, maybe." And if that were true, maybe it also meant other parts of his dreams wouldn't happen. Should he tell Uzziah about these other, more disturbing bits?

As if seeing Adan's indecision, Uzziah said, "Ben told me you had another nightmare last night."

"Yeah, you could say that." Adan turned a ring circling his pinky finger while Uzziah walked to the sink in the corner and washed his hands.

"Tell me about it later, and we'll work through whatever you're feeling. But the messenger will be here soon, and you need to be gone when he arrives." Uzziah crossed the padded floor, his mouth drawn. "Stay close to Sam tonight, and don't go out on your own."

Not this again. "Uzziah, I walk this city alone all the time. Why do you worry so much?"

"I want you to stay safe. All of you."

Smoking Worlds. *He* was the only one Uzziah tried to nanny over.

"And keep your marks covered." Uzziah nodded toward Adan's hand where the marks and the ring hid under his sleeve.

Adan threw his hands up. "Why did you give me the marks if you want me to hide them? And you had to know Garran would be angry. You didn't make my life any easier, you know." Adan's run-in with Garran wasn't over. Plus, these marks had made his dreams more intense, more vivid.

"Your brother will come around."

Adan fought to keep from rolling his eyes. Garran was *not* his brother, but Uzziah often referred to the twelve as such.

Uzziah smiled his infuriating, secretive smile. "Well, best not let Garran see the ring for now. All will be revealed soon."

"That's cryptic." Shaking his head, Adan started to leave. He wouldn't get anything more out of Uzziah. But he had to know one thing. He paused.

"Yes, Adan?"

"My dreams of the distant future…" Adan cringed, but Uzziah only raised a brow, waiting. "Will they come true? They seem so distant and… foreign."

"I couldn't tell you. You're the only Dreamer I've ever met. Perhaps you can change the outcome by changing your path."

Adan pressed the ring harder against his finger, relieved, but only slightly. How would he know when to change paths?

Uzziah clamped a hand on his shoulder. "You can't help what you dream, Adan. All you can do—all anyone in your position can do—is figure out what good you can do with the Gifts you've been given."

3

Evie's legs burned as she matched Joram's longer stride. He—unlike her—visited Sector Five often and refused to take any detours.

"How often do you deliver messages?" she asked on a breathless huff as her gaze darted about. The humans didn't seem to notice two of the Maker's Marked walking among them.

Joram kept his pale blue eyes fixed ahead. "Oh, every so often, but not to this particular Guardian. He's one of the hundreds in Sector Five. Around twenty live here in Shura."

Only twenty? Her fingers balled into fists. Now more than ever, wouldn't it be essential to have more Guardians on the ground? The Deceiver was on the move in the lower sectors. The danger to humans —to them all—was greater than ever.

But she checked the human emotions that threatened to bubble up. She wouldn't succumb to them, even if she did occupy a mortal body.

As they passed a busy storefront, she brushed her fingers along a neat row of feathery white masks. From inside the poorly lit costume shop, her reflection stared back—a darker, more human version of herself.

"Stop it," Joram hissed as she lifted her sunglasses for a better look. "Come on."

She trotted back to his side, catching his suppressed grin. She was probably acting like an unruly child.

She smiled and said hello to a passing pedestrian who'd donned an elaborate white feathered mask. Evie's lips spread wider at the grin she received in return. A skateboarder bumped her elbow.

"Sorry," he yelled over his shoulder.

She rubbed her arm. This was more fun than she imagined.

Today wasn't just any day for the mortals flowing around them like water. Today marked the beginning of the Festival of Alvar, a yearly celebration honoring the fabled Guardian, the Truth-Speaker. Many pedestrians wore the usual festival costumes: light clothing ranging from white fitted pants and T-shirts to long, flowing cream-colored dresses. White ribbons trailed them on the breeze. Dazzling blue eyes peered from white feathered half masks.

The two companions paused at a stoplight. A familiar row of skyscrapers glittered before them. She'd been gazing at this skyline from her screen in the Control Room this morning. These buildings had been lit from behind as the sun awoke. She'd been lost in thought about this moment, anticipating her walk in the sun among the humans. She'd caught herself, looking around at the other Watchers to make sure no one noticed her strange reverie. They'd never understand her longing to escape the Control Room.

Now the skyscrapers reflected the afternoon sun, and she committed the shape and colors to memory. Who knew the world would look so alive?

"Let me show you where we are." Joram pulled a portable device from his pocket. His fingers flew across its surface, luring a map of the city onto its glossy screen.

He pointed to a throbbing blue dot. "We're here, and here's where we entered the sector." He dragged his fingers across the screen to reposition the map. "This is where we're going. Not much farther. But I want to make one quick stop before we arrive."

The word *walk* blinked onto the street sign.

Her stomach fluttered as she stepped onto the crosswalk.

Mere hours ago, she was watching humans, watching *him*. Unlike the other Watchers, she'd become restless after a morning on the Control Room floor. No one else fidgeted. No one else daydreamed. Did she really fit in?

Her gaze had flicked to the folder icon on the screen covering her desktop. Labeled Research, it contained many things, including her more secret findings. The Watchers nearest her worked on their assigned tasks. Muffled conversations rose and fell, and low-volume city noises floated from the enormous wall of screens.

Evie touched the icon, and the folder revealed its contents. A few quick finger movements brought her to a buried folder called Dreamer. She pressed the locate icon, and a video window spread over the smooth surface.

She'd smiled when she saw dark curls bent over a book. She smiled now, thinking about it.

She'd wondered what text he read. Was it the book he acquired earlier in the week? Or some new adventure?

Now, she thought of that book again. Would he be sitting in his apartment lobby, perhaps reading it when they arrived?

"What are you grinning about?" Joram's amused voice wrenched her from her thoughts.

"Nothing. Just excited." She nodded to his fingers. "Where'd you get the communicator?"

He slid it into his pocket. "Krystopher gave one to each Guardian. I'm a Travel Coordinator, so I have a few to communicate with them as needed while I'm here. Though, they prefer for me to meet with Guardians in person when I have a message to deliver." He tapped his jacket pocket. "Like this letter."

His purpose for being in Sector Five was to deliver a message from Krystopher, the personnel director and one of her few close friends in the Control Room, to Adan's Guardian, Uzziah. What might Krystopher have to say to a Guardian on the ground?

Joram held the cream-colored envelope toward the sun as if trying to see through the thin paper, then tucked it back in his pocket.

"Will your device communicate between here and the Control Room?"

"Nope. And they've never worked between sectors either, even back when the Maker allowed travel between them. I've been dabbling in the communication systems, though. They need some new tech."

"Did you ever travel between sectors back then?" She might as well be an infant compared to him. She wasn't around during those dark days before Sector One fell. Though he was formed eons before her, Joram didn't look it in the way humans would expect. They'd both pass for late teens or early twenties here.

"I didn't become a Travel Coordinator until Sector Five was well underway. The Maker had already destroyed the intersector portals. I worked as a Guardian for Sector One and then for Two until… well, you know."

Though she didn't know the particulars, she did know Sector One burned well before she was even a thought in the Maker's mind. "So, you ended up in the Sector Five Control Room?"

"Yes, and perhaps I'll transfer to Sector Seven when it's finished."

What would her future look like since the Maker had canceled promotions for the only job she'd ever wanted? "Indefinitely," he'd said. What a devastating word, laced with so much uncertainty. Did he mean she could apply for Guardian again in a few years? A hundred years? A thousand?

And what would happen if they found out about this clandestine trip?

A ripple of cooler air ruffled her hair. She shoved the locks behind her shoulders and tried to send her worries away with the wind.

"What do you think Sector Six is like?"

"Who knows." Joram chuckled. "No Guardians. Precious few Watchers. No telling what the humans are like by now."

Evie shuddered. Rules against Guardian and Watcher influence were strictly enforced, probably making Sector Six a barbaric land.

"Why did the Maker ban Guardians from Sector Six?" she asked as a man in a white suit and matching feathered mask shoved between them. He raised an arm, loosing an earsplitting whistle.

As they passed a slowing taxi, Joram reclaimed the space between them. "It happened just after he discovered the Deceiver had moved on to Sectors Two and Three. The Maker tried to safeguard the portals, but it didn't work. So he destroyed them. Perhaps eliminating Guardians from Sector Six was an experiment—a trap of sorts. They never made it public, but there must be measures in place to alert the Control Room if anyone uses a Gift in the sector. That's why Guardians and Gifted humans aren't allowed."

A trap?

Joram paused at another streetlight. "Here we are. Stop number one. This may be the most important stop we make, so prepare yourself." His eyes twinkling, he gestured to a shop across the intersection. Ava's Pastry House.

Evie laughed.

They crossed the street, and Joram opened the door with a soft ding. "Wait here, and don't talk to anyone."

Evie leaned against rust-colored brick as he ducked inside.

A man and woman sat on dainty chairs around a table next to the entrance. They sipped their black drinks and chatted about the weather.

"What a perfect day." The woman sighed.

"It is now." The man waved a hand toward the clear sky. "I heard a storm is moving in."

Evie looked up, as did the woman. "You're kidding. That will ruin a few parties. Maybe they're wrong. It wouldn't be the first time."

The man raised his cup. "Here's hoping."

Their cups came together with a clink.

Evie smiled up at the sky. Rain! How she'd love to feel the drops on her skin! But she'd be well away by then.

A statue in the distance snagged her attention. Positioned past the next intersection, the smooth stone formed two enormous outstretched hands. The fingers held five smooth, round spheres. She'd sketched it once in her private quarters, away from the prying eyes of those who would wonder why she'd do such a thing.

They must be very close now.

Just this morning at her desk, she'd watched the Dreamer. The hood of his light-gray jacket rested on his back, and he'd pulled its worn sleeves over his hands. His fingers held the book flat on his desk.

He sat in a quiet classroom—his advanced math class—with about twenty others. Students sitting in neat rows faced a watchful woman.

This was all part of her research. After all, if the boy was what she thought he was, his Gift would be powerful indeed. Not even the Guardians could read the future.

Some students hunched over papers, scribbling away. Others read or stole glances at portable devices when the teacher wasn't looking. A girl leaned to the side and whispered something to the Dreamer. He glanced up, and Evie caught the flash of brilliant blue.

Evie slammed her headphones over her ears and cranked up the volume. But when the girl whispered again, Evie still couldn't make out the words. The boy smiled, a bit forlorn, displaying a single dimple on his honey-toned cheek, and whispered something back.

When a stern voice screamed his name through her headphones, Evie'd jumped, bumping her knee on her desk. The Watcher to her right peeked over as she dialed down the volume and gave him an apologetic grimace. He'd turned back to his report, hiding a grin. He, like many others, was good-natured about her oddities. To her other side, her best friend, Alizah, watched her with a raised brow. Evie lifted a shoulder.

"… something you would like to share with the class?" the teacher was asking.

"No, ma'am."

"Then keep quiet."

Adan returned to his book. The girl watched him from the corner of her eye.

Sighing, Evie used a finger to drag the video to her screen's top corner. She opened a text file called Background. This document contained everything she'd learned about Adan Andree's childhood. Even after hours of research, Evie still couldn't begin to guess where the Dreaming Gift originated, if that was what plagued him. None of his ancestors seemed to have it. A human came to possess a Gift in only two ways: either inherited through birth or through marks bestowed by a Guardian.

She continued to peruse her notes. A bell rang in her headphones. Adan closed his book, grabbed his backpack, and left the room with his best friend, Sam. Evie closed the video rather than follow them down the hall. She had no desire to sit through a history class.

Her afternoon dragged on until Joram popped in to wish her luck on the upcoming promotional announcements.

"You're a shoo-in."

But there were several applicants.

"You're the most qualified. Of course, you'll get it. In a few hours, you'll have your Guardian marks. Besides, Krystopher *is* the personnel director."

Evie forced a smile, but Joram must have read her worry because he lowered his lips to her ear. "And if you don't get promoted, I can always take you to Five."

She'd sucked in a quick breath and darted a glance around.

But he'd only laughed. "Might be better than waiting for the next promotion years from now."

She nodded toward her supervisor's office, where he conversed with both Krystopher and the Maker. "They'd never allow me to go with you to deliver your message."

"They don't have to know." A devilish grin crinkled his cheeks.

Horns blared, yanking her back into the present. She jumped as two humans yelled from car windows.

"Reckless," Evie muttered, standing on the ground in Sector Five.

"What?" Joram held something wrapped in delicate white paper.

"Nothing. What's that?"

"It's called a cinnamon bun. Try it."

She took the roll and slid her first bite of human food into her mouth. She gasped as doughy sweetness exploded on her tongue. Did all food taste like this?

Joram chuckled. "Shocking, right?" He started walking again. "That's one thing humans have gotten right over the long years. Food."

After a few more blissful minutes, Evie licked the last sweetness from her fingers. Joram slowed, seeming lost in thought.

"It's not too far now, but I don't think you should go in with me. Or even into the neighborhood, really. The Guardian I'm visiting might recognize you for what you are, and you can't walk around inside with sunglasses on."

"Maybe I could wait in the lobby? Or outside?" She winced as her voice rose to a whine. Seeing the Dreamer was the reason she asked Joram to smuggle her along. Her envy had been more than she could bear after the unceremonious shattering of her dreams. And now he wanted to leave her out of this part?

"We can't risk it. If you stay in this area, there are restaurants and outdoor shops. You can explore more parks and bridges that way."

That thudding in her chest quickened. How could she argue? He was right, after all.

Joram rested a hand on her shoulder, likely mistaking her hesitation for fear of being left alone. "Hey, you'll be fine. This will be a fun adventure. You might not get this chance again for a while." He patted her shoulder, his last words slicing her.

Then he pulled the communicator from his pocket. "I'll be meeting with Uzziah, and then I have some other stops to make." He powered on the screen. "I brought two of these today so we can communicate. The humans call them cell phones."

Evie took it, and Joram issued a quick lesson on using the map application.

"Meet back at the portal by six. The time is at the top. I'll comm you if anything changes."

"Fine." She slid the device into her back pocket.

Six o'clock. Almost three hours.

"Here, take this in case you get hungry or thirsty." He held out a few green bills but didn't let go when she reached to take them. "You could get into a lot of trouble if anyone finds out you came here without permission. Don't talk to anyone, don't let anyone see your eyes, and don't go near Uzziah's building."

When he let go and walked down the sidewalk and around the next corner, she crossed her arms.

She should do what Joram said. Stay around here, explore, eat.

Then, unbidden, an image of the Dreamer walking home from school teased her. She saw him shoving his unruly hair from his face, then plunging his hands into his pockets as he made for home—the very place where Joram traveled.

She should stay. Do the right thing for once today. But Adan was probably almost home now, that single dimple forming on his cheek when he spied his little brother running to meet him.

Evie hustled to peek around the corner. This was small-time compared to what she'd already done.

After she'd followed Joram for another block, her steps slowed. He'd mentioned that only *she* would get into trouble if this little adventure were discovered. The Maker would be angry, and both her supervisor and Krystopher would look bad. If they found out, they might never forgive her.

4

Coffee Connection—the familiar sign swayed overhead as Adan strode toward his favorite park down Twelfth Avenue. As he moved past, the shop's door swung wide and spilled one of its patrons onto the sidewalk.

"Hey. There you are. I thought you might be working today." Sam nodded over his shoulder, where Adan spent three afternoons a week serving the local caffeine addicts. Sam held a large frozen concoction in one hand and an elaborate festival mask in the other. The price tag still dangled from its corner.

"No. Uzziah's busy, so I'm with Ben tonight."

Sam's face fell. "So you aren't going to Nora's party? She was going to ask you."

Adan shrugged. "She did. But I told her I couldn't."

"Bad luck. Sorry. You want to get a coffee or a smoothie or something?" Sam, prepared for Adan's refusal—a result of his need to save every penny—added, "I'll buy."

"You're not buying my coffee. Besides, I'm meeting Ben at the park." As Adan's best friend, Sam meant well. He just didn't get Adan's aversion to accepting the occasional handout. Coming from a family with money, he probably never would.

Adan started walking again, and Sam fell into step beside him.

"So, what are you doing tonight?" Adan asked, and Sam launched into his plans.

When he'd finished and Adan didn't respond, Sam scooted forward, walking backward in front of him. "You want to talk about your dream?"

"Not really. What's there to say? I'm a freak of nature, and now I'm marked as one for everyone to see." Adan held out his arm and yanked his sleeve back. Swirling black marks snaked along the back of his hand, up his forearm, and disappeared under his shirt.

Sam flipped back around. "People wait their whole life hoping to be Guardian Marked."

"But everyone's going to think I should be Strength Gifted, and I'm not. I've no proof of what I can do. I'm not even sure *I* believe it."

"People born with a Gift ask Guardians to mark them all the time."

"I know, but why?"

"I don't know. So people can see they are Gifted? It's prestigious." He shook his head. "Uzziah thought you'd be happy."

"Dreaming isn't a Gift people know anything about. Why'd Uzziah think I needed to be Marked? I never asked for it. Not to mention, Garran's ready to kill me."

Sam chuckled. "It was awesome. Did you see his face when Uzziah announced it was you? Classic. Too bad Uzziah didn't let us go to your marking ceremony. He should've forced Garran to watch."

Adan didn't comment.

"You didn't tell us everything that happened in your dream."

As the other boy watched him with wary eyes, Adan ducked his head. Asphalt disappearing under his shoes, he stuffed his hands into his pockets.

"Oh, come on." Sam nudged him with his elbow. "You've had some crazy dreams over the years. And now, out of nowhere, Uzziah says your dreams may be showing you the future. What does that mean for all the crazy stuff you've told me? Are the rest of us going to bow down to you or something? And are you in danger of whatever wakes you up at night?"

Adan forced a smile. Sam didn't know the half of it. "I've always told you I think Uzziah's a little on the crazy side. It's nothing. My dreams never amount to anything."

Well, almost never.

Sam saluted with this coffee. "I hope you're right. All I know is whatever you saw scared you. A lot. I hope you never meet it face to face."

"Believe me, me too."

They parted ways, and Adan made his way to the park. He strode under the statue of two outstretched hands and ran his fingers over the smooth nameplate. *The Maker's Hands.*

Then he crossed the bridge over the pond at the park's center and found a secluded bench where he contemplated his dream, his marks, and his nemesis.

Garran, the hulking nineteen-year-old, inherited his Strength Gift from his father. Over time he'd become an enormous jerk, making his fits of anger terrifying. Only Uzziah could stand against such raw power if Garran ever decided to become aggressive.

You're going to be a disappointment to every person you come across. No one had ever stated Adan's fears so bluntly.

Last night, when Uzziah announced he intended to give one of them the markings of their inherited power, every head turned to Garran. Every head but Uzziah's.

A murmur spread through the group as Uzziah explained Adan possessed the inherited Gift of Dreaming. The Guardian called it an honor. Right. More like a *burden*. And now this burden made his friends jealous as Uzziah lead him away to be marked among the Gifted.

All Adan had ever wanted was to be normal. Find his mom, be a normal kid, have a normal family, sleep a normal night. Or save up enough money to give Ben a normal life in an apartment away from all the Guardian drama and competition.

But, last night, Uzziah pushed his goal further out of reach.

Adan spun the ring on his pinky finger. The black Guardian marks snaked out of his sleeve and swirled down his hand and around that same finger. He tilted the ring side to side, and when the sunlight caught the tiny prisms circling its flat surface, colorful rays reflected.

"It will help with your dreams," Uzziah had said when he presented it in secret after Adan's marks were complete.

What a joke.

Last night, Adan's dream had been more real, more detailed, yet more impossible than any before it. He'd woken in a panic, yelling out in fear.

"What happened?" Sam asked after pulling him into the hallway, followed by Ben. The three of them huddled together on the smooth hardwood floor.

Adan told them about the dream and the path and Uzziah's visitors. He left out the part where they knelt before him.

"Then, suddenly, there was this bright otherworldly light. It came from something big, but I couldn't see what. I shielded my eyes and walked toward it. I couldn't keep my feet from taking a step and then another and another." Adan had been dreaming of the strange light for as long as he could remember. It had always been present in the fog, but recently, it became more prominent.

"The light grew brighter, and I had this feeling like someone was coming. A shape formed in the light."

Adan had paused to look down at Ben. The boy watched Adan with wide sapphire eyes. Adan played it down. "And I think they were trying to attack me."

Ben gasped.

"It's just a dream," Adan promised. Just a dream. Ben, of course, believed him. If he told Ben a portal from Sector Two deposited giants in their living room Ben would believe him.

Sam eyed Adan, aware he'd left something out. He and Adan both knew the marking ceremony changed things. These dreams weren't just dreams.

Now, from the park bench, Adan cursed the wretched marks that pulled and ached all the way up his arm and across his back. He longed for them to fade. They would be easier to hide when they healed, becoming a few shades lighter than his skin.

He slid his book from his back pocket and ran a finger over the designed golden spine. Resting his elbows on his knees, he flipped it open, then read aloud in a whisper. "'You are my Marked One.'"

Adan shook his head. "Nolan, did you have this much trouble?" he asked the story's protagonist as he scratched at the charred skin on the back of his hand and shuddered at the image of his laughing classmates.

He sighed, tucking back into the book's worn pages where words let him be someone else, somewhere else. With all the mind control he could muster, he shoved the dream out of his head. Even the part he didn't tell Sam. The part where a golden blade had flown end over end toward him out of the light and plunged deep into his chest with a sickening thud.

5

Evie rushed around the next corner, narrowly avoiding what might have been an unfortunate crash with a food stand. But she didn't see the boy.

"Wow," she panted to herself, "he's fast."

She bent, rubbing an odd pain in her side.

Yellow vehicles filled the street as white-clad pedestrians floated down the sidewalk. The press of bodies dizzied her.

She'd followed Joram easily enough. When they arrived at Uzziah's corner, she'd spotted Ben, Adan's nine-year-old brother, running out of their apartment. The boy yelled to the smiling doorman, something about Adan and the park. She had thought to wait for Adan, but this might be her best chance. After only a few blocks of her following him, his bobbing head disappeared.

I'm an immortal Watcher—a trained warrior. I should be able to keep up with a human child. Her mortal heart didn't listen. How could it when it thundered so? Her breaths came fast, and her lungs burned. *Am I dying?*

Finally, accepting death wasn't upon her, she plucked Joram's communicator from her pocket. Her blue dot pulsed near a green rectangle on the map, and she could only hope this was where Ben headed.

When the dot arrived, she let out a breath as she passed under the statue of outstretched hands.

This park occupied only a single city block, but the tall skinny trees provided ample shade for city dwellers. Several of those inhabitants lounged on the soft grass.

She'd wasted many a work hour watching Adan in this very park. She took notes on his behavior, paying particular attention when he napped—how his eyes shifted behind his lids or how often he spoke aloud or jerked awake. He came here to read or do homework or hang out with Ben. On the best days, he'd tell Ben about his dreams.

He has to be here. Ben had run off this way.

A sparkling pond beckoned from the park's center where a carved footbridge arched over its middle. She strolled up the creaking planks, running a hand along the smooth handrail. From here, she could see almost from one end of the park to the other. Only a pocket of space hid behind a handful of boulders.

Evie stepped in a slow circle, noting each human. No Adan, no Ben.

Her shoulders drooped until an excited shriek sounded from the direction she'd come. *Ben?*

No, not Ben. Another, younger child stood between a man and a woman, holding their hands. They walked to the edge of the pond, and the boy released their hands to peer into the water. When he moved away, the man and woman drew together as if tugged by a magnetic force. Their fingers entwined. The man brought their clasped fingers to his mouth, kissing the back of her hand. They gazed at each other in that secret way Evie never understood. The man leaned in and whispered in the woman's ear.

Evie drummed her fingers on the handrail. This moment wasn't for her, though her simmering curiosity of what was between them continued to burn.

Proceeding across the bridge, she veered off onto a pebble path cutting a narrow line through the green. Yellow flowers swayed, and she plucked one to examine its delicate makeup. Something about it felt strangely familiar. How beautiful for something so insignificant. Hoping to commit its form to memory, she placed it on her palm. Perhaps she'd sketch it later.

A breeze ruffled her dark hair, and before she could react, the wind lifted the flower from her palm and deposited it into the pond. It floated peacefully atop the water just out of reach. From the other side of the pond, the boy looked at it and then at her.

She offered him a weak smile and then set to walking again, already making plans to go back to Adan's apartment and start a fresh search. She wouldn't likely see him now. Her steps slow, she kicked at the pebbles.

The path forked, and she followed it around the boulders to the hidden area beyond.

She stopped, breath hitching.

There he was. Adan the Dreamer. Sitting at one end of a park bench, only ten paces away. His head bent over a golden-spine book.

Evie stood motionless, heart thundering. She took in Adan's dark curls shoved back by a mask atop his head. His elbows balanced on his knees as he held the book before him. He flipped the page, brow drawn. A leaf fluttered to his sleeve, and he brushed it away.

Catching herself, she glanced around. No one noticed her blatant staring.

What book held his attention so? Was it the same novel he'd been reading yesterday? She should find out. For her research, of course. Surely, it wouldn't hurt to sit on the other end of the bench.

She smoothed her hair and adjusted her sunglasses. Then she crossed to the park bench and settled onto it, resting a forearm on the armrest.

Adan shifted in his seat, and brilliant blue flashed her way. The corner of his mouth darted up, and then he returned to reading, unaware of the turmoil his gesture caused her.

He sighed and shook his head, and such profound curiosity overcame her that she had to clamp her mouth shut to keep from asking him what was wrong.

A happy squeal bounced down the walkway. It was the child from the pond. The boy's parents swung him high between them.

As Adan let his book fall closed, a finger marking his spot, she peeked at its golden spine expertly engraved to mimic a mass of thin vines. Once, a lock may have circled the pages but had long since been stripped away. The words *One's Raining Fire* spread over the front in golden letters. It was the same book, an adventure story about a mortal tasked with building a portal to escape the antagonist of his world. Though believed to be fiction, it was full of Guardians and Watchers and the elusive Deceiver. Many mortals no longer believed in the Watchers, the Deceiver, or even the Control Room, but this book told about them with accuracy.

Evie leaned forward, tucking her hands under her thighs, and bit her lip to keep from grinning at the irony of Adan unknowingly sitting next to a Watcher.

The boy and his parents passed in front of them, and the boy, noticing Evie, darted forward, holding out a newly picked yellow flower. Her eyebrows rose, and a smile stretched apart her lips. She took the bloom, and the boy dashed away.

Bringing the flower to her nose, she hazarded a glance at Adan. He watched the boy retreat and then met her eyes again. A single dimple folded into one cheek.

Her heart raced, and her cheeks warmed under his attention. Traitorous human body. She looked down at her feet, not knowing what to do or say, and he returned his attention to his book.

She imagined herself saying something clever about the flower or the book to make him laugh. But she couldn't imagine what those words might be.

After a time, Adan snapped the volume closed. Seeming agitated, he rotated a ring on his pinky finger.

Angry, black swirls curved over the back of his hand. What other things did she miss during all the times she was away from her workstation?

" 'Amid disquieting thoughts from the visions of the night, fear and trembling seize me…' "

"'… making my bones to shake.'" Evie finished in an equally quiet tone.

Adan's head whipped around. He fixed her in place with those piercing eyes. "You've read *One's Raining Fire*?"

Startled, she darted her gaze away. She hadn't meant for him to hear. But wouldn't it be rude to ignore him now? To get up and walk away as Joram would expect?

Had she read it? Of course, she had. Well, at least she'd started it. Several days ago, when she first noticed him with it, she'd searched the Guardian archives and downloaded it to the screen in her private quarters. When she learned the text mentioned Watchers, her curiosity had hardly been contained. What would Adan learn about *her*?

"I've started it. I'm not quite done, though." She met his gaze, and the corner of his mouth quirked into a half-smile, revealing the dimple again. How she cursed this human body for making her feel as if she were running a race!

Adan angled toward her, stretching his arm across the back of the bench. "What do you think so far?"

Trying to mimic his relaxed manner, she angled toward him. "I like it." Was he simply being polite? No, his face was expectant. "I enjoy the idea of portals, and Nolan's an interesting character. I think you're farther along than I am." She nodded to the book. "What about you? Do you like it?"

"I agree about the portals. The idea of traveling between worlds is intriguing. Nolan's okay, but I hate how everyone thinks he's a fraud."

Evie chewed her lip. *How much will he share with me?* "Do you think Dreaming ever existed, or did the author make it up for his story?"

His gaze snapped up too quickly. This was likely the reason he'd sought the book. Nolan was a Dreamer. Precious few books mentioned the rare Gift.

"Yes. I think it probably did." He adjusted his sleeve.

Uzziah must have given Adan the mark. But why did he do it, if the boy already possessed the Dreaming Gift through birth? Evie could hardly ask the question, so they fell into an awkward silence.

Adan glanced up the path behind Evie in time to shield himself from the impact of an overexcited nine-year-old. Ben bounced into him, and Adan maneuvered the boy into a playful headlock.

"Where've you been, little brother?"

"Hey." Ben struggled until Adan released him, dark curls splayed wildly. "I was getting a mask and a snack." He held up a crumpled bag and unraveled a strip of white cloth from his pocket. The mask wasn't a half mask like Adan's, but rather a cut of fabric with two holes. He put the holes over his eyes.

"Here, let me," Adan spun him around and tied the cloth onto Ben's head, making his hair stand even more on end. As Ben grinned, Adan clapped him on the shoulder. "You look great. No one will recognize you."

"I bought the cheapest one, so I could get a snack." Ben held up a brown sack and noticed Evie, who was smiling at the exchange.

"Hi." She gave a little wave. "I like your mask."

"Thanks." The boy's grin deepened.

"This is my brother, Ben." Adan patted the boy's shoulder. "He's nine."

"Who are you?" Ben asked.

Evie peeked at Adan, who lifted a brow.

"Evie," she answered after a pause. No reason not to give her real name, right? "Nice to meet you, Ben."

The boy wriggled away from his brother. "Where's your mask? You aren't even wearing white."

"Maybe she didn't want to dress up today."

"But why wouldn't someone want to dress up?" His mouth flattening, Ben eyed her dark-gray shirt.

So she shrugged. "Well, I don't have a mask from last year, and I haven't had a chance to get one yet."

"Oh, I know a great place. Over there." He pointed toward the street. "It's where I got mine. Can I help you pick it out?"

"Ben." Adan gave her an apologetic look.

This was her chance to excuse herself and leave.

"Here, try this." Ben handed her something like a fried pastry and then shoved one into Adan's hand as well. "Adan smashed it just now, but it should still taste good." He plucked a third from his bag and crammed it into his mouth. Cheeks bulging, he wiped his hand on his pants. "Yep. It does." Then he trotted up the path, the ends of the white cloth floating behind him. "Let's go, guys."

Evie's lips twitched, and Adan's cheeks took a rosy glow. Did he want her to go? Even if he did, should she? Realizing she shouldn't know his name, she said with mock incredulity, "How could I possibly go mask shopping with you? I don't even know your name."

There. Ball back in his court to borrow a phrase from her years of watching humans.

"Adan." He smiled. "My name's Adan." He stood, stowing his book in his pocket, and took a few backward steps up the path. Seeming unsure, he tilted his head in Ben's direction. "What do you say, Evie?" There was that half-smile again. "Want to go mask shopping?"

Her stomach fluttered at her name on his lips. This was a bad idea.

She got to her feet and turned her head toward the way she'd come— past the lonely flower in the pond and to the portal where Joram would later be waiting. She twirled the perfect flower in her hand. Adan beckoned with a hopeful expression.

Yep, this was definitely a bad idea.

6

Wearing her new mask with pride, Evie spent an hour walking with the Andree brothers. They explored several shops and even picked up more snacks.

Luckily, she'd found an inexpensive festival mask built onto a pair of sunglasses. The style wasn't Ben's first choice, but it kept her golden eyes hidden.

Were she in Sector Four, she'd likely not have to cover her eyes. There, all had hazel irises, from deep caramel to almost yellow.

But here, blue eyes looked out from every human face. Not only that, but each donned a similar golden-brown skin tone. She'd asked Krystopher once why Sector Five was the only sector with a minimal range of color. All others had varying shades from almost pure white to deepest brown. He'd said the Maker loved variety, but Jesiah was trying to make it difficult for the Deceiver to blend in, should he find a way to cross into Five. She touched her mask. It was easy to blend in if you knew how to do it. What a disturbing thought.

But those thoughts were for another day. Today, she shifted down the street with the exhilarated people of Shura. Families and friends moved along in their light-colored finery like a swirl of white clouds. Perhaps her dark shirt *was* the rain cloud in the distance, a threat on the horizon.

Adan asked about her school and home. She evaded most by claiming to be from out of town. Not a lie. The best way to avoid talking about herself was to keep him talking.

"What do you want to do when you finish high school?" she asked.

"Honestly?" He scratched his nose. "I have no idea. I wish someone would tell me what I should do with my life. What my purpose is." He pulled at his sleeve. "I'm not interested in the plans my classmates throw around."

"Adan's saving money so we can get our own place," Ben said.

Adan frowned at the boy. "We live in a group home. I'm a trainee for a Guardian. I'm thankful for it, but I want Ben to have a normal life. I don't feel like we belong there long term, you know?"

Evie knew the feeling. "I have a job I don't think is right for me. I don't really fit the mold."

"What's your job?"

"Um… it's a desk job. I work with… surveillance equipment." She shrugged. This was true enough, though vastly understated. "Perhaps I'll be promoted soon."

"Or get another job."

"Right." If only it were so easy.

Though she already knew many things about him, she listened, enrapt to hear from his lips that his favorite book was a fantastical adventure. His favorite drink was something called a latte—though he usually bought black coffee because it was cheaper—and his favorite subject in school was history.

They walked on, passing through another retail section. She paused before a window holding a glorious display of fighting knives. She leaned toward the window, almost able to feel the polished blades.

"Knives, huh?" he asked from over her shoulder. "Interested in weaponry?"

"You could say that. I have some training in knife fighting."

"Really?" He narrowed his eyes as he stepped next to her. Their elbows were almost touching.

"Yes, really." She sent him a challenging smile.

He laughed, palms out. "Okay, okay. Remind me not to pick a fight with you."

She smiled as they moved to catch up with Ben, but it slipped away. *No, you won't pick a fight with me. You won't ever see me again.*

Adan pulled Ben into another playful headlock, ruffled his curls, and then—like a good big brother—helped him retie his mask.

She'd never researched a specific person before. Before Adan, she'd been on a mission to learn all she could about Guardian gifts. And before that, to learn everything about Sector Six, which was admittedly not much. Her quest for knowledge about Gifts and how they passed through birth or the Guardian marks led to a brief memo on Dreaming.

This piqued her interest, and after digging around in the archives, she'd found a single file about the Gift.

A newer memo affixed to it simply read, "Andree?" The part of her that thrived on discovery had become obsessed until she'd unearthed Adan and Ben. Only Sector Five held the surname, and Evie had gone through many Andrees before finding Adan and suspecting him of having the Dreaming Gift. She'd made time to check in on him every so often. But, after an eerie incident when Ben fell off his bunk bed, Evie had been unable to keep herself away from that Dreaming folder.

Would she ever see him in person again? Time passed differently in the Control Room. Adan would grow old and maybe even pass from the sector before Krystopher promoted her to the field. *If* he ever did.

Adan led them to a street party occupying an entire intersection. A band played on a stage as white-clad bodies moved to a fast rhythm in the fading light. Pulling their masks over their eyes, Adan and Ben plunged into the throng. Ben beckoned for her, and she followed. She'd never been in such a crowd. But, before long, laughter slipped out as she bounced along with everyone else.

After a while, they meandered to an area filled with round tables. Adan snagged one, and they sat, breathing heavily. Evie's throat felt strange. Her skin glistened with a light sheen, and her hair stuck to the back of her neck. She smoothed it over one shoulder, letting the cool breeze brush her skin.

"This is awesome." Ben drummed his fingers on the table.

Adan pushed his mask atop his head. His knee bounced to the rhythm, and he glanced her way. He smiled when he caught her eyes on him. She grinned and looked away, heat flooding her cheeks. Hopefully, her mask covered the rosy skin.

He placed his elbows on the table and turned the ring circling his pinky finger. Before Evie could stop herself, her hand had reached out to his, and with one finger, she touched a black mark crossing the back of his hand. When he froze at her touch, she jerked away.

"I'm sorry. I just…" She tried again. "Does it hurt? It looks new."

He shifted his hands to his lap. "No. It's fine, and yes, it's new." He opened his mouth to say more but, probably not knowing how to explain, shut it again.

Sensing he didn't want to talk about it, she pointed to Ben's brow instead. "Now that scar looks like it has an excellent story."

Adan brushed Ben's hair away from his eyes. "Don't all scars?"

Ben swatted his hand away and touched the rough patch of skin. Evie already knew the story. She'd been watching that evening, months ago.

"I fell off the top bunk." An air of pride lifted Ben's voice.

"Oh, really? How did that happen?"

He shrugged. "I had a bad dream."

"What did you dream?"

"I sometimes dream about the computer lab at school. You know how in dreams it's the same but different?"

Evie nodded, though she had no idea what he meant, having never slept in her existence.

"It's like that. Sometimes I hear people talking about boring things from the next room, but I can't ever go closer. But that day"—he pointed to his scar—"I heard a man's voice, and he was super mad. But I didn't hear anyone else. I think he was watching a scary movie. There was screaming, and then he rewound it and watched it again. He got madder and madder, and I was afraid he'd find me. He yelled, and then I saw his shadow coming toward the door. Then I was falling and… boom." He flailed his arms.

"Then what happened?" How much would they say about their little chat afterward?

"Nothing. I wasn't scared or anything. Right, Adan?"

"No way. He wasn't scared. He didn't even cry."

Ben beamed, but Evie knew better. He'd been terrified. He'd hardly noticed the pain on his head in his fear of the man from his dream.

But that wasn't what had spoken to Evie that night.

Adan had prodded the boy with questions, trying to find out what might be causing his nightmares. Ben admitted some children had made fun of him for not having a family and for being a little boy under a Guardian's care. What use did Uzziah have for such a weakling?

Ben told Adan he wished he were tougher and not so different from the other kids.

Sitting side by side in the hall outside their bunk room, he'd asked, "Why can't we have a normal family like everyone else? It's not fair."

Adan pulled him close. "No, it's not fair. But it's okay to feel sad. Having emotions and even crying doesn't make you weak. Being scared or happy or sad or longing for a family isn't bad. It makes you human. It's the way you were made."

While Ben was quiet, Adan ruffled his hair. "I've had this dream lately that a Watcher is keeping an eye on us."

Evie's eyes had gone wide, just as Ben's had. Evie, from her Control Room desk, and Ben, from the floor next to Adan, had said in joined whispers. "What?"

"Yep." Adan rubbed his brother's back. "So there's nothing to worry about. We're going to be fine. And I'll walk you home from school for the next few days."

Ducking his head, Ben picked at the hem of Adan's sleeve. "But what if I have a bad dream again?"

"Hmm." He slid his arm from Ben's shoulder. "I have an idea. Wait here." He disappeared around the corner, and when he returned, he knelt in front of Ben and offered him something from the palm.

Evie used two fingers to zoom in on her screen.

Mercifully, Ben asked the question she wanted to voice. "What's that?"

"It's a Watcher." Adan held out a carved wooden figure. "It's from Asher's board game, Guardian Quest. He won't miss it. He never plays anymore. Keep it with you to remind you you're safe."

Ben ran his thumb over the smooth surface. "I'll keep it in my pocket."

Adan's smile softened his sad face. "Good. Ready to go back to bed?"

Evie gripped the edge of her desk. Had Adan dreamed about a Watcher? Or was it a story he made up to appease a child? How could she find out if they made no further mention of the game piece?

In the exhilarating city square, sitting on a chair at a table surrounded by humans, the boys laughed together. Ben reenacted his fall again, and she laughed, too.

No, these two boys didn't live in an ideal situation. It was far from perfect, but they did have each other.

Something in her chest stretched and grew. It felt like a hole—a gaping space that hadn't been there before. It accompanied an emotion she couldn't quite name.

After that day, Evie had been unable to look away. She found endless excuses to check in on them. Excuses she need only tell herself since no one else even knew who they were. Drawn toward them as if she were a part of their little family, she liked to think she was, in a way, tucked away in the pocket of a nine-year-old. Watching. Protecting.

Ben tugged on Adan's sleeve and whispered in his ear.

They both stood. "Evie, will you save our seats? We'll be right back."

"Sure. I'll be here."

They walked away. Adan got in line for one of the many vendors, and Ben stepped into a public restroom.

Something tapped Evie's head. As she reached up to inspect, a drop of water plunked onto the table. She prodded the silvery dome with a finger. Another drop, then another. *Rain!* Liquid continued to dribble from the sky.

She extracted Joram's communicator from her pocket and glanced at the time. It was later than she'd thought. She tucked it away, and then her gaze flicked to where Adan stood. This time she caught *him* staring at *her*. He smiled and ducked his head as she'd done only minutes before. The gesture sent her pulse into thudding.

She diverted her attention back to the dancing mob and drummed her fingers on the table. The crowd thinned as the sun dipped below the buildings and dark clouds rolled in.

Through the parting bodies, a tall figure stalked into the horde. Face shining with wetness and anger, Garran—Adan's archenemy of sorts—shoved dancers aside as he made his way in Adan's direction.

Evie's fingers paused. What was he going to do?

The glint of a blade winked at his side.

She surged to her feet as the rain began to fall in earnest.

"Adan," she called.

He looked up, shielding his eyes. "What's wrong?"

When she was only a few steps away, a man plowed into her. His shoulder snagged her mask, and the impact sent her stumbling.

"Sorry," he yelled, not slowing.

Adan helped her to her feet.

"What's..." he began to ask, but his words fell away. His eyes flared at the edges, his lips parting. Water dripped from his curls, and he raised a hand as if to touch her but then thought better of it. "Evie?"

Her mask was gone. It lay useless at their feet.

Adan took a step back. "Who are you?"

"I…" How could she explain the golden eyes?

"You're a Guardian." His voice wasn't fearful. Guardians weren't something to be feared, but a hint of betrayal tightened his lips as he realized she'd hidden her eyes from him all afternoon.

No time to explain. "Garran's coming."

The Strength Wielder was closing in, almost on them now.

Adan glanced at the boy before facing her. Something like surprise or suspicion narrowed his eyes. He started to say something else but snapped his mouth shut. "I have to go. Tell Ben to go home and wait for me there."

He sprinted away.

Evie stood motionless. Garran barreled past. Three others she vaguely recognized followed.

Should she help Adan? She didn't have a weapon, but she could fight.

Ben emerged from the restroom and stood under an overhang. He peered around the almost deserted intersection.

No, she couldn't leave Ben. She picked up her mask and slid it onto her face.

"The party's ruined," Ben whined as she joined him. "Where's Adan?"

"He had to go. He said to wait for him at home."

"He had to go?"

He'd see through any fib she told him. "Garran showed up, and he was mad." The skin between Ben's eyes crinkled as he chewed his lip, so she added, "But Adan got a head start, and he looked really fast."

"He is! He's the fastest one."

This made Evie feel marginally better. Should she follow now that she'd given Ben the message? No, Ben was right. He'd be fine. Plus, she couldn't leave a child to walk home in the rain.

"I should take you home. Do you know the way?"

"Yeah. We need to go that way." He pointed the way they'd come.

"Okay, then. After you."

After a short while, it was clear Ben wasn't sure how to get back to his apartment building. They crisscrossed the streets, darting from one overhang to another as rain spattered the pavement.

Then Ben saw a landmark he recognized, and his pace increased. They rounded the last corner and took cover under his building's overhang. The doorman was gone, and pedestrians had deserted the sidewalk. Cars sped past with blazing headlights.

"Do you think Adan will be all right?" she asked.

"Yeah, he's fast. And when Garran gets mad, he just yells, and then it's over." Ben shrugged. "Hey, how do you know Garran anyway?"

Another mistake. Evie put a hand on Ben's shoulder. "I have to go now. You go on upstairs, okay?"

He nodded.

"It was nice to meet you, Ben." She meant it. "Tell Adan I said bye."

She couldn't force a smile. She'd never see the Dreamer again, and she didn't even get to say goodbye.

As if reading her mind, Ben asked, "Will I see you again?"

She lifted a shoulder. "Who knows?" An honest reply. Maybe she would return before he died of old age, and his soul went to the Waiting Place. Maybe. She waved as he opened the door and went inside.

She ducked back into the rain, her shoes squishing on the pavement.

Everything looked different in the dark. She paused under a doorway and fished the communicator from her pocket. When the screen lit up, the words *Where are you?* flashed across its surface before going dark. When she tried to pull the message up again, nothing happened. She shook the device and tapped it on her other hand.

Nothing.

Her heart sped as she sprinted through the rain in the direction she thought she was supposed to go.

After ages of running through the drenched streets, she recognized the familiar skyline from this morning. This street carved a direct path to the park. Her legs ached, but she didn't dare slow.

Evie rounded the last corner and sprinted into the trees. It was dark now, and the shadows cast eerie shapes across the lawn.

She spotted Joram huddled over his device in a copse of trees. He stood upon the portal, his form already fading. He'd started the return procedure.

Evie raced across the limp grass. "Joram. Wait."

Eyes widening, he raised his palms in an I'm-sorry gesture. "I can't stop it," he said as if from a great distance. Water dripped from his chin, and he faded before the droplets splashed onto the metal disk.

She rushed atop the portal, calling his name. She spun, stomping her feet on the surface, having no idea how to activate it. Nothing happened. No tingling fingers. No disappearing Evie. No stark, clean Control Room.

Panic gripped her as the first clap of lightning lit the sky. The answering boom vibrated through her body, and she dashed out of the trees and across the street. She stepped under the awning of a bank that had long since closed and stood in the darkness with her back pressed against the bricks.

"He left me," she whispered, and her heart thundered as another fork of lightning ripped at the sky.

7

Children. His fellow trainees acted like three-year-olds.

Sam sat huddled, hiding in the slowing rain, waiting to see what the biggest toddler of all was going to do next. Garran crouched below in the narrow alleyway like a pouting child.

Sam perched on a fire escape landing far above Garran and his two cronies, Todd and Stella. The others had gone to bed, believing the excitement to be over.

Sam certainly hoped it was.

As Adan's best friend, Sam would gladly wait in the rain. A lookout of sorts. Well, maybe not gladly. But he'd do it.

He'd never seen Garran so angry. Jealousy plagued the other boy—it plagued them all. But Garran had begun to lash out more. No telling what he might do after last night's marking ceremony.

Their Guardian was stronger than Garran, but Uzziah hadn't been around when Sam stopped in the apartment earlier. If only the man allowed his trainees to have cell phones.

Below, Todd broke the silence. "Garran, let's go home. He's not coming, and I'm soaked."

Garran glared at the other boy. "I'm not going anywhere. He always comes this way. Thinks no one knows about it."

They sat in a dead-end alley mostly hidden from the street. Large discarded boxes and concrete blocks cluttered the space.

This particular passage had once been Sam and Adan's "shortcut." One could scale the uneven brick wall until they reached the drainpipe, shimmy around the corner, and climb down the other side right to the back door of Uzziah's building. It wasn't shorter, but it *was* secret.

Sam leaned against the brick wall for a wait. He dug his baseball out of his pocket and tossed it up and down.

Garran would go in. But what if Adan showed up first? Sam wasn't sure what he might do about it even if Adan did creep into the shadows. None of them could stand against Garran and his otherworldly strength.

What was it Garran wanted? What would make him happy? Sam would never pull the answer from the Strength Wielder's pea-sized brain.

He flipped the baseball to his other hand.

Todd and Stella started playing a game with dice. The rain had slowed to a drizzle, and the occasional car splashed by the alley.

Maybe Sam should make himself known. Try to talk some sense into the idiot. "Garran, Todd's right. Go in. He's not going to come this way."

The others looked up, their startled faces a tan flash in the dim light. Garran rolled his eyes. Sam may be the second-largest boy, but Garran held no fear of him. Sam was not Gifted and was not a favorite.

"Go home, Sam. This has nothing to do with you."

"Good idea. Let's all go in." When Garran ignored him, Sam continued. "What's your endgame here? What are you going to do? Uzziah already gave him the mark. You can't change that."

"He needs to be put in his place. He thinks he's better than us. Even than you."

"You don't even know what you're talking about."

"Now that he has the marks, he'll be more arrogant than ever. And he'll believe everything he's ever dreamed. I'll make sure he knows otherwise."

Sam shook his head. Okay, so he'd thought the same thing. *Would* Adan's visions come true? Sam had always seen him as a boy who had nightmares. But now?

Gravel crunched halfway down the alley.

Oh boy.

Adan had crept in. He probably couldn't see Garran and the others behind stacked boxes. He could only see Sam high above.

An I-told-you-so smirk parted Garran's lips. "Here comes the Dreamer," he whispered.

Sam shot to his feet, grabbing the slick handrail. "Run, Adan."

As Garran, Todd, and Stella stepped forward, Adan turned to run, but John, another of Garran's lackeys, blocked the way.

Flame it. How had Sam missed the other boy there?

Adan took his chances with John. But all John needed to do was slow him down. Garran barreled toward Adan.

Sam climbed down the fire escape, jumping the last feet. He yelled and pulled at Garran, his efforts useless against the Strength Wielder's raw muscle. Garran pounded Adan's face and then tossed him farther up the alley where he'd be trapped. The Strength Wielder was holding back. Otherwise, Adan would be out cold.

Todd, Stella, and John fanned out, preventing Adan's escape.

Adan stumbled to his feet and backed into the corner. Blood gushed down his chin, and dark stains speckled his hoodie. Adan's eyes were wide, though one seemed in the process of swelling shut. His hair hung, dripping over his brow. His fingers twitched, and a twinkle reflected in the streetlight.

Garran pointed at Adan's hand. "He told me you had it, that Uzziah gave it to you."

Who told him what? The others looked equally confused.

Adan glanced at his pinky finger but said nothing.

"An enhancement ring," breathed Stella. She and the others stared at Adan's hand.

"A what?" Adan asked. Then, as Garran prowled closer, Adan backed farther into the corner.

"When did he give it to you?"

"Garran, stand down." Sam lifted his palms. "He's done nothing wrong."

Something ugly distorted Garran's face. "Nothing? Yesterday, he not only received marks from a Strength Wielder—which happens only once a year, by the way—but Uzziah also gave him his only enhancement ring. That marking ceremony should have gone to me. I've been here the longest. And that ring should be mine."

Sam stepped back, a shudder coursing over him. He no longer recognized this boy. Where was the fun-loving boy he first met years ago in Uzziah's atrium? "What happened to you?"

The decision to act narrowed Garran's already beady eyes, and Sam was flying backward into the gravel.

Sucking air into his lungs, he regained his feet. The Strength Wielder hadn't spared him another thought but turned back to Adan.

Adan, though faster, was only able to avoid Garran's iron grip for a few minutes. Garran trapped Adan in the corner and seized him by the collar. Sam ran forward as the Strength Wielder punched his best friend in the face. He pulled at Garran from behind. Adan crumpled to the ground, and Garran kicked him.

"He's going to kill him," Sam yelled to the others.

Todd, Stella, and John stood openmouthed. They hadn't planned on something so drastic. They rushed forward, calling for Garran to relent. Together, they clutched at Garran's trunk-like arms. Garran backed away, breathing hard, the four of them still clinging to his body.

"That ring should be mine," he bellowed again.

Sam rounded on him. "You're right. Maybe it should be yours. Take it, but leave Adan. Look what you've already done." He gestured at Adan's bloody and almost unrecognizable face.

"He needs to pay. He tricked Uzziah into giving it to him."

"Yeah." Sam took a breath. "Yeah. He should pay. Let's leave him here. He can shiver in the alley all night. Look at him. There's no way he'll be able to walk back home. He can't even stand up."

Relaxing his clenched fists, Garran seemed to be considering his words.

The four boys stood pressed together as if expecting an explosion.

Garran shook them off, nodding. "That's a good idea. Yeah."

He scanned the deserted space. Having come to a decision Sam couldn't begin to guess, he walked to a spot below the fire escape. Garran knelt, taking hold of something solid. With a mighty roar and the grinding of metal, he jerked back as the object gave way. Garran tossed a mangled padlock to the side and pried at the heavy, rusted double doors of a long-forgotten storage basement. He flung them open with a resounding clang and stalked back to Adan, leaving a dark opening visible. A staircase led into inky blackness.

The rain picked up again, splashing into Sam's eyes and dripping off his nose. He and the others squinted at Garran. What did he mean to do?

Garran took Adan by the ankle and dragged him toward the gaping hole. Adan's fingers scrambled to find purchase on the graveled surface, though his eyes were barely open.

Garran's plan clicked into place in Sam's mind. But, when he moved to stop him, Garran swiped him out of the way. The others made no move to block him. He stopped just short of the opening and grabbed Adan's left hand. The Strength Wielder tugged the enhancement ring from the Dreamer's finger.

Adan's swollen and bloodshot eyes found Sam, and Garran gave one final tug over the opening. Adan thudded onto the stairs and tumbled into the darkness. He landed on his back, and a sickening thud resounded as his head hit the concrete floor.

Leaning over the edge where a slice of light found Adan's face, Sam mouthed, "I'll get you out. I promise."

Adan's eyes fluttered closed as Garran slammed the doors shut with a final, earsplitting clang.

Hours later, Sam lay on his back in the bunk room, touching the corner of a swollen eye. Ben and a few others slept.

Sam cut his gaze to Garran, hoping he'd fallen asleep. He hadn't. The boy sat on his bed, rotating the enhancement ring over his swollen knuckles. The ring was too small for Garran. The Strength Wielder seemed to be debating what to do about that.

In the alley, Garran had hauled an enormous concrete block to the basement door and slid it on top. Only a Strength Wielder would be able to dislodge it. At this hour, the basement would be blocked off from the apartment building above. Adan was stuck, and he'd likely passed out. Sam hoped he had. It would be a mercy.

After that, Garran had announced they would all be going up to their apartment. While Sam tried to think of an excuse to stay, Garran issued a ridiculous number of threats.

Uzziah remained absent.

Later, pretending to go to the bathroom, Sam had tried to sneak out. Garran punched him in the eye for it.

Under Garran's watchful glare, none who were in the alley had spoken to the other trainees, and now all was quiet.

Ben had been waiting for them. Sam didn't dare recount the story, but he told the smaller boy not to worry. Adan was fine.

Sam turned his head on his pillow. Todd squirmed under his gaze. Garran's cronies hadn't expected things to get so out of hand.

Olivia, another trainee, stopped in the doorway. She held out a box, giving it a shake. "Anyone want to play Guardian Quest?"

"Sure," Asher answered.

They exchanged a few bewildered whispers as they cleared a space in the center of the room.

"What about you, Sam?" Olivia asked, picking at the corner of a pillow she'd pulled into her lap.

Sam shook his head. When she frowned at his stony silence, he rolled over, facing the wall. Later, he'd sneak back down.

Footsteps padded past as a few others joined the game.

Sam blinked, his eyelids heavy. He pictured himself strong enough to stop bullies like Garran. If Sam could only match him in strength, then they might well keep him in check. What a dream.

It'd been an early morning and a long day, and now Sam's adrenaline rush crumbled like a wasted sector.

He listened to the whispering drone as the others set up their game, shuffling the pieces, rustling hands over the ground, shifting weight on the hardwood floor.

He pulled a blanket over his head.

Seemed many things went wrong this holiday evening. The others loaded Guardian Quest back into the box. One of the game pieces had disappeared. They wouldn't be playing tonight after all.

The Watcher was missing.

8

Evie shivered, sitting cross-legged on the damp portal. The cold metal bit into her skin, but she didn't dare move. Joram would come back for her. Why hadn't he come back for her?

After the lightning subsided, she'd returned to the disk and huddled in the rain all night. Mercifully, it had slowed to a drizzle. Now dawn was minutes away, and soon early morning commuters would fill the streets. Already the occasional pedestrian meandered by.

By now, word of her crimes had reached Krystopher. Had he decided to leave her? And wasn't that what she wanted? To live in Sector Five?

But she had nowhere to go, no Guardian Mark, and no Guardian Gift. No, she'd never wanted to live on the ground as a… *human*.

She needed a plan. She'd decide how long to wait, then take action. She needed food, shelter, and sleep. Her energy winding down, she blinked and tried to keep herself from yawning. She failed.

Where would she go? Uzziah offered her only logical answer. She cringed. "Hello. I'm Evie. I'm a Watcher, and I was left by accident. Oh, and I pretended to be a human to two of your boys yesterday."

She shivered. Two hours. She'd wait two hours.

Rubbing her hands together, she wished for gloves. As the thought crossed her mind, her hands did seem to warm. She held them before her. Yes, definitely warmer—and tingling.

This is it! She stood, bending her knees. She wouldn't fall this time.

Relief washed through her as the tingling sensation grew. The feeling of fading—of coming unwound—shivered down her body. She felt very far away. The green of the park blurred until her feet rested on a different surface. Blinking into familiar golden lights, she stood, hands still raised before her, in the Transportation Room of Control Room Five.

But her relief vanished as surely as the green park. The wide eyes of not only Joram, Krystopher, and Alizah were fixed on her but also Gavrie, her supervisor, and before them all, Jesiah, the Maker himself.

Evie's pale fingers flew over her workstation screen. She logged in, scanning the tasks she'd missed, and pulled up her assigned vidfeeds from various sector locations. On a normal day, she'd push one to the massive wall of screens. Alizah would do the same. But today was not a normal day.

"Everyone's staring," Alizah noted from her desk next to Evie on the Control Room floor.

Evie raised her head. Sure enough, countless pairs of golden eyes flicked her way.

Great.

Their desks, along with hundreds of others, faced the long, busy wall. Screen after screen of footage from Sector Five covered its length and width. One showed a park not so different from the one Evie was in yesterday, another showed a rooftop high above the city, and still others displayed city streets, vast farmland, and tropical beaches. They moved and changed as Watchers adjusted their view or pushed a new image onto the wall. The Watchers looked after humans from behind desks forming perfect lines across the spotless, pale-gold Control Room floor. They guarded and protected, and most of all, they watched for signs of the Deceiver.

"What were you thinking?" Alizah's strawberry curls bounced around her worried face.

Gavrie, their supervisor, had sent them back to their work areas to wait. Nothing like this had ever happened, so there was no measure to guess what kind of punishment would be dealt.

"It seemed harmless. I've wanted to go for so long. When they took the promotion away, I was so angry." Evie flicked a lock of her long hair out of her face and huffed. "Then, when Joram suggested it… I don't know… I just thought, 'Why not?'" Resting her head on her chair back, she regarded the pale-gold ceiling. "What have I done?"

"I can't believe Joram was so careless. *He* should've known better." Alizah swiveled in her chair. "What do you think they're discussing in there?"

Evie lifted a shoulder. Krystopher, Jesiah, Joram, and Gavrie had been in the office for several minutes now. After they'd seen to Evie's return, they questioned her. She told them of the places she'd gone and seen and about the ruined communicator. She left out, however, how closely she traveled with her human companions. She didn't name them.

"Joram waited for a while." Evie rubbed the shivers from her arms. "I was already late, but I saw him leave. What did they say when I didn't show up for my next shift? That was hours ago."

"They comm'ed your private quarters, but, well, obviously, you weren't there. At first, Gavrie seemed annoyed. He asked where I thought you might be. I don't think, in all this time, anyone's ever just not shown up." Alizah cut her gaze to Evie. "You're a legend."

"Yeah, some legend." Evie stared at the ceiling again. Her eyes prickled. How strange. No one cried here. She willed it away before anyone noticed.

"You'll get a long-winded lecture, of course… and perhaps a Death Guardian glare."

When Evie raised an eyebrow, Alizah grinned. "Chin up. It will be fine. I'm sorry you were trapped in the cold for so long. I was worried. We all were. I never thought to ask Joram. It wasn't his shift, so no one wondered about him." She studied Gavrie's office door. "He returned hours before telling anyone he left you. Fear of Jesiah's wrath must have made him try to take care of it on his own."

They sat in silence.

Then Alizah nudged her. "I probably shouldn't tell you this, but Krystopher rescheduled the promotions."

"What?" Evie jolted upright, banging her knee against her desktop. An unfamiliar sensation tightened her chest. *What have I done?*

"Before we realized you were gone, he announced they'd reset the promotion dates. They'd only postponed them because they wanted to wait until after Jesiah's trip to Sector Seven. It's going to happen in about three weeks across all open sectors."

Evie slumped in her chair. It had all been for nothing. All she'd had to do was wait a lousy, sacked-sector three weeks. She lowered her head to her hands.

Alizah rolled her chair over. "Gavrie's coming."

Evie sat up. The slick black surfaces of the touchscreen desks reflected his perfect posture. The man was not smiling beneath his narrowed golden eyes.

"Evie." His eyes caught the reflection of the flickering screens, their brightness in stark contrast to his dark skin. "A word, please."

He led her down the short hallway toward his office.

As they approached, Krystopher stepped out with Joram and stood next to the bench outside Gavrie's door. Joram met Evie's eye. "Sorry, Evie. I tried to bring you back, but I was having technical difficulties. The sequence had to recharge."

Evie nodded but said nothing.

"Go on, Joram." Gavrie crossed his arms. "Rest. We'll expect you back at the start of your next shift."

Jesiah, the Maker, walked into the hall from Gavrie's office and put his hands in his pockets. Feeling small under their assessment, Evie sank onto the bench.

"You too, Evie." Gavrie tilted his head toward the door leading to her private quarters. "It's not officially your shift. You can go for now."

Evie straightened but didn't stand. She glanced between them. "But what's going to happen? Will I be punished?"

Jesiah emitted a commanding presence in any room, but in this confined space, he was radiant. "To be honest, we haven't decided. We're going to take some time to think about it."

Evie studied her hands as the others cleared out. Waiting longer might be worse than any punishment.

"So, what did you think, Evaniah?"

Jesiah's deep voice startled her. The Maker stood a few paces away, a curious glint to his eye. Only he called her Evaniah.

His short silver hair glistened as if more than reflecting the light above them. His crisp white button-up shirt always immaculate seemed more blindingly so today. He'd discarded his tie, making him appear more relaxed.

"About what, sir?" She remained seated. Should she rise?

"About Sector Five."

Her eyebrows shot up, her mouth slid open, and she snapped it shut.

Jesiah laughed. Warm and rich, his laughter always seemed like she'd once imagined sunlight to be. "Was it all you hoped it to be? I don't often get to talk to someone immediately after they've experienced one of the sectors for the first time. Especially someone who wanted to go as badly as you did." His eyes twinkled as he sat next to her.

Evie ducked her head. She'd never spoken to the Maker one-on-one. Sure, she'd sat in on his meetings, and he talked to everyone on occasion and learned their names. But now, he sat, curious, asking about her illegal adventure like a human asking about the weather.

"It…" she began, throat dry. "It was amazing." She shuffled her feet. Surely he didn't have the time for her limited opinion. But his expression was open and hopeful. "More than amazing. Beautiful. As the sun was setting, the sky was the most stunning color. The trees, the water, the warmth."

She closed her eyes, smiling, remembering. "And the humans." She thought of Adan and tucked her hands under her thighs. "I loved it. Well, until the end, at least."

"No, I suppose your time in the rain was not your finest." He pushed his sleeves up and rested his elbows on his knees. "But I'm glad to hear you speak well of humans, Evaniah. Many believe they aren't worth the effort. That they aren't worth preserving." A wistful smile. "But I… am quite fond of them."

Her head jerked up. How could anyone discount *all* humans? "There were some whose emotions ran hot. They let their humanity weaken them." At this, Jesiah frowned, but she continued. "But there were others who didn't. Others who were kind and good."

Adan and Ben, the family in the park, the many dancing, smiling mortals. Her lips curved into a smile. "They're worth it."

"I'm glad you think so. Though I don't think being human is a weakness. Strong emotions make them different from those in the Control Room, but that's not a bad thing." He sat back, removing his elbows from his knees. "I'm leaving now to visit Sector Seven. I won't be here when Gavrie speaks with you later today. I've left everything to his good judgment."

"I'm so sorry, Jesiah. It was rash and stupid."

"I forgive you."

Evie searched his eyes. "How can you forgive me so easily?"

"People who hold grudges are fools who have unknowingly erected a prison around themselves. The key to their freedom is in forgiveness. Of course, I forgive you. It does neither of us any good not to."

He stood.

"What's it like?" Evie blurted. "Sector Seven, I mean." Humans didn't yet inhabit it. A blank slate for Jesiah to fill. "Is it true it's filled with strange creatures? Predators?"

Jesiah patted her shoulder. "I'm sure you would love it. And yes, it is." He peeked at his watch. "I'll have to tell you about it another time. You know we have rules for a reason. They're meant to protect both you and the billions of humans in the sectors. I'm trying very hard to contain the Deceiver's lies. I can't afford for him to cross into the newer sectors. The lies he spreads cause humans to do things that aren't so different from a Watcher who makes a rash, emotional decision. One who doesn't think things through or consider who they might harm in the process."

Hunching her shoulders, Evie pressed her hands deeper under her thighs, and her heart… *hurt.*

"Please don't break my rules again."

"I won't." And she meant it.

Evie lunged at her invisible opponent in the cavernous training room. She'd needed something active to keep her mind from worrying. Her body was in top shape. She trained hard, and her immortal shell needed little prodding to perform the moves. Many believed learning mortal style hand-to-hand and weapon combat was a waste of personal time. But it represented one of the few pastimes training her for anything human-related. Her weapon of choice had become the dagger, and she'd completed all her marks, earning the label of Immortal Warrior—a useless title. But it filled the time.

Finished with her last round, she moved on to the rock-climbing wall and lifted herself off the ground.

She dangled above the padded floor when footsteps echoed across the space. Krystopher smiled as he approached and she dropped to the ground.

"How are you feeling after your little adventure?" He crossed his arms over his broad chest, pulling at the round Maker's mark stitched onto his shirt.

"I'm okay. A little embarrassed."

Krystopher chuckled.

Evie kicked at the padded floor. "What brings you to the training room? Since you don't have workers to train for new jobs, I thought you'd be tinkering in the lab. Aren't you working on a new kind of portal?"

"That's going to have to wait a few weeks. I'm joining Jesiah in Sector Seven, and I wanted to speak with you before we leave."

A thin package rested across his palms. "This is going to seem strange to you, but I have something I want to give you."

"I break the law, and now you're giving me a present?"

"Believe me. It's not some sort of reward."

She took it, turning the unbending white-wrapped parcel in her hands.

"I think you may have gotten into something bigger than traveling unsanctioned." He scratched his head, looking into the distance. "I'm not sure why," he paused. "Well, I felt I needed to give this to you. There may be a time you'll need it. I don't know when or where or why."

When she started to open it, he raised a hand. "Not now. Later." He glanced at the door. His premonitions were something of a legend in the Control Room.

She tucked the gift into her bag.

He straightened. "Well, I'm off. I'll be gone for a while, but I don't think Gavrie will deal too harshly with you." He clamped a hand on her shoulder. "You'll be fine. Take your punishment with dignity and get back to work."

When he'd almost reached the door, her every muscle tightened around the desperate question breaking free. "Are my chances of becoming a Guardian lost forever?"

Not breaking stride, Krystopher looked over his shoulder. Was he smiling? If he was, she more felt than saw it. "That's yet to be seen, Evie."

<<<<<>>>>>

After showering in her private quarters, she slid into a chair and activated the screen on her dresser's surface. She accessed the human literature archives and opened *One's Raining Fire*.

In it, Nolan, a zoologist, received his plans to build the first-ever portal. The schematics came to him in a dream, and Nolan had begun the building process in the rooftop garden of his office building.

Nolan bent to examine the round base, which would be the anchor for the structure. He wondered, not for the first time, if he was crazy. If anyone found out about this, they would certainly think so.

Needing something for her fidgeting hands, Evie pulled a sheet of paper from her desk. A sketch should do the trick. She set her workstation to read aloud as the flower from the pond came to life under her attention.

One's Raining Fire continued in a computerized voice.

The Guardian returned later, disturbing Nolan from a fitful sleep full of visions of an all-consuming fire. Glad to escape his dreams, he listened as the Truth-Speaker provided further instruction. How could it be? The key to the Deceiver's capture rested around him—around Nolan, Krystopher's Marked. Nolan would send the Deceiver home to face his judgment.

"What if I can't do it? What if I can't follow the plans?" Nolan asked the Watcher.

"You can. Everything you need will be provided."

"But what if I don't want to?" He lifted his palms, breath quickening. "I have a family to think of. I have two sons, and my wife is with child."

"Search your heart, Dreamer. Does this feel right? Does it feel like the right thing to do?"

Nolan closed his eyes and waited. A slow breath filled his lungs and then passed through parted lips. Listening to the Still Small Voice, he lifted his chin and opened his eyes. "Yes."

"Good. Because, for you—for every man—if we know the right thing but don't do it, we have already failed. The fire from your dreams is coming, Nolan. Prepare."

Evie paused the playback and examined the flower she'd drawn. Why had the shape seemed familiar? As she traced her finger over it, trying to touch that place in her memory, a light flashed, and a soft beep sounded. The comm system on her dresser hailed. She pressed the receiver, hoping to see Alizah, but a different face appeared on the screen built into her mirror.

"Hello, Ariel. Did you need something?"

"Evie, Gavrie would like to see you in his office."

Well, hello to you, too. Not that she expected different from Ariel, Supervisor Gavrie's no-nonsense assistant.

Evie gathered her sketch and stowed it on a high shelf in her closet with hundreds of other drawings. Once she'd changed into her off-duty attire, soft gray pants, and a pale-gold short-sleeve shirt, she threw on a light jacket and filled the pockets with Krystopher's gift and Joram's communicator. She'd return it while in the Control Room.

Alizah passed her in the hallway. "Something's happening," the other Watcher said, "and I don't think it's good."

"What do you mean?" Evie quickened her pace. Was this meeting not about her punishment?

"Several people came rushing in, and Gavrie led them straight to his office. He sent for Joram too."

Evie half-expected a mortal heartbeat to accelerate inside her chest. "Who were they?"

"I only recognized Remiel. I hadn't seen him since he transferred out of Sector Five."

"When did they arrive?"

"Half an hour ago."

Evie chewed her lip. She and Alizah entered the Control Room and crossed the space toward Gavrie's office. Several faces watched them pass with knowing disapproval—not a good sign. Gavrie met Evie at his door, but instead of letting her in, he gestured for her to follow.

She frowned at Alizah, who paused, watching them retreat. "Can Alizah come?"

"No, only you for now. I'm sure the others will fill her in."

As they exited the space, Evie peeked over her shoulder. Another Watcher was already whispering in Alizah's ear. Her gaze, which never left Evie, held unmistakable alarm.

No. Not good at all.

9

Adan walked along the dark path, this dream somehow hazier than the last. Was it the loss of the ring?

The sun hung below angry gray clouds spanning the vaulted sky. Trees cast long shadows across a never-ending trail.

Then the path widened where a single snowy tree stood. Though the weather was warm, fluffy white clung to wide branches as muted sunlight cut through like quivering daggers.

A small form knelt in the open space. With a twig, Ben drew intricate patterns in fine sand.

Adan ran to him, but as he approached, Ben shifted into someone else. Sam stood, disrupting the circular shape in the sand. He faced the trees where Garran stalked out, eyes swirling to black. A shadow of a bear followed him. A snake slithered in the yellow grass below the trees.

Garran sauntered over to stand next to Sam. Together, they faced Adan. Each took a knee and bowed low.

Adan touched his own fine clothes, elaborate garments more like a costume from a medieval movie set. When he lifted his head, the boys were gone.

Within the trees, a face peered back at him. The stranger spoke in urgent warning—a warning Adan couldn't hear. He jogged closer, but an anguished battle cry split the unnatural quiet. Adan dodged a knife as it sliced through the still air.

His attacker moved in a cloud of golden light, pale hair wild on the growing wind. The assassin lunged, sinking a dagger deep into Adan's chest.

Adan fell back, grasping at the wound as blood blossomed on his fine shirt.

The face leaned over him, but the blinding light swallowed all detail. A single tear fell from the silhouette and landed on his cheek.

<<<>>>

Adan jerked awake, sprawled on his stomach. He groaned and rolled onto his back. His entire body ached. He rubbed his face. One eye was nearly swollen shut. The other eyelid opened as his jumbled thoughts shifted. Garran. Adan shot upright and winced.

What happened? There'd been festival celebrations, Ben in a park, Evie, Garran's fists, long darkness. Then… what?

Adan sat on an unfamiliar bed. Skin grating against a dingy feather mattress, he stood in a cell formed by gray stones. A sturdy metal door and—*iron* bars crisscrossed the window upon it. Light filtered through more bars on another window—long and narrow—high in the wall.

He yanked the door handle. When his fingers wrapped around it, his knees buckled as the crackle of an electric current pulsed through him.

He hit the ground and panted, trembling on all fours.

Was this a joke? "Garran? Sam? This isn't funny."

No answer.

He stood and touched a quick finger to the door's metal. Another crackle. Another jolt of thunder in his veins.

His breath quickened, and a bead of cold sweat slid down his back.

"Hello?" His yell echoed down a hallway beyond the door. "Ben?"

Think. Just think. What had Uzziah always taught him? Stay calm. Stay focused. He paced. A bucket rested in the corner. A cup of water waited next to the door. A chain snaked across the stone floor. One end attached to an open shackle. The other bolted to the wall.

His stomach turned.

He pushed the bed beneath the window, stood on it, and looked out. Grass swayed before his eyes. The narrow window rested just above the earth, putting this dingy room mostly underground. The green spread into the distance to touch a forest where tall trees shot into the sky. And beyond that—mountains.

Shadows stretched long, marking the time as either dawn or late evening. Either way, he wasn't in the city. And if the mountains were any indication, this basement was a long way from home.

How did he get here? How much time had passed?

A memory flashed. The trunk of a car. A blindfold. Darkness.

Panic returned. He'd been in the dark for hours. He'd heard voices and then been assaulted by blinding light as the door to his basement prison opened. Someone with a flashlight tied a cloth over Adan's eyes and fixed something to his ankle. They shoved him into the trunk. The pain over his body had been nearly unbearable until he felt a jerk of electricity.

He couldn't remember any more. Had he passed out? He yanked his pant leg up and groaned. Oh, why couldn't it have been another bad dream? A metal band encircled his ankle. Balancing, he gripped a bar crossing the window. Something crackled.

Several minutes later, he awoke on the disgusting mattress, staring up at the electric bars crossing the high window.

He squeezed his good eye shut, willing himself to remember. He tried turning the ring on his pinky, but the finger was bare.

Right. Garran took it.

Peering at his hands, Adan recalled a strange feeling.

Just as he grabbed at another memory, voices carried through the window from outside. He shot to his feet as two sets of boots stalked past. When they crossed out of sight, a door creaked, and footsteps pounded overhead and then downward toward him. He backed against the wall across from the door and snatched the bucket, brandishing it over his shoulder.

A stern face appeared in the tiny window. Dark eyebrows drew together over the strangest eyes—bright green, like two shining emeralds.

The man chuckled at Adan. "He has spunk. I'll give you that."

His deep vibrato wielded a strange accent.

"He's Gifted." This person didn't have the foreign accent and stood just out of view. "A Strength Wielder—and only recently Guardian Marked. He has yet to use it in my presence. I want you to find out how powerful he is."

The eyebrows in the window shot high. A gleam of greed darkened those bizarre eyes as the man whispered, "Guardian Marked. Most you bring me possess only a watered-down inherited Gift. This is rare, indeed." His eyebrows lowered, his gaze remaining on Adan. "And blue eyes. How strange. Where did you find him?"

"That's none of your concern."

The green-eyed man frowned. "How is he contained?"

"He's shackled. Here is the activator."

The man took something and looked it over. "Where do you acquire such things? This one looks even better than the last."

"Again, that's no concern of yours, but you'll have ample opportunity to try it out."

The man cocked his head. "Boy, I want to come in and have a chat. But first, put the bucket down and attach that manacle on your ankle."

Was he kidding? Adan wasn't going to chain himself to a wall. "No."

The man started to raise his arm, but the other one cut him off. "Adan, be reasonable. There's no way out of the room. We'll simply wait you out."

An opening appeared at the base of the door, and a hand pulled the glass of water from the room. The opening closed again.

"The only reasonable thing to do is to put on the manacle—and there's no reason not to. You want to do what he says."

As the man spoke in his mild way, Adan began to relax. He was right. Adan could see no reason to resist. He dropped the bucket and clamped the heavy iron onto his leg.

The door opened, and careful not to touch its metal surface, the green-eyed man stepped in, revealing his short stocky body and graying dark hair. He held something before himself with nervous fingers. "Hello, Adan. My name is Captain Edward Curtshaw, former captain of the guard for King Alexander. You will be in my care for a time. I understand you are new to your Strength Gift. Not to worry, we shall find out exactly what you can do."

"What are you talking about?" Adan stared at him, unable to look away from his eyes. *Strength Gift? King?*

"You will find out soon enough." The captain offered a pleasant smile. "Now, take off your shirt. I would like to see your markings."

Adan's outrage must have shown. The captain looked back at the other man who still didn't show his face.

"Show him what your little device does."

Adan followed the captain's gaze to his hand, tensing. The captain rotated a palm-sized metal box and pressed a button on the side.

Electric pain shot up Adan's leg, and he jerked onto his knees and then flat to his belly. Electricity pulsed through him in waves. When it stopped, he panted on the cold stones.

Adan tipped his head toward Captain Curtshaw, and the man recoiled. He held the device before him. "Do as I say."

Adan stayed on the ground but moved one leg into view. The manacle circled one ankle, and the horrible metal band—an electric ring —circled the other. His breathing shallowed, and his heartbeat thundered as if it wanted freedom from his chest like Adan wanted freedom from this room. A bead of cold sweat dripped down his temple and splattered onto the dusty floor.

"Allow me." From the hall, the other spoke. "Adan, there's no reason to continue to resist. We mean you no harm. Show the man your marks."

Adan felt himself nodding. He stood, clutched the corner of his bloody T-shirt, and yanked it over his head. Standing tall and shirtless, he met the captain's gaze. He would not cower. Then he turned, displaying his entire left shoulder and back.

The captain's hungry eye devoured the swirling marks. A smile touched his lips. The blackened marks started around Adan's pinky finger, curled over the back of his hand, and around the length of his arm. They curved from there to the edge of his clavicle and over his shoulder. Sweeping around to his back, they fanned around his shoulder blade, swooping up and stopping at a point below his neck. There, it swirled into a circular pattern. According to Uzziah, the complete design was specific to the Dreaming Gift. To Adan, it resembled every other mark he'd seen.

"The others I've seen are of a more subtle variety. Their markings were not blackened like this boy." Captain Curtshaw sent a questioning look over his shoulder into the hall.

"As I said, they are new. They'll fade with time."

"I've never seen any so newly given," the captain murmured. "Incredible."

Adan faced the man and scowled. Why had he taken his shirt off?

"We'll be off right away. We journey together, strong one." Captain Curtshaw smiled and left the room, closing the door behind him. They'd left him chained to the wall.

"Try to find out how strong he is. There may be more to him than meets the eye. He was made for something particular."

"And what would that be?" the captain asked.

"I don't know." Then, more to himself, the hidden man added, "But I'll enjoy thwarting whatever those plans might be." Louder, he said, "I'll check in from time to time. He's from far away and will need to be taught your customs. He may lack knowledge of everyday things. You'll teach him. Keep his mark hidden."

Their voices faded up the stairway until the door snapped as they exited the house.

Adan sank onto the bed and wadded his shirt in his hands. Anger sparked in his blood, igniting that buried ember. He put his shirt on and leaned forward, balancing his elbows on his knees and resting his head in his hands. The ember burned bright, not only toward these strange men but also toward Uzziah for giving him these accursed marks. If his arm was free of them, would he be in this situation?

Adan lifted his head. *They don't know I'm a Dreamer. They think I'm a Strength Wielder.*

Icy threads of suspicion began to unfurl. Why had Uzziah insisted the marking go to him and not Garran? For what purpose? And why had the circumstance been kept secret? The marks were only for show because he'd already inherited his Gift. Uzziah said they'd allow Adan to embrace the Dreaming Gift and be who he was meant to be. The marks had also been a neon sign for these psychopaths, pointing right to him.

What do I do now?

Adan examined his hand. One streak of the mark had already faded. It should take months for the black scars to flake away and the freshly healed skin beneath to show. He traced the faint skin-colored bevel with one finger and remembered Evie doing the same.

Evie, who looked at him with guilty golden eyes.

His gut roiled. Why had she sat next to him? But hadn't *he* started the conversation? And... she knew Garran's name. He stood, heart accelerating. Ben. Adan had entrusted Evie with Ben. Had Ben ever made it home?

He let out a roar as a door slammed overhead. Then he pulled at the manacle and cursed himself for going along with the man's suggestions. *Be stronger.*

He made himself look compliant as Captain Curtshaw opened the door again and strode into the room. The other man, from outside the door, said, "Adan, the captain is going to toss you a key. Unchain yourself. Then we're going to take a walk outside. There's no reason not to. It's what you want, isn't it?"

Yes. Yes, it's what I want.

Even as Adan felt himself relaxing, he ground his teeth and fought for control of his actions. His mind strained in two directions. The captain tossed him a key, and there was no division on this point. He wanted out of the chains.

They clanked to the floor.

The man with the soothing words ascended the stairs.

The captain stood like a nervous lump at the door, holding his tiny remote.

Adan rose. What was it he wanted to do?

Ben. Find Ben.

His thoughts focused. His mind warred with itself, but perhaps he could win the battle.

"Come on." The captain nodded toward the open door. "After you."

Adan moved with deliberate slowness. Overhead, the front door opened and closed.

"Hurry up," the captain demanded.

Adan dragged his feet. He may not be a Strength Wielder, but Uzziah trained him well in hand-to-hand combat. As he stepped toward the captain, Adan shot out a hand, grasping the captain's wrist. Using the momentum, he twisted the other man's arm, and the remote clattered to the floor. He shoved the startled man into the electric door, where he jerked before crumpling to the stone floor.

It was all very quick and quiet. Adan grabbed the remote and sprinted up the stairs. Pausing at the top, he peeked around the corner. He couldn't see the other man through the dirty window next to the back door. So he ran the other way across a drab living area and out another door.

He darted across the lawn and into the woods. A dirt road split the forest, and he angled toward it. Then he sprinted around tree trunks, determined to keep his lead. Once in their car, the two men would overtake him in minutes.

Adan lumbered on. Pain shooting through his body with every stride, he stumbled onto the deeply riveted dirt road. Checking that all was clear, he crossed and carved a path parallel to the road, within the trees.

He ran on like this until he paused at an intersection.

Distant clopping drew his ear, and he ducked back into the forest. A horse and carriage trotted into sight. A man and woman sat side by side on the sturdy metal structure. How far from Shura had his captors brought him?

The couple chatted. "Are you going to see your brother today?" the woman asked.

"No, he's gone to Inevah for a few days. Perhaps I'll see him next month."

"Ah, that's right. I hope he's not delayed. I hear rebels have been making trouble."

"Ha. Rebels. That's a myth. Probably a bunch of troublesome young folk. The lot of them are likely to end up in jail by year's end. Just you wait."

Their carriage bumped along and out of earshot. *Inevah? Rebels? Where am I?*

Adan wiped the sweat from his face, crossed the road, and followed. If they traveled to a town, then that's where he wanted to go. Maybe he could borrow a cell phone.

As he jogged along, he flung the remote to his electric shackle into the woods toward a faint roar. A river?

Fifteen minutes later, a farmhouse materialized through the trees. A barn and several cows dotted the grassy fields. Soon, more farms spread over the land. Swaths of the forest had been cut away for cattle and crops.

At one point, he darted between a house and barn. He hid, watching the road, but still didn't hear the rumble of an engine. He leaned against an ancient plow to catch his breath. An old windmill turned with a soft groan. A line of clothes fluttered in the breeze. A cow lowed in the distance. No truck. No tractor.

Strange—like going back in time.

Weariness pressed on him, as did the sun that had crept higher in the sky. Morning then.

The road wound into a town. Squat buildings scattered around, and further in, they formed a perfect square around a vast, bustling space.

Pedestrians threaded around each other, scurrying off to one place or another. Adan covered his marked arm with his other hand. The black swirls would stand out if the captain came asking about him. Cringing, he swiped a dark leather jacket thrown over a porch rail. He'd return it later.

Keeping his head bent and his hands deep in his stolen pockets, he moved toward the town square. Passing unnoticed proved impossible, what with his bloodied clothes and swollen face. Pedestrians gave him a wide berth.

The dirt gave way to a cobblestone path, and for the first time since waking, Adan heard the putt of an engine. A motorized bike rumbled by. The contraption—ridden by a dark-haired boy about Adan's age—was made from metal piping. A pole rose above the rider, and at the top, perched the smooth surface of a solar panel. Adan stared openmouthed. A cloud passed overhead, and the engine sputtered out. The boy shot an offended look at the sky and then pressed a button between the handlebars. Two pedals folded out with a clang. He fitted his boots to them and began pumping across into the pedestrian-packed square.

Adan blinked, a shiver coursing through him. *Where am I?*

He moved in a slow circle, feet light on the dusty cobblestones.

Shop-goers meandered along the booths. Many donned leather jackets or vests, and a few ladies wore puffy ruffled skirts.

But perhaps more interesting than the strange clothing was the wide variety of skin tones. Some matched Adan's golden shade while others were pale, and still, others were as dark as chocolate. Dark hair rested on some heads, while others sported a lighter shade.

Where am I?

Something bumped into Adan's back, and he whipped around to see an older man tip his hat. Eyes hooded by bushy gray eyebrows sank into the deep shadow lining his face.

"Do you know how far it is to Shura?" Adan asked.

"Shura? Never heard of it." The man strolled away, eyeing Adan's bloody T-shirt and swollen eye.

Shura was the largest city on the continent. How could he not have heard of it?

A woman in a puffy dress sauntered by. Adan tried again. "Do you have a cell phone I could borrow?"

"A what, dear?" She busied herself by straightening her skirts with fingers much lighter than his own. She seemed to try very hard not to look at him.

"A phone. I need to call my Guardian."

"Guardian? I don't—" She finally lifted her gaze. "Oh my." She took a step back. Adan did too. "Your eyes." He was thinking the same thing. "They're bl–blue."

They stood staring at each other. Then she scurried away with one last glance at his face. Her eyes were dark as night. So dark Adan couldn't distinguish the iris from the pupil. The black orbs were set in a face that could otherwise pass on the streets of Shura.

A man wearing an elaborate weapons holster clopped past leading a horse. A woman pumped water from a spigot. A man whose eyes were light brown—almost gold—chased a toddler over the cobblestones. The child clung to a handmade doll. A teenager with orange hair darted through the crowd like a flame.

Where am I?

He scanned more faces and then sucked in a breath when he found a familiar pair of green eyes locked on him. Captain Curtshaw hustled in his direction. Adan whirled and sprinted behind a building. He ran the length and darted into an alley. Ducking behind a pair of trash bins, he sat with his back pressed against the stone wall and his head in his hands.

Think. What am I missing?

On a horrible night, years ago, he'd been huddled with Ben in an alleyway not so different from this one. They'd run away from a horrific foster home, and when Adan thought things couldn't get worse, a stranger tried to steal his backpack and all the things they owned. This marked the first time Adan had been in a fight, and they'd only narrowly gotten away. He never wanted to feel so helpless again.

Now here he was, hiding in an alley, helpless.

He stood and peered around the corner. Men and women sat around wooden tables eating breakfast within a restaurant across the street. They dined merrily as if the world hadn't flipped upside down. A man glanced his way.

Adan looked at his hands as a memory tried to surface. But it eluded him when something hard smacked against his neck. He reached up and found a round object suctioned to his skin. The last thing he saw was the wide eyes of the man in the restaurant before, once again, a sharp jolt of electricity zapped through him and everything went dark.

10

Sam's mind whirled as the high afternoon sun streamed in the floor-to-ceiling windows. He sat on a couch in their apartment with Ben curled in a ball at his side. The kid had finally fallen asleep. It'd been well over twelve hours since he'd discovered Adan's absence from the basement.

Uzziah paced nearby until he plopped into a chair across from Sam. "Let's go over it again."

"Okay." Sam sat forward, careful not to disrupt Ben.

"One—you saw Garran drag Adan into the basement." Uzziah lifted a finger. "You came upstairs and fell asleep." He raised another finger. "Two—when you woke up, Garran was sleeping, so you rushed outside and found Adan gone. Right?"

"Right."

"Three—you came back and woke Garran while also discovering Ben was gone. Neither Garran nor anyone else knew anything about either boy, and that's when you came to me."

Sam nodded.

"Then Ben returned, saying he knew where Adan was, and he took you to a parking garage on South Eighth, but Adan wasn't there. Ben says he followed a black car on his bike."

"That's right."

Ben had led him to the lower level of a nearby parking garage and the gate of a chained storage area nestled in the back corner. They couldn't get in, but clearly, Adan wasn't there.

Ben had been inconsolable since. Uzziah alerted the authorities of Adan's disappearance, and a full-scale investigation began. The police searched the garage, but they saw no reason to enter the clean, empty unit without a warrant.

"Then," Uzziah continued, "the two of you came back, and I confiscated the ring from Garran. He admitted to beating Adan and throwing him in the basement, but then claimed to have no idea what happened to him afterward."

Sam rubbed the back of his neck, his whole body tense. "Ben says he followed Garran downstairs during the night. But I never heard anything, and when I woke up, Garran was asleep."

After shifting Ben's head to a pillow, Sam stood and paced. He pulled his baseball from his pocket and rolled it between his hands. "Garran was ready to kill Adan, and maybe he would have if I hadn't been there." His chest tightened, and his voice rose. "Garran did something to him. And he knows where he is."

Ben stirred but didn't wake.

"Calm down. Think about what you're accusing Garran of."

Sam's chest labored under his heavy breathing. "I wish you'd been home last night. Where were you?"

"Another Guardian asked me to pay them a visit." Uzziah shook his head. "Only when I got there, he didn't have any new information to share. It was as if he didn't know I was coming." He raised his hands. "I'm sorry I wasn't here."

Sam tossed the ball until it slipped from his fingers and rolled out of reach under the console. He leaned his forehead against the enormous glass window overlooking the city. "I told him I'd come back. I *promised*."

Uzziah moved next to Sam. "You're not to blame."

"I have to find him. But I don't know where to look."

Ben groaned and jerked in his sleep. "Zuh," he mumbled and rolled onto his back, rigid. "Find him," he whispered and thrashed, now mumbling incoherent words.

Sam rushed to shake him until he cracked his eyelids open.

"I..." Ben started, rubbing at his eyes. He sat up and stared at the floor.

"Ben, are you all right?" Uzziah asked.

Ben blinked at him and then at Sam. The boy pulled something from his pocket as he whispered, "It was so real."

Sam frowned. Ben clutched Asher's missing game piece.

"Why don't you tell us?" Uzziah lowered himself on Ben's other side.

"I was dreaming about the computer lab at school again. I could hear people fighting next door, and they argued about how a boy got there. Some of them thought he should be killed." Ben lifted wide eyes to Uzziah. "Then a weird-looking girl came into the lab and started to type. I thought they might be talking about me, but she didn't see me."

"Then what happened?" Sam asked.

"She worked on the computer for a while until she found what they were looking for. She was excited. It looked kinda like an architect drawing. She didn't stay because someone called her back."

Uzziah patted Ben on the back. "It was just a dream." He rose and walked to the sink across the room. "Would you like something to drink?"

Ben rubbed grubby hands over his face. "Someone said the girl's name, but I can't remember it."

"You mumbled a lot while you were asleep. You said, 'find him,'" Sam offered.

"Yeah. The girl said someone has to find him first. Anything else?"

"Not really." Sam shrugged. "A lot of sounds we couldn't make out. You tried to say something like 'buh' or maybe 'zuh.'"

Ben straightened, staring ahead. "That's it. Ali-*zah*!"

Uzziah stiffened at the sink. "What did you say?"

"I heard the name Alizah. The girl."

A low breath whistled past Uzziah's lips. "What did she look like?"

Ben huddled closer to Sam. "Well, her eyes were like yours, but her hair was orangey. Her skin was really pale."

Uzziah sat on the coffee table, facing Ben. "You dreamed about the computer lab at school?"

"Yeah. Well, I think that's what it is. It was fancier than the one at school."

"Ben, did the girl say where the boy had gone?"

"No." Ben's knuckles whitened over clutched fingers. He held the game piece in a death grip.

The Guardian studied Ben with his golden eyes. A storm was brewing in them, and something like dread tightened his features. Then he grabbed a notepad and pen from the end table. "Ben, can you draw what was on the screen you saw—the architect drawing?"

"Maybe." Ben bent over the pad. He drew a rough shape a bit like a curved arbor. With a shrug, he handed it to Uzziah. "It was way better and had more words and stuff on it."

His eyes widening, Uzziah traced his index finger over the lines on Ben's sketch. "A Watcher in the Control Room matches Ben's description. Her name is Alizah."

Sam raised a brow. "Uzziah, what are you thinking?"

"We need to go back to that parking garage. Break in if we have to."

11

Evie followed Gavrie down the long hallway to Joram's office in the Sector Five Travel Center. As they approached, she peered through the viewing window next to the door and drew a slow breath through her nose. She'd never thought much about smell, but a new contrast emerged. The Control Room environment was always pleasant, always mild, and always the same.

She touched the smooth window, where, beyond, workstations lined the dimly lit room. She'd been ecstatic to see this place when she'd been interested in promoting to Guardian.

Now, she wished to be far, far away from Joram's door.

They entered the space. Slick black screens hung on gray walls where footage of every portal in the sector could be called up in real time. Only one screen flickered, displaying a regretfully familiar metal disk. She rubbed her arms, even though none of her previous excitement shivered through her.

Next to the screen, a single step led to a much larger metal disk—the powerful Control Center portal. Joram sat on the step, and Evie frowned at him. He half-heartedly returned the gesture. Two others stood together, watching their exchange.

"Evie, this is Dina, Guardian supervisor for Sector Six," Gavrie said.

Evie inclined her head toward his equivalent in Sector Six. What could she possibly want with Evie?

"And this is Remiel, her assistant." Gavrie crossed strong arms over the smooth fibers of his gray uniform shirt. "They bring news of a Gifted inhabitant from Sector Five—a boy—who has illegally crossed into Sector Six."

Evie's brow shot high. She waited for them to continue, but they watched her. She cleared her throat. "How is that possible?"

"Does your surprise indicate you know nothing about it?" Dina asked. "Even though you took an unsanctioned trip to Sector Five? And visited the boy's home?"

Her mouth went dry. A terrible feeling bloomed in the pit of her stomach. "Wh–Who is in Sector Six?"

Dina and Remiel exchanged a glance.

"What is his name?" Evie demanded.

"Calm down, Evie." Gavrie touched her elbow.

Remiel flipped through the papers on his clipboard. "Adan," he said. "Adan Andree."

She shook her head. "Adan." Her voice emerged on the air whooshing from her lungs. "What do you mean *crossed over*? That's not possible."

Gavrie's brow furrowed, and he lowered his arms to his sides.

Supervisor Dina answered. "That's what we thought. Until his power tripped our alarm, and there he was on our screen. As you know, the Gifted aren't allowed in Sector Six per Jesiah's request."

Apprehension blossomed within Evie. Adan? In Sector Six? Alone?

Gavrie lifted a hand and glared at Evie. "You know this boy? I assured them you had no contact with anyone on the ground."

Evie turned her attention to the floor when she was sure sector fire was about to erupt from Gavrie's ears.

"You *talked* to him yesterday?"

"Yes," she admitted on a whisper.

Joram stood. "I saw her with him. I told her to stay away from Uzziah's building, but I followed her when I saw her at the street corner beside it. She found the boy in the park. He didn't seem to be expecting her. I didn't think much of it, and after watching them for a few minutes, I delivered my message."

She rubbed the shivers from her arms again. He'd followed her and watched her? With Adan?

"When I got back here and waited for the portal to recharge"—Joram went on before she could defend herself—"I dug into her video logs. I wanted to figure out what she was doing—why she was late." He straightened and faced Gavrie. "I shouldn't have taken her, and I'm sorry. It was reckless. I should've told you the moment I got back, but I hoped to fix the situation before anyone found out. The portal took ages to recharge. And I shouldn't have accessed her vid logs without telling you. I was just…" He lifted his head, facing Evie with something akin to pity. And perhaps some jealousy? "… curious. As it turns out, she's been watching the missing boy for months."

All eyes turned to her, probably wondering the same thing. Why would someone watch a specific mortal if they weren't ordered to do so? It was a strange thing to do. Watchers kept a distant eye on the population. Her interest on a personal level was another of her oddities —one she'd kept secret.

Her shoulders drooped, and she raised her palms. "I was curious about his Gift. And about those who train under Guardians. That's all."

Had Joram opened the files on her desktop? Surely not, or he'd spill that incriminating information as well.

Gavrie's eyes narrowed, a muscle twitching on his jaw. "So you met with this boy? Even though you left out that little detail when you recounted your time on the ground to me."

"I told you I met two of Uzziah's trainees. Adan and his brother, Ben, were those two."

"Saw them." Gavrie stalked closer, his hands clenched. "You said you *saw* two of Uzziah's trainees."

Evie avoided his golden gaze but straightened her shoulders. "I met them. I talked to them. I was with them for hours."

Gavrie braced one elbow in his hand and pinched the bridge of his nose with his other hand. "So what is he doing in Sector Six?"

"I don't know. Truly, I don't." Turning to face Dina, she felt the muscles around her eyes soften. "Is he okay?"

Remiel hugged his clipboard to his chest after a pause. "We don't know. We have minimal Watcher interactions with the people in Six, also per Jesiah's request. That means our surveillance is limited. And Guardians, of course, aren't allowed."

"I thought you said he showed up on your screen."

"He did." When Dina nodded toward a workstation, Remiel moved toward it. "We have a still shot of him sometime after his power first surged. We haven't been able to locate him again." Remiel inserted a metal disk, and a photo spread over the desktop. With a flick of the wrist, he sent the image to one of the wall screens. It flared to life, casting a bluish glow over their faces.

Evie drifted closer. There he was. Adan. Sleeping. His hoodie was gone, and blood splattered his T-shirt. Full lips pulled his battered face into a frown. She stood with her mouth open, and Gavrie stepped beside her. He and Joram both watched her.

Oh, Adan. Her fingers twitched with the desire to go to him. To erase his bruises from the screen. "What happened to him?"

"We don't know," Dina answered. "We were hoping you could tell us. There's nothing else to go on. We only know his name after coming here and using the Sector Five human facial recognition database. It's taken hours to find a match."

"There are no other still shots or videos?" Gavrie asked.

"No, nothing. We aren't even sure where this is. We only obtained the general vicinity."

"Joram, can you please get Alizah and bring her here?"

When Joram left the room, Dina asked, "Are his marks glowing?"

They bent closer.

"It's hard to say by the way the light from the window is hitting him. It's not the best photograph." Remiel tapped a pen on the desktop. "But I see no reason why they would glow while he slept."

Evie squinted. Yes, it seemed as if the marks were glowing. If they were, then Adan's mind was lost somewhere in a vision. She glanced at the others. This photo didn't capture him sometime *after* his power surged. This was *when* his power surged. *They don't know he's a Dreamer.*

Gavrie pivoted from the screen, rubbing his temple. "What caused this photograph to be taken?"

"We have this measure in place to alert us if someone uses a Gift in the sector. It is as a safeguard against the Deceiver to keep him from crossing into it." Dina crossed her arms and tapped her foot. She lifted her chin. "Is this boy the Deceiver?"

"No," Evie blurted, then cringed. No one had asked her.

Gavrie cleared his throat. "I find it unlikely. According to the reports I've read this morning, he's been with the Guardian Uzziah for some time. If he is, he's integrated himself among the humans with great success."

"There's no way. I could never believe it." Evie balled her fists at her side and raised her chin like Dina. "I know when he was born and where he's lived since then. Besides, the Maker trapped the Deceiver in one of the early sectors—probably One or Two—after he destroyed the intersector portals. Everyone knows this."

"That's true, but somehow, this boy found a way. And he didn't go willingly."

Dina rounded on Evie. "Did you take this boy to Sector Six?"

Evie jerked her chin up higher. "No. How could I?"

"There's no other explanation. How did you do it?"

How did I what? Evie nearly stamped a foot. "I didn't do it. I wouldn't even start to know how."

"Are *you* the Deceiver?" she asked, meeting Evie's volume.

Evie sucked in a breath, and even Gavrie gasped.

Remiel put a hand on Dina's arm.

"That is impossible." Gavrie angled his body in front of Evie. "Evie was the last Watcher Jesiah created. The Deceiver's movements have been on record for far longer than she has been in existence."

Dina opened her mouth to say more. But Remiel pulled her aside, and they bent their heads over the clipboard, speaking in soft voices.

The Deceiver had eluded capture for eons, and he had somehow managed to keep his identity a secret. He walked among the humans undetected, spreading his infectious lies. Ever since he escaped Sector One's destruction, the Guardians believed him to be locked in Sector Two or Three. Guardians and Watchers hunted him always. How could Dina believe it to be her?

Evie pushed this insult out of her mind and faced the Dreamer. She touched his onscreen face and ran a finger over the smooth surface, wincing at the bruising. How did he get there, and who had hurt him? Was it Garran?

Anger at the Strength Wielder burned in the pit of her stomach, even as sadness and worry churned in the recesses of her mind. She'd never before felt such an onslaught of emotions while in the Control Room— while in this immortal body. She sucked in a ragged breath.

Gavrie watched her, then bent close so only she could hear. "You don't know what happened to him?"

Holding her elbow, he guided her into the hall. One hand braced on the cool, gray wall, she told him every detail of her time with Adan. She gave special attention to her final moments with him, including Garran and his out-of-control rage.

When she finished, Gavrie paced, hands in pockets.

"Gavrie?" She took a step toward him, palms lifted. "You have to find him. If the rumors are true, it's a harsh and wild place. What if he's hurt?"

The slightest smile tipped one corner of his lips. "Be careful of putting on a human body, Evie. The emotions running wild in them can lead one down a path they never meant to take."

She looked away. Of course. That would explain her idiotic behavior: the human body. And yet, these emotions had started long before she ever put on the human form. She shook the thought away. "How did he cross over?"

"I don't know." He scratched his neck. "If neither you nor Joram found a way to take him to Six, then how did he get there? Someone found a way. Sector Six has stringent guidelines for Guardian and Gift interference. The fallout will land on your shoulders whether you had anything to do with his disappearance or not."

"Me?" She jerked her head back, spine stiffening. "What do you mean?"

"It doesn't look good, does it? You traveled—*unsanctioned*—to Sector Five the day one of its citizens appears in another. Of course, everyone would assume either you or Joram had something to do with it. And Joram is a less likely suspect because he travels to the ground all the time. He scheduled that trip."

She wrapped her arms around herself, squeezing her elbows. "I'm so sorry. Should I work in the Sector Six Control Room for a while? Stay until I can locate him, and then the Travel Coordinator can take him home? Maybe Adan will trip the alarm again."

"That's not the way it works. Sector Six doesn't have a Travel Coordinator because no one goes to the ground. They already have a few Watchers—five, I think—and they don't want you in the Control Room. They don't trust you. Besides, I've already suggested that." He pinched the bridge of his nose. "They have something else in mind for you." He turned, pacing again, saying to himself, "I wish Jesiah and Krystopher were here."

"Where are they? Can we contact them?"

"They're on the ground in Sector Seven. There's no communication system in place for Seven at all. This situation is out of my hands. It's Sector Six's call."

"What are they going to do?" Evie let her arms drop to her sides. "Just tell me."

Gavrie opened his mouth to speak, but Supervisor Dina opened the door. Alizah and Joram rounded the corner, and Dina beckoned them into the Travel Center. "Gavrie, we've waited long enough. Evie needs to come with us."

Alizah's eyes went wide, and Evie's head whipped to Gavrie. Her supervisor sighed. "Evie, you'll be portaling with them to Control Room Six. I've already spoken to Joram about what will happen now, and he's going with you to assist."

She swallowed. But he'd said they didn't want her in Sector Six's Control Room. "Please tell me what's happening."

Gavrie looked to the other supervisor, who met his gaze. "Against my advice, they've decided you will go to Sector Six in person."

"What?" Evie and Alizah said in unison.

"They and Joram will explain everything when you get there." Gavrie braced both hands on her shoulders. "I'm sorry. I'll see what I can do. But you're a part of this mess, and now it's your part to fix it. I hope to see you back soon."

"You can't do this." Alizah was saying as a dull ringing began in Evie's ears. "We know almost nothing about Sector Six. There's no telling what the people are like or how dangerous it is."

"They want me to go *now*?" Evie's breath quickened as she pulled away.

Gavrie's hands dropped to his sides. "There's nothing I can do. The decision's been made. Alizah, you can go with Evie to the Sector Six Control Room to see her off."

He gave her shoulder one last pat, then strode away.

Alizah wrapped an arm around her.

Joram ushered Evie and the others onto the portal. "I tried to talk them out of it," he said in a quiet voice.

Her hands began to tingle as the group faded from the Travel Center. In moments, their feet were planted in an almost identical room, light-years away—the Travel Center for Sector Six.

She stood motionless in the spotless workplace, Alizah's arm still draped over her shoulder. The Watcher's voice rose as she argued with the others, but Evie couldn't focus.

Alizah stepped back as Remiel slung a heavy backpack over Evie's shoulder. *What am I supposed to do?* The ringing in her ears quieted as her mind cleared. "So I'm going to Six as a Guardian? How am I to find him?"

"No, you'll go to Six as a *human*," Supervisor Dina said. "Nothing more. Guardians aren't allowed in Six. We'll send you to the portal closest to the area in which we believe our system photographed the boy. Then you'll search for him." She pushed a door open. "Remiel and I will be in the Control Room. We want to prepare our sensors to see if we pick anything up as you arrive. Good luck, Watcher."

"Wait." Evie shifted toward her.

"The Travel Coordinator can answer any more of your questions and will give you your final instructions."

The door closed behind her.

That's it. That's all Evie would get from them? She clutched Joram's arm. "What do I do if I find him? Take him home? How?" *This is happening too fast.*

He flipped a switch on the portal and jerked his arm away from her. "How do you still not get it?" He glared at the door where Dina had disappeared. "Evie, you won't be taking him home. We don't know how to get him there." He took two deep breaths, then touched her chin, tipping her face his way. "Unless, of course, you do… know how to get him home."

"I don't!"

He released her with a nod. "Then you are to kill him. He is a contaminant in Sector Six. Those were Dina's exact words."

Kill him? An uneven breath raced into her parted lips. She might have made an inaudible sound in protest, but Alizah voiced what Evie was thinking. "Are you crazy? She can't do that. There is no precedent for this. Krystopher and Jesiah would never allow it."

A muscle twitched in Joram's jaw. "I want to agree with you, but don't forget they're the ones who put the rules in place. The whole point was to keep it separate and prevent the Deceiver from traveling between sectors. Remember Sector One?"

Alizah paled.

Evie shivered. The Maker had declared Sector One a total loss. "Alizah, what does he mean?"

"Jesiah himself destroyed it. He and his Death Guardians."

Evie's fingers wound around the backpack strap. "But it was uninhabited… wasn't it?"

Alizah's gaze drifted to the floor. "No, it wasn't."

Joram shrugged. "He won't concern himself with the death of one mortal child." He walked to the computer and began typing in the procedure. "Look, I'm sorry this is happening. I'm only doing my job. They asked me along because no one here has ever sent anyone to the ground before."

"Then why do they have a portal?"

"I don't know. Because they set it up like all the other Control Rooms. Jesiah probably changed his mind about Guardians in Six after they built it."

"You did this. It's your fault this has fallen on me." She let the backpack drop to the floor. "I won't do it."

"You will. You have no choice. And they've given you three weeks to complete the task. If you don't, you'll be left there. As a mortal." He grabbed her pack and helped her into both straps. "Dina thinks you will fail. She suggested they summon the Death Guardians if you don't make your deadline. You'll stay there until you age and die."

As Alizah paled even further, Evie shook her head and backed away. "Left? A mortal?" The pack hit the wall, and she slid to the ground.

"Don't you think we need to talk to Krystopher first?" Alizah rounded on Joram. "This is madness."

"I need you to leave the room."

A speaker crackled from a corner near the ceiling. "The Control Room is ready. Get on with it. Send the other Watcher out."

"Alizah, get out." Joram entered the procedures into the console. "One Sector Six human coming up." He was programming her Sector Six appearance, but she couldn't find it in herself to offer an opinion. "He won't recognize you. That's good. He won't know who did it as he dies."

"That's helpful." After glaring at Joram's back, Alizah knelt in front of Evie. "I'll find out what I can and try to reach Krystopher," she rushed her whisper. "And there may be a way to warn Uzziah. He'll know what to do. Be careful." She grabbed Evie's hands.

Evie clung to her friend. If she couldn't do it—if she couldn't *kill* Adan—she'd never see Alizah again.

"What do I do?" Evie whispered.

"Find him," was Alizah's firm reply. "Then we have three weeks to figure something out. I'll do everything I can."

"Alizah, go."

"But—"

"Forget it," Joram cut her off. "There's nothing you can do. Get out."

Alizah backed away from Evie, holding her hands until she could no longer reach. Evie's hands fell to her side as Alizah closed the door and moved to stand by the viewing window.

When Evie's hand brushed her side, the parcel Krystopher had given her bumped it. She'd taken it to her private quarters. Unwrapping the white paper revealed a sharp golden dagger. Possibly the best weapon Evie had ever seen. An intricate weave of golden vines and thorns etched the hilt and wove over the polished metal to meet and circle a single point on the back of the grip.

Her heart sank.

Somehow, Krystopher had known. He'd known she would need it. Surely, he would never want her to kill a human, but he'd given her the weapon to do it.

"Stand on the portal," Joram said.

"Why didn't you come back for me?" Evie pushed to her feet and moved toward the portal.

"I couldn't. There's only enough power for one trip there and back before the portal has to recharge. By the time it was primed, Gavrie had already realized you were gone." He rubbed the pinched spot between his eyes. "Look, the whole thing was a bad idea."

Evie crossed her arms. Joram wasn't absorbing any of the blame or taking any punishment. "How do we know you didn't take the boy to Six?"

His face hardened, fingers freezing over the touchscreen. He faced her. "I came back, remember? I'm not the one who spent an entire night in the sector unsupervised." A pause. "I'm not convinced it wasn't *you*. It's interesting you're trying to shift blame."

"I didn't have anything to do with it." Her fists clenched, even as regret and fear took root deep inside.

Joram rolled his eyes. "Look, I'll help you if I can. Maybe rig up an old monitoring system, help Alizah find a way to communicate with you."

He picked up something from the console. "There are clothes and food in the pack. Dina also provided some coins and a few things to trade." He opened his palm. "And here's a watch with your countdown. Wear it, so you'll know how much time you have left. Be back on that portal in three weeks. I've clocked in your return procedure."

Evie closed shaky fingers over the cool watch face. The countdown had already begun.

"And, Evie, it's a blood portal. It's not like the one in Sector Five. When you return to it, bring some of the boy's blood. That's the only way to activate it."

She twisted her fingers around the watch, imagining the feel of a knife hilt in her hand. "Joram." Her throat closed over her whisper. She tried again. "What if I can't do it?"

"You're an immortal Watcher destined to be a great Guardian. Don't throw those dreams away. That's what you want, isn't it? It's everything you've been working toward for far longer than that boy has been alive."

Evie nodded.

"He'll age and die. His life is a moment in time. Yours will be forever, and in a little over three weeks, Krystopher will reinstate the Guardian promotions. This is your chance to achieve everything you've ever wanted." Joram reached toward the console.

Her fingers began to tingle.

"Remember, you're no human. Keep your emotions in check. Slay him, and come back home."

Alizah gave a feeble wave from the viewing window, her features tight.

Joram was right. Evie could do it. She had to.

She gripped the strap of her new pack. This task was a small thing compared to the immortal life stretching endlessly before her. Joram offered an encouraging half-smile.

The last thing she saw before she faded.

Part II

*And that prophet, that dreamer of dreams,
shall be put to death.*

Deuteronomy 13:5

12

For the second time, Adan jerked awake not knowing where he was. He struggled to a sitting position and clenched his teeth at the pain along his ribs. Flakes of dried brown came away when he touched his puffy face.

He'd been dreaming again. This time, the assassin stumbled out of the light, almost as if they'd been shoved. He, as always, couldn't discern a face in the blinding glow. As he'd brought his hand up to shield his eyes, the dreaded blade had flown hard and fast toward him. Again, it sank deep into his chest. As he lay dying, the light faded. The assassin was gone, but a large archway stood where the light had been.

Now awake, he attempted to shake the horrible memories. How many times had he played out his own death?

He put his feet on the floor and settled into a soft rug. The dimly lit and relatively clean room little resembled the last. No chain protruded from the wall. A bowl of water perched on a stand next to a rickety wooden chair beside the decent, though old-fashioned bed. A sliver of light escaped around a gray drape stretching from floor to ceiling over smooth gray stone walls. He pushed the fabric aside and sucked in a ragged breath.

Checking for an electric current and finding none, he placed both hands around the thin metal bars crossing a tiny window and gaped at the spectacularly disorganized metropolis far below. It stretched for miles, and where the streets of Shura divided it into perfect squares, this city wound a maze of curved and irregular paths.

Rather than glittering skyscrapers, these buildings stood much closer to the ground. Only three or four rose higher than a few stories. Squinting, he made out what might be a cobbled surface. Was that another horse-drawn wagon? And a wall to encircle it all? Pedestrians moved along the cobblestones, and he had the sudden feeling of looking into a strange new habitat—like he peered into another world.

The city gave way to forest, and mountains rested in a hazy line.

"Where am I?" His unused voice came out in a throaty whisper.

The sun was beginning to set. He let the curtain fall back in place. What day was it anyway?

After he'd peered out the bright window, the sudden darkness unnerved him. He let his eyes adjust and dragged the chair over, draping the curtain over its back. He found no light switch or bulb—not even a lamp. When the sun drifted below the horizon, complete darkness would envelop.

He padded to the closed door, dread creeping into his belly. He stood with his feet apart and swatted at the handle. No charge. But it didn't budge. He put his shoulder to it and shoved. Nothing.

"Don't try coming through!" a voice bellowed from beyond, and he jumped. "We have stun pellets. We'll have you down afore you can step from the room."

"Come now," another, deeper voice joined in. "We've been twitching for a fight. Break down the door, and we might let you play before we send you back into oblivion."

His eyes wide, Adan backed from the door. When the backs of his knees hit the bed, he sagged onto it. The mattress groaned, and the men chuckled.

The icy fingers reclaimed their grip, tightening his stomach. "What's happening?" he said in little more than a whisper.

He rubbed his neck and felt the soreness. Something had hit him and suctioned there.

He rumpled something folded on the foot of the bed—a light-gray, long-sleeve shirt. *No chance.* He turned away, but the bloodstains streaking down his chest caught his eye. He sighed and unfolded the shirt.

The sleeves bore holes he could hook his thumbs through, bringing the fabric over his entire mark. Good. Once he'd changed shirts, he rummaged around, still wearing the same dirty jeans, tennis shoes, and electric ankle ring.

His golden-spine book still nestled in his back pocket. So he pulled it free and slid the photograph of baby Ben from the worn pages.

"Please be okay," Adan whispered to the image.

Something clicked. Then the door handle began a slow downward arc. He returned the photo to the book and stuffed both into his pocket, moving to the furthest point from the door. The handle gave way.

A head of reddish hair peeked around the door. The newcomer's gaze went to the bed, but then hazel eyes widened as they found Adan crouched across the room.

"Relax." The boy about Adan's age gulped. "I'm only bringing you dinner." A tray proceeded him into the room. His accent was similar to Captain Curtshaw's, though a little rough around the edges.

This was the strangest boy Adan had ever seen. How did he coax his hair into such a color? And what about his eyes? They were the palest brown, almost yellow. Flecks of other similar tones even painted through the irises. They reminded Adan of a dimmer version of Uzziah's Guardian eyes.

The boy stood several inches shorter than Adan. An off-white shirt hung over his tattered pants. The visitor's eyebrows stayed high on his head until he offered a nervous smile, lifting his cheeks where a spattering of spots spread to his light-skinned nose.

He crept forward, placing the tray on the bed, eyes never leaving Adan's. Was he… afraid?

Ah, he thinks I'm a Strength Wielder.

Just when the mutual staring started to get awkward, the boy said, "Your eyes are—strange." He squinted. "I've never seen anything like them."

My eyes are strange?

Adan said nothing but strode to the open door and came face to face with three armed guards. Two held wicked curving blades, and the other gripped a strange, shiny gun. It pointed at Adan's face. He shuffled back.

The red-haired boy shrugged. "Sorry, but you won't be going anywhere today. Come back in and leave the brutes to their self-importance."

As the guards glared over Adan's shoulder at the boy, Adan followed his advice.

The boy rolled his eyes. "Idiots." He shook his unruly hair off his forehead, regarded Adan, then gave a firm nod that sent it bouncing wildly again. "I like you. You have gusto. But, if you didn't, you wouldn't have three armed guards. Did they do that to your face?"

Adan touched the mushiness on his cheek and swelling up his eye. He could only imagine the bruises forming there by now. "No. Who are you?"

The boy straightened. "I'm James, Healer, and current property of Captain Curtshaw. But, I'm curious, who are *you*? So much secrecy surrounds your arrival."

"I'm Adan. Where are we? What city is this?"

"This is Inevah. Welcome to the greatest city in the Great Valley. Well, that's what they tell me anyway. Since I've been here, I've never been outside the castle walls."

Adan drew his eyebrows together. Inevah? The Great Valley? And what did he mean *castle*?

James cocked his head when Adan said nothing. "So, you're not from around here? That explains your accent."

"Do you know how far we are from Shura?"

"Shura? Never heard of it."

"What do you mean you've never heard of it? It's one of the biggest cities in the world." Was Adan overseas—stuck in some ancient city where no one had even heard of Shura? "You said I was the reason for secrecy. What do you mean?"

"I mean, they snuck you in through the back gates." James gestured out the door. "They swore the guards to secrecy. They swore *me* to secrecy. And they said not to let anyone see your unnatural eyes."

Now that was going a bit far. "You've never seen blue eyes before?"

"Never." The boy stared again.

Adan cleared his throat. "I don't know why I would be a secret. Everything's a haze." He paced, talking to himself. "One minute, I'm put in the trunk of a car, and the next, I'm here in this weird city straight out of a movie."

A frown pressed James's lips white and wrinkled up his spotted forehead. "I didn't understand most of what you said."

Pressing a hand to his aching temples, Adan sank onto the bed, careful not to disturb the tray where a cup of soup and a fist-sized loaf of bread sat. "I must be in a dream. That's what this is. They've been so real lately." He blinked as if doing so might wake him up. It didn't.

He had to be missing something.

"I can see you're confused," James said. "Maybe you've forgotten something. Perhaps it will come to you. Or perhaps it won't. Many who end up here don't remember how they arrived or even where they came from."

What? This was becoming more and more bizarre. Adan knew where he came from, but the beating he took was making things foggy. He jerked his head up. "What about you? Why are you here?"

"I've come to deliver food and to heal your wounds, of course. Now, if you don't mind, let's get to it." James rolled up his sleeves. Little brown marks like those on his face dotted his pale arms.

"You're a Healer?"

"Yes. Where does it hurt the most?" James asked.

Adan lifted the corner of his shirt, exposing an angry purple bruise.

"This might hurt a bit." James closed his eyes and placed a hand on the bruise.

Adan squeezed his eyes shut. He'd been healed this way before.

He sucked in a breath as James's power flowed through him. A pattern on the Healer's other arm began to glow. The glow was muted, though, compared to Uzziah's marks, and it covered only an area on the inside of his wrist.

The tingling increased within Adan's torso until he hissed in pain. Then it faded and, in a dull throb, spread over his body to his other bumps and bruises. He reached up to feel his healing lip. The power whispered across his back, over his shoulder, and down one arm.

He peeked at his hand, the black scars of his mark flaking away. Yes! They'd be much easier to hide this way.

James kept his hand on Adan until his wounds no longer throbbed. Finally, the Healer pulled away and sat back, his breathing ragged.

Adan inspected himself. "Incredible." This boy was much more powerful than Stella. "You're Guardian Gifted?"

"That's the rumor. Supposedly, long ago, my ancestors were given Gifts by Guardians, though most believe that to be a legend. Others think I evolved. But who would call this a *Gift*? It's the reason I'm a prisoner."

The skin pinched between Adan's eyes. Was he here for the same reason?

The glowing mark on James's wrist faded to normal. The shape had a fairly abstract pattern resembling a coil of snakes forming a tight circle.

"Is your mark only on your wrist?"

James rubbed the mark, his brow furrowing. "All the Gifted have to be marked in this way. It's the law."

"The law?"

"If you're not already marked, they'll mark you." He paused. "Are you strength marked?"

"No," Adan answered honestly as he examined his dinner. Now that pain wasn't on his mind, the hardy smell demanded attention.

"Next time a Sodorran representative is in town, they'll require that it be done."

No time to fret over that now. He needed to find out where he was and how to get home. He stood and paced again.

"So we're in a town called Inevah. But what's this building? This room is higher than anything else out there."

"You're in the castle, of course. Captain Curtshaw lives in this wing most of the year. He used to be captain of the king's guard, but now, he is sort of a financial advisor. You'll see others like me. We're in his service all hours of the day."

Adan strode to the window. Though he couldn't see the castle, he could tell it was massive. To the left and the right, curved towers rose into the sky. Below the castle, the broad city wall and the long row of shorter buildings formed the sides of a triangular courtyard.

"Okay, so I'm in a castle. Whose castle?"

"King Alexander's, of course. Where have you been? Hiding under a Strength Wielder's boot?"

Right. If one found themselves in a castle, then they should assume there is a king.

"What about a queen?"

"No, she died years ago. His Majesty never remarried. But he does have two sons. Prince Mason, who's away, and Prince Hagan."

"Okay." Adan rubbed his temples—throbbing despite James healing his wounds. Sure, history was his favorite subject, and kings and castles sounded like his favorite kind of social studies lesson. But. This. Was. Different. "So how do I get out of here? I want to go home."

"You don't even know where you are, and I don't know where your home is. Which way would you go if you did escape?"

Laughter from Adan's guards carried under the door.

James lowered his voice. "Your best bet is to find a way to be useful. If not, you'll be sold—whether you're Gifted or not. Then there's no telling where you'll end up. This castle is an excellent place to listen. And perhaps wait for the right moment."

"What happens now?" Adan ducked his head and rubbed his temples again, not wanting to know the answer.

"Rest, Adan. Eat. You'll start your testing tomorrow."

13

Again, Evie found her feet planted firmly on the ground, her wonder at occupying a human body long gone. How could she do what they asked? Stepping off the portal, she sank to her knees in the tall grass and hung her head.

Her chest tightened, and her breathing came in great heaves. A moan escaped her lips. Tears pooled in her eyes, and she snapped them shut. She leaned back and tilted her face toward the sky. She would not cry.

I am no human.

She opened her eyes. Trees surrounded her, but no skyscrapers boxed her in, no city noises filtered through, only wind and leaves and her shallow breath.

A violet six-winged butterfly landed on her arm, tickling the sensitive skin of her wrist. It crawled to her thumb where she shook it off, and it fluttered away to hover near a patch of yellow flowers.

She was probably the first of Jesiah's Marked to set foot in Sector Six in a millennium. How had it come to this?

Taking a deep breath, she observed this fragment of the Maker's most mysterious sector. To one side loomed the steep rise of a cliff. She walked the other way to a clearing and stopped on a rock ledge high above a wide valley. Her lips parted, and she sucked in a ragged breath. Had she ever imagined anything so beautiful? A forest rolled its way across the land like a tufted green carpet. A winding river cut through the middle and disappeared around the hazy outline of purple mountains. They formed a jagged line across the blue sky that topped the expanse like an enormous dome. Within it, puffy clouds drifted on the same wind that ruffled long tendrils of her hair.

Far in the distance, the rise of buildings cut a wide hole in the trees. Evie squinted and shielded her eyes. A crooked city sprawled in the space. Surely, she wouldn't need to venture so far from the portal.

A relieved sigh passed her lips when she noticed a town of smaller buildings nestled in a cozy cluster near the river. Around them, thin streams of smoke rose from tiny homes dotting areas of cleared farmland. Much closer.

Adan has to be there.

In Watcher Training, she'd studied each sector—each sector but Six. Even her research yielded spare facts: Jesiah opened it to humans last, making it the youngest working sector, and no Gifted humans or immortals were allowed. With no Guardian influence on the ground, she'd wondered what the people would be like. But now, civilization before her proved these people builders, engineers, and survivors.

But what other kinds of creatures lived here?

The tilt of the afternoon sun conjured images of sharp teeth in the inky shadows. She'd better make it to the town before dark.

She knelt, slid the bag from her shoulder, and unzipped it. But her fingers shook, and a strange sensation zinged through her at the sight of her skin. She dropped the pack and inspected her arms—fair and lightly dusted with freckles. Her annoying human heart quickened as she yanked a lock of hair around and held it in front of her face. Pale strawberry blond fluttered in the breeze. It reminded her of a lighter version of Alizah's curls.

Pushing thoughts of her best friend aside, Evie dug into the pack and found a strange assortment of objects: an empty bottle, a handful of gold coins, a pocketknife, and a pot. Another compartment held a blanket, soap, and a change of clothes. The black pants and stiff white shirt were an exact duplicate of the off-duty attire under her jacket.

The last compartment contained the strangest objects. Evie removed an ornately carved wooden bowl, a fancy brush, and a box painted pale gold. The words *Guardian Quest* scrolled across the top. She'd seen Adan and Ben with this game. These must be the items to trade.

She shoved her hand to the bottom of the bag and touched a scrap of paper.

She traced the words on it—*Do what you have to do and come back to me. ~Joram*

He must have stuffed it in the bag before she arrived at the Travel Center.

"I will, Joram. I have to," she whispered a promise to herself and to him.

Then she repacked her bag and peered across the valley. A road crossed through the forest and veered in an arc lining up with the river. If she reached the river, then this path would lead her straight to town.

She patted her jacket pocket, glad to feel the hard metal of Krystopher's dagger.

Her lips parted when Joram's communicator jostled inside her pocket. She removed it and pressed the power button. A soft breath whistled from her mouth when the screen flickered to life. She navigated its settings, then sent Joram a message only to have it returned as an unavailable connection. The map application didn't work either. She slid it into her pack. Worth a try, at least. She'd try the built-in solar charger later—just in case.

Shadows lingered under the trees, but when she stepped into them, they weren't as dark as she feared.

When a thin stream snaked into view, a strange, primal longing filled her mind. Her throat ached. She sank before a gentle spot, filled her bottle, and then drank deeply. *Human bodies and their many needs. Humans are weak.*

She walked on until the stream met the river and turned back to gaze at the mountains. Shura, Adan's city, was beautiful in its own way, but this—this was raw beauty: rolling hills, snow-capped mountains, raging rivers, and then miles and miles of forest. For the first time, Evie saw Jesiah as an artist, this land his canvas.

By the time she reached the dusty road, the sun hung low, and the forest sounds had grown disturbingly loud. The almost full moon lit the sky, though darkness hadn't descended. A bird squawked, and Evie jerked her head toward the sound. Leaves rattled high in the trees.

A snap echoed from the shadows. Two flashing red eyes reflected from the dark. She fumbled her golden blade from inside her pocket and held it out.

She never knew a human heart could pound so fast. A dull ringing strained her ears, and then another snapping noise came closer this time.

She began to jog. What should she do?

Ahead, a horse and carriage rounded a bend in the road. She sprinted toward it, put her dagger away, and approached the strangers. Two men watched her with raised brows. The carriage stopped, and the men jumped down on either side. A window nestled in their transport behind the bench where the men had been sitting.

Evie slowed, noting their wary faces. One pulled a short sword from its sheath, and the other nocked an arrow to his bow, though he held it pointed to the ground. Their gazes darted between her and the forest.

Evie stopped a few paces away.

"What is a Huldan doing alone on the Sodorran Road?" the swordsman asked her.

"I'm on my way to town," Evie said. "But something was following me." She looked back over her shoulder but saw nothing. Another creak sounded among the trees, and she whipped her head toward it.

The archer spun and let his arrow fly, then stomped in after it.

The other man pointed his sword at her chest. "Show me your wrists."

She flinched and did as he asked, brow pinched.

He eyed the inside of her forearms with something like disappointment. "Are you a diversion?"

"I don't know what you mean. I'm just trying to get to the next town." She took a step away. "I'll be on my way."

"No, you don't." He blocked her with his sword. "That's a strange jacket." He poked at it with his sword tip, and a fray appeared. "And the rest of your clothes too. Looks very fine for the likes of you. What's in your pack?"

"Nothing." She hooked trembling fingers over the strap.

The archer reemerged holding a fluffy animal. He yanked his arrow from its middle, and blood coated his fingers. Tiny hooves dangled from the sheeplike body, and a pointed nose protruded from a lifeless face. Long ears drooped down its back. A herbivore?

The swordsman snorted a laugh and sheathed his sword. He reached for her jacket. "I'll have that. And the pack too."

Startled, she tried to back out of reach. But in one move, he grabbed her sleeve, and she stumbled toward him. She reached for her dagger, but he pinned her arms at her sides.

The backpack snagged at her shirt collar, and the man paused. She struggled, but his iron grip didn't give. What was she thinking? What was all her training for?

"Take a look at this." Her captor growled as he forced her head into a bow and pushed her hair off her nape. A lengthy pause followed.

She thrashed again as fingers grazed over the place where Jesiah's Mark swirled on her skin. "Don't touch me."

They ignored her. "I've never seen this mark. Should we take her?"

"He'll want to see this."

"Load her up. Might mean a big payday."

"No!" Evie yelled, kicking.

The swordsman lifted her and carried her to the back of the wagon. He grunted when she connected with his shin. The archer pulled keys from his pocket.

Though she thrashed and screamed, her captor didn't loosen his grip.

Another groan came from the window at the back of the carriage. "Help," a girl's voice croaked. Fear seized Evie. Someone was already inside. It was a cage.

Before the archer could unlock the door, an arrow thwacked the carriage. The three of them paused as it vibrated in the near darkness, less than an inch from the swordsman's face. The man released her and pulled his sword free. Evie stumbled to the ground.

Shadows emerged from the darkness as humans descended upon them. At least six masked figures.

She pushed to her feet and ran for the trees, clutching her backpack straps, footsteps pounding behind her. She tripped over a log and sprawled onto the damp ground. Hands grasped her and hoisted her up. She screamed.

"Shhh," urged a voice. "Get down. Don't you know how to creep along quietly?" A girl, judging from the voice, peeked out of a black face covering. "Get down." She jerked Evie into a crouch behind the underbrush.

Evie shuffled back, breathing heavily. "Who are you?"

"One of your saviors, it seems. What are you doing out here alone?" The girl glanced back the way they'd come, and moonlight caught in her eyes—eyes the most brilliant green Evie had ever seen.

"Nothing. I'm trying to get to town."

The girl eyed her, snatched her hand, and turned over her wrist. "What did they want with you?"

"They were trying to take my things. What are *you* doing out here?" Evie pointed at the girl's face mask. "Wearing that?"

"Rescuing the girl."

The voice in the cage. "Why do they have her?"

"Because she's Gifted. Why else?"

Gifted? There were no Gifted humans in Sector Six. Only Adan. "Are you sure it's a girl? Not a boy? Dark hair, blue eyes?"

"Blue eyes?" The girl snorted. "It's a girl. I'm certain."

Of course. That would've been too easy. "What were they going to do with her?"

"Sell her in Sodorrah, I suppose."

Sell her? To who? Evie groaned and massaged her temple. Too many questions, too much to take in.

The masked girl faced the fight. She'd slung a bow over her shoulder and gripped a knife in one hand.

"Why aren't you fighting?" Evie asked.

Something twisted up her features. "My cousin won't let me. I'm here to keep watch. Thought I'd make sure you were okay." She shifted to her other foot. "So. Are you?"

Now that her breathing had slowed, Evie felt weary to her bones, though she didn't think any were broken. Her stomach growled. "I'm okay," she said. "I'm hungry, though?"

The girl laughed. "Is that a question? Either you are, or you're not."

Right. The scuffling was coming to an end, and Evie wanted to be on her way. "How far to the next town?"

"You're almost there. A little farther that way. It's called Soli."

"Is there a place I can stay? A hotel or something?"

"There's an inn and a restaurant if you can afford it."

"Thanks." Evie stood and started walking away.

"Hey, wait. If you wait a minute, we can walk you. It's not safe."

Shaking her head, she kept walking. She'd learned her lesson. She couldn't trust humans, and she didn't need help. "I need to go. Thanks for checking on me."

"Well, at least tell the innkeeper Lena sent you," she whispered. "Hey, you dropped something."

But Evie was already creeping back onto the road.

Darkness had descended on Soli by the time she arrived, but several lamps lit the night. Humans milled about the square, and she trusted none of them.

The Inn at Soli sign swung over a cheery establishment. Piano music drifted out the open door. It must be the place.

Keeping her dagger where she could reach it, Evie told the first woman she came across that Lena sent her and she needed a room and food.

"I don't work here, girl." The young woman eyed Evie's uniform. "Check with Patty." She pointed to a plump woman clearing tables in the corner. Other patrons gawked.

Patty, a more friendly human, led Evie up the stairs and to a room with a bed. A writing desk and wooden chair filled most of the remaining space. "We have pork stew tonight. Will you have it now, or do you need a moment?"

The discomfort in Evie's stomach answered for her. "Now, I think. Also, I'm looking for a young man named Adan. He has dark hair and blue eyes, and he's rather tall."

"Blue eyes?" The woman chuckled. "You need some sleep, dearie. I haven't seen anyone like that." A warm smile bunched her full cheeks up under her eyes. "Will you join us in the dining room, or would you like to eat here?"

"Here. Thank you." She'd had enough interactions for one day. She'd eat her first full meal in private and then tackle her next fear. She eyed the bed.

Evie threw her pack on it. Huh. One of the compartments had come unzipped, and the golden Guardian Quest box was gone. At least, she'd lost nothing else.

Movement drew her attention, and she locked eyes with the mirror posted by the door. Only the bright golden eyes and basic structure were familiar. Messy reddish-blonde hair framed her pale face, and light freckles dusted her cheeks and nose.

"Who are you?" she asked her reflection. The pale-haired stranger didn't answer. She only frowned.

Evie sank into the chair and put her head in her hands, suddenly drained. This body was so tired, and it ached in so many places.

Her mind reeled with all she'd endured in only a few hours as well as the things she'd seen and heard. Gifted humans lived here in Sector Six. Bad people prowled the shadowy roads, but good people lingered also. And no sign of Adan.

A few days ago, exciting possibilities lay before her. Tonight, she plotted murder in a dingy room in Sector Six.

Not for the first time, fear struck her that Jesiah had no place for someone like her among his Marked. She'd always felt different—like a bright golden flare among their soft sophistication. This would've never happened to anyone else in any Control Room. She couldn't come up with any reason Jesiah had made her. So why did he?

She pondered this and other dark thoughts involving her sharp golden blade until Patty returned with soup, a hunk of bread, and advice on where to buy clothes.

As Evie savored every nourishing bite, she decided that tomorrow was a new day. She'd search this tiny town and find Adan. Pulling Joram's note from her pocket, she gazed at the scrawl of letters. She *would* do what needed to be done, just as he asked. She would return home.

She locked the door, pushed the desk in front of it, and moved to the bed. Her confidence wavered. She'd feared this moment, drifting off into unconsciousness—into complete unawareness. What was it like to sleep? Would she dream? Would someone sneak up to her room and pick the lock while she rested in a senseless state?

Her mind fought against it, eyes fluttering and then snapping open again. What if she never awoke?

After a long and miserable hour, she relaxed, and without knowing it happened, she drifted.

<h1 style="text-align:center">14</h1>

"Adan," Evie's voice broke the silence. Adan stood transfixed, watching her. She wore all white, and a beautifully feathered mask covered the top half of her face. Her bright eyes peeked out like golden lanterns.

He'd been walking along the wooded path when she stepped out of the shadows and onto the sand, peering into the dense forest. She'd called his name, searching, but didn't seem to hear when he answered. Now, she rotated in a circle as if not quite sure what to do next. Her skin glowed with a soft golden light.

She glided past the snowy tree and disappeared around a corner.

Adan started to follow but halted when a black bear lumbered out of the trees, blocking his way. It paused, standing tall on hind legs, but, like Evie, it didn't seem to see him.

Birdcalls echoed from where a flock of blackbirds circled in a swirling dark cloud.

The bear huffed a groan, lowered its front paws to the ground, coating them in a puff of sand, and sauntered into the forest.

When Adan turned back, he found the smooth bronze archway before him. It stood taller than a man and wide enough to walk through. Anticipating the assassin, his heart began a wild rhythm. But, where before the arch glowed from within, today its depths were a rippling black. He walked forward, daring a closer look. He could almost see a reflection rippling on the surface. The swarm of birds landed in the trees around him, their calls spurring him onward.

The archway rested on a flat circular disk where a round swirling pattern had been stamped. The numbers one through five spread across the curved top of the arch, each encased in a perfect circle. Next to the five, however, a roughly carved six was scrawled onto the smooth surface—as if a child had drawn it.

A memory, something real, not some fantastical dream, wove through his brain. The imperfect six began to glow. The birds squawked in earnest. His eyes went wide as the memory solidified. Light filled the space inside the archway. The birdcalls were almost deafening. The golden gleam of a dagger flashed, flying end over end in his direction through the blinding light.

<<<>>>

Adan awoke with a yell. His heart raced, and his ears rang with phantom birdcalls. He must've fallen asleep sometime during the night. The glow of his marks cast eerie shapes over the dark walls. The soft light was already fading. Placing a hand on his chest where the blade had been about to enter, he sat and remembered.

That night, after he'd fallen in and out of consciousness during the awful car ride, the trunk had opened. Bright light crept in the edges of his blindfold. His legs didn't want to move. He could hardly move at all. He'd been dragged along a concrete floor and then pulled atop another surface. He steadied himself against a thin hard structure. Peeking out the top of his loose blindfold, he could see something arching over him. Numbers lined the top like in his dream. He felt weightless, and his head seemed as if it were going to split in two. He shut his eyes against a flaring light and was about to pass out again when solid ground met his feet. He stumbled, falling to his knees in soft grass. The blindfold fell, and he saw an arch of flowers before falling forward onto his face. He'd been so dizzy.

"Welcome to Sector Six, Strong One," a man's voice said. Adan's eyelids drifted downward as a cool finger traced the marks on his hand. "What is your purpose?" the stranger asked himself. "What does he hope you will do?"

Then there was nothing.

Adan hitched a breath and sat up. His frantic heart didn't slow. "Sector Six?" he whispered, unable to think beyond these two words. "That's not possible."

He stood, walked to the window, and tugged the drapes aside. The sun was already creeping upward, painting the old-fashioned buildings with brilliant light and harsh shadows. It could easily be in Sector Five, couldn't it? In another part of the world?

But the people in town yesterday… The woman and her black eyes. The way she looked at his blue ones. No one here had ever heard of Shura.

"No." His mind dismissed what his memory was trying to force him to see. He wouldn't believe it.

The man had asked, "What is your purpose?"

This Adan had struggled with for as long as he could remember. If his birth was an accident and if his mother didn't want him, what *was* his purpose? Why was he here? Had even his world been unable to keep him? Bitterness bubbled up in his chest. A resentment that made him angry at the world, at his mother, and at the Maker.

He paced to work the tension from his body. And what about Sam? He'd promised to get Adan out of the basement, but Sam never returned.

Adan fell back onto the bed and draped an arm over his eyes. *Don't panic.* Fear and anger weren't going to get him out of this room.

A hysterical laugh escaped his lips. "I'm in a castle. Locked in the tower of an actual castle." Sobering, he whispered, "Am I really in another sector?"

A tear leaked from his eye and fell to the mattress. If it were true, then even if he got out of this room, he had no idea how to get home.

Getting back to Ben was the priority, and escape was the first step. He'd figure everything else out later.

Footsteps clomped in the hall.

"Focus." The man who brought him here never showed his face. He had also refused to tell the captain where Adan was from, so the captain didn't know how to get him home. Adan needed to find out who the stranger was.

Keys rattled, and James pushed the door open. "Hey, Blue. How'd you sleep?"

Adan shrugged.

James held out a tiny white case. "I'm to show you around today, and Captain Curtshaw wants you to wear these eye coverings."

Adan opened the box. Other than the electric devices he'd had the displeasure of experiencing, this was the most advanced thing he'd seen so far.

"Contacts?"

"Pardon? Is that what you call them? The captain says they'll tint your eyes brown. I've never seen anything like it. He doesn't want anyone to see your eyes." James was staring at Adan's eyes again as if he were some three-headed dragon.

Adan wasn't opposed to blending in. He lifted a contact to his eye. "Did he say why he wants to keep me a secret?"

James cringed as Adan attempted to force it onto his eye. "He keeps all of us a secret. The blue would draw too much attention." He paced the room. "But you. You—he kept secret even from the other Gifted captives. Maybe he hopes to keep you for himself."

Great.

"Also, he probably doesn't want the king to find out what kind of operation he has going on here."

The contact slid into place. "This would be a lot easier if I had some eye drops or something."

James laughed. "Whoa, one blue, one brown. Now you *really* look strange."

Adan scowled.

When he forced the other contact in, he stood. "What operation?"

"So many questions. Come on. We'll talk on the way." The boy led him down a dim hallway, and Adan's guard followed a few paces behind.

James lowered his voice. "The captain has moved several Gifted people through here since I came along. He uses the king's facilities for his testing. Inevah is a free city, so I doubt the king knows the captain is keeping *special guests* in his castle. Captain Curtshaw will make it look like you're a guest in his home, though we both know you're not going anywhere. I'm not sure what the endgame is, but he has an outside employer. The captain tests the Gifted before they move on. His employer requested these extra guards for you."

Could he mean the other man in the basement—the one who kept his face hidden? "Who's the employer?"

"I don't know. I've never seen him."

"What does he want with us?"

"I'm not sure. The most powerful Gifted are sent to Sodorrah. I don't know what becomes of them there. As for myself, I serve as Healer for the captain and his family. And anyone else he pawns me off to." They reached the end of the long hallway and took a staircase down to the main floor. "Others Gifted in strength are kept around to help with building projects or anything else. Water Movers have their uses."

"How many are held captive here now?"

"A handful of us live here permanently, and a few others, perhaps including you, are passing through."

"This is all too much." Adan rubbed his face. "What am I doing today?"

"First breakfast. Then strength testing."

"James, I'm not Strength Gifted."

James glanced sidelong at him.

"I'm not." Adan threw his hands up.

"Then you're going to have an interesting day."

With that, James pushed through a door, stepping into a crowded dining area. Two burly young men stood at either side of the opening. Three long tables striped the room where groups sat huddled together. Two more muscled figures—one man and one woman—stood like statues at the only other exit.

Touching Adan's arm, James slowed their pace. "Those are the guards for the rest of us"—he indicated himself and the twenty or so others seated throughout the room—"the *special guests*. The guards are all Strength Wielders, of course. Idiots. They think they're better than the rest of us because they get special privileges. That's how the captain keeps them controlled." He rolled his eyes. "Even though they're prisoners like us."

The same electric ankle band Adan wore wrapped around each guard's ankle.

"How many are there? Just these four?"

"No, there are six more. They take shifts, and there's always one at each exit from this wing."

Adan followed James through a line along the back wall where an older woman filled plates.

"Hello, Hattie," James said as she passed him his breakfast.

"Good morning." Hattie handed Adan a tray and looked him over. "Ah, the new one. The one with all the guards."

"Hattie, this is Adan. Looks like the captain hasn't decided what to do with him yet. Hattie's not Gifted, but she's not allowed to leave either. She's one of us."

Hattie shook her head, a motherly smile forming. "You know it could be considered rude to always point out that someone is *not* Gifted."

"Correction, Hattie is a *gifted* chef. She tends an orchard and cooks the food. You'll find no better feast in all the Valley." James finished with a flourish and a wink while Hattie mumbled something like "oh, stop" and shooed them on their way.

He led Adan to the end of a long table where two others were already seated. "Guys, this is Adan. Adan, this is Grace, a Water Mover."

A dimpled girl with dark-brown skin and light-brown eyes smirked back. "Welcome to Inevah Castle where all your dreams come true."

James snorted. "And this is Thomas. Our resident Strength Wielder."

Thomas inclined his ashy blond head. His black eyes peered from skin only slightly lighter than Adan's—a soft golden tone.

"The captain has found him to be less compliant than the typical guard." James gave him a conspiring grin.

Thomas returned it. "I have no intention of cooperating."

"He's the reason we now have two guards at each door."

Hattie, the cook, took a seat, setting a plate before her. "How is it today?"

"Wonderful, as always." Thomas shoveled a portion in his mouth.

Grace pushed a long black braid over her shoulder. "So, Adan, what can you do?"

Adan met her level gaze. They watched him expectantly. *Here we go again.*

"Nothing. I don't have any of those abilities." He avoided their stares by looking at his plate. A cut of fried meat he truly hoped was chicken perched atop a mound of rice. Not typical Sector Five breakfast food. He spooned some into his mouth so he wouldn't have to elaborate.

"Uh-huh." Grace waggled both brows. "You have an army of guards. You were hidden away for an entire day. The captain sent James to heal you. *And* I hear you won't be staying in the dormitory with the rest of us."

Adan shrugged and swallowed. "I don't know."

"You have to be a Strength Wielder to have that kind of guard."

"I'm telling you, I'm not. The captain thinks I am, though."

"That might not bode well for you today. Though, you wouldn't be the first to try to hide it. No one wants to give up their secrets and get the mark." She held up her hand, revealing the inside of her wrist. They all bore the strange mark.

"Look, I don't know what to tell you. All I want is to get out of here. Has anyone even attempted to escape?"

"Look… Adan, was it?" Thomas bristled. "We try to help people who come through here. I'm not going to lie to you—turnover is fast. You're different, or at least the captain thinks so. But if he doesn't find a use for you, you'll be out of here like all the rest. And I don't mean out of here like back home. I mean out of here like dead, sold, or down the road to Sodorrah."

"He's right." James picked at his food with a bent fork.

When Thomas sighed and looked away, Grace patted the giant's arm in mock sincerity. "Though, according to Thomas, being shipped off to Sodorrah might be the best chance of rescue." She laughed when he scowled.

"For your information, when the prince visited the captain a few days ago, I overheard the word *rebel* several times. I'm sure of it."

Grace rolled her eyes. "How many times do I have to tell you? The rebels are a myth. No mysterious rescuer is lurking outside the walls."

They ate in silence, and Grace stared at her drink. Swirls of clear water rose in intricate patterns. The others didn't seem to think this strange. It splayed out in a fanlike shape and froze in place. Grace, obviously feeling Adan's stare, looked up. "What?"

"One of my brothers is a Water Mover. I've never seen him do anything like that. Now, I think maybe he's not very good at it."

Grace smiled her first real smile. It made her look less harsh and more like a girl who wanted a normal life.

"Did he have training?"

"Fighting, yes. Water moving, no."

"What about your parents or grandparents? Surely one of them is a Water Mover. Is *that* your Gift?"

"No, I'm not a Water Mover. And he's not my brother. More of an adopted brother, though not even that, officially." Uzziah's urging them to see each other as a brotherhood must have worn off. He didn't regularly call anyone but Ben his brother. "Besides, he's Guardian Marked. I don't think his Gift was inherited."

Blank stares gawked at him. "What do you mean, it wasn't inherited? All Gifts are inherited."

"He was marked. You know… by Guardian." Huh? Just confused faces.

Grace let the ice formation drop into her glass, and the glance she shared with Hattie spoke of how loony they thought he was.

"Guardians are a myth," Grace said. "Just like the rebels."

Adan's last thread of hope faded. He wasn't in Sector Five anymore. He was sure of it.

"Never mind," he said. "I'm probably wrong." This felt too much like school. He might as well have fallen asleep on the table and woken with a shout. Always the outsider. Always the strange one. Would he ever fit in?

"I do have a biological brother. He's nine." His gaze drifted to his plate. "I'm all the family he has."

"At least you remember your family." Whew. Grace allowed the topic change. "I can almost remember faces, but just when I think I have it, they're gone."

Adan started to ask what she meant when a clatter rang across the room. Someone had flung a plate against the wall near a group of six wide-eyed prisoners.

"Oh boy," James whispered.

The room went still as a guard stalked over to investigate.

"Whose is that?" he bellowed, pointing at the tray. All seated near the mess still had a plate in front of them.

Adan and his companions sat in stony silence. When no one near the guard answered, he yelled again. This time one of the younger ones darted his eyes toward the door.

The guard—and everyone else—followed his gaze to where the largest Strength Wielder shielded the main entrance. Behind him, a girl crept toward the open doorway. Her brown face melted into fear. Her distraction hadn't worked. The boulder-like guard threw out a hand to stop her, and the doorframe fractured. His wrist began to glow, releasing his power. The girl cringed away, and with only the flick of her hands, she threw water from a nearby glass into the guard's face. He reached for her arm and slung her over his shoulder. The raw force broke her arm, and she screamed.

Across the table, rage mottled Thomas's face. He sprang to his feet and ran for the girl. Before he could make it, one of the other guards pulled a gun-like device from his pocket. A circular disk shot toward Thomas and suctioned to his thick calf. The leg jerked and gave way, crashing Thomas to the floor.

Chaos erupted. Three well-dressed men and two more Strength Wielders barreled in. Guards dragged Thomas away.

A guard rounded on Adan and his companions, who'd risen during the commotion.

"Sit," he ordered.

They did. The group nearest the spilled plate filed out.

Adan's heart slowed, and all became quiet again.

"What will happen to them?" he asked.

Hattie pushed her tray away. "I'm not sure,"

A muscle flexed in Grace's jaw as she stared at her fisted hands. "When I tried to escape, I was beaten and locked in a dark room for days."

"Should we help them?" Adan leaned closer.

James shook his head. "We'd end up punished along with them. I'll heal the girl's arm later."

"What was that thing that took Thomas down?" Adan rubbed his neck. "One was used on me yesterday."

"A StrengthShock. It helps keep the Strength Wielders in line."

It seemed entirely too modern for this city. "Will he be okay?"

James nodded as a stern-looking man with a sharply pointed nose strolled near. "Stop your whispering. Finish up, and move on." They sat back and picked at their food.

"Act natural, Adan. Make them think you're unaffected." An uncaring guise covered Hattie's face better than any festival mask could. "We'll get our revenge. Besides, you need to concentrate on your testing today."

Still shaken, Adan cleared his throat. "I have no idea what that means. How will they test me?"

Mirth skittered from Grace's lips. "Probably best not to give you too much to think about."

"Not helpful." He scooped the last of his rice. "Any tips? I'll fail them all. I don't have any gifts like yours."

Grace stood, grabbing her tray. "We'll see. They'll make you reveal your secrets." She walked away with one last piece of advice. "Oh, and try not to die."

Adan's mouth fell open as she strode from the room.

"Don't mind her." James elbowed him. "It's not so bad. Besides, I'll be there to heal you."

Somehow, this didn't make Adan feel any better.

15

Evie's feet ached, and she lamented again the absence of her flawless immortal body. She'd run out of water an hour ago and was relieved to find herself back at the inn.

She shuffled into the dining room and made for the stairs. The innkeeper, Patty, paused to give her an approving nod. Evie had taken her advice and purchased new clothes. A pair of dark pants hugged her legs, and sturdy hiking boots clopped up the stairs as Evie made her way to her room. When safely inside, she shed her sleek dark jacket and threw it onto the bed.

She examined herself in the mirror. Her ponytail sagged on the back of her head, and strands of light hair fell in a wild halo around her face. She pulled at the hair tie, letting the long locks fall over her new, fitted, cream-colored shirt.

Her golden eyes shone with unnatural brightness, even in this poorly lit room. No wonder the humans often did a double take in her direction.

She sagged onto the bed and tested Joram's communicator. Still no signal, just as the other times.

This morning, she'd woken from her slumber rather than slept on for all eternity. She remembered having been somewhere else—somewhere strange and fantastical. She'd dreamed. But now, she couldn't remember the details any more than she could conjure Adan's blood on her blade.

Had it been too much to think she could walk up to someone in town and ask, "Where is the blue-eyed boy?" and they would direct her straight to him? She hadn't heard a peep about him all day. She had tried not to think about him as she searched the town. Sure, she'd asked passersby if they knew of anyone meeting his description, but that was solely about location. She tried not to think about how he looked in the photograph—beaten and bruised. How he had smiled at her only days ago, or how his dimple quirked and his beautiful eyes lit and full lips curved.

"Stop it. You're doing it again. What's wrong with you?" She had a job to do, and she meant to do it. Her future depended on it.

A savory smell wafted up the stairs, and her tired feet carried her back to the dining room. She found a table and sat with her back to the wall, watching the patrons, hoping for and dreading the sight of piercing blue eyes.

Chairs scraped on the wood floor, and forks clanked on the plates as murmured conversations rose. A waiter wandered over, and she ordered the special.

A musician played a merry tune on a guitar, and she relished the feeling of doing something so normal in the human world—eating at a restaurant, listening to music.

More humans trickled in, and the noise grew to a dull roar. A bookshelf near her held several board games. She found a battered copy of Guardian Quest, the game she lost in the woods.

With it in hand, she returned to her chair and sifted through the box. When unfolded, the game board covered much of her table. She placed each of the wooden figures next to it and then grouped the two golden Guardians and the pale-gold Watcher together. The three of them wore corresponding labels on their bases. The remaining six pieces were unpainted and identical. They represented the humans. One of the humans had the word *Deceiver* stamped onto its base. It blended in perfectly. Evie set the pieces on the board where their names were labeled: Guardians, Watchers, humans. There was no place for the Deceiver. Where did it fit in? She had no idea.

Her food came, and she pushed the game aside. The swinging door kept a steady open and close rhythm as the place filled. Most avoided her dark corner. Then a group of five young men took a seat two tables over. She kept her head down, not wanting to draw attention.

They leaned together in whispered conversation. After ordering, they sat until one of them began to drone on. "The entire area was founded by a group of settlers who traveled from across the sea. When they arrived, they couldn't agree on much of anything, so half of them settled Inevah, and the other half traveled farther inland to Sodorrah. They—"

"Stop with the recital. We came here to listen, not talk." Something clattered to the floor. This boy's weapons belt had slipped to the floor.

"Yeah, you're the mask of stealth," another boy said on a laugh.

"How would you know anything about this place anyway?" one of them asked the know-it-all.

"I found a book store and traded a knife for it."

"Are you kidding me? You traded one of our weapons for a book?"

"Hey, knowledge is power."

"Both of you, shut up," the largest boy growled, and they silenced.

A party of older men sat at the table between Evie and the boys. The newcomers seemed to know the waiter and ordered right away.

Evie went back to her dinner. She moved the game pieces around the board until she keyed in on the older men's conversation.

"It's getting out of hand. I was born and raised in The Valley, but I don't like what I'm seeing—Sodorran soldiers combing the land, looking for the marked. The Sodorran steward is gathering them up, claiming they are his." Bending forward on his elbows, he lowered his voice. "I saw them take one yesterday. His mark was strange, though. It was different."

The five boys stiffened and came to attention, as did she.

The other men leaned in. "How was it different?"

"Well, it was still charred, so I could see it well. It was bigger than the others."

"Can you draw it?"

"Oh, I can't draw."

"Try." His companion prodded a napkin across the table.

The man pulled it close.

Evie sat higher, nudging the game board. One of the pieces fell over and rolled off the table. She left it and scooted back, trying to appear at ease. The men didn't notice, but she still couldn't see the drawing.

"I don't know, something like that." He passed the napkin back to his friend. "The mark went all the way up to his sleeve and down onto his hand. And I'm telling you"—he tossed his pencil onto the table and sat back—"he had blue eyes."

The other men chuckled. "Oh, really? And how long had you been in the drink before you saw this blue-eyed boy?"

"Believe me. Don't believe me. I don't care. I'm telling you what I saw." He drummed an index finger on the tabletop, hitting it there again like a period after each sentence. "He was hiding between Omer's shop and Gina's. A man I didn't recognize caught him unaware from behind. He used some shiny device I've never seen before. I don't know how he did it. But the blue-eyed boy collapsed, and then two people dragged him back down the alley and out of sight."

He waved a hand. "Now, I don't like to get into other people's business, but I got up and walked around to the back. They put the boy into a wagon and covered him up. One guy was stocky with graying brown hair. The other..." He shook his head. "Well, I don't rightly remember what he looked like. Anyway, the stocky man told the other he was going to go around to the south entrance of Inevah to avoid the rebels."

"Ridiculous," one of his companions scoffed. "One"—he held up a finger—"the rebels are a myth. Just a bunch of youngsters causing trouble. And two"—another finger—"the marked are always taken to Sodorrah, not Inevah."

"Not always," interjected the third man. "I've heard tell there's some sort of operation in Inevah—a dealer of the captured Gifted—and they're at odds with these supposed rebels. It's rumored they rescue the marked ones as they're transported by caravan near the city. They have a leader now, you know. The rebels. The man with a falcon inked on his arm."

"All right, Bernie, we're listening. So what happened after that?"

The man sat back. "Before I could do anything, the wagon took off down Main Street, moving away from town. No doubt headed to Inevah. The stocky man drove the wagon, and the other stayed behind. I returned to my dinner."

A loaded silence hung over the group.

He folded his arms across his chest and jerked his chin up. "I didn't want to get involved."

Evie squirmed in her chair, needing a look at the drawing. She bent to pick up the game piece, and as she did, she peeked around Bernie's elbow.

One of the boys at the far table leaned forward, and his gaze also cut to the drawing. A smudged arm with a swirl of black protruding from a crude sleeve scrawled across the napkin. The boy met Evie's eyes, both caught snooping. Her eyebrows drew together as he turned away. She sat up, holding tight to the small figure. She knew that face. Placing the Deceiver on the game board, she exhaled as a new worry tightened her chest.

Another Sector Five trespasser sat two tables away—Adan's best friend, Sam.

16

Adan stood dripping as he heaved rapid breaths of glorious air. He'd been sure they were going to drown him this time. The location of this torture was a hidden courtyard. Apparently, this outdoor area within his wing of the castle was once Captain Curtshaw's private garden. It stretched wide, providing a secret place to test his latest subjects.

High castle walls enclosed the space, and three stories up, a balcony overshadowed the length of one side. Someone watched from the shadows.

Adan sank to his knees, spewing dirty water as the warm morning sun rose over the castle to begin its arc overhead. Since most tried to hide their gifts, the captain and his guards were willing to make them use those powers. Their initial strength tests failed, resulting in a broken arm. James now sat weakened to the side after healing the injury.

"Dunk him again." Captain Curtshaw stepped away to protect his spotless suit. His patience waned, and he'd resorted to testing for other gifts. Back in Sector Five, even the weakest Water Mover could force water from the bucket so he could breathe. Adan, however, couldn't move a single drop and was likely to drown before this ended. He tensed as dread overtook him.

The Strength Wielder, who Adan had begun to think of as the Boulder, seized Adan's hair and dunked his head again. He thrashed and pushed against the rim. Just when he thought it might tip, the Boulder righted the bucket and shoved his face in deeper. Adan's lungs were near bursting when the beefy hand released him and he flew backward out of the water. He sucked in a mighty gulp of air and fell onto his side, spewing. Ears ringing, he thought only of his burning lungs. Someone was yelling nearby.

"Clearly, he's no Water Mover. Why do you continue to dunk him?"

The Boulder gaped at the captain who ground out his words. "We test them for everything when a Gift does not show itself."

"Be that as it may, my employer requests you stick to strength tests."

A tall, finely dressed young man had materialized amid Adan's sputtering. The man brushed at his black pants and straightened a tailored black jacket. When he noticed Adan's gaze, he smiled but took a step back and shoved his dark hair from his eyes. Adan got to his feet. This was the first person he'd come across whose height allowed them to meet him eye to eye.

In an accent similar to the captain's, the man said, "I'm Joromy, and you must be the captain's new friend."

Adan scoffed, and Joromy laughed. "I suppose *friend* is not the right word. Come on, one final test, and you'll be done for now."

When the captain glared at Joromy, the two exchanged some silent but mutual insult. A muscle twitched in Captain Curtshaw's jaw. "Fine."

He and his Strength Wielder followed as Joromy led Adan to a secluded corner. They crossed over worn remnants of a brick path to a space where rocks sprawled in the shadow of the stone wall.

Adan rubbed his recently healed arm. "I can't move those, you know."

"Are you sure?" Joromy nodded to the rocks. "Give it a go."

"So you just want me to pick one up?"

"Sure. Can you?"

"Maybe the smaller ones." Adan approached them.

"Try them all. Start with the smallest."

Adan bent and picked up a rock about the size of a melon. It was heavy, but he could lift it. He moved to the next one and was barely able to get it off the ground before dropping it again. He could only move the third one in a tilting motion.

"I can't pick this one up."

"Just keep going."

Adan stepped in front of the next rock. This was ridiculous. He bent at the knees and coiled his muscles. The rock gave almost no opposing force, and Adan toppled backward with the momentum. He fell onto his back, knocking the breath from his lungs. This rock weighed less than the first one.

A smug grin uncoiled Joromy's lips as Adan frowned and got to his feet and brushed at the dirt caking his wet shirt. "What was that about?"

"That was my idea. Someone trying to hide their strength would pretend they couldn't lift the rock. But someone with nothing to hide" —Joromy's eyes twinkled—"or someone very smart. They do that. It's funny every time. Come on. I'll walk you inside."

Adan scowled and glanced at the captain, expecting him to argue, but the man motioned for James to follow.

Joromy pushed through the double doors to a hallway near the dining room. "Well, Adan, it's been an interesting day for you."

"Yeah, I guess." Adan's wet socks squished inside his tennis shoes. "You mentioned your employer. Is he the man who brought me to the captain?" *And perhaps the only person who knows how to get me back home?*

"As a matter of fact, yes."

"Who is he?"

"Someone influential in Sodorrah. I'm his assistant."

"Can I talk to him?"

"Oh no, I think not." Joromy started to clap Adan on the shoulder but pulled away as if afraid to touch him. "The captain would like you to get cleaned up now. Perhaps the Healer can escort you." After Joromy and the captain shared another glance, he retreated down the hall.

Captain Curtshaw spun in the other direction, calling over his shoulder. "Healer, take him to clean up."

James led the way, keeping his mouth shut until they were out of earshot. "Whoa. How did you attract *his* attention?"

"Why? Who is that?"

"He works for the steward of Sodorrah. He visits often and watches the testing, but I've never seen him come into the courtyard. What did he want?"

"Nothing, really. He wanted me to stick to the strength test." *And Joromy's employer knows I had a marking ceremony with a Strength Guardian.* "What's the Sodorran steward's name?"

"I've never heard him called anything but Steward."

"What does he look like?"

James shrugged. "He never comes to this part of the castle."

"Is Joromy one of the Sodorrans who gives the marks?" Adan gestured toward James's hand.

The Healer was quiet as he opened the door to a new hall of the castle. "I don't think so. But it might be hard to say since no one remembers who gave them their mark."

"What do you mean? Do they put you under?"

"Put you under?"

"Like, give you a drug to make you pass out?"

"No, no, nothing like that. The Gifted will remember someone walking in, they remember getting the mark, and they remember obeying what the person said, even if it wasn't what they wanted to do. But they won't remember the person who marked them after they leave. No one can describe them. Is it always the same person? Is it several people? Is it a man? Is it a woman? No one remembers."

Adan's brows drew together. The man outside his basement prison who'd stayed carefully hidden—the man Adan had obeyed though he hadn't wanted to…

They walked on until James chuckled and eyed Adan's soaked shirt. "I take it you're not a Water Mover."

"Obviously not."

"You can't move water. You say you're not a Strength Wielder. So what are you? What *can* you do?"

An excellent question, and Adan feared the answer was *nothing*. What would happen to him then?

Would James tell the captain if Adan revealed the truth?

Best to keep it a secret for now. Dreaming amounted to nothing anyway.

17

"Okay. This isn't working," Sam said after stumbling across a deep rut in the dusty road.

"What should we do?" Chase's voice came out of the blackness.

The moon slid behind a cloud. Not a star marked the sky—or a streetlamp. It was never dark back home. Even on camping trips, they had the luxury of a flashlight. This complete darkness unnerved him.

"We could try to make torches," Elias said on a yawn. Their day of searching in the sun had worn them out. It wasn't late, but they couldn't travel the two hours to Inevah like this.

"Let's make camp." Sam let his pack drop to the ground. "Chase, can you get a fire going?"

"Probably. Give me a minute." Chase's movements seemed loud as Sam's ears compensated for his lack of sight.

Chase, who'd earned his place with Uzziah because of his uncanny outdoorsman skills and his decent talent in archery, was unmatched in his ability to find and use what he needed in the wild.

As Sam listened to him rummaging, he touched a finger to his still black eye. He winced, and his mind flitted back to Ben. He'd had to leave the boy behind. This was no trip for a nine-year-old.

"I'm going!" He'd screamed in their apartment living room. "You can't stop me!"

Uzziah, patient as ever, laid a hand on the boy's shoulder. "You're too young. That's my final word."

Ben fled with tear-filled eyes, and Uzziah gave Sam and each of his companions a set of low-tech weapons. He sent them off to pack, but during the flurry, he'd drawn Sam aside.

"I want to give you one more weapon. Don't tell the others yet. It may keep Garran in check."

An argument erupted in the dark forest. Sam sighed, wincing as he adjusted his pack.

"According to most survival guides, you need a flat piece of wood to use as a fireboard, and we need to make a fire bow. That kindling should be arranged differently," Asher prodded in his usual know-it-all fashion.

"I know what I'm doing." Chase kept his response quiet.

"Where is your fireboard?"

"Don't need it. Can you bother someone else?"

"If you don't make a fire bow, you'll chafe your hands."

"No, I won't."

"It'll take twice as long. You need a bow. Do you have twine?"

"Asher, I have a lighter," Chase confessed as a flame lit the dark. He held it near a bunch of sticks he'd arranged in a teepee formation over dry leaves. Chase smirked. "Any more helpful advice?"

"Uzziah told you not to bring anything like that."

Chase rolled his eyes as Asher launched into a recital of the information he'd learned in one of Uzziah's books about what Sector Six might be like after all this time—preindustrial, possibly medieval. Asher trailed off muttering, "But not a place for automatic lighters."

Asher was not as talented in the physical sense. He could hold his own in a knife fight if need be, but his Gift was in wisdom. He was well read and had a photographic memory. Chase often teased him about being gifted in the art of useless information. But more than that, when his Gift made an appearance, Asher would know without reason the choice he should make. This feeling only came on him occasionally, and he described it as a strong hunch or a push in the right direction. The Gift could be useful if it worked on command. But Asher couldn't summon the knowledge he desired at will. He'd had no hunch as to where Adan might be.

Chase continued to nurture the flame, and the growing glow illuminated Elias's bright-red tennis shoes. He hadn't bothered to get out a different pair after the Alvar Party, and they didn't blend in.

When the fire was steady, Chase pushed himself to his feet. "Hey, I need some firewood. Dry stuff."

After the darkness, the campfire made their site positively cheery. Sam nodded. "Okay, you heard the man. Firewood. Dry stuff."

Everyone lumbered off into the trees. Everyone except Garran. He sat on a log and picked at his nails.

A frown tightened Sam's lips. "Garran, help us find firewood."

The Strength Wielder looked up. "I don't take orders from you."

"Yes, you do." Sam's fingers twitched at his side, and he adjusted his new gloves. "Uzziah put me in charge."

Garran stood. "I will lead this group. I have no intention of dying while we try to rescue a piece of arrogant filth."

Elias, Chase, and Asher returned to the firelight, arms full of branches. The green of their tinted contacts reflected the dancing flame. The clouds parted for the moon, casting an eerie glow over them all.

Best to move on now. Sam picked up a branch and tossed it at Garran's feet. "Okay, make a pile by Garran, and he can keep the fire—"

"What did I tell you?" Garran stood, his fingers twitching. "*I'm* leading."

Sam crossed his arms. "I don't think so."

"What did you say?" Garran's hands went to fists. He lurched.

So this was happening. Sam bent into a fighting stance. "I said, I don't think so."

Garran attacked, but his eyes went wide just before making contact. Like lightning, Sam whipped Garran around and forced him to his stomach, pressing his face onto the dried leaves at their feet. Sam knelt beside Garran and held his arms at a painful angle. Garran bucked and growled, but Sam didn't move. He looked up at the other boys, whose mouths hung open. He could sense the light from his marks reflecting on his collar. Chase dropped the branches he'd been holding.

"I will lead this group." Sam's tone dared anyone to disagree. Chase, Asher, and Elias nodded. Sam glanced at Garran's back and then back at the other boys. As the faintest of smiles curved Chase's lips, Sam couldn't help but answer the silly grin with his own.

Garran's muscles eased, and Sam, schooling his features, stood and stepped back to let the boy stand.

Garran whirled. "What is this?"

Sam ripped a glove from his fingers and let his arm dangle at his side. The other boys gaped. Swirling, light-leaking scabs protruded from the back of Sam's hand. And there, resting on his pinky finger, was Adan's ring.

"What is that?" Elias gawked.

Sam shifted, lifting his palm. He twisted the ring on his finger with his other hand. "It's an enhancement ring."

"Yeah, but where did it come from?" Elias asked as he turned to Asher.

His not-always-useless information poured from his lips. "Enhancement rings are rumored to have been forged by the Maker himself, though no evidence can back that up. Not even the Guardians know." He met Sam's eyes. "But I don't know how *you* ended up with one."

Garran spat on the ground and wiped pebbles from his face.

"Uzziah gave it to Adan." Sam faced Garran. "Someone took it from him, but Uzziah got it back. He gave it to me, and now, it is mine." Sam shoved his glove back on. He shouldered past the others and picked up a handful of dry kindling. "Like I said. Firewood. Dry stuff."

The others made a pile on the ground. Garran tossed a branch onto it, though his look promised retribution.

Chase whispered, "That was awesome."

Sam smiled as he bent to scoop up a handful of dry leaves. *Yes. Yes, it was.*

Half an hour and several Asher versus Chase arguments later, a decent fire blazed. Sam sat atop his sleeping bag, staring at the flames. He tossed a baseball up and down. They'd each spread their bags near the warmth, and all was quiet.

Garran stared up at the sky, fingers clasped behind his head. He opted, for now, in favor of stony silence. His eyebrows were drawn in what might be anger mixed with confusion. Sam couldn't fathom what storm brewed in his pea-sized brain.

Garran hadn't wanted to join this rescue mission, but Uzziah forced him along.

When Uzziah ordered the brute to get packed and cover his blue eyes, Garran made the mistake of saying he wasn't going.

The older man moved with inhuman speed across the room and pinned Garran to the wall with a forearm across the throat.

Uzziah had hissed in his ear. "This started with you, and if you don't help bring Adan back, then your time with me is over. You'll never be recruited by another Guardian."

The boy's world revolved around his elite status, and his family would never allow him home after being so dishonored. So Garran came. And now Sam had to put up with him.

Chase laughed. Lying on his back, he peered straight up. He giggled again, and this time he didn't stop but clutched his stomach.

Sam and Elias shared a glance.

Elias threw a twig at him. "Guys, Chase is losing it."

Sam felt his lips turn up as Chase continued to giggle. "What are you laughing about?"

Chase rubbed his eyes and gasped between outbursts. "I can't believe Adan asked some Sector Six lady if he could borrow her *cell phone*." He broke into another fit.

The others relaxed, and more chuckles rumbled around the fire.

Elias rested on an elbow. "I bet she thought he was some sort of alien."

"At least he didn't say, 'Take me to your leader,'" Sam finished in a robotic tone.

All but Garran cackled. Then their laughter faded, and only the insects and the popping fire filled the void.

"You should've seen her eyes," Elias whispered. "They were black as this night was before our fire."

Chase flicked a leaf from his sleeping bag. "I saw a kid with bright orange hair."

"We're a long way from home, boys." Sam folded his arms across his chest and hunkered down on his sleeping bag. The story about Adan was funny, but they all knew what it meant. Adan didn't know where he was, and now he'd moved on to a bigger city. How would they ever find him?

Yesterday, the bronze archway had deposited them in a garden near a town called Soli. The portal stood among several statues, and a vine of yellow flowers tangled over its height, hiding it. This archway was a replica of the one Ben led them to in the parking garage and a reproduction of the drawings in his dream. All intersector portals were supposed to have been destroyed long ago, but someone had restored these. They'd even added Sector Six to its travel capabilities, etching a hand-drawn six across its top to match the perfect one through five already there.

After not finding Adan waiting on this side of the portal, they made camp and then began an organized search this morning. They split up, and late that afternoon, Elias returned with a lead. He'd spoken with a lady who'd seen a boy matching Adan's description. She didn't know where he'd gone after asking to borrow her cell phone. They'd grabbed dinner at the local inn, where they caught a break.

With a lead to guide him, Sam made plans to get on the road to Inevah early the next morning.

As his companions began to still around the fire, he eyed the trees and their many shadows. He couldn't shake the feeling of being watched. Chase also watched the forest with sleepy eyes.

Just as Sam felt himself drifting, a snap sounded outside their circle. He peered into the dark. Movement! He sat upright, and the others did the same. As he got to his knees, a shape detached from the shadows and crept away from the firelight to dart behind a tree. Sam put his fingers to his lips and rose. He slid one of his daggers from his holster. Creeping behind a tree, he stooped where the intruder couldn't see him.

The others began to rise, grabbing weapons of their own, but Sam motioned for them to lie back down. They did, pretending to dismiss the disturbance. They rested their heads, and Elias adjusted Sam's sleeping bag, making it look more like someone was in it. Then they waited.

Not ten minutes later, another sound creaked behind Sam. Chase met his gaze.

Sam gripped his dagger, heart pounding. Another crunch in the leaves, this time behind Sam's hiding tree. This idiot must have a few screws loose to risk sneaking into a camp of armed men.

A light glared in Sam's eyes. The mark on his hand was glowing. He fumbled to cover it, but his dagger tumbled into the dry leaves. Light also peeked from his collar, and he covered it with his left hand, sending a glow over the entire campsite. His companions narrowed incredulous eyes at him.

"Sam, your pack." Elias bolted upright.

A hand grabbed Sam's pack and then disappeared behind the tree. The retreat was loud after the long quiet. Sam pushed to his feet and spun to follow the thief, his stronger muscles propelling him faster than he'd ever run. A slight but nimble figure skittered in the moonlight. The others crashed through the forest behind him.

As he drew closer, he could see that this wasn't an adult. This was a boy. The child was scrawny and probably only came up to Sam's chest. Sam was almost on him, and the thief knew it. He lunged as the boy threw himself behind a sapling. Sam's hand missed the boy, and he swiped the tree instead. It bent to the side, roots exploding out of the ground in a spray of dirt. As the trunk cracked and splintered to the ground, the momentum sent Sam tumbling.

He landed beside the boy, who gaped at him. "Sam, you almost crushed me."

Huh? He gawked at the boy as the others rushed to surround them.

"Ben! What are you doing here?" Chase shrieked, voice cracking.

The boy ducked his head as Chase tugged him to his feet. "I wanted to help, but no one would let me."

Sam sat up, still dumbfounded. "Ben… Why are you…? Where…?" He groaned and raked his hands through his hair. "How did you get here?"

"Same way you did," Ben replied in a voice suggesting Sam asked the most ridiculous question he'd ever heard.

Elias hunkered before Ben. "How did you know what to do?"

"Easy, I watched Uzziah show you."

Sam sighed. "This is just great."

Asher helped Sam to his feet.

"Hey. Wait a minute." Sam eyed Ben. "Why did you steal my pack?"

Eyes wide, lips quivering, Ben offered the vision of skilled innocence. "I was hungry."

"Wipe that angelic look off of your face." Sam rolled his eyes. "I'm not buying it for a second."

Ben shrugged, unaffected.

Sam loosed a breath. *This isn't good.* Ben, blue eyes blazing, in Sector Six meant more complications to deal with.

Asher clapped Ben on the shoulder. "Come on. Let's go back to the fire. You can tell us how you found us."

Ben walked away, digging into the bag still over his shoulder. "I'm starving. Sam, don't you have any food?"

Sam rubbed his forehead. *What now?* Chase and Elias meandered away, trying not to laugh as he wiped dirt and leaves from his clothes. He smirked and stepped around the downed tree. It was as big around as his thigh.

I knocked over a tree. He fell in behind his friends.

Chase glanced over his shoulder and said too loudly, "Hey, Elias."

"Yes, Chase?"

"Do you remember when Sam was trying to hide and his body flashlight came on?"

"Oh yeah, and did you see how he dropped his weapon when he tried to hide it. Classic."

"Shut up," Sam muttered. He'd never live this down.

18

Evie perched in a tree high above the boys' abandoned camp. *What a bunch of idiots.* This was like watching some great comedy show. *Humans.* Since they'd left everything behind, unprotected, she slid to the ground to investigate their provisions. Like her, they were well stocked after their time in Soli.

She inspected Sam's strange weapon holster. She'd seen it on him and thought it a bit extravagant. His dagger still lay in the dry leaves where it had slipped from his grasp. She rolled her eyes.

Their simple but modern sleeping bags were most certainly from Sector Five. They'd prepared for this trip—as if they planned to cross over into Six.

Voices drifted from the direction the boys had disappeared, and she scrambled over their bedrolls to her perch in the canopy. She needed information, and she couldn't very well walk up and ask. For now, she'd listen.

How was it that seven Sector Five residents, including Adan, had now crossed over into Sector Six? How did they do it? And some of them were Gifted. Had they tripped another alarm? Would the blame fall on her? Would she be tasked with exterminating them as well?

She'd waited for the boys to emerge from the restaurant after the helpful tip on Adan's whereabouts and had spotted Ben doing the same. Perhaps she should've alerted Sam, but she hadn't thought of it. So she'd spent the last few hours following the follower.

Now, she'd learn all she could and move on. She didn't need humans slowing her down.

The boys lumbered into camp with all the stealth of stampeding elephants.

"I told you." Ben was saying through a mouth full of bread. "I slept outside your campsite last night. Then I followed Sam all day."

Chase sank onto his sleeping bag, brushing at the fabric. He frowned at a rumpled and dirty corner. His gaze darted to the trees, and he scanned the darkness. Evie melted further into the shadows.

"Yeah, but how'd you know how to work the portal?" Sam passed Ben a canteen.

Portal? Evie nearly gasped.

"Easy." Ben gulped a swallow. "I rode my bike to the parking garage and watched Uzziah teach you how to draw the symbol."

"You're crazy." Elias cuffed him. "What if you never found us?"

Ducking away, Ben yawned. "It wasn't hard. I could hear you right when I got here. Asher and Chase never stop arguing."

Sam gave the culprits a look. Chase threw his hands up. Asher scowled.

Hope welled inside Evie. Was there an intersector portal here in Six? Did the Maker miss one when he set out to destroy them?

Or had it been restored?

This meant one also hid in Sector Five.

But that wasn't her concern. *There's a portal, and these boys know where it is.* Adan must've happened upon it and fallen through. Then Uzziah sent the others after him. If she could help these boys find Adan, then get them all back to the portal and back home… Easy. The Sector Six employees had assigned her another task, but given the circumstances, wouldn't they want her to change her plan? There hadn't been a way to take Adan back. But, now, she'd found one.

She glanced at her watch but couldn't see it in the darkness. Since her arrival, she'd watched it, noting the time evaporating away—ticking down like the numbered days of a mortal. More than a day had passed since her three-week countdown began. Twenty days left.

"Ben, did you bring anything with you?" Elias nudged the boy. "Food? Water? A sleeping bag?"

"I didn't think about it."

"So, you haven't eaten anything all day?" Sam widened his stance and crossed his arms.

"I had a granola bar."

His brow rose. "Where did you get it?"

Ben peeked around Sam to where Garran was lying on his bedroll away from the group. "I borrowed it from Garran's bag while he took a nap," he whispered.

"Garran was sleeping while we searched for your brother?"

At Ben's nod, Sam scowled in Garran's direction but didn't confront the boy again.

The boys questioned Ben until the poor kid's sleepy lids drooped low over sapphire eyes. Sam and Chase arranged for Ben to lay between them, and before long, Ben was fast asleep.

Soon, Asher, Elias, and Garran settled into sleep as well. Chase's eyes, however, searched the trees.

"What is it, Chase?" Sam asked in a low voice.

"An uneasy feeling—like someone's watching." The two of them continued to cast watchful eyes over the area. "Should we take Ben back through the portal tomorrow?"

"Definitely. It's not safe, and Uzziah's probably freaking out."

"I could take him in the morning while you guys sleep. It's not that far."

Sam shook his head. "No way. We're staying together."

Chase shifted in his bedroll. "Do you think Ben was telling the truth?"

"Yeah, I mean, he was right. The portal was there in the garage."

"No, I mean about the other part." He gestured to Garran.

Sam followed his gaze.

From Evie's vantage point, Garran resembled an enormous, slow-breathing blob.

When Sam didn't answer, Chase tried again. "Do you think Garran went back to the basement? Is Adan missing because of something he did?"

Evie sat straighter. *What?*

"I don't know," Sam said. "I don't want to think so, but you should've seen him. He was so mad. I've never seen him like that. He pulverized Adan's face until we talked him down."

Well, that explained Adan's bruises.

"Well..." Chase drug the word out, rubbed at his eyes, and huffed. "Whether Garran was involved or not, Uzziah believes Adan came through the portal, and he didn't do that on his own. It begs the question, who helped him… or took him?"

Indeed.

"I don't know." Sam propped himself up on an elbow facing Chase. Firelight glowed in green eyes, odd in his face. "But judging from Uzziah's reaction, it can't be good. Whoever it was, they took Adan through a portal that's not supposed to exist. Ben didn't get a good look at whoever was driving the black car."

"What else did Ben say?"

"He heard Adan yell from the trunk of a car, and so he followed on his bike. At the time, I wasn't so sure. I mean, he's just a kid, and he was scared for his brother. But I let him take me to the garage. He'd heard a clanging noise and followed it. When he got to the bottom floor, a bright light came from the storage area. The gate was locked, so he came to get me. You know the rest. I got there, and it looked normal. The police didn't find anything. But when Uzziah saw the portal, everything changed. That's when he gave me my marks and told me we had to go get him."

"Why didn't Uzziah come?"

"Guardians are banned from Sector Six. But I got the feeling he didn't want to alert anyone that we were crossing over and thought we could travel unnoticed without him. It was all really weird."

The boys quieted, but Evie's heart pounded in her ears. Garran had beaten Adan and locked him in a basement. Something hot and foreign boiled in her veins, and she clenched her teeth and closed her eyes, fighting the urge to jump down and teach him a lesson with her golden dagger.

Not because she had a soft spot for the Dreamer, of course. That would be ridiculous. But because the Strength Wielder had started all of this trouble. Garran was to blame for her predicament.

Evie breathed slow and steady, willing herself to think. Was it a coincidence this had all happened on the day Uzziah marked Adan among the Gifted? And who would she have to deal with when she arrived to take back what belonged in Sector Five? Too many unanswered questions.

Chase's soft voice rose again. "What happens if we don't find him?"

Sam stared into the distance. "I don't know."

Evie knew. These boys would go home. They'd return to Uzziah, their families, and their lives. But not Evie. She'd stay here, alone, to age over the next decades until this mortal body quit. All her dreams would fade as she did. There'd be no promotion to Guardian. She wouldn't regain her immortality or receive a Guardian Gift.

She let out a silent breath. *Will I ever find the Dreamer?*

The Dreamer… Her mind flitted back to the street party only a few nights ago when she caught Adan watching her. *He* had been watching *her*. The corner of her mouth tilted up—such a strange jump in emotions.

She settled against the tree and tried to shove all thoughts of blue eyes, dark hair, and a single dimple from her mind.

As the moon slid behind the clouds, the hint of a smile curved her lips. She whispered, commanding herself to remember, "You are *not* a human."

19

"Try again. You can do this."

For the last half hour, Adan had been attempting to wield a weapon similar to a crossbow. Aware of every eye on him, he braced the weapon and loosed an arrow. It fell nowhere near the mark.

James scratched his head. "Unbelievable. I've never seen anyone do this poorly."

That helped. Adan scowled.

Grace sauntered over from where she'd been freezing water and hurling it as a weapon at her targets. "The mystery continues." Her eyes narrowed. "He can't even use the most common weapon. Most kids master it by the time they're five."

A whistle blew.

"Next station." The sharp-nosed man also served as the weapons trainer. He looked bored unless he had the pleasure of leering at Adan's inadequacies.

"Come on." James led Adan to the next station.

Adan's nostrils flared as he tossed the bow onto its rack.

After yesterday's testing, he'd learned that, today, under close supervision, all the "special guests" would attend weapons training. James said most people in Inevah knew how to fight on some level and they were all more valuable to the captain if they were skilled combatants.

Thomas the Strength Wielder was back, as well as the five accomplices caught in the escape attempt. They all sported new bruises but seemed otherwise okay. Only the Water Mover who tried to slip through the door was still absent. In all, twenty special guests gathered in the courtyard. Even Hattie was present.

Adan exhaled when James handed him two curved blades. One for each hand. About six inches long, they bent into a broad arc. Despite the weapons' unfamiliar half-moon shape, he felt more confident. He'd been training in knife throwing and fighting since age thirteen. He'd even placed in a few competitions for Guardian-trained athletes.

More blades gleamed on a rack against one of the stone walls.

James picked up a pair. "These are my favorite."

Adan stepped back, bending his knees, and took a few slow swings. "I can't believe they let us handle knives."

"Well, not really. Take a closer look."

Adan touched a finger to its dull edge and smooth, rounded tip.

Though everyone had moved on to their stations, those nearest Adan continued to cast glances his way. He weighed the blades in his palm and performed a few practice moves, eager to prove he wasn't a complete waste.

Then he faced James. "What do we do?"

"We spar." The Healer arched a brow, then lunged.

Caught off guard, Adan took the dull point of James's blade in his side. Though it wasn't sharp, pain still throbbed. He scoffed at the Healer, who wore a wide, annoying smile.

Adan bent as if hunched in pain and then sprang toward James.

James's eyes widened before he slid to the side, avoiding the blade. His smile broadened. Adan couldn't help but return it. And they sparred, exchanging swing for swing while their feet shuffled up a puff of dust. Others around the courtyard paused to watch. The two of them were evenly matched, and other than James's first swing, neither gained the upper hand. So Adan wasn't the worst at something.

"Not bad, Blue," James said as he and Adan stepped away from each other—both grinning.

"Yes, not horrible." Even the weapons trainer had stopped to watch. "Though, you'd likely be bleeding out from self-inflicted wounds, were you using real blades." The sharp-nosed man jerked his chin toward their legs. "You would've cut your thighs a number of times already with your blade edge. Let me show you." The weapons instructor launched into a demonstration, letting them follow along trying the techniques.

After this, the group completed two more stations where Adan made a fool of himself at the long sword and then again at the wooden staff.

Dejected, he followed the others into the castle. As they made their way down yet another hallway under the watchful eyes of Captain Curtshaw's Strength Wielders, Adan tried to make note of every turn.

The women veered into a separate doorway, and the female guards followed. The men entered another opening across the hall.

Adan slowed. A bath the size of a swimming pool dipped into the ground. Steam rose from it, creating swirls that slid along the ceiling.

James gripped Adan's arm, pulling him the other way. "Looks nice, doesn't it? Too bad. We don't get to use it. We get the bucket."

He indicated a basin. No steam rose from this water.

The others, including Thomas, whose bruises spread over his entire body, had already stripped off their clothes and dipped sponges into the water. They worked quickly, shivering. While James dumped his shoes and clothes to the floor, Adan hesitated.

"No privacy here. You'll get used to it." James walked to the basin.

Adan glanced around. That wasn't what bothered him. Had the captain decided not to keep his marks a secret?

Telling himself he didn't care, Adan faced away from the others and stripped off his shirt. As he undressed, the room quieted. Muttered whispering echoed through the stone chamber. When he walked to the basin, everyone gawked.

James tested the water and shivered. "You said you weren't marked."

"No, I didn't." Adan picked up a sponge someone had discarded onto the floor and dunked it into the cold water. "I said I wasn't strength marked."

James frowned but didn't comment.

Adan gasped when he ran the sponge over his torso. Even during the hardest times in his life, he'd had hot water for bathing. This was an unexpected kind of agony. He could sense the others sneaking glances at his mark. This felt familiar—Adan, the oddity.

"I bet he drew those marks on himself." Boulder, the brute who'd held Adan's face in the water bucket, stood a few paces away with two other guards. They chuckled. "Is that why you're here? Those marks?" He laughed with the rest. "They'll find out soon enough that you're useless."

Adan didn't have a retort. The marks probably *were* why he found himself here. He didn't want to admit they gave him crazy dreams. Oddity indeed.

James tilted his head to the side and wrinkled his nose. Blue eyes, cluelessness toward everyday things, and now the strange marks. What did he make of it?

The guards taunted Adan long after he'd dressed, and they made their way to the dining room. During the meal, Adan sat with the same group, and despite his protests, James filled the ladies in on Adan's strange marks.

Wishing to change the subject, Adan observed the different groupings around the dining hall. "Why do they separate based on eye color?" he asked his companions.

The group who caused trouble yesterday was bruised and downcast. Though their skin tones ranged, every member of that group had the same bright, yellowish eyes as James. Another group consisted of those with light-brown eyes like Hattie and Grace, and the third group had deep-black eyes like Thomas.

With his tinted contacts, Adan would probably fit best with the brown-eyed group.

"Seriously, where do you come from?" Grace asked.

Hattie answered Adan's question. "They don't trust each other. It's been that way for as long as I can remember."

Huh. What was so different about each of them? They all looked the same amount of strange. Likely, the only difference between one to the next was simple biology. "Your group is the only diverse group here."

Hattie laughed. "It hasn't been an easy road. That's for sure. But we are those who've been trapped here the longest. Everyone else has come and gone, and yet we remain. All we have is each other." She gestured around the group, and they nodded their agreement.

Adan might never fully understand their culture, but *that* he could grasp. Being trapped together with these people already made him feel a bond different from any he'd had before.

He shifted, unsure of his place. "So why am I sitting here? I've only been here a day."

Laughter still shone in Hattie's light-brown eyes. "Perhaps because you sat down or because James was assigned to you or maybe something else entirely."

20

As the sun reached its peak, Evie pulled a strip of dried beef from her pack. She continued to the gates of Inevah but found, however, her stomach had soured along with her mood since the foul morning.

Foot traffic had increased over the last hour, and she tailed the dispirited Sector Five boys.

Earlier, they had returned to Soli intending to send Ben home through the portal. They'd led her to a lovely garden. But, from her hiding place in the trees, her heart had raced as Sam sank to his knees and gathered a handful of wilting yellow blooms. She listened as the boys yelled and searched. The portal was gone. All that remained were the cut-away flowers and a perfect empty circle in the sand. Sometime during the night, the portal had vanished—or been moved.

Fear rolled through the boys like a tide. And her hopes plummeted as her new plan, one allowing Adan to live, vanished as well.

Sam and his companions took a long time to pull themselves together. Evie didn't mind. She needed a moment herself. She'd cast aside her assassin's mindset and was loathe to put it back on.

Sometime later, they turned back toward Inevah and made progress down the dusty road. As they traveled, she tried not to think about these trapped boys who had no way of returning home. They were not her problem.

She reached into her pocket and gripped Joram's note. *Do what you have to do…*

Reminding herself of what she wanted—not what she had to do—was the best way forward. She wanted her immortality, the Guardianship, and home. And she'd do anything to get those things back.

Unlike the boys who shuffled ahead of her, she still had a way home. A portal, a dot high in the mountains, would take her back to the Control Room. She *would* kill Adan and go home. Nineteen days remained.

She held her head high as she wound through the crowd of humans.

Leather belts and dark jackets hugged many bodies, and a few more extravagant outfits sported brighter colors, shiny embellishments, or even voluminous petticoats. At least half carried weapons strapped to their bodies with overcomplicated holsters. Sam fit right in. His holster held many knives and wrapped in an intricate pattern around one thigh, like a western cowboy warrior. She managed a grin as he adjusted them for the hundredth time.

Her golden weapon remained hidden in her jacket. No other she saw matched its craftsmanship.

The strange city sprawled in every direction, and she slowed. How would she find Adan? Where should she start?

The boys passed through the soaring city gates where soldiers stood guard. They took no weapons nor questioned anyone. She strolled through and loosed a breath once inside.

Since the boys were here, she'd stay close for now, not hunt out Adan on her own. Not that she worried after them, of course. She wasn't their protector.

The dirt path faded into smooth stone, and the street narrowed, closed in by shops and homes. Front doors stood wide, and laundry flapped from strings connecting second-story windows.

They arrived at a city center where pedestrians meandered around a circular fountain. Inevah castle rose in the distance, its towers reaching for the sky.

The boys came together, looking over a map the talkative one acquired from a vendor. She bought her own map and a loaf of bread and rested on the lip of the fountain.

An argument erupted among the Sector Five boys, and Ben, apparently bored, meandered away to peruse the market. An oversized hoodie hung from his shoulders, and the hood, as Sam had instructed, remained low over his blue eyes.

Sam had also told Ben to stay close.

The boy moved around the open space, eyeing each vendor's offerings. The attendants watched him, likely marking him as a thief. As he moved farther away, she checked over her shoulder and rolled her eyes. The older boys' heads were still bent over the yellowed parchment. She'd have to watch Ben herself. Just this once. She huffed, settling onto the fountain halfway between Ben and the others.

The tinkling of glass snagged her attention. Ben, hand outstretched, stood before shards of sparkling glass.

"I hope you've money to pay for that," came a gruff voice.

Ben stiffened.

Uh-oh. Evie squinted back at the other boys, willing them to glance this way. They did not. Whirling back, she watched Ben try to slip away. The man, who had a scruffy pointed beard, grabbed Ben's shoulder from behind. Two other young men stepped up as Ben tried to push the man's hands away. But his grip was firm, and, with his other hand, he ripped the hood back from Ben's head.

"Did you hear what I said? You'll p—" The man froze, looking into Ben's wide eyes.

"Oh, now you've done it," Evie hissed to herself. She whirled in the neglectful boys' direction and shouted, "Sam!"

Sam jerked his head up and met her eyes. She spun to Ben, planning to intervene, but the boy twisted out of the ridiculous hoodie and sprinted down a nearby alleyway. The three men charged after him. She didn't look back as her boots pounded the cobblestones.

<h1 style="text-align:center">21</h1>

Sam glanced up from haphazardly inked streets on brittle parchment to find a familiar face. Bright golden eyes blazed from pale skin before the girl strode in the opposite direction. Her light reddish ponytail swished behind her.

The girl from the tavern?

Movement caught his eye. Ben. A man, a stranger, gripped his shoulder.

Sam stepped forward, startling the others. "Ben?"

Ben, too far away to hear, pulled free and ran. He hurtled in the opposite direction, disappearing between two buildings. The man and two others rushed after him, and the girl followed at a sprint.

"Ben!" Sam shouted again as he raced after them. By the time he reached where Ben had disappeared, the boy and his pursuers were no longer in the alley. Sam dashed through it and stumbled onto another, busier street. It narrowed and curved at each end, hiding its length from view. Doors stood open along the sidewalk, and side streets veered off.

"Ben," he shouted again, halting in the roadway. He turned in a wild circle, searching for a crop of dark hair. His comrades rushed to a stop around him.

"What happened?"

"Where's Ben?"

"What'd you see?"

Sam's body buzzed. "Ben was running. He came this way, but I lost him." He put his hands on his head. "Someone was chasing him."

"What? Who?" Chase panted, peering around at the pedestrians.

The others did the same.

"I don't know." Sam grabbed at his hair. "Let's split up. Meet back here in an hour." He pointed at a sign to their right. "Diamond Bakery. Asher, you're with me."

He sprinted away, not waiting to see if they followed his instructions. He ran to the left down the busy street, almost crashing into a man on a rusty scooter. What might Ben see as he ran through this area? Where would he go? The entrance to another side street offered a logical path.

"Anything?" he called to Asher, a step behind.

"No."

Flaming, useless Gift. Sam entered the narrow space at a run. Asher's feet pounded behind him. "Ben!" he yelled.

They wound through what felt like a maze until they spilled out into an intersection of three streets. Sam spun, looking down each one. A biker sped past. Pedestrians watched him with curious eyes. He put his hands in his hair again. *Where did he go? Think.*

He spun toward Asher, who paused beside him. The boy stood serene, eyes closed. *Come on, Asher.*

Just as Sam was beginning to lose hope, a faint glow reflected on Asher's jacket collar. Yes! Asher's utterly unreliable Gift was mobilizing.

The boy's eyelids popped open. "This way." He formed the shortest sentence Sam had heard him say in years.

Asher sped down the street and then hooked a left. No hesitation slowed his movements. They rounded a corner and came to a metal gate spanning the alley's width. The bars were thick, and a brick wall rose into the sky above it.

Sam shook the bars. "Ben!" he yelled again.

Asher's brow furrowed, his marks no longer glowing.

Beyond the gate, boxes and crates stacked in neat rows before the other end of this alley curved out of sight. Sam growled and shook the bars again but only managed the faintest glow from his marks.

But… Yes! Ben barreled around the corner.

"Ben!" Sam craned to see around the boxes.

The boy, not yet hearing their call, ran toward them into a mirror of their dead-end path. The bars would trap him like them.

Sam called out again.

Spurred on by the sound, Ben hurtled around the boxes and slammed into the gate.

"Ben, are you okay?" Sam practically yelled through the bars. They faced each other, both holding onto the unyielding metal.

"Sam, I didn't mean to. I didn't mean to break the glass. Can you tell them I'm sorry? Even after I climbed the fence back there, they kept coming."

The three men emerged around the corner and slowed. They crept forward, smug. Ben was trapped, and they knew it.

"Is that a door?" Asher whispered, pointing to the wall behind a stack of boxes.

"Try it, Ben," Sam said.

Ben pushed the stack, leaving enough space to see a narrow door in the redbrick wall. He put his shoulder to it. "It won't open. There's not even a handle."

"Ben, I can't get through, and they're coming. Hide, and I'll talk to them."

Ben scrambled out of sight.

"We know you're in there," rasped a breathless voice. A pile of crates hid the man, but when his lined face appeared, eyes as black as the night sky went wide at the sight of Sam and Asher at the gate.

"Mind your own business, Inevite. You're on the wrong side of the river."

Weren't these men Inevites? This was Inevah, after all.

"Hey, there's been a misunderstanding. The boy's with me. If he broke something, I'll pay for it."

The man stepped around a stack of crates and took in the bars holding Sam back. He relaxed and scanned the space. "Such strange eyes," he said. "My employer collects those with strange markings. The boy might fetch a nice price."

The other men crept around the boxes, spreading out.

So this wasn't just about broken glass. Sam's stomach turned.

"He's with me, and I'll be walking away from here with him." At least, he sounded more confident than he felt.

"Oh? And what are you going to do about it?" The man chuckled as he poked around, sliding nearer to Ben's hiding place.

"Look, I can pay you. Just leave him alone."

A scrape issued from Ben's corner, and the man swung his head toward it.

"Ben, run!" Sam bellowed.

Ben slid between the boxes and hurtled down the alley retracing his steps.

"He's coming," the man warned.

The other two men approached, and one grabbed Ben from behind, pinning his arms in a bear hug. Ben kicked, but the man was too strong. The other seized his legs, and the man at the gate grinned at Sam. Then the man joined his comrades walking the other way.

"Ben!" Sam and Asher yelled. Sam shook the gate, and his mark began to glow. He gripped two bars, threw his head back, and roared. The metal groaned under his force, but it didn't give. Sweat trickled down his forehead, and the glow began to fade.

A slender form dropped to the ground in front of him on the other side of the gate. He gaped at the newcomer. When she turned, a charge zinged through him. The bright eyes of the girl from the inn—the light-haired girl who'd shouted his name from across the square. She'd shed her jacket and now held a wicked dagger that gleamed even in the shadows.

"Go back that way and turn left, then take the first left after that." She gestured behind him. "Meet me at the other end. Follow the sound." Without waiting for a response, she wove through the boxes.

He and Asher shared a look. "Stay here and watch for Ben," Sam said. "If I don't come back, go back to the bakery."

Sam charged out of the alley. He almost sprinted past the next left but caught himself and doubled back. High walls blocked the afternoon sun, casting these pathways into deep shadow. As he ran around crates, shouting came from ahead. *Follow the sound.* He skidded around a curved wall as the golden dagger flashed with skilled use.

The three men had produced weapons, and Ben huddled against the wall. Sam reached to climb over a low gate when the girl screamed and fell against the bars. Her back pressed against the metal, and a faint glow peeked through her thin white shirt from a circle below her neck. The light faded, and the girl was once again a whirlwind of movement. She carved her way through her opponent, taking him down with a blow to the temple. One of the men pulled a short knife and rounded on Ben. The girl threw her blade at the attacker. It sliced into his shoulder, and he screamed out. She ran to him and yanked her dagger free, flipping it to knock him out with the hilt. He slumped as Sam hauled himself over the fence. The remaining man, the one with the pointed beard, skidded to a stop, outnumbered and trapped.

A predator made prey.

"Get out of here." The girl stepped to the side and threw her chin toward the gate. Sam did the same, and the man hurried between them, scaled the fence, and disappeared around the corner.

Sam met the girl's eyes. They stood, taking each other in until Ben cried out.

Sam rushed to him and gripped him in a bone-crushing hug. Tears ran down Ben's cheeks, and Sam knelt to wipe them away.

The girl stood over one of the unconscious men, her eyes wide.

"Are you okay?" Sam joined her. The sight was foreign and wrong. As if he were watching some action movie back in Sector Five.

She gaped at his bleeding shoulder. "I've never done that before."

Wasted worlds. He assumed anyone that skilled at sparring had some practice—at least in this crazy sector.

"Who are—" he started to ask, but she'd already retrieved her blade and was walking away. "Hey, where are you going? It's a dead end." He jogged to catch up, motioning for Ben to follow.

"I dropped my things into the alley before I jumped." She was all business now, but her hands were shaking.

"What's your name?" He took Ben's hand. The boy was shaking too.

Didn't seem she was going to answer.

"I'm Evaniah."

They reached the alley's cluttered end, and she strode within the boxes and out of sight.

Sam paused to tie Ben's shoelaces. "Asher?" No answer. Rustling gradually grew frantic from where she'd disappeared.

"It's gone!" she shouted. When he moved closer, she strode out knuckles white. "It was right…"

Her words faded into the shadows. Her golden eyes widened as she stared behind Sam.

He whirled. At least fifteen people had crept into the alley. They wore cloths over their faces where strangely colored eyes peeked out. More figures watched from high windows, and another three emerged from the door with no doorknob.

Evaniah backed away and joined him.

"Drop the weapon, Huldan," one of the men said.

She stiffened, then released the dagger as if realizing they addressed her. It clanged to the ground.

"What do we have here? Trespassers?" A tall man, presumably the leader, strode forward.

"Morris, look at this," one of the bandits said from behind Evaniah. "What happened to the gate?" He ran a hand along the bent bars. They bowed outward, not far enough for a person to pass through but enough to draw attention.

Evaniah met Sam's gaze, holding his stare.

"Look at his mark," she whispered so only Sam could hear. An inked falcon peeked from below the leader's pushed-up sleeve.

The man with the falcon-inked arm.

Rebels.

22

Evie shifted, and her thigh brushed something—or someone—resting next to her on the hard bench.

Sam?

"Can I take this off now?" she asked no one in particular as she tilted her head, trying to see through the thin slice of light below the cloth tied over her eyes.

"Fine," a gruff voice rumbled.

Footsteps drew near, and the blindfold lifted over her ponytail. She squinted into the sunlit hall. Seconds later, Sam did the same and inched away from her.

A muscled man returned to his perch across from them. His thick, dark fingers clutched a sheathed long blade.

Sam eyed her. No doubt, he'd been replaying the last hours in his head and came up short on answers about her and how she came to be sitting next to him.

Muffled sounds echoed under a door where the falcon-marked man talked with Ben. The three of them—Sam, Evie, and Ben—had been taken on a winding journey before arriving here. Though blindfolded, she'd the sense they traveled through the more obscure and shadowed city passageways.

Sam had whispered to Ben not to tell the strangers where they were from. Was Ben taking Sam's advice?

A door creaked. "Yeah, so Sector Five is way different from this. And the food here is gross. I hope we find Adan soon so we can go home."

"You've got a crazy story, kid." The man laughed as he followed Ben into the hall.

Now that she could see him properly, Evie studied the rebel leader in his dirty work boots, dark pants, and black leather jacket. A scruffy beard covered the brown skin of his face. He scratched his jaw.

Ben sighed and flopped into a chair next to their guard who grunted and pointed his blade in the other direction. "Do you think those men are dead? I've never seen a dead person before."

They weren't dead, but it could have gone that way. What if she'd killed one of them? What would Krystopher say? And would those men be in the Waiting Place now? All by her hand.

"No, they're not dead," Morris answered.

Ben brightened. "Don't be mad at Sam and that girl. They were trying to save me."

"You don't know her?"

"No," Ben said.

"Well, I'm going to have a chat with each of them. Ladies first." The man gestured to the open door, and she followed him into a cluttered office. All manner of trinkets and volumes cluttered the bookcases on one wall. Books stood in uneven piles around the room, and maps were strewn over the desk. The man eased into a wooden chair and gestured to a similar one across from him.

Evie sat.

A light flickered overhead, and her gaze followed a cord winding away from the simple bulb and out the open window. From there, it attached to a solar panel.

The man leaned forward, resting his arms on the table. The light gleamed in kind black eyes—a stark contrast to his rough appearance. She'd thought him older, but now, she guessed he'd walked the sector no more than three decades. Muscles twitched under the falcon covering his golden forearm.

He noticed where her eyes had landed and frowned. "You've heard of me."

"Yes."

"What's your name?"

"I'm Evaniah." She might as well stick with her given name since she'd gone by Evie in Sector Five with Ben. She doubted the kid would recognize her either way, what with her lighter hair and freckles.

"And what's a Huldan doing roaming the streets of Inevah with two people, one a blue-eyed child and the other an Inevite, who she doesn't even know?" When she didn't answer, he went on. "But more importantly, why were you trespassing?"

"I didn't mean to trespass. I was trying to help the boy." It wouldn't do for her to say she and Sam were searching for the same person. How would she explain it?

"I'm in Inevah because I'm searching for someone." She lifted her chin toward the door. "I think these boys are looking for someone as well. In Soli, we overheard a conversation about two men who captured a boy and brought him this way."

"Unfortunately, that's become a common occurrence."

Evie rested her forearms on the desk to mirror him. "We also heard about a falcon-marked man who's been causing trouble for the captors. Perhaps that man might've heard something about these kidnappings."

He unrolled his shirtsleeve so it covered the strange mark. His gaze never left her.

"Look… what was your name again?"

"I didn't say." He sighed. "It's Morris."

"Look, Morris, I was hoping you might have heard something. Anything. The people who took the boy knew to avoid you."

His eyebrows rose. "You heard of me in Soli?"

Evie didn't deny it as she picked at a thread hanging from the arm of her chair.

"That's not comforting."

"If it makes you feel better, others said they thought the rebels were a myth."

Morris shifted, sitting back with a creak. "How do I know you're not a spy?"

"I'm no spy. I don't care about you or what your rebels do here. I only want to find the person I'm looking for and go home."

"How did you find me so easily?"

"Find you? You stopped us, not the other way around. I was helping the boy, and you happened to be there." She drew her eyebrows together. "With a dozen men," she whispered to herself. "We ran right into your backyard, didn't we?"

He frowned. "How did you know where to find us?"

"We didn't. If you want to know how we found our way, you'll have to ask Ben. He's the one who picked the path." At his silence, she plunged on. "How do you know when they're going to move a prisoner? Where's the best place to ambush them?"

"So many questions. I don't trust you, Evaniah. My trust is earned. Only then will I consider helping you."

Trust? Evie crossed her arms and forced a laugh. "I don't need your help. Just tell me where, and I'll go alone."

He pursed his lips. "I've never seen a Huldan fight like that." He shuffled the maps on his desk, gaze still not leaving hers. "Just so you know, I don't have information about anyone transported in the last day. And I'm not telling you anything about the prisoner transports or how I find out about them. Not only because I don't trust you but also because attacking a caravan alone is suicide—ridiculous and arrogant. You'll end up hurt or killed." He rubbed between his eyes. "Will your *friend* Sam be asking for the same?"

Evie shrugged, balling her fists. "How should I know? The first time I saw him was yesterday in Soli."

She cocked her head and watched Morris. "Strange, isn't it? Have you ever seen anyone with blue eyes before?"

He relaxed and tilted his head to the side. "No, I haven't. It is curious. Some of my older texts mention blue eyes." He gestured toward his books on the floor. "But that's a different subject altogether."

She opened her mouth to demand he tell her when her attention caught on a book atop a disorderly stack. Stifling a gasp, she slid from the chair and knelt before it.

"What are you doing?" Morris lurched to his feet.

She picked up the dingy volume and ran a finger over a title that may have once been embossed with shiny gold. *One's Raining Fire,*" she breathed.

The door creaked behind her. "Hey, Morris," a female voice spoke as the door clicked shut. "Did you see this kid's eyes? And why's Charles glaring at an Inevite like he wants to flay him?"

Evie stood, startling a beautiful girl whose green eyes widened.

"It's you." The girl laughed. "I hope you didn't come to get your game back. I already gave it to my cousin." Her gaze flicked to a shelf behind Morris. Evie's lost board game, Guardian Quest, perched on a low shelf.

The suspicion on the rebel leader's face didn't ease. "You two know each other?"

"This is the girl we met on the road. Remember me?"

Evie wouldn't have recognized her if she'd passed her on the street, but given the mention of the game, it must be her green-eyed rescuer. "Lena, right?"

"That's right. How'd you end up *here*?" Lena pulled her long, dark hair into a messy bun. Her loose cream-colored tunic accentuated warm golden skin a shade lighter than her cousin's. Aside from the green eyes, the girl would pass as a Sector Five citizen.

"It's a long story."

"They always are." She slipped past Evie, grabbed the golden box, and started from the room. "Come on. You can tell me while you show me how to play this."

Unsure, Evie followed.

"I thought Morris would know how to play Guardian Quest, but—"

"Estalena," Morris cut in. "Can I have a word?"

"Wait here." Lena rolled her eyes and stacked the game atop the book in Evie's hands. "I must be in trouble if he's using my full name." The girl shut the door, leaving Evie to stare at the wooden planks.

Sam, still sitting on the bench, cleared his throat. "How was it?"

"Okay. He wanted to know why we were trespassing."

"Are you free to go?"

Evie glanced at the armed man across the hall. "I don't know. I'm being kidnapped by the girl to teach her how to play Guardian Quest. Only I'm not sure how to play."

Ben stood. "Oh, we know how. I could teach you."

Evie smiled at the eager boy as Lena emerged from the office and Morris called for Sam.

"I'll watch Ben for you," Evie offered.

Sam nodded, wary, and closed the door.

Evie turned to Lena. "What did he say?"

"Oh, he doesn't trust you." She smoothed stray hair behind her ears. "He thinks you're trouble. But when I told him about meeting you on the road, I was able to talk him into letting you stick around in case we hear about your friend."

Stick around and conspire with humans? This was not how she saw her search playing out. She'd agreed to go along with humans once before in Sector Five and look where that had gotten her.

But since her mental list of leads was hovering around zero, perhaps this was her best option. Not because she needed help, but because she might be able to glean useful information before heading out.

"Do you have a place to stay?" Lena asked.

Evie shook her head.

"Morris will help you out. I'll talk him into it. Come on. We'll wait over here while you explain the rules of Guardian Quest. You, too, Blue Eyes." She held her hand out to Ben, who jumped up and took it with an eager smile.

Lena led them into an adjacent room where late afternoon sun streamed in a window. Ben was already chatting as Lena goaded him. Just like that, a bond was formed. Was it always this easy for humans?

An unpleasant feeling crept into Evie's chest—in that hole, she'd discovered back in Sector Five. Something like longing, bitterness, and sadness. She hugged her arms around herself and pinched the inside of her elbow. This human body that coated her... She was acting like one of them, letting weakness seep in. *Snap out of it.*

She shoved the feeling away.

23

"This way." Evie scooted into line as Morris grumbled and shouldered a heavy metal door. Tromping ahead of her, Sam, Ben, and Lena followed the rebel leader through a dark and cluttered building and up a steep staircase.

Light spilled in the upper-level windows. From the outside, Evie might've thought the place abandoned. Perhaps that was the point.

With a kitchen and a table at one end, mattresses rested against the other wall, some on bed frames, some not.

Morris crossed his arms. "This is one of my rooms in the city. You can stay here for a few nights. We'll see if news of your friends crosses the river." Addressing Sam, he said, "I sent my guard, Charles, to the bakery to fetch your companions."

Sam's worried brow softened a bit. "Thank you, Morris."

When Morris only scowled, Sam tried to fill the awkward silence. "So, how many places do you have in Inevah?"

"I don't know you nor trust you." Morris waved a hand. "Don't ask questions."

He rested that hand on his cousin's shoulder. "I'll be back later. Get them settled."

"Sure." She flashed the winning smile that had worn him down earlier. He rolled his eyes and stomped down the stairs. He'd have happily dumped them in an alleyway with nothing but a cheery Death Guardian glare, but Lena wanted to help them. Seemed the girl didn't have a lot of friends.

"Bathroom is downstairs." Lena swept an arm around the room. "Take any bed you like."

Ben ran for the only bunk. "Sam, I don't think that guy likes you."

"I don't think he likes either of us." Evie moved toward the mattress farthest from the others.

"He's not so bad." Lena kicked at a messy pile of old newspapers. "Morris has a lot of people to protect. He's not likely to tell strangers much of anything." She stooped to pick them up and tossed them toward the corner. "You have to admit you're a strange group. Inevites rarely cross the river. Huldans don't leave the mountain. And people never have blue eyes. Not to mention your strange accents."

Ben's legs dangled from the top bunk. "Everyone from Sector Five has blue eyes and talks like this. Well, a few people have gold eyes like Evaniah. Uzziah—"

"Ben." Sam jammed his hands on his hips. "What did I say?"

The boy frowned and plopped back on the bed with an exaggerated sigh.

"See what I mean?" Lena crossed her arms.

Evie bent to rummage in her bag. When she glanced up, Sam was frowning at her. He stared at her golden eyes.

No time to worry about what he thought of her. She needed information, and Lena seemed willing to talk. "I don't know much about Inevah. Can I ask a few questions?"

"Sure." The green-eyed girl plopped onto a mattress and leaned against the wall.

Evie sat, crossing her legs. "This is Inevah, yet you don't call yourself an Inevite. And you said they never cross the river. What's that about?"

"Inevites—the Green Eyes like Sam here—are the city's original inhabitants. Well, really, they're the Great Valley's original inhabitants. Native Sodorrans also have green eyes."

"But *you* have green eyes." Sam braced his back against the wall, tossing a baseball up and down.

"Yeah, but I wasn't raised with the Green Eyes. My mother wasn't a Green Eye." Lena picked at the corner of a pillow. "My father must've been, though. That's what Morris says. Most of us are refugees from Sodorrah. We call ourselves the Arvad. The non–Green Eyes. We stick together because the Inevites don't accept us."

"Why not?" Evie tapped her fingers on her leg.

"Many reasons. They believe the city is theirs, and I guess it is or was. Mostly, though, very few of the Green Eyes are Gifted. They fear us. Many more of the Arvad, those with other-color eyes, are born Gifted. Though many Arvad aren't born with a Gift, the Inevites assume we all have some scary power. Sodorrah passed a law in the Valley saying every person with a Gift must be marked. A pattern is inked here." She pointed to the inside of her wrist. "Of course, the Arvad try to hide their Gift to avoid the marking. The marked ones are the poor souls who disappear into caravans like the one you nearly ended up on, Evaniah."

Evie stopped tapping. "Why do people leave Sodorrah to come here?"

"Some are kicked out, some escape. Over time, we've formed a sort of family here on our side of the river. Communities have also started in Soli and other villages. And in the mountains, of course."

"Yeah, you mentioned that. So the Huldan look like me. Who are they?"

"They're a group of Yellow Eyes who moved to the mountains and into hiding. It's rumored the Yellow Eyes are the most likely to have Gifted offspring. They stick to their mountain hideaways to protect each other. Morris thinks they're cowards for not standing up for others and themselves."

Lena cocked her head. "I've never seen a Yellow Eyes quite like you. Most have eyes of a more brownish-yellow color. Some call the color hazel. But your eyes are so bright—more like gold."

Sam raised a brow at Evie.

"But who am I to judge someone based on eye color? I'm a Green Eyes living among the Arvad. Neither side of the river accepts me." Lena cleared her throat. Then she smiled, eyes a bit too bright. "Who's ready to teach me to play Guardian Quest?"

Ben, ready to do something other than talk, jumped down, and they spent the next half hour discussing rules and strategy. Evie relaxed and laughed along with the others.

"Don't play against Asher," Ben said. "He always wins. It's annoying."

"That's true," Sam said. "He's weirdly good at this game."

After a while, Lena's head snapped up. "Shhh. Listen."

They froze. A door closed downstairs. Then shuffling feet and low voices approached. Sam gripped the hilt of his blade, but when the voices rose into range, he relaxed.

"According to this, the Green Eyes were the only ones here for centuries. The other colors, the Gifted, aren't mentioned until more recent years. This scholar believes—"

"Asher, give it a rest."

Ben jumped to his feet. "Chase! Asher!"

Morris's man, Charles, entered, followed by four falsely green-eyed boys. They yelled out when they saw Ben, and Chase swallowed the smaller boy in a hug. Elias and Asher grinned and patted him on the back. Even Garran seemed relieved. Sam joined them, and Evie—Evie cringed over the hole in her chest.

It stretched and grew. She lowered herself against the wall next to Lena. How was it that, sitting in a room full of eight other humans, Evie had never felt more lonely? She rubbed the chill from her arms. She'd feel normal again when she returned to the Control Room.

Chase spotted Evie and Lena first. He jerked his head, swinging his floppy hair to the side. "Sam, introduce us to your friends."

"Guys, this is Evaniah and Lena."

Chase displayed a perfect, pearly white grin as Elias elbowed his way next to him. Sam continued the introductions, and they already assessed how pretty Lena was with her long dark hair and emerald eyes.

After a moment, they were looking at her in much the same way. Evie's cheeks grew hot.

Charles, acting as their guard, settled in a corner and tucked into a fresh newsprint he'd brought with him. The rest relaxed around Guardian Quest, and Sam impressed them with how Evie rescued Ben. Lena even asked Evie to share pointers on wielding a blade. Chase offered to help in a training session.

The other boys had dispersed to look for Ben but had regrouped at the bakery. Asher had arrived to tell them Sam and Ben had been captured by a group of masked men. They'd fought over what to do next until Charles arrived.

"It was like every murder mystery ever written." Chase slumped against the wall. "Don't trust the stranger who offers to lead you back to their lair." He glanced at Charles. "No offense."

The man didn't glance up from his pages.

Elias kicked off his red shoes. "Yeah, so we had another fight about whether to follow the stranger who claimed to know where you were. But Asher felt like we should follow, so we did."

Chase chuckled. "I knew we were walking to our death."

With the game forgotten, the group continued to chat. When the conversation turned to Adan, Ben's face fell. Lena put out a hand to him, and he joined the girls on the wall, sitting on Lena's other side.

"Hey, if anyone can find your brother, it's my cousin. He helps people all the time."

Ben tried to smile, but fat tears pooled in his eyes. One escaped and slid down his round cheek. Seeing this boy cry stirred something strange. Evie's chest tightened. It felt like the bottling of—something.

Ben leaned his head against Lena's shoulder, and the girl ran her fingers through his hair. She whispered to him and rubbed her knuckles over his cheek.

How does she know how to do that?

"Why don't you tell us about your brother?" Lena asked.

"He's the best." Ben stood and held his hand up. "He's pretty tall, like up to here. I only come to his chest." He stepped over Lena and plopped back down, this time squeezing between Evie and Lena. They both scooted, catching each other's eye.

Chase muttered to Elias, "Sure, if he does it, it's fine."

They scowled at the boy.

"What do you and Adan like to do together?" Lena nudged him with her shoulder.

"Well, we like to go to the park. We play catch with a baseball sometimes. Adan helps me with my homework."

Lena mouthed "Baseball?" over Ben's head.

Evie shrugged. "It's a game." This could be a fun way to find out more about the Dreamer. "Does Adan like to do homework?"

"Not really. But he does like to read."

This she knew. "Do you also like to read?"

"Yeah. But I like funny books, and Adan likes grown-up ones."

Lena ruffled his hair. "What do *you* like to do for fun?"

"I like lots of stuff. Video games, baseball, basketball, riding bikes."

She squished her eyebrows together, probably having never heard of these things.

Ben continued. "But I want to start training with the other guys. They won't let me, though. I'm *too young*." He said the last bit with the same disdain Lena had used when saying her cousin wouldn't let her fight.

Evie pulled her knees up, scraping her boots on the worn wood plank floor. "And what does Adan like to do for fun?"

"He likes to hang out with me!" Ben's head popped up along with the corner of his mouth. "But besides that, he likes to train in our gym. He used to be the worst at fighting. But now, he's one of the best."

"He must've trained hard."

"Yeah, he thought Uzziah would make us leave if he didn't do a good job. But he would've kept us."

Perhaps that was true, though that Uzziah recruited Ben and Adan proved strange. They were not the usual type. Guardians never took on a child who wasn't old enough to begin training.

Lena, hardly able to keep up with the strange conversation, grinned at Evie over Ben's head.

Ben sobered, and this time, he rested his head on Evie's shoulder. The others went on talking while she reached over and brushed her knuckles over Ben's cheek. His eyelids drooped. He ran a finger over the watch circling her wrist, so she pulled her sleeve over the too-advanced accessory. Ben dropped his hand and blinked, staring at the floor.

Sam scooped him up and deposited him on the top bunk. Sam stood on the bed frame as he whispered to his best friend's little brother.

Evie's thoughts turned back to that friend as she rearranged the pieces of Guardian Quest. *Where are you, Adan? Are you hurt?* As Ben said, Adan had skill as a fighter. He could hold his own.

She might not have an easy time sinking her blade into the boy when the time came. Not only because she didn't want to but also because Adan was a well-trained opponent.

What if *he* killed *her*?

Sam returned, still gripping his baseball. "Who's ready to play?"

Charles, the guard, ignored him, but everyone else perked up, even Garran, who stopped sulking long enough to join the circle.

"It's a six-person game, but there are seven of us." Sam crossed to Ben's bed and returned with the worn wooden Watcher Evie had seen Adan give Ben months ago. He set the game piece among the human figures. It stood out in dingy contrast. "We'll pretend this is one of the humans. Now, we each roll to see which order we'll choose." The dice moved around the circle. Evie rolled a two, giving her the lowest score. Each player chose a human figure, and those with the highest roll also got to select a Guardian or a Watcher, allowing them special advantages. When her turn to choose came around, the only figure left was Ben's Watcher, the makeshift human.

She picked it up, the unnerving coincidence not lost on her.

"The idea is to be the first to the end of the path. The more people you have in an alliance with you when you win, the more points you get. Look at the base of your human figure, but don't let anyone else see," Sam said. "If yours is the Deceiver, keep it secret. Your job is to lure the others into an alliance. If the Deceiver wins, everyone loses points, especially those aligned with him."

After everyone peeked at theirs, the game began.

Evie took a moment to catch the rhythm of the game, but she loved the strategy. They asked questions and made alliances and tried to ferret out the Deceiver. Everyone volleyed to ally with Evie, for they knew her figure was not the enemy.

And so the game moved forward, drawing them ever closer to the end.

Evie aligned with Asher and Sam. Elias accused Asher of cheating. Sam pointed out a nervous twitch near Garran's eye, after which, no one wanted to join with him until Lena felt sorry for him and aligned against Chase's recommendations.

"He wants you to feel sorry for him. If he's the Deceiver, that's part of his game. The Deceiver can only win if he reaches the end and has human alliances. But the humans with him lose twenty points, and everyone else in the game loses ten. The Deceiver wins even more points if he has Guardian or Watcher alliances. You have a Watcher."

Lena lifted a shoulder, and Garran, for once, looked grateful as they laughed and jostled for position on the board.

"Morris told me once this game is based on a book," Lena offered after her turn.

Asher perked up. "Really? What book?"

"I'm not sure. Morris's copy is ancient. It's something about fire. *Raining Fire,* maybe?" Her eyes brightened. "Oh, Evie, it's the one you borrowed today."

Evie reached into her pocket as Asher said, *"One's Raining Fire?"*

"Yeah, that's it." Lena leaned forward. "Have you read it?"

Evie drew the book from her pocket as the coincidence fueled her nerves: Evie the human Watcher playing the human Watcher, the game based on a book, Adan reading that book the day he was taken? And now she held a copy of the book in her hands. She tucked it back in her pocket. Hidden away, her fingers brushed at the pages.

Asher rolled the dice. "I've read it. I read it from start to finish the day I got it. I did some research and found a few people who think it's a prophecy that hasn't been fulfilled." He studied the game board. "I bet the board represents Sector One, and the players represent the humans and immortals who helped the Truth-Seeker trap the Deceiver." He moved his figures, one human and one Guardian, closer to the finish, pulling his alliance, Evie and Sam, with him. As he handed the dice to Elias, he said, "It's funny, I found the book using my Gift."

Blinking those big green eyes, Lena jerked her head up. "Gift? You're Gifted?"

"No," Sam cut in. "He means he has a knack for finding useless items in bookshops."

His Gift led him to the book? "Why'd you read it so fast?" Evie asked. "Was it that good?"

"It was good, but also"—he glanced at Sam—"I had a strong feeling Adan should have it, so I finished it to hand it over. It's what he's reading now. Or was. I wonder if he finished it before—well, you know."

The group quieted, letting the rolling dice speak for them.

"Oh, look. Here's the garden where Nolan made his escape." Asher pointed at the board near the end of the path. Yellow and red flowers lined the trail leading to the winning golden archway. "Nolan said the flowers were like a river of color. 'In a river of blood and gold, the Deceiver waited.'"

Evie hadn't read this yet. Unable to stop herself and hoping to get them talking, she said, "I've read part of it. The hero, Nolan, was a Dreamer."

Five dark heads whipped toward her.

Chase gave Asher a shove. "You never stop talking, and you forgot to mention *that* little tidbit?"

"I never thought it was important."

"What is it? What's a Dreamer?" Lena picked up the dice, but she didn't roll them, waiting.

No one answered.

Evie's fingers stilled over the book in her pocket. *Relax.* "Nolan was coveted for the Gift. He could see the future in his dreams. Many wanted to use him. The antagonist, the Deceiver, hid among the humans. He could control people with his words."

Lena snorted and shook the dice in her hand. "That sounds like the steward of Sodorrah."

"What do you mean?" Evie sat straighter.

"You've heard rumors, right? They say he can make most people do whatever he wants just by saying it." Lena tossed the dice onto the table. "One lady, not too long ago, even claimed he made her forget the name of her hometown. But no one can ever look into these things because no one remembers the steward's face. Or so they say." She slid her alliance into place, only four spaces from winning. "No one can find him if he doesn't want to be found."

She passed the dice to Garran, whose face had gone ashen. He tossed them onto the board. Were his hands shaking?

Evie gripped the book hidden away in her pocket. "So you're telling me the person who's gathering the marked to Sodorrah can control people using only words?"

"That's the rumor."

Garran bumped his and Lena's figures to the space just before the end.

Evie released the book and rubbed her forehead. She took up the dice with an uneasy feeling, but Elias put out a hand to stop her. "Wait. At this point, when the person whose turn it is has the opportunity to roll a winning hand, the Guardian in last place can choose a human— hopefully, the Deceiver—and use the blood weapon on them. If he accidentally chooses a human, that human is out of the game, but if he chooses the Deceiver, the Deceiver is sent here." He pointed to a space on the board marked Immortal Holding. A familiar golden pattern covered the area, but Evie couldn't quite remember where she'd seen it. "The Deceiver then loses two turns and all of his alliances if the other players are smart. And that last-place player, my friends, is Chase."

Chase sat forward, studying the board. "Ah, being last pays off. Elias, who do you think should get the ax?" The two boys bent their heads to talk it over, reaching a decision almost immediately. "Garran," Chase announced.

Garran scowled, and a collectively held breath released as he lifted his figure and proved he didn't hold the Deceiver. He removed his character from the board. Suspicious gazes glanced around the room, no one trusting anyone else.

"I think it's Chase," Sam announced. "He effectively stalled the game because now Lena has to move back five spaces. He has a chance to catch up if Evie doesn't roll a seven."

Chase scoffed as denial bubbled up.

"Of course, it could also be Elias." Lena gestured to him giving a bit of a bow. "And he knew Chase distrusted Garran and would waste the blood weapon on him."

Sam rolled his baseball between his palms. "You're right. I hadn't thought of that."

They were both right.

"Evie, it's your turn," Asher said. "Roll a seven, and we win."

Evie cupped the dice and shook them in her hand. No one spoke; no one moved. She flipped them out with a splay of fingers.

When they came to a stop, Asher stood with a whoop. "Yes! Seven. The winning streak continues."

Evie smiled and slapped Asher's outstretched hand, but her thoughts had drifted somewhere else. They'd snagged on another memory from the book. She bent over the archway inked onto the game board. Nolan, the fictional Dreamer, had been given plans to build a portal to escape his sector. Was it possible that the Deceiver, the real Deceiver, who had a talent for weaving lies into his victims' heads, had done something similar? The Control Room believed he was locked away somewhere in Sectors One, Two, or Three. But what if he wasn't? What if he'd found a way to escape to the one loosely monitored sector? What if the Deceiver was here?

Asher continued to gloat, but Sam didn't rejoice. He watched with a self-satisfied grin.

"Sam?" Elias raised his eyebrows. Elias was holding up his and Chase's figures so everyone could see their clear bases.

"Wait. What?" Asher asked. "No. No. No."

Sam tipped over his figure, and sure enough, the word *Deceiver* was stamped on the base. Evie had lost. She'd been utterly misled.

Sam laughed. "Looks like the Deceiver wins again."

Later, as Evie lay restless on her mattress, pondering what she hoped were unlikely possibilities, a soft click bounced up the stairs. Propped on an elbow, sketching flowers and bugs and other fascinating things, she whipped her head up at the sound.

Charles, still perched in his chair, had fallen asleep with his chin on his chest. Evie faced the door and feigned sleep, clutching the golden dagger under her blanket. A stair creaked. Then someone appeared in the doorway. Morris. He scanned the room and, spotting Charles, strode to him on silent feet.

"Charles." Morris shook his shoulder.

"Wha—" The man's head jerked upright, and his eyes focused. "What is it? What's wrong?"

"A shipment's being moved from the castle. It's headed down the Sodorran Road."

Charles's eyes went wide. "How'd you find out?"

"Jimmy heard someone at the tavern mention it."

"Someone mentioned it?"

"Yes, probably a drunken off-duty gate guard."

"Someone *mentioned* a secret shipment on our side of the river? Doesn't that seem strange?"

"Yes, but we have to act. They're keeping their movements quiet after our last raid. It could be nothing more than stolen goods. But it could be"—Morris jerked his head toward the sleeping room—"*someone*. Let's scope it out and make sure it's a fight we can win."

Charles rose, grabbing his weapon. They exited on silent feet.

Evie hesitated before throwing her blanket aside. She laced her boots, stood, and sheathed her blade. Someone moved behind her. Sam and Chase rose as well.

"Guys, what are you doing?" Lena whispered.

Sam buckled his holster and met Evie's eyes. "Are you thinking what I'm thinking?"

Only if you're thinking, "Stay out of my way, Strength Wielder." But she gave him a quick nod. If someone was on this shipment, and if he happened to have blue eyes and a dimple, she was going to be there.

<h1 style="text-align:center">24</h1>

"Come on, or we'll lose them."

Sam adjusted his holster as Lena motioned him and the others forward. The moon cast eerie shadows across the dark alleyway. He crept along, feet shuffling on the cobbled road as they left the city.

Chase moved silently in front of him. *How does he do that?* Sam stumbled, and Evaniah bumped into him from behind.

"Sorry," came her faint whisper.

She peeked at the Strength Wielder behind her. Garran brought up the rear, and she seemed almost as uneasy about it as Sam.

Garran, who Lena had cheerfully invited along, looked ready for a brawl. That could be good or bad, depending on how this played out. Asher and Elias stayed behind to look after Ben in case something happened and they didn't return.

Lena pushed through trees at the city wall where they climbed over and dropped to the ground in deep shadow. Homes and businesses lined these roads as well as if the city walls had filled to bursting and spewed forth the overflow, letting the structures tumble out.

Their motley group darted through the outskirts until the city gave way to a forest on what Lena said was the Sodorran Road. Once here, Chase tracked Morris with ease, pausing to adjust the bow Lena loaned him.

After a while, Chase halted, motioning them to hang back. He slid through the trees on silent feet and returned.

"They've stopped and are hiding in the trees. We could hide high on the hill across from them."

When Sam motioned him forward, Chase led the way. They settled on a rocky ledge sheltered by gangly trees. Their vantage point rose above the road where it snaked between two hillocks.

"Did he say anything about timing?" Chase wondered aloud.

"Not that I heard." Lena wrapped her arms around her knees. "Guys, I don't know about this. Morris will kill me if he finds me here."

"We're just watching," Evaniah whispered.

Sam sat, clearing pebbles from beneath him. "She's right. We'll hang back."

They hunkered in silence until Chase, with a flick of his unruly hair, tried for conversation with Lena. "So, your cousin seems more like your dad. Do you live with him?"

Her green eyes caught the moonlight. "He raised me. When he was sixteen, he and my mom tried to escape from Sodorrah. My mother was protecting me. I'm not Gifted, and I look like I'm from the Great Valley." She gestured toward her face. "Green eyes and all. They would've taken me from her. During the escape, my mother was killed, and my dad, who Morris says was a Sodorran guard, was captured and executed for helping us."

Silence followed.

"How awful." Evaniah reached out a hand to touch Lena's arm, but she let it drop before making contact.

Lena lifted a shoulder. "The incident spurred Morris to help others. Maybe he's trying to make up for not being able to save my mom. Since then, he's been rescuing the Gifted and trying to get the Inevite royalty to wake up and do something. That's how he became the leader. He can be intense, but he's a good man." She dipped her chin, picking at her dark pants. "Even though he can't forgive himself for what happened."

"I'm sorry, Lena." Evaniah placed a hand on the girl's arm as if unsure how to touch or comfort someone. "How old were you?"

"I was only four. I don't remember much, though I was old enough to. Morris says my mind has blocked the trauma." She shrugged. "That's one thing I have in common with the Arvad. I have a broken memory. Most of them don't remember their past or where they came from. Morris was four when he and my mom were brought to Sodorra. He says my mom never remembered anything from before then. Morris's memory is sketchy in the same way mine is."

Their voices died away, and Lena pulled a loaf of dry bread from her pack. She broke it apart and passed the pieces around.

Only the rustling leaves and the melodic insects broke the hushed night.

Sam closed his eyes. His last conversation with his parents had been heated. They lived a short two-hour train ride from Shura, but both worked constantly. A few weeks ago, they made plans to attend a weapons contest where he would compete against other Guardian-trained students. Then his mom called to say they couldn't come. He placed third out of fifty target throwers, and no one was there to see it. His mom claimed they couldn't get away. She'd pled with him to forgive her. He had not. After those last words spoken in anger, he hadn't even called to tell them he'd be traveling. What if he never returned?

Lying on their bellies, Lena and Evaniah crept toward the rocky ledge to peek across the valley. Chase crawled out and flattened next to them. Garran stared into the blackness.

If Sam's parents were neglectful, Garran's were overbearing. They set crazy expectations for him. Sam had spied them giving Garran an earful after a hard-fought competition. Apparently, taking second in staff combat wasn't good enough.

At least they showed up.

Garran hadn't been himself for the last few days. Not that Sam was complaining. Garran's usual self wasn't pleasant. The Strength Wielder's brow was drawn, and he gazed toward the road with a glassy expression.

"What is it?" Sam asked. "You look like you're on the verge of solving a mystery? Have you figured out what one plus one is?" Sam smirked.

Ignoring his barb, Garran furrowed his brow. "I…" He rubbed his eyes. "I'm remembering things. Or not really remembering, because it was always there, but things are… coming into focus. Like fog is lifting."

Sam fought the urge to roll his eyes.

"What have I done?" Garran whispered so low Sam wasn't sure he meant for him to hear.

Sam's brow pinched, and he opened his mouth to demand that Garran explain when a pebble hit his leg.

Evaniah pointed toward the road. "They're coming," she mouthed.

He and Garran inched forward. Two horse-drawn wagons materialized in the moonlight. Together, they carried four armed soldiers, and four more crept along on foot.

"This is good." Lena nodded. "Only eight."

Along with the creaking of the wheels, anguished words drifted through the forest. They came from inside the lead carriage.

"Please. Let us go. They would never know."

"We want to go home," another voice sobbed.

Both voices were female, but that didn't mean Adan wasn't among them.

"Shut up. Guards, stay alert." Sam wasn't sure which soldier had spoken. Moonlight cast hard shadows across the road, and still, no sign of Morris emerged.

The soldiers around the carriages peered into the trees. They were ready. Expectant.

A branch snapped like a gunshot near the road. The sound came from this side of the valley, and Sam craned his neck to see. The soldiers swung their weapons toward the noise.

Everything spun into swift action. Two men, presumably Morris's people, yelled as they burst through the trees and attacked the soldiers. The soldiers met them, blades flying, and the clash of metal ricocheted up the hill. The rebels wore dark clothing and dark cloths over their faces. There was no way to tell if one was Morris. The other soldiers jumped from the carriages and closed in, outnumbering the two rebels.

"Look." Evaniah pointed across the valley. More dark figures crept from the brush on the other side. They felled two of the eight soldiers from behind. As the other six became aware that more rebels were upon them, they fanned into a tight defensive arc behind the carriages.

Hands snaked from the barred window of the front carriage, where the continued pleas of those inside rang out.

"Help us."

"Run."

"Don't leave us."

"It's a trap."

Sam's brow creased.

The eleven rebels spread out to surround the six remaining guards. One of them, Charles, had lost his face covering. Sam could just make out the round swirling glow of the Gifted Mark on his forearm. With unnatural ease, he swung an impossibly thick mace. Strength Wielder.

"Surrender." Morris's rasp was barely audible across the distance.

"Oh, I don't think so," came a sandpaper voice from one of the soldiers. "Now!" he yelled.

The back of the rear carriage burst open, and two enormous men bounded out. They wore thick leather armor and chain mail and carried swords in both hands. Even more disconcerting were their bright glowing marks.

Sam straightened to get to his feet, and Chase put a hand on his shoulder. What should they do?

The two Strength Wielders rushed at Charles. The other guards broke formation, colliding with the rebels. The clang of metal and the cries of battle echoed through the valley. The three Strength Wielders tumbled into the trees, and after only a few seconds, the two surprise attackers returned, leaving Charles unmoving in the dry leaves.

A guard moved into one of the rebel's defensive blocks, running him through the gut. The rebel fell, clutching his middle, and slumped into stillness.

"No," Lena whispered.

Even as the word swirled around her, the commanding soldier yelled, "Don't kill them. He wants them alive."

With the only rebel Strength Wielder dispatched, the two Gifted soldiers made quick work of disarming the others. They knocked out two rebels and held the other at knifepoint.

A Strength Wielder disarmed the last rebel with an easy backhand. The blow likely broke bones, and the man fell to the ground. His face covering slipped to the side, and blood gushed from his nose. Morris. He tried to get up, but the raspy-voiced man kicked him in the ribs. Morris fell back with a moan.

"Morris." Lena moaned as well as she shifted into a crouch.

Evaniah grabbed her shoulder. "Shhh."

The lead guard towered over Morris. "So you're the fabled rebel leader. We've been looking forward to this moment." He laughed, an awful, grating sound. "Off to the gallows for you. Your rebellion will fall before your neck is stretched."

"You may kill me, but the rebellion will continue. The people won't stand idle much longer. They'll demand action from Inevah."

The man laughed again. "You're a myth to the people. Most aren't even sure you exist. No one of importance knows what you're about. The rebellion dies with you."

"Does the king know what you transport in this caravan?" Morris asked.

The voices within the carriage had quieted, but Sam could still hear whimpering—all that remained of a short-lived hope.

"You and I both know the king doesn't see all that happens in The Valley. You should know by now he sees only what—or *who*—he wishes to."

"What do we do?" Lena hissed.

"They want them alive. The soldiers won't kill them," Evaniah said.

"They *will* be hanged. To the Inevites, it will look like any other punishment, but it will be a clear message to the rebels. The soldier is right. The cause will be lost—and my only family with it." A tear slid down Lena's cheek. She clenched her fists before her, facing the horrors below. "No way can we take two Strength Wielders, but once they get them back to the castle, they'll be out of reach."

Evaniah stared at Sam. Her knowing gaze bored into him. He'd never used his strength in a real fight, and neither he, Garran, nor Chase had ever fought outside the combat ring. He ducked his head, not wanting any of them to see the weakness within. What if he died? What would happen to Adan? To Ben? He couldn't waste his life here.

One of the prisoners moaned, "Please, Maker, save us."

Evaniah's head jerked toward the carriage, and something in her changed. Her face hardened into concrete determination. She drew her golden dagger, and finally, she touched Sam.

She must've seen his reluctance. Her knuckles whitened on the weapon's hilt. "I don't know what the future will bring. If you'll find your friend tomorrow or the next day or next year or never. But I do know you can do something for the people down there. The rebels *and* the prisoners. Use the Gifts you've been given."

She flicked her gaze to his hand, where the enhancement ring was tucked under a glove. Who was this girl?

Hope lit Lena's green eyes. "Please, I beg you. We can work together." She reached for her bow and drew it over her shoulder.

Choose the right thing, not the easy thing. Wasn't that what Uzziah was always trying to teach them?

"Perhaps—" Evaniah started as she turned, whipping her light ponytail over her shoulder to gaze toward the mountains. "Perhaps you came here for more than finding a lost boy." She seemed to be talking to both Sam and herself. When her golden eyes met his again, they'd morphed into something fierce. "If we know the right thing to do but don't do it, we've already failed. We'll have failed these people as well as our own conscience. You'll have failed even Adan, who might be locked away and depending on someone just like you to choose their own right thing."

Even she looked surprised by her words.

Fidgeting with the leather buckles of this holster, Sam faced the carriages. The guards kicked and pushed the rebels—those who had taken him in and given him a place to sleep. They would die if he didn't act. Resolve hardened his chest. It would be up to him and Garran. A hard glint steeled Garran's eyes. He nodded once, jaw set, and they drew their weapons.

Sam hissed a set of instructions, and they crept down the hill, weaving through the trees. Soldiers herded the rebels toward the carriage doors.

When Sam and Garran were almost to the tree line, an arrow whizzed by, striking one of the Strength Wielder soldiers in the upper arm. His sword clattered onto the rocky path, and he loosed a low bellow.

Sam slowed and urged Garran forward. "Take the injured one. We need to disarm them." Garran growled his assent and left all traces of stealth behind. He crashed through the trees, and the guards whipped their heads in his direction.

Morris's eyes went wide as Garran barreled toward him, but he recovered and lowered his shoulder to ram a distracted guard as Garran's fist met the injured guard's jaw. The other, bigger Strength Wielder moved to join his comrade, lifting his enormous sword. Sam plowed through the trees, tackling the man into the side of a carriage.

Sam's opponent swung his sword around, but Sam grabbed his wrist, pinning it against the carriage. Wasted worlds. His power was stronger than this man's! Much stronger. He beat the wrist against the wagon until the soldier dropped his weapon. As Sam was about to plunge his dagger into the man's gut, his opponent brought his knee across Sam's wrist and held it low against the carriage's splintering wood. Sam's blade slipped from his sweaty fingers. The other man went for the fallen weapons, but Sam kicked them under the carriage. Just as well. He was more confident in a fistfight anyway. The other man lunged, and they pummeled each other in a tangle of fists.

Sam was dimly aware of the fighting around him. He caught glimpses of Evaniah's shining dagger and Garran's gleaming sword.

Sam had trained in hand-to-hand combat from a young age, and he smiled as the other man realized he was outmatched in both strength and skill.

Chase crept from the trees behind Sam's opponent, flipped his blade, and let it fly. The soldier yelled out and fell to his knees.

Blood blossomed from his back as he tipped and fell flat to his face. Chase and Sam gaped at the body. This was not how he thought victory would feel. Chase retrieved his blade, and they crept around the wagon to help the others.

But the battle was over. Their two groups had eliminated all soldiers. Evaniah's blade had found two, and arrows sprouted from others. Morris and his men had helped Garran finish off the remaining Strength Wielder. Bodies lay strewn about in the moonlight, though after a quick count, Sam was sure one soldier was missing.

All fell silent but for the heavy breathing of overexhausted bodies. Lena sauntered from the trees, bow in hand. Morris's men relaxed when they saw her, and she gave them a crooked grin. "Looked like you could use a hand."

They laughed, too tired, injured, and shocked to do much more.

Morris, however, was not smiling. "What are you doing here?"

But Sam didn't hear her answer. Instead, he followed Evaniah to the front carriage.

"Adan?" she said, seeming filled with both hope and dread.

Wide eyes peered out the window where filthy hands clung to the bars. "There's no one here by that name," a voice croaked.

Sam's heart sank. He met Evaniah's eyes. They shook off their disappointment and did what they came down the hill to do. One of the rebels calmed the horses as Sam used a stone and his strength to break the lock. The others, including a limping Charles, lumbered over and helped the prisoners out. The half-starved people mumbled their thanks, and an older lady even pulled Sam into a fierce hug.

In all, seven prisoners had been packed into the carriage. Evaniah's ashen face revealed perhaps the first genuine emotion he'd seen on her. She was moved, as was he, by the gravity of what they'd done as well as by the disappointment they shared. She was right; this was the right thing to do. She met his eyes, and he gave her a nod.

Morris spoke to the prisoners using a speech he'd probably delivered many times before. "My name is Morris, and you're safe. I won't make you do anything you don't want to do. You can leave now if you like, or you can come with us until we can help you go wherever it is you want to go. The choice is yours."

Two young men with amber eyes mumbled their gratitude and melted into the trees. Morris began calling instructions and questioning the remaining five. The older woman was with a man who might be her son. They held to two children, one a young teen and one about Ben's age. They requested a place to stay. The remaining captive, a bruised teenage girl, appeared to be alone. She'd seen more food than the others. Her dark skin wanted to melt into the shadows, and only her bright hazel eyes betrayed her on this moonlit night.

"What's your name?" Morris asked.

"I'm Tula," she said. "I'm from Hulda."

"That's in the mountains," Lena hissed to Sam and Evaniah. So this girl was one of the Huldan who Morris considered cowards.

"A group of my friends and I were taken about two weeks ago while on a foraging run. Some were ungifted, and I don't know what happened to them. Myself and five others were sent to Inevah castle and marked." She held her arm out, displaying a swirling circle inside her wrist. "They're still there."

She had everyone's full attention now.

She clasped her hands and leaned in. "Can you help me get them out?"

Morris wiped his bloody nose on his sleeve. "You've been a prisoner at the castle for two weeks? Do you know why you were being transported?"

"I tried to escape. It wasn't a good plan. I see that now."

"Was there a boy named Adan there?" Sam blurted.

Tula scrunched up her eyebrows. "I've never heard that name."

"Were any new people brought in over the last few days?" Morris asked.

"We were the most recent catch until the day I tried to escape. One boy was brought in the night before."

"Did he have blue eyes?" Chase blurted.

"What? No. He was at breakfast the morning I made my move. I didn't look at him closely, but I would have noticed that."

Evaniah shifted in the dark, her golden eyes like two tiny lanterns. "Tula, how long ago did you try to escape?"

"It seems like much longer, but it was only yesterday morning."

Sam whispered under his breath, "The timing is perfect."

Morris rubbed his jaw. "It's not much to go on."

"But it's something. What should we do?" Sam asked.

Morris opened his mouth, dissent hardening his face, but Evaniah cut him off. "We have to go to the castle. It's our only lead."

"That would be suicide."

"Perhaps." She let out a long breath as she wiped sweat from her brow. "But we have to investigate, and we need to help this girl."

"Let's start by gathering information." Morris stood straighter. "We know almost nothing about the castle or the way the guards work around it."

"Fine," Sam and Evaniah said at the same time.

Morris turned back to Tula. "I think we can help each other."

The girl's shoulders relaxed, and she nodded.

"Morris?" Lena slipped past her and touched her cousin's arm. "Someone in the castle knows you're in the city, and they want to silence you before you gather more supporters. They set an ambush for you, and it almost worked. Don't you think it's time the rebels became more than myth?"

Morris and his men shared a look. A few of them grinned.

"You're right, and we have a few ideas." The rebel leader tucked her under his arm as he steered his cousin and the others back to investigate the aftermath.

"Can I help?" Lena scooted out from his arm.

"No chance." Their voices faded into the dark.

Evaniah meandered away, and Sam watched her back. He had questions for the golden-eyed girl. But, before he could move to catch up to her, Garran approached.

The Strength Wielder stuffed his meaty hands in his pockets. Blood splattered his face, but he didn't seem to care. "Sam, I have to tell you something."

Here we go. "What is it?"

"It was me. This is my fault."

"What are you talking about, Garran?" Sam yanked up the corner of his T-shirt to dab at the blood seeping into his own eye. "Use more words."

"I remember now. It's all coming back. I did do it, what Ben said I did."

Ouch. That cut stung. He tried again, lighter. It never hurt like this after the training circle. "What did you do? Spit it out."

Garran's throat bobbed. "I sold him. I sold Adan to the man in the black car."

Sam dropped the corner of his shirt and finally met Garran's uneasy gaze.

Garran ran a hand through his blood-sprayed hair. "I took the money. I put him in the trunk of that car." His jaw clenched. "The man's been coming to me for months, asking me about Uzziah's ring and my inherited Gift. I think he wanted me, but somehow, he heard about Adan. That day, he made me do it. He made me *want* to do it."

25

"Who are you?"

Evie jumped at the unexpected hiss. She'd been watching the road disappear under her feet as she trailed the humans.

Sam sidled next to her, matching her slow pace.

She'd been avoiding the boy, knowing his questions demanded answers. She'd been avoiding them all. The humans were not helping her growing erratic emotional state. Earlier, the captive's cry for help from the Maker had shaken her, had convicted her. She didn't regret the aid she'd given, but she couldn't afford to be distracted. She had a job to do.

She lifted her chin, peering straight ahead. "You know who I am. I'm Evi—Evaniah."

"Do you need me to list the things I know about you that don't add up?"

No. She knew them quite well.

He ticked them off on his fingers. "You knew my name before I met you. You know things that other people don't seem to know. You don't know the things other people do know. Blue eyes don't surprise you. You have a mark on your back that glows."

Nosy, sacked-sector human. She spun around. "My mark doesn't glow."

"Uh, yes. It does. I saw it."

She frowned, returning her gaze to the road, and reached back to touch that spot just below her neck. "None of those things mean anything, Sam."

"Maybe alone they don't, but together they do. You referred to this place as Sector Six. I've never heard anyone but my Guardian refer to a place as a sector in normal conversation. But the strangest thing you've done is to walk up to that carriage and ask for Adan. You said you were searching for someone." He lowered his head, watching her. "Is it a coincidence your missing person has the same name as my missing person?"

She'd made too many mistakes. But who was he, this human child, to question her? She paused on the road between two homes looming in the darkness. "You're one to talk. What are you hiding under those gloves? And under those—" She glared at his falsely green eyes but stopped. Here she was, giving away more.

"See? How do you know that?"

They faced each other now. She couldn't pretend to be from this sector. What could she say to get him off her back and out of the way? The Control Room hadn't explicitly forbidden her from telling anyone the truth. "Okay, fine. Yes, I'm searching for someone. His name is Adan. He has dark hair and blue eyes, and he shouldn't be in Sector Six."

Her gaze slid back to her feet as Sam's eyebrows crept toward his dark hair. "You know what I think?"

"What?" She jammed her hands on her hips and cocked her head. "Enlighten me."

"I think you're a Guardian. The eyes give you away."

She snorted. *If I were, I wouldn't be in this mess.*

"Fine, don't tell me, but at least answer this. Why are *you* looking for him?"

She kicked at the road. "All I can tell you is, for the moment, our goals align. We *are* going to find Adan. My future depends on it."

She stalked away, and Sam hung back, not trying to catch up. Then he called, "What do you mean, 'for the moment'?"

She picked up the pace, fleeing further questions. Her watch vibrated against her wrist, reminding her another day had slipped away. With trembling fingers, she reached into her pocket and gripped Joram's note.

"Do what you have to do," she whispered to herself.

Part III

And they said one to another, behold,
this dreamer cometh.

Genesis 37:19

26

"You're useless, boy."

Adan squeezed his eyes shut and rubbed his forehead as Captain Curtshaw paced.

"He said you would be Strength Gifted. It's been almost a week of tests. Still nothing."

Adan's jaw clenched. "I'm telling you—I've *been* telling you—I'm not."

The early morning sun streamed in the man's open office window. So far, their little meeting wasn't going so well.

When the captain turned his head, Adan glanced around to glean some resource for his escape plot—a plot that was going about as well as this meeting. Books lined organized shelves along the wall, and papers lay in neat stacks across the desk. The only object of note was a dull silver letter opener atop a thick envelope. It glinted below the logo of a bear's head where bold black letters inked the words *The Den*.

The captain paced behind his desk. "You're not a Strength Wielder. You're not a Water Mover. You're not a Healer. What are you?"

Adan said nothing.

Someone knocked.

"Come in," the captain ordered.

The Boulder shouldered his way in, an object pinched between his fingers. He wiggled it. "I found this in his room."

Adan hitched a breath. His golden-spine book dangled from the Strength Wielder's fingers. "It was on his bed."

"Let's have it then." The captain flipped it open.

Adan released his breath. Ben's photograph didn't fall from its place.

Chuckling, the captain read aloud. "'In a river of blood and gold, the Deceiver waited. His only hope rested in the death of Krystopher's

Marked. Together, the Deceiver and his immortal'—What is this rubbish?" He scoffed, flipping the book closed. "Fiction? Did you steal this?"

"What? No. I brought it with me. It was in my pocket." Adan held out a hand. "Can I have it back?"

Captain Curtshaw stepped onto a stool behind his desk. He slid the book between two others on a high shelf. "You don't need such distractions."

Light tapping sounded at the door.

"What now?"

The Boulder exited, throwing a smirk in Adan's direction as a prim woman entered. "Darling, are you joining me for dinner with the prince this evening?"

The captain's head jerked up, mouth tight. "I have business to attend."

"Very well." As a relieved smile touched the corner of her lips, she shifted her focus to Adan. "And who is this?"

"Nobody. He's here on a trial basis," the captain said, turning away.

Adan grimaced in her direction, but her attention had already moved on. She eyed a low shelf behind the desk, scowled, then walked out the door.

When the door closed, a decision solidified in the older man's eyes. He walked to the door and opened it, calling down the hall. "Vincent, escort him to breakfast. I don't want to look at him again."

Smoking Worlds. The Boulder had a name—Vincent.

Before the thought could solidify, the captain fisted Adan's shirt, lifting him from his chair, and thrust his nose so close Adan could count the pores. "I don't have any more time to waste on you. I don't care what he says of you. You're nothing." Captain Curtshaw shook Adan, then released him and walked to his desk. The next words came so low they may not have been meant for Adan's ears. "You may not be Gifted, but your strange eyes might be worth something."

What?

The captain sank into his chair as the Boulder grabbed Adan's arm.

Adan's breathing shallowed. *What does he mean?* "Wait. Listen, I'm not sure what my captor was hoping for, but I do have strange dreams sometimes and—"

"You have strange dreams?" The captain cut him off with an incredulous laugh. He picked up a stack of papers, and the letter opener clanged onto the wooden surface. "Don't start begging now. I've heard it all before. I don't have time for you, and I meant it."

He waved toward the guard who shouldered Adan into the hallway. "I have more important business to attend to." Then the captain smiled to himself. "Like purchasing the most profitable tavern in Inevah."

"You didn't let me finish." Adan started again, but the door slammed shut.

"Start moving before I make you." The bulky man-child stepped closer.

"All right. I'm going." Adan approached the staircase.

He'd been born with the most useless Gift. The captain and everyone else thought he was a complete joke. His dreams wouldn't save him. He needed to escape.

Last night, another mind-bending dream left him sweating. He saw Evie and the bear and the birds and other animals that flitted in and out of his dreams.

He'd grown wary pacing below the deafening birds. He'd heard a soft crunch and a bleat and found a small horned ram facing him. It pawed the ground, lowered its head, and charged. Not knowing what else to do, Adan lifted his foot and met the animal's blow with a boot against its head. The tiny animal staggered and ran into the trees. A snake slithered in the shadows.

A tree towered from the center of the path. Its branches spread wide, casting their shadows over Adan. An eagle passed overhead and into the dark clouds. A beautiful, vibrant green dressed the tree, but for a spot of red. The spot bled down the trunk until crimson rivers oozed from the bark and spread to the branches. It pooled at its foot, and a puddle crept toward Adan's feet. Blood dripped from the leaves. A swollen drop splattered onto Adan's face. When he touched it, his fingers came away coated in red.

Then he was sitting up in bed, soaked in sweat. He touched his cheek to see if there was blood. There wasn't.

Useless. A useless dream.

If only Uzziah had Gifted him with strength. Then he'd have a bargaining tool. The ember of anger buried inside Adan burned hotter.

He growled, and the guard beside him chuckled at the feeble outburst.

Two men passed them in the hall. "… negotiate the purchase of The Den. We shouldn't accept less than what the advisor told us.…" And they were gone, the captain's investment, no doubt.

The Boulder gave Adan a nudge toward the dining room.

Grace and James were already sitting at their table. Adan got his tray and plopped it next to James. Grace jumped, and the elaborate ice formation she'd been forging came crashing down.

"Hey," she said. "What happened to you? Someone steal your puppy?"

"Nothing," Adan mumbled.

Hattie sat on Adan's other side, and then Thomas arrived, almost bursting with energy. "I have news," he hissed. "You're not going to believe this. The guards were talking about a caravan that left the castle four days ago to travel to Sodorrah. It was meant to be a trap, but it didn't work. It has to be the rebels. They killed every soldier, but one. The captives are all missing, and—get this—they even killed the two Strength Wielders who went along as part of the ruse. The soldier who made it back said the other group had three Strength Wielders, and one was the strongest he'd ever seen."

A wide grin spread over Thomas's face, and he thumped his hand on the table, drawing attention. "I told you the rebels were real."

The others wiped the shocked expressions from their faces and went back to eating as a guard ambled by.

When the guard was clear, James pointed his spoon at Thomas. "We have to find a way to contact them. They could help us. And we could help them."

Thomas stabbed a bite of slimy egg onto his fork. "If I get out of here, I'm joining up."

Adan pushed his food around his plate. He was all too happy to find someone to help them escape, but he wouldn't be joining the rebels. He had to find a way home.

The others began talking about an event the captain was rumored to be hosting tomorrow. He hardly listened until Grace sent a splash of water into his face. "What's with you today? Your head's under the Huldan mountain."

He wiped his eyes. "I've failed all the tests. What will happen now?"

No one had an answer, but their grim expressions weren't comforting.

After breakfast, the weapons instructor in the practice yard was as frustrated with him as ever.

"Keep the blade out from your body," the man shouted over clanging metal.

Then he barreled forward, grabbing Adan by the collar. "Get your head out of the sky, or you can spend some time in solitary."

Adan gasped and nodded.

"I know what's in store for you, boy." The instructor's hot breath seethed into his ear. "Tell you what. I'll give you one more chance to show us your worth." Louder, he called to Adan's least favorite guard. "Vincent, come teach him a lesson. No weapons."

The trainer shoved Adan away as the Boulder stalked over.

Oh boy.

Adan had fought Garran in the training ring. It never turned out well. But Adan was surprisingly good at evasion. His only hope with the Boulder, as it would be with any Strength Wielder, was to move faster, be smarter, and stay out of reach. Adan crouched into a fighting stance. The Boulder did the same. The instructor backed away. The clanging around the courtyard quieted.

With a yell, the Boulder barreled forward. He was so big and cumbersome—and not to mention the warning yell—that Adan easily sidestepped him. The bigger boy, who'd been expecting an immediate impact, staggered forward and whipped back around. He attacked again and again, and Adan continued to evade his iron grip.

Yes! This Strength Wielder was much less skilled in hand-to-hand than Garran. Here, they probably fought with weapons almost exclusively.

The Boulder was slower, too. Adan was the fastest of Uzziah's trainees, and he used that to his advantage now. He slipped behind the enormous boy and put a fist in his kidney. The Boulder hardly noticed. *Great.* This was turning out to be a fight to see who would become exhausted first.

The Boulder's swings grew increasingly wild. When he threw his body and momentum too far to one side, Adan used his leg to sweep below the Strength Wielder, knocking his feet off balance. Adan spun, giving him another shove. The guard fell forward onto a knee, one hand flying wide and the other reaching to catch himself. Adan put a kick in his back, planting his sole on the boy's tunic where the crest of Inevah was pressed into the fine leather. Adan blinked. An odd sense of déjà vu brushed at his mind. His foot hadn't sent the other boy down completely, and the Boulder was back on his feet.

While Adan was distracted, the Boulder ended the match. The Strength Wielder landed a punch across Adan's face. Adan took the blow at an angle, lessening the force. But his vision blurred, and he stumbled. The Boulder threw him to the ground, pulling his arms behind his back. Adan's face pressed into the dusty brick path. His cheek throbbed, and blood stained the ground under him.

The Boulder would've kept up a stream of punches, but the instructor called him off. The pressure left Adan, and he flipped onto his back, breath ragged. James leaned over him, grinning.

"Not bad, blue."

Adan cringed at the nickname.

"Back to your stations," the instructor shouted. The man didn't offer any praise, but he also didn't insult Adan. Improvement?

Adan started to walk back with James when his attention caught on the bloody brick where his face had been flattened to the ground. No, not the bloody brick—the bloody *tree*. Etched on each block was the mark of the mason, a broad oak. Adan's blood was soaking into its branches.

He jerked his gaze to the Boulder. The boy sauntered toward the other guards. The crest on his back—a ram's head circled by a ring of thorns—still held Adan's dusty footprint.

Adan reached up as he had in his dream and brushed his fingers along his cheek. Blood stained his fingers. A bird squawked in the distance.

He'd dreamt of this moment.

27

Adan slipped a shirt over his dripping hair in the chilly bathing room. Would it be so difficult to give them a towel?

Thomas struggled next to him, forcing still-wet feet into leather boots. "Another missed opportunity," he grunted under his breath.

"What do you mean?"

James shook out his hair and pitched his voice low. "He means we've been working on an escape plan centering around one of Captain Curtshaw's auctions. He's having one tomorrow."

Adan's eyebrows crept higher, and James launched into details. The others had worked up a strategy. But it wasn't ready.

"… and then if we all had an excuse to be down there, we could fight our way to the alley behind the block. And then…" James snapped his fingers in a voilà gesture. His almost-plan was full of holes and what-ifs. A reason for them all to be asked down to the courtyard on auction day, for one. It wouldn't likely get that far.

"The alley is the key." James pounded a fist into his hand as they filed into the hall with the other special guests. "It's the only exit not guarded by Strength Wielders. A few people stand guard near the opening, but their only job seems to be keeping unwanted visitors away from the illegal market."

They quieted as guards shuffled them along to the dining room, Adan pulling at his damp shirt.

"So, what do you think?" James whispered when they joined Grace and Hattie at their table.

"Well… you guys need to fill in the gaps. A lot of things could go wrong. Why would someone like Thomas or even Grace be needed in the square?"

Rubbing his temples, James ducked his head, then fisted his hands in his reddish-blond hair, yanking it in all directions. "I don't know."

"Do you know what's beyond the alley?"

James stabbed his fork into a suspicious-looking glob on his plate. "No."

"What we need is outside help." Thomas propped his elbows on the table and steepled his fingers. "A diversion."

Adan shrugged. "Yeah, maybe." He could ask more questions to tear apart the feeble plan, but he'd let it rest.

Should he tell his friends about his Gift and what he'd discovered in his dream? He clenched his fork in his fist. He couldn't stand seeing their disbelieving or, worse, pitying faces. He'd tell them, and they'd pretend to understand or be concerned. Then, later, he'd catch them sharing incredulous glances when they thought he wasn't looking. It had all happened before.

Instead, he said, "What did you mean when you said the auction is illegal?"

"Illegal—as in against Inevah law."

"I know what illegal means." Adan scowled, tapping his foot on the stone floor. "What's illegal about it? And isn't it here at the castle?"

"The main auction is within the law, but it's a front for what brings in money. Captain Curtshaw's auctions are well known in The Valley and beyond. People will come from all over, but by dusk, they'll have run off any reputable bidders. Then they bring out the less reputable items."

"Like…?"

"Like stolen goods, illegal imports, weapons… and people."

Adan's head snapped up, a sickening sensation twisting up his gut. But dinner was over. A guard ushered him up the long staircase to his room high in the castle wall.

He removed the colored contacts and splashed his face with water from the basin, catching his reflection on the surface. His blue eyes rippled back.

You may not be Gifted, but your strange eyes aren't without worth.

Closing those eyes, he allowed the thought that had been swimming around, untethered in his mind. *He's going to sell me at the auction.*

His stomach roiled. Willing himself to calm, he paced. He pried at the door and then the window, almost making his hands bleed. His old friend panic clawed in.

Adan forced himself to breathe. Perhaps it would be easier to escape if some auction winner took him away from here—away from the thick rock walls, the heavy doors, and the long, labyrinthine hallways with guards around every corner.

But now, he had nothing to lose. He would try to escape. Tomorrow, he'd put one of his crude plans into action.

With that settled, he undressed, flopped onto his bed, and considered his dreams. Could they give him a means of escape? He squeezed his eyes shut and wished for a solution to come to him.

Today, he'd been certain his dream was of an actual moment. Maybe if he looked hard enough, he'd see what needed to be done. If he could interpret this dream, perhaps he would find a way to change the future.

Change the future. If Adan could do this—see the future and alter it— then he was the valuable commodity Uzziah tried to make him out to be. Had the Guardian been right about him all along?

What did he know from his dreams? There was the bear, the birds, the possible warning, the watching snake, and the archway. What else? He fidgeted. How would any of it help him? After hours of coming up with nothing, he drifted to sleep.

The path was brighter this time. "Pay attention," it seemed to say.

Ahead came a flash of white. Evie jogged away and around the corner. He wouldn't follow her today.

He turned and found his friends—his fellow trainees from Sector Five—watching him. They shuffled in the soft sand.

No, they weren't all friends. Garran stood among them.

Adan glared at the boy, condemning him, allowing his anger to burn bright.

Garran studied his feet.

The hatred slipped from Adan like water from a cupped hand when another, bigger feeling came over him at the sight of Ben peeking from behind Sam's back. Ben stepped forward to stand next to Sam. Above bright sapphire eyes, dark curls moved in the soft breeze.

"Ben," Adan breathed.

The boy reached a hand to Adan, beckoning. How would Adan ever get back to him?

The bronze archway loomed behind the boys.

No. Not now.

But it didn't glow—not yet. The boys knelt low on one knee and then drifted away like smoke. A snake slithered in the underbrush.

The bear lumbered onto the path, and Adan tilted his face to the sky, expecting them this time. Yes, a dark shadow of birds flew toward his place in the woods. They landed in the trees and, as before, began their deafening serenade. This time, the bear didn't saunter away. It let out a mighty roar toward the sky.

Think, Adan. What does it mean?

As if on some silent cue, the birds descended on the bear. The bear fought against the birds, but with so many, they'd gouged out its eyes. Blood streamed down its face. The birds used their beaks as tiny daggers on the bear's skin. The blind beast swatted with its front paws. The birds evaded his claws until a swipe made contact with a single blackbird streaked with brilliant gold. It landed at Adan's feet, flopping a broken wing.

The snake slithered forward and grabbed the bird in its jaws, swallowing it whole. The snake returned to the trees. The bear stilled as the birds pecked away at its flesh. Blood soaked its dark coat. Then, just as they came, the birds, as one, soared away into the sky. The bear's body began to flake away as if made of ash. As if it had been burned.

Think. A bear destroyed by a flock of birds. Hadn't he seen a bear yesterday? A drawing of a bear.

But the archway loomed and delivered his assassin in a riot of blinding light.

Adan sat up, eyes wide. For once, he wouldn't dwell on the golden blade.

Focus on the bear. No, not the bear. The Den.

The Den was the tavern Captain Curtshaw planned to purchase. Something was going to happen to it. Would an actual flock of birds do something? No, that was silly. What did Adan care if the captain's investment got smoked? There had to be something else. What about the single bird? Could he have stopped the snake from devouring it?

He flopped onto his back, slinging an arm over his eyes. Where was a means of escape in this? He tried to sleep again—to dream—but after a half hour, he gave up. There'd be no more dreams tonight.

He dressed and replaced the brown contacts. He paced, muttering to himself. Answers evaded him until, right on time, footsteps clomped along in the hall.

If this was like any other day, it was James and a guard, here to take him down to breakfast.

Adan moved close to the door. James wouldn't try to stop him, so when the lock clicked and the door cracked open, Adan darted past the startled Healer. He raced by the guard and sprinted full-tilt toward the stairs. The guard yelled out, and his heavy footfalls pounded behind Adan.

He took the lead and bounded down the stairs three at a time, then veered in a sharp left at the bottom. The other way led toward the dining hall—and the guards. But he didn't know where this hallway led.

He burst into a vast, open space—a rotunda—and smack into the back of the Boulder. He stumbled forward, but the force knocked Adan back against a pillar. Adan spun, noting the other people about. He sprinted for the only other door, but another guard cut him off.

Shouts reverberated all around.

"Catch him."

"Don't punch him. No bruises."

"You. Guard the back door."

Guards surrounded him, then forced him to the floor.

"Don't harm him." A familiar voice came closer. "Not the face."

Adan stopped struggling as the Boulder pulled him to his feet.

"Ah, Adan. We want you looking your best for your big moment this evening."

Adan sagged but wasted no time conjuring another escape idea, this one from the dining hall at lunch.

As if the captain had read his mind, he said, "Take him to his room and stand guard the rest of the day. But feed him. I don't want him to look weak. He can stay there until evening."

Adan's heart sank. He thought again of the dream. It was his only tool. Maybe the dream was not about how to escape but about how to stay.

Find a way to be useful. Hadn't James said that days ago?

When the guard began to turn him away, Adan said, "Wait. The Den tavern is a bad investment."

The captain, who'd already started walking away, turned his head but didn't stop. "And what would you know of such things?" He snorted out a laugh and continued on, not waiting for a response.

"No. Wait." The Boulder gripped Adan more tightly and started backing him out the other way. "I dreamed a flock of blackbirds destroyed a bear. It looked like the bear on the papers in your office." Even as he said it, it sounded ridiculous, but Captain Curtshaw paused, eyeing Adan as if puzzling something out, trying to remember something on the edge of reason. But he shook his head and left the room.

Adan's head drooped, and he didn't protest as the Boulder led him back to his room. They passed James, who watched, bewildered, in the hall.

"Get the Dreamer some food. He's having some alone time today," the guard sneered.

The Boulder shoved Adan into his doorway and leaned against the frame. "Now, you have plenty of time to have another one of those fancy dreams."

Laughing, he slammed the door.

28

Adan peered out his barred window. In the triangular courtyard below, pedestrians congregated near a raised platform, their indistinct conversations wafting upward. The auction was about to begin.

The clever location, well away from the main castle gates, nestled next to Captain Curtshaw's wing and tucked into the space where the palace jutted from the city wall.

Only four paths led away from the courtyard. Thomas was right. The second was the only unguarded exit. If he were to run through it, he'd need to take an immediate right to avoid being trapped in by the city wall. Tightening his shaking fingers around the bars, Adan mapped a route in his mind.

A few doors away from his path to freedom, a man in an apron stepped onto a tidy porch. A wooden sign swung over his head. It likely bore the face of a bear. The Den? Adan's brow rose. He'd never noticed it before. The man swept his stoop and returned inside as someone lumbered up the steps to the platform, somehow signaling the start of the auction. The crowd pressed near.

Adan moved away from the window, not wishing to see more. He settled for pacing.

James arrived with dinner.

"Any miraculous ideas for me?" Adan asked.

"No. I'm sorry," James whispered. "But Thomas did hear Captain Curtshaw talking you up to a ship captain from the Southern Isles. If he gets his hands on you, no telling where you'll end up. Overseas most likely."

Overseas? He felt as if a fist had tightened around his heart. He dropped onto the bed.

He must've arrived here by some long-lost intersector portal, and he'd have to leave that same way. He couldn't leave this area.

"James, what am I going to do?" Adan put his head in his hands.

"You have to escape. Try the second alleyway. Spot the people acting as lookouts. Few others will care enough to stop you. The captain's guards are under orders not to harm you, so you should have a chance to look around. Oh, and the captain sent this for you to wear."

Adan unfolded the bundle of cloth—a simple, light-colored shirt, similar to the long-sleeve hoodies he wore back home.

"I think he's planning an onstage reveal." James cringed when he took in Adan's horrified face.

Adan gritted his teeth and balled the shirt, throwing it across the room. "I'm not wearing that."

"Adan, they'll dress you if they have to. Change clothes and save your defiance for outside the castle walls."

When James stood to leave, Adan rose with him, and the Healer pulled him into a quick hug. "If you escape, tell the rebels about us. And if you don't escape, don't give up. We'll look for you if we ever get out. We'll be watching from our window. Good luck."

After slapping Adan on the back, James ducked out of the room.

Adan tried to eat but gave up as his stomach turned. He changed and paced until he heard footsteps in the hall. When the door opened, it revealed three guards.

"Let's go." The Boulder flashed a nasty smile.

Another sneered. "Showtime."

Adan fell into step behind the Boulder, and the others followed him.

They marched through the hallway and down the steps. Just as the main door came into view, Captain Curtshaw strode alongside Adan, joining their long walk.

"Ah, Adan. This is where we part."

The captain held the stack of papers labeled The Den. Adan nodded to them. "It's a bad idea. My dreams showed me."

The captain's steps slowed, but he chuckled. "Turning a profit relies on more than dreams, boy."

"Think what it would mean if I'm right. Don't send me away."

Stopping, the captain said, "Enough. Put your hood up."

Adan did. Captain Curtshaw held out a hand. "Now, give me your eye coverings."

Adan froze.

"Now." The man flicked his fingers.

The guards glanced at each other, raising their brows.

Adan poked at his eyes until he'd extracted both contacts and placed them in the man's outstretched hand. He didn't look back up at the captain, though he cringed as the man chuckled. "That's it. Keep your head down until the right moment. You'll know when. Oh, and have you heard of the shock stick?"

No reason to acknowledge him.

"No? Well, let's just say you'll find out if you step out of line." The captain stepped aside. "All right, move on. He should be up soon."

Adan and the guards passed through the doors where two additional guards joined their procession.

Stepping out among so many people after over a week with the same handful of prisoners reminded him of Shura's busy streets—pedestrians jostling for space.

He didn't dare look up, but he peeked from under his hood. The main entrance into the courtyard was just ahead. People and guards blocked the way. *Not yet.* The Strength Wielders herded Adan into the first alley—a staging area of sorts.

A cage, already holding four others, waited in the shadows. Guards pulled a young woman from it. She ripped free of her captor's grip and sprinted for the alleyway's other end. The guards near the cage as well as three of Adan's scrambled after her.

This was his chance. Everyone was intent on the girl.

Adan barreled after them. The guards didn't look back or notice.

Fire zipped under his skin. An electric shock rocked his muscles and sent him to the ground. He lay still before he took a knee to right himself. His body didn't want to obey.

Thick boots approached, and another shock jarred his body. Yelling out, he fell onto his face.

"I was hoping to use this," the Boulder said. "Get up."

Adan managed to stand on wobbly legs. Shock stick indeed. The captain's guards ushered him back to the cage.

Guards dragged the girl—who they'd apprehended—into the courtyard and up the platform stairs. Adan looked away, not wishing to see more.

Captain Curtshaw strode forward. "This one's next. Quick now, before the sun is down. Dust him off." His guards patted Adan's dusty shirt.

Then they shoved him forward. Adan kept his head low, painfully aware of the shock stick bobbing along beside him. What should he do? He shuffled forward as they guided him to the foot of the steps.

"Up." Captain Curtshaw gestured with both hands as the Boulder raised his weapon.

The guards spread around the platform. There was nowhere to run. No opening.

Adan climbed the stairs at a snail's pace.

The hefty auctioneer began his speech. "And now we have a young man who, I'm told, is special," he roared with enthusiasm. "It's all been very hush-hush, but I'm sure we're in for a treat. Though item number 743 is not Gifted, he's said to be interesting to look at. Shall we have a look?"

All Adan saw were the wooden planks before him.

The auctioneer's heavy footfalls came closer. "Well, let's see you then, boy." He rubbed his hands together, chortling. "Don't keep us waiting."

The crowd quieted. Then agitated muttering drifted through them.

"Now," the captain whispered. "Now. Take your shirt off now."

The Boulder began walking up the stairs.

"Uh-oh. Looks like he needs persuasion," the auctioneer sang merrily.

The crowd jeered.

Adan shuffled farther from the guard and closer to the platform edge. He reached up as if to pull his hood back as he prepared to jump, make a run for it, and hope for the best. Three, two—

An explosion split the still air. Adan crouched to keep from stumbling as the earth moved. At the opposite end of the courtyard, flame and smoke lit the sky behind the gathered crowd. Auction-goers ducked and screamed and then shifted into chaos. Every head turned away from where Adan stood forgotten on the stage.

Going with his first instinct, he took a running leap off the platform. The guards didn't even notice. He sprinted for the second alley, bumping into frantic people as he ran, only to find a bottleneck at the entrance.

The auctioneer bellowed for calm but trailed off with a gurgle. An arrow jutted from his beefy neck. The screams around Adan spun into a full panic. Black-clad figures stood upon the rooftops shouting and firing into the crowd. Few arrows found a mark, but some of the auction-goers drew arms and shot back. Flames licked the sky behind them.

More dark figures darted in and out of the retreating crowd. They yelled out, increasing the panic, but few engaged with their weapons unless to defend themselves.

Were these the mysterious rebels?

Near the platform, the Boulder brandished his electric weapon, shocking anyone who ventured within reach. The Strength Wielder hadn't yet noticed Adan, who shouldered his way toward the alley. One of the rebels jumped from a low overhang. The Boulder caught him midjump with a shock to the hip, sending him sprawling onto the ground. Looming over the limp body, he poked at the rebel, delivering wave after wave of electric agony. Then a new threat emerged, and the Boulder moved on to his next victim.

Did the other assailants know their comrade was down? Should Adan do something? No, this was his one chance. The crowd was starting to push through, and soon he'd be able to run far away. Across the courtyard, the castle doors burst open, and soldiers poured into the space. The rebels seemed to melt away. They disappeared into the night, leaving one of their men behind.

Adan blinked. The grounded man's foot twitched.

The fallen bird.

Guards would arrive to gobble up this creature. The path to freedom lay ahead. But… the blackbird. Growling, he hustled forward, slinging the stranger into a fireman's carry. The rebel was lighter than Adan had imagined and not wholly unconscious. He ran down the now-open alleyway. As he emerged onto the street, he slid to a stop.

Soldiers swarmed the road.

He slunk into the shadows.

What do I do?

He wouldn't be able to carry this person very far. People continued to stream past, not paying him any attention. A narrow door burst open on the wall behind Adan, and two people sprinted out carrying buckets. Having no other options, Adan hauled his load inside and closed the door. He stood in what must be the back room of one of the businesses lining the courtyard. Mercifully, it was empty. Boxes piled around, but it was too open and exposed for proper hiding. He spotted another door in the corner and rushed to open it—a broom closet. Intending to drop his load and run, Adan lowered the stranger's feet to the ground. Shouts echoed in the alley. Maybe it was better to stay.

As sweat dripped down his back, he wrapped one of the assailant's arms around his neck to hold him up. Then he closed the door, shutting them into the cramped space. With no room to spread out, it was almost completely dark.

Great. Now what?

He should've left the stranger. Now they'd both be caught. How could he have been so stupid?

To offset the weight, Adan put an arm around the stranger's waist— around a slim, feminine waist. The dark figure groaned, trying to stand. A very girlish sound.

Adan's brow rose. A girl. She coughed and reached up, probably to pull the cloth from her face.

"Shhh." Adan mimicked the best Inevan accent he could muster. "They're still out there."

She stiffened and tried to step back but met the wall.

"Hey, it's okay. We're hiding in a closet. You got knocked out, and soldiers showed up."

"Wait… what?" She eased her arm from around his neck and stood on her own two feet. He let go of her waist and dropped his hands to his side.

"We're hiding. A guard got you with the shock stick."

She sucked in a sharp breath. "Oh yeah… right. Um, thank you. Who are you? You sound familiar."

"Nobody. Just someone who wants to get far, far away from here. How about you?"

She snorted as if to say, "If you don't tell me, I won't tell you."

Fine. Next question. "Are you with the rebels?"

Laughter rushed out, making her shoulders tremble. "If I were with the rebels, I wouldn't be likely to tell you, would I?"

Was that a yes?

They listened. Shouts still echoed from the alley and beyond.

She sighed, her breath fluttering against his chest. She was rather tall, but still half a head shorter than him. Their bodies and faces were only inches apart in the cramped space. "Where are we exactly?" she asked.

"The back room of one of the buildings surrounding the courtyard. I'm not sure what it's called, but it's not The Den."

She laughed again. Adan liked her laugh. It reminded him of someone, though he couldn't decide who. "I should say not. It's probably ash by now."

Right, the fire. He shivered at an image of a dead bear crumbling to ash. He smiled in the dark. He could see the future. The captain would search high and low for him now. His lips turned down. That would make it even harder to escape.

She shuffled her feet. "Do you know this area?"

"No. Not really."

She sighed again. "Me either, but I've looked over several maps. Do you know what's beyond this building and across the back street?"

"No."

"Really? You don't live around here?"

"No."

She seemed to be growing more suspicious. "Uh-huh. What were you doing here then? Buying humans?" He stiffened, and she noticed. "That's it, isn't it? You're hiding because you're afraid of the king's guards."

"No." He jerked back a little too forcefully. "I wasn't buying anyone. I was the person being bought."

A pause. "Oh... I, um, I'm sorry. I didn't think of that. Wait. You could've gotten away, but you hid me instead?"

"Well, yeah. I guess I did."

"I don't know what to say. Thank you." Under her breath, she added, "Humans are so unpredictable."

"What?"

"Oh, nothing."

Adan opened his mouth to say something else, but she touched his waist, grabbing at his shirt. "Shhh."

They listened. The backroom door banged open, and sets of feet pounded on the floor.

"Search everywhere." It was Captain Curtshaw. They'd both be caught. What would happen to her? Adan was probably safe. The captain had to see his value now. No telling what would happen to the girl.

He put his hand on the small of her back and drew her close. He leaned down until his lips were almost touching her ear. She smelled of lavender. In the quietest voice he could manage, he said, "Listen. I'll be okay. He'll take me back in. But not you. You stay here. I'll distract them."

She tipped her head, whispering in his ear. "I can't let you do that. If it weren't for me, you'd be long gone."

He *had* thought of that. But… "You have to. Just pass along a message if you run into any of those rebels. There are both Gifted and non-Gifted prisoners held in the castle by Captain Curtshaw."

Her cheek brushed the stubble on his. "Okay, I'll pass it on. I mean… if I run into any, I'll tell them."

Adan smiled, turning toward the door. "You do that."

"Wait." She grabbed his shirt again. "Can you think of a way the rebels might contact anyone inside the castle?"

The voices were getting closer. They were almost out of time.

"The main sleeping quarters are on the third floor overlooking this courtyard. There are several windows. If I'm caught, I'll tie a cloth to the bars of my window that's higher up. I can't think of anything else. Maybe you will." He turned them in a tight circle. "Back into this corner, and when I open the door, don't move." He felt, rather than saw, her nod.

Someone was walking this way.

He cracked the door and then peeked over his shoulder. The rebel was in shadow, but he didn't miss her bright eyes go wide under a low hood. Locks of golden hair escaped around a beautiful face. Something like shock passed over her features.

Oh, right. The weird blue eyes.

Oh well. He gave her a parting smile and pulled his hood low over his brow. She opened her mouth to say something, but he put a finger to his lips. He opened the door and, leaving it cracked, sprinted for the exit. Shouts and heavy footfalls thundered after him.

29

Evie stood statue-like in the closet. Her mortal heart pounded in her chest. It was him, Adan. In the closet. With her.

How could she be so stupid? She'd thought she was the only one to mask a bad accent successfully. She touched her face where his cheek had brushed against hers and stopped the ramblings of her frantic brain. Shouts echoed in the alley. A voice yelled in agony. Had the guards gotten their hands on him?

The footsteps receded, and all was quiet. She put her head in her hands and replayed their exchange.

Adan had saved her. He had picked her up and carried her to safety rather than running away to his own freedom.

This both irritated and thrilled her.

He'd been so close in this tiny closet. His hand on her waist. His cheek pressed against hers. His lips at her ear.

Snap out of it. Think.

If the guards recaptured Adan, then the rebels could find a way to rescue him and the others from the castle. *If* they kept the Dreamer around long enough.

She'd been in the closet for several long minutes before it occurred to her that, had she known it was him, she could've killed him and been done. She could've taken up a drop of his blood and disappeared toward the mountains. The golden dagger in her boot mockingly dug into her ankle. She could've made it to the portal by noon tomorrow and left Sector Six behind forever.

Then, uninvited, an image of Adan appeared across her mind. He'd glanced back as he prepared to create a diversion to save *her*. She'd caught that flash of blue eyes and the crooked half-smile.

Closing her eyes, she shook her head. She was lamenting a missed murder opportunity of the one who'd saved her. A wretched feeling weighed on her heart.

I'm ready to be free of this mortal body.

There was no recognition in his eyes. Her skin and hair were different now, and she'd worn a half mask almost their entire time in Sector Five. He wouldn't know her. Another unpleasant feeling twisted her gut.

The more she thought about it, the less she wanted to tell Sam and the others she'd found their friend. What if they knew she was the one to kill him? It would be better to hide her informant's identity. Sam was already suspicious and would get in her way, but she could lead them to Adan later, and then make it look as if anyone could have finished him off. The boys would be devastated, but they'd have closure. They wouldn't search for him indefinitely. Yes, she'd keep Adan a secret for now. In the meantime, she could help the rebels save as many prisoners as possible. This would be her redemption of sorts.

Wiping the sweat from her brow and hardening her resolve, she thought of the clean Control Room and her promotion to Guardian. She checked her watch. Fourteen days left. No problem.

Faraway voices drifted from outside, but the storage room was quiet. Testing weak legs, she crept into the cluttered back room. She shed her jacket and pulled the black face covering from around her neck, exposing her light-blue shirt. Tossing the jacket into the broom closet, she flipped the black cloth, unmasking a pale-orange pattern. She used this as a headscarf to hide her light hair. The darkness would shield her freckles, and no one would mark her as a Huldan.

She peeked out the back door. Shouts bounced down the alley from what must be the courtyard, and long shadows flickered across the cobbled ground. Humans darted around in the firelight. She stepped into the alleyway and closed the door. No one noticed.

The other end of this street was quiet and dark. She should walk away and disappear into the blackness, but she hesitated. How would she know if the guards had detained Adan? What if he'd escaped?

Making up her mind, she slunk along the dark wall until she rounded the corner and emerged into the fire's dancing glow. The courtyard was in chaos. A crowd had gathered to watch The Den burn, and those closest passed water buckets. The blaze was almost under control.

She stepped in a small circle, searching every face until the castle doors burst open. Four men herded a hooded figure toward the fire. Adan, his eyes lost in shadow, clutched his side and walked with a slight limp. Was blood dripping from his nose?

This was because of her—because he'd saved her.

But if they recaptured him, why were they leading him back out here?

She squeezed into the line to pass buckets. From here, she was close enough to hear one of the men—the oldest. He tapped a flat piece of wood at his feet.

"How did you know this would happen? Are you in league with the rebels?"

"I told you. I dreamt it. I've been dreaming of the bear and the blackbirds for days. And only last night, I dreamed that the birds killed the bear. The bear crumbled to ash. Besides, I'm not from here. How could I be working with anyone?"

The man folded his arms and paced, shooting glances down at the charred tavern sign.

"Because of the auction, this place has been one of the most profitable businesses in the city. I was to sign papers to buy this tavern this evening."

His gaze bore into Adan, but Adan kept his head down and his eyes hidden. "And did you buy it, sir?"

"I did not. Because of what you said, I decided to wait."

"You told me I was being ridiculous."

The man smoothed his salt-and-pepper hair back, but only succeeded in making a mess of it. "I did think so until you told me what you saw." Light from the burning tavern danced across his face. "When you said it, I remembered having a similar dream last night. I dreamed of the bear and the birds. Only I forgot about it until you mentioned it." He slashed a hand through the air, then slammed it into his open palm. "I've changed my mind. You will stay."

Adan's posture sagged. "Yes, sir."

"Take him to his room."

When the captain waved them away, they shuffled back to the castle. Evie passed buckets until Adan and his escorts were well away from the fire. Then she approached the blackened sign. She nudged the charred plank of wood with her toe. The Den was branded near the top, and below that, the bear's head carved its way across the surface. A red bird with open wings flew across the face. It was little more than a splatter of crimson.

The rebels, at least those who'd been invited along on this raid, had practiced drawing this falcon modeled after Morris's marked arm. It was to be painted in places across the courtyard. The rebels were making themselves known, claiming they were more than a myth and wouldn't stand for discrimination against the Gifted.

Had Adan dreamed about this raid? This fire?

Evie smiled. The Dreamer had seen them coming.

She nudged the sign with her toe again. The red paint had dripped into the bear's eyes, making them appear as if they'd been plucked away.

What else had Adan seen while he was sleeping?

After leaving the blazing fire behind, Evie crept toward rebel headquarters. Hidden in a warehouse basement, it was not too far from the apartment Morris continued to loan Evie and her new Sector Five friends.

It appeared that Morris trusted them, however reluctantly. They'd all spent the last days planning the raid on the auction as well as asking around about a blue-eyed boy.

With Sam, Evie had searched Inevah for word of Adan in case he wasn't at the castle. They'd separated and worked their way through the neighborhoods. Lena even joined them when she wasn't at school or headquarters.

Because no lights lit the Inevan streets, the city shut down after dark. Evie had spent hours with Lena and the boys at their borrowed apartment. They talked, played games, and bantered well into the night. At first, she shared little but listened with fascination to their lively conversations.

One evening, when they thought no one was listening, Sam and Garran meandered into an argument. Who was worse: Garran's wealthy parents who thought nothing short of perfection was acceptable, or Sam's who were too busy working to come around.

Playing cards at the table, Lena and Evie glanced up when Sam said, "At least your parents come to our competitions. And you get twice as much spending money as me."

Garran rolled his eyes. "At least your parents don't freeze your accounts when you don't win a gold medal."

Evie hoped Lena wasn't paying attention to this ridiculous exchange.

Evie didn't know much about Garran's mom and dad, but she did have a vague knowledge of Sam's. From what she could tell, they worked hard to make the money for their son to be Guardian trained. "At least you have parents," she whispered after Lena had descended the stairs. "Sounds like your parents love you and want what's best for you. Lena's parents were killed trying to escape from Sodorrah. She was born in captivity." Evie regarded Sam. "Is it possible your parents are busy working hard to pay for your lifestyle?"

Sam didn't respond.

Later, Lena asked Evie about her family, but Evie had shrugged. "I don't have parents either." A bond had formed between them after that.

During the evenings, the girls often teamed up in Guardian Quest, and during the day, they partnered in group weapons training. At night, while Lena returned to Morris's place, Evie visited Nolan the Dreamer in her mind's eye as she pored over *One's Raining Fire* in the dim candlelight. Never before had she read anything from an actual bound book. She relished the crisp pages. But at these times, her human body somehow relaxed, and her mind threatened to drift into oblivion. She'd jerk awake and demand it to stay alert. But, still, her lids grew heavy, her head bobbed, and then, when she could fight it no longer, she'd sleep with the book still propped before her.

Fight training had become one of Evie's favorite things about Sector Six—gritty, no-rules fighting. While learning new techniques, she shared her knowledge. True to his word, Chase helped Evie teach Lena the knife fighting basics.

The rebels were loud and boisterous. Often they raised their voices, but smiles and laughter came just as freely. And Evie was growing accustomed to these humans.

Now, she had much to tell them.

When the hideout came into view, she meandered down an alleyway as Lena had taught her. She scanned the warehouse in a crowded neighborhood on the Arvad side of the river and waited until the street was clear. The first level housed all manner of discarded items. If anyone were to search it, all they'd find was a hoarder's amount of junk.

The quiet space appeared unoccupied.

She stopped in front of a shabby bookcase and reached between two volumes. She pulled three times on a piece of twine that wound behind the books, down the wall, and into the basement. After a moment, she looked down at a tiny mirror on the bottom shelf and waved. The mirror joined a series of mirrors giving the rebels in the basement a decent view of her. The barely visible eye in the glass widened and disappeared.

Then the bookcase swung open.

"It's Evaniah. Guys, she's back."

She peered into a rectangular hole in the ground. Sam's face came into view, and something like relief and anger first slackened, then twisted up his features.

Evie stepped forward and descended a long ladder to a vast bustling room. The original entrance to the long-forgotten basement had been removed and built over years ago.

Her legs wobbled when her feet hit the stone floor. She'd made it back.

The relief didn't last, though, as angry faces scowled at her.

Only Lena smiled and yanked her into a hug. "Charles said a Strength Wielder took you out. They lost sight of you after that. What happened?"

"That's not the right question." Morris shouldered through the crowd. The band of rebels made a wide space for him. "What were you doing there? I told you to stay here. I *ordered* you to stay here."

"I know, but—"

"There's no *but*. If I give an order, it's followed. If that's not how you like to work, then you can leave and never come back."

"I wanted to help. I *can* help."

"That may be, but given how quickly we put this together, I wanted only the most experienced people out there. Your inexperience could get people killed. Charles was injured because he left his post to try to save you."

Evie glanced at Charles, who wore a bandage over one arm.

In all her existence, no one had ever yelled at her like this. She hadn't meant to do anything wrong. Her impulse to go where she wasn't allowed had been strong. Like a day not long ago—only nine days ago—when she'd been in the Control Room fighting that same impulse. She lost the battle with herself then, and she lost it today as well. Neither time had she considered what her actions would cost others.

Tears pooled in her eyes, and she willed them away. *Watchers don't cry.*

Morris sent the rebels back to work, and only Sam, Lena, and Charles remained.

"Are you okay?" Evie asked Charles in a whisper.

"Only a scratch."

"It could've been much worse." Morris folded his falcon-inked arm over the other across his chest.

She swallowed hard, still looking at Charles. "I'm sorry."

Morris jammed his hands in his pockets. "So? What happened?"

She cleared her throat. "A Strength Wielder attacked me with his shock stick."

"Shock stick?"

"Yeah, the weapons they were using. It sends an electric pulse into the body. It's unpleasant, but there's no lasting damage. He shocked me several times, so I passed out."

Charles scratched his chin. "Where do they get these strange weapons?"

"I don't know. But we need to find out." Morris loomed over her. "So, you were unconscious. What then?"

"I woke up in a broom closet with a stranger. He'd picked me up and hidden me away in one of the shops."

"A stranger?" Morris tensed, letting his arms drop. "Evaniah, were you followed here?"

"I don't think so."

"Did you consider the person may have been playing you to follow you?"

"Listen, it wasn't one of the king's soldiers, and it wasn't anyone attending the auction. He was a prisoner… the one on the auction block when The Den blew."

Morris pressed his lips into a fine line, but Evie plunged on. "He created a diversion for me but was recaptured. And not by the king's soldiers. After things quieted, these guards—these Strength Wielders—escorted him into the castle."

"Charles, grab a few people and run the perimeter in case she was tailed."

"There's more." Evie shoved her hair behind her ears as Charles left. "People are being held in the castle by Captain Curt-something."

"Curtshaw."

"Yeah, that's it."

"The three prisoners we rescued said as much."

"Prisoners?"

"Yes. We built the entire operation around a diversion to allow us to get prisoners out of the holding cage." Morris turned haunted eyes to the floor. "If we'd started earlier, we could've saved more. But they were sold and are beyond us now."

So much responsibility rested on this man's shoulders.

Sam, who still glared at Evie, fisted his hand. "The prisoners say they haven't seen anyone with blue eyes, but there's a boy with strange marks on one arm. He's there. Adan's in the castle." He pounded the fist into his palm. "I know it."

She forced a smile. "Excellent."

They didn't know her savior was the boy in question. She stretched her muscles and slid her sheathed dagger from her boot.

Glancing at Morris, she said, "The boy who saved me is going to tie a cloth outside his window. This is your chance. If I can contact him again, we can formulate a plan working with the prisoners on the inside."

Morris's brow rose.

With a little clap, Lena grinned. "That does change things."

"He'll trust me. I need to be the one to do it."

Morris ran his hands through his hair. "Okay. Scope it out. We'll start working out what we need from him. Did he give you his name?"

"No. And I didn't give him mine."

His regard sized her up. "Will you need backup?"

Sam shifted, looking hopeful, but it wouldn't do for him to see Adan.

The dagger and its sheath heavier in her hand, Evie shook her head. "I should work alone."

"Okay, then. See if you can make contact." Morris strode away.

Sam watched her with his usual suspicion. "You should've told me you were going to follow them. We didn't even know you were gone. I would've gone with you." He held her gaze, then, lowering his head, walked back toward Ben and Chase where they were setting up to play Guardian Quest.

Lena patted Evie's shoulder. "A rebel within the rebels. I like it." Her green eyes twinkled, and Evie forced a laugh.

"That's me, I guess."

"Just don't let it get you killed. I don't have many friends, you know." Lena gestured toward Ben. "Want to play?"

"Not this time."

Lena sauntered away.

A human considered her a friend?

Evie slipped the dagger from its sheath. Turning the blade, she imagined plunging it into Adan.

Grimacing, she caught her reflection in the polished metal. Surely that couldn't be the Watcher staring back. This mortal was stricken— pulled apart like the tingling space between two portals. In that frozen time where one was seized between two worlds, yet belonging to neither.

Who are you? the girl seemed to ask.

"I'm an immortal," Evie whispered back. "And I *will* do what it takes to be a Guardian."

30

Evie gripped the castle wall, fatigue plaguing her mortal muscles. Maybe this wasn't such a good idea.

Yesterday, after sleeping well into the afternoon, she'd returned to the castle. Pale yellow fabric flapped in the breeze—outside a very, very high window.

Now, in the dark, high above the cobbled courtyard, she questioned her plan. Her climbing experience was limited to the training room. But how different was it, really? So, hand over hand, she hauled herself upward. Her feet found purchase on the uneven stone as her fingers dug into the spaces between them.

She rounded a corner, completing what she hoped was the trickiest stretch of the climb. And a low breath slid from her lungs. She hazarded a glance downward. Lights in windows dotted the blackness beneath her, but none reached high enough to touch her.

She continued, ticking off the points of her plan: get Adan to provide maps and locations for Morris to rescue the others, gain Adan's trust, and then lure him to the window and slit his throat. No problem. Like a Watcher blending in with humans. Easy.

Her heart warred, but he was only a human. Killing Adan would protect the other Sector Five boys.

Completing her task would give them a chance to get back home without meeting the Death Guardians the Sector Six Control Room had threatened to send.

If only she could squash this human side—this emotional side. No other Watcher would have such trouble carrying out this task. Her makeup was so unlike any other Guardian or Watcher she must've been Jesiah's greatest mistake.

She was almost to the marked window when her left hand slipped. She yelped and held tight with her right while digging in with her toes. Her loose hand found purchase, and she closed her eyes, breathing deeply, muscles trembling.

"Hello?" came a low whisper from the window above her head.

"It's me." She clung to the wall and climbed another few stones until her face was below the window.

"How can I help you?" His arm snaked out the window as if to grab her and haul her up.

As much as it would help right about now, he was no Strength Wielder.

"You can't. Just give me another second."

His arm disappeared as her toes found a jagged stone to hold her weight. Clinging to the metal bars with both hands, she drew herself up and looked in the window.

Her breath caught. Adan was grinning, that single dimple catching a shadow on his cheek. His dark curls fell almost to his eyes. She couldn't help but smile back.

"You made it. I'm glad you didn't fall to your death." He cringed, appearing to regret his choice of words.

Evie laughed and peeked below her. A mistake. "Not yet, anyway." Once she'd settled her grip, she relaxed. A candle burned near the window, and dim light revealed brown eyes. This explained why the other prisoners hadn't seen a blue-eyed boy.

Adan, frowning at her confusion, stepped closer. "Are you okay?"

"Yeah, it's just, you look… different."

His face shifted into understanding—not entirely relieved. "Oh yeah, I was… wearing eye coverings when we met. They make my eyes blue."

"Oh." She nodded, understanding more than he knew. "So, are you okay? What happened after you left me?"

"Oh, it was great. The Strength Wielders tackled me to the ground. Cracked a few ribs."

"I'm sorry." She really was.

"I'm okay. A friend healed me."

His head jerked toward the door. "Get down," he hissed, moving back into the room.

Evie shimmied to the side so her face was out of view. The door creaked, and silence held. Then Adan said, "What do you want? Does the captain need me?"

"I heard voices," a deep voice replied.

"You know, hearing voices is a sign of dementia."

"A sign of wha—" Then louder, the stranger said, "I heard you talking."

"Would you like to look under my bed? I'm the only one here. Is there a rule about talking to myself?"

Another pause. "There is now. Go to bed."

The door slammed.

"You still there?" A low whisper from the window brought Evie shuffling back.

"Nope. Fell to my death." When Adan granted her a grin, stupidly, she grinned back.

"We better keep it down. I'm not allowed to talk to myself anymore."

"I heard. That's a shame because you seem like you'd be good company."

He flashed his dimple again.

Evie shook herself. *Back to business.*

"Listen, I'm not going be able to hang on out here much longer." She shifted her grip. "We're working on a plan to get you out of here. What I need is a map of the castle. Guard and captive locations, entrances, exits, and anything else helpful. I brought paper if you don't have any."

"I don't."

She tried to maneuver her shoulder bag to her front. It was more difficult than she'd imagined.

"Let me help."

She hesitated. "Okay. Grab this strap on my shoulder and pull it around until you can reach in." As he came closer, she was aware of the blade strapped to her hip. All she had to do was grab it. She wouldn't have the information for Morris, but she'd be done with this adventure. She could go home.

Flattening herself against the jagged stones, she grasped tighter with her right hand to free her left. Adan reached out the window and brushed a stray lock of hair from her neck. She froze. His eyes met hers. He pulled at the strap.

Just do it. Her fingers twitched toward her dagger. *Be done.*

He opened the bag and withdrew the supplies. His face was very near now. She stared at him. His dark lashes almost brushed his golden cheek as he examined the rolled paper and pencil. He caught her staring, and they gazed at each other. Did he sense the tension within her?

It would be wrong not to get the information needed to rescue the others. She could wait a little longer.

His eyebrows drew together, forming a crease between his eyes. "You look familiar."

"Oh… I get that a lot. Guess I have a common face."

She tried to make him smile, but his features remained thoughtful.

He took a step back. "That's definitely not it."

Evie flushed. "Have you met many Huldans, then?"

"Not really. I guess there's no way we've met before."

"Doubtful."

But his brow didn't relax. "What's your name?"

"Don't worry about my name. Tell the others we're going to think of a way to get them out. I'm sure there are people they want to get back home to—people who are looking for them."

"Must be nice to have someone looking for you."

"You don't think anyone is looking for you?"

"Oh, they probably are. They're just looking in the wrong place."

Evie wanted to encourage him—wanted to tell him his brothers were searching in the right place and she'd help him get home. But that was a lie, and she couldn't force it from her mouth.

Wondering if he would answer, she asked, "What's *your* name?"

"No way. If you don't tell me yours, I'm not telling you mine."

She smiled. "Fine."

Her fingers were starting to sweat. "I better go while I still have strength. We'll find a way to get your friends out. Be patient. This will take careful planning. I'll be back in a few days to see if the map is ready."

"Okay." He glanced down at his new paper and then back at her. "I look forward to it."

She slunk away down the wall and cringed. Pathetically, she, too, looked forward to it.

Traitorous human heart.

31

Adan fell onto his bed, exhausted. Though Captain Curtshaw had sent him to bed early, hoping to get more useful dreams out of him, his daily schedule was intense. What with training and testing under the Sodorran Joromy's watchful eye, performing his menial tasks, and now joining the captain in his office, Adan was weary. Not to mention, for over a week since Evie's first visit, he stayed up most of the night drawing maps and writing out information the rebels might need.

The captain grilled Adan with business questions. Should he do this? Or should he do that? A few dreams may have helped the captain's business dealings, but Adan had no idea what advice to give. Luckily, he'd taken business classes back in Sector Five and was able to speak to the man knowledgeably.

Though Captain Curtshaw had doted on Adan, he was growing frustrated. He had, however, learned Adan was good at math. Plenty of others back home were better than him at this kind of thing. But here… here he was some kind of genius. Seemed they rated less emphasis on education in Sector Six. Adan had been keeping the captain's books. Unexciting as it was, it did allow him a good look around. Not that he'd found anything useful, though his golden-spined book still sat on the top shelf behind the captain's desk.

Now, Adan fidgeted with his blanket. *I should get up before I fall asleep.* He still needed to sketch the atrium he'd run to during his escape attempt. He wanted to finish before the girl arrived.

His lips turned up as he thought of her. She'd scaled the wall three times since her first appearance, each time asking for specific information about the castle or the guards or the captain. They plotted and planned together, hoping to discover the perfect opportunity to escape. The two of them were the whole of the communication channel between the rebels in the city and Adan's friends in the castle—the Inside Rebels as James called them.

The rebel girl still seemed shocked Adan had given up his escape opportunity to save her. What he didn't tell her was he was reasonably sure she would've died had he not stepped in. He had changed the future by changing his actions. In his dreams, he'd stood by and watched the golden-streaked bird's demise. But in real life, he had stepped in. He might not have noticed her or cared if he hadn't already dreamed of that moment.

He was also certain it was what he'd been meant to do. Whether for good or ill, he didn't yet know.

He did know, however, when the girl would make the climb to his window. Her bird form would appear in his dreams the night before. Adan, so lonely in this tiny room, found himself keeping her until she insisted she needed to go, leaving him all alone again. Of course, she *was* the one hanging off the side of a wall.

He couldn't shake the feeling that he'd met her before. She rarely talked about herself, though he'd tried time and again to pry information from her lips. She'd smile her infuriating smile and change the subject. He told her all about Garran and the man who brought him here, though he didn't mention the portal or Sector Five. She'd asked him to describe his kidnapper, but of course, he couldn't. He'd never seen the man.

The rebel often asked about his life before he came here, and he said more than he intended. Sometimes, when he asked her a question, she seemed as if she wanted to answer but would think better of it. It was maddening. The mystery of her kept him guessing, and she was on his mind far too often.

He sat up, listening for movement. Nothing. He'd yet to get used to this—the silence. No ambient street noises, no random sirens, no snoring boys in the next bunk. He'd longed for privacy in Uzziah's apartment. But now, he wished for that crowded bedroom. Sadness pressed on him, but he pushed it away. For Ben, he'd stay strong.

Adan moved to the desk, but after an hour of sketching, he could no longer hold his eyes open. He settled his forehead on the wooden surface to rest.

His thoughts returned to the girl. She still hadn't given him her name, though he'd given in and revealed his on their second meeting.

Nights ago, she surprised him by asking, "What does one wear to the Festival of Alvar?"

"They celebrate that here?" he blurted before catching himself. "In Inevah, I mean. I… thought it wasn't common in this area."

"It's in a few days, and I hear it's a big deal. I guess you can't help me with my wardrobe choice?"

"No, I guess not." He smiled. How strange that people celebrated the same holiday in both sectors.

"Have you ever been a part of the celebration anywhere?"

"Yes."

She studied the window sill before glancing up through her lashes. "What was it like?"

"Well, people take off work early. There's plenty of food and music. People dress up in light-colored clothing." He shrugged. "It's pretty fun."

"Sounds fun. What did you do last year?"

"Well, it wasn't a year ago. We celebrated about two weeks ago in my city. I hung out with my brother. And a… friend."

It had felt like she was fishing for more than festival information when she'd pretended to examine the bars before her. "Oh? Who was the friend?"

The corner of his mouth lifted. "Her name was Evie. I'd only just met her."

"So, you spent the entire festival with your brother and someone you'd just met?"

"Yeah, pretty lame, I guess. She hadn't had a chance to find out about my flaws."

Her golden eyes shone. "Hmm… Cryptic." She opened her mouth to ask something else but shut it again.

"What?"

"Why did you hang out with this girl all evening? Did you… feel sorry for her?"

He'd expected her to ask him what his flaws were. She rarely said anything he expected. "Why do you want to know about a person I spent an evening with once? Obviously, I haven't seen her again." His voice turned bitter, though not at her. "That was the night I was brought here." Eons ago.

"I don't know." She lowered her head. "Something to talk about, I guess. You almost done?"

"Almost." Adan set back into his drawing of the practice yard, labeling the location of each station. But he wanted to tell her about Evie.

"I hung out with her because she was fun to be around. She was nice to Ben and nice to me." Something warmed him as his lips spread. "She couldn't dance." The girl looked offended as if he'd just insulted all women, so he fished to redeem himself. "She… she was beautiful. But most of all, I had thought we had a lot in common. We'd read the same books, and we both liked weapons."

Her eyes had gone wide. "What do you mean *had* thought you had a lot in common? You don't anymore?"

"I'm not sure. It might've all been an act." He paused, the paper blurring before him. "Sometimes, I think she may have had something to do with my kidnapping."

Her fingers squeezed around the bars. "What makes you say that?"

"I never saw her there, and Garran handed me over to the stranger. But it's strange, isn't it? I meet this girl who's willing to hang out with me and my little brother all evening. She hides her Guardian's eyes the whole time, and then that night, I'm brought here."

The rebel at the window seemed at a loss for words—confused.

"Oh, right." He waved a hand. "You guys don't have Guardians. Never mind."

His heartache started anew. "I left Ben with her. That was the last time I saw him. I left him with a stranger who may have been responsible for my kidnapping." He put his head in his hands. "I'll never forgive myself if something's happened to him."

She'd tried to smile. "I bet your brother's fine." She sounded so confident. "He's worried about you, but I'm thinking he's safe."

"I hope you're right."

"I'm… I'm sorry for everything you've been through. Truly, I am."

<<<>>>

Adan's feet scuffled on the worn path running through the never-ending forest of his mind. So much for staying awake.

A sound drew his attention. The golden-streaked bird rested on a high branch above his head.

"Hello, little rebel," he whispered. "See you soon."

Ahead, Evie, dark hair flowing over a white dress, glanced up at the sound of his voice as if he had called out to her. This time she was wearing her half mask rather than carrying it. Long ribbons flowed eerily behind her like the slow-moving tentacles of some lazy sea creature. She stood near the snowy tree, and its white flakes drifted across the path around her. The strange girl lifted a palm, and one rested on her outstretched hand.

They gazed at each other. Her golden eyes caught the low sunlight as it filtered through the snow-covered tree. Then she continued up the path as usual. She'd stopped calling his name some time ago. Adan peeked up at the bird to see what she made of this strange girl, but the bird was gone.

Ben tumbled from the trees, feet crunching on the dry leaves. Worry etched his features, and for the first time, he spoke aloud in Adan's dream. "She's been deceived. Adan, I'm scared."

The boy took a knee and bowed before him. When Adan started forward to comfort him, Ben melted back into the trees. Sam, Chase, Garran, and the others waited for him there. A strange girl with hair like flames loomed behind them in the shadowy depth. She watched Ben.

They moved away and out of sight, and Adan tried to follow. Something pulled at his leg. A broad silver band circled his ankle. It wasn't like the one he wore in the waking world.

Frustrated, Adan huffed. When he turned back, a wooden structure spanned the path—a platform holding a single sturdy block. The block had a circular indent across its top, and a long curved blade leaned against its side. An executioner's block? A mesh sack lay atop the block where the guilty party's head might rest to await death. It looked to be filled with... what? Some sort of fruit? Juices from the fruit dripped onto the surface, creating a dark-red stain.

A circle of gold, like an enormous glittering ring, rolled over the platform and landed at Adan's feet. A crown. Its polish faded, and it tarnished before his eyes. James, who'd never before appeared in Adan's dreams, stepped around the platform and picked up the crown. The drab finish morphed into brilliant gold—James's Gift at work.

The Healer tossed the crown overhead, deftly catching it again. He set it on the wooden structure, which was now a sturdy throne. James walked away, disappearing into the trees.

Now, the path was clear, but for the archway several paces ahead. Nothing Adan did ever changed this part. He'd been dreaming of some version of this for months, years maybe. Nothing kept it from coming.

The archway began to glow with its mysterious light, and his reflection rippled on the surface of the shimmering nothingness between worlds. Though his features were blurred, they moved like water in the translucent center. His likeness held a knife. He drew his arm back and let the blade fly. The golden blade plunged deep into Adan's chest, this time near his shoulder.

Though he felt no pain, his fear was real. Blood spilled down his front, and he fell to his knees and onto his back. Blinding golden light surrounded him, and a figure appeared above his body, features lost in silhouette. His assassin reached to grab the knife hilt, and a tear landed on Adan's face. His hands began to tingle. When the figure moved away, the golden bird was back, and she threw her head back and squawked into the sky.

"Adan?"

Adan sat up, fighting the bedsheets tangled around his legs. Clutching his chest, he felt his heart race.

I'm going to die.

If he didn't find a way to change the future, he'd perish at the end of a blade.

"Adan?" A hiss from the window. The barred window framed the rebel girl's worried face.

Great. Of course, she had to see him wake up from his nightmare like a child.

"Are you okay? Bad dream?"

Adan rubbed his face. "Yeah. Something like that."

Her brow drawn, the rebel took him in. She opened her mouth to speak, but nothing came out. She closed it again as her gaze rested on his hands. The marks that glowed during his dreams were only just fading. He hid his fists in his lap and sat on the bed, facing away from her.

"You're Gifted," she said.

He started to deny it, but no point now. The girl had already seen.

"What's your Gift?"

"It's complicated."

When she didn't say anything, he put his thumbs back in his sleeves and shifted. She was watching him, but she didn't pry.

"I have news. We've decided to carry out the plan during the festival."

He stood. "That's only four days away."

She glanced at the watch circling her wrist. "Lots to do between now and then."

He had to get his book and, more specifically, his photo back from Captain Curtshaw.

They went over the details, and he explained what he and his friends had in mind.

When they'd made their plans and there was nothing left to say, she hesitated at the window. He didn't want her to go, and perhaps she didn't want that either because she said, "Tell me about your family."

How much should he say?

Leaving out anything about Sector Five, he told her about Ben and Sam and the others—and about Uzziah and how Adan lived with him and not his parents.

When he finished, she said, "You seem angry now."

"Well, it's not the ideal situation, is it? But that's not what I'm thinking right now. I feel bitter—angry at them. No one prevented this. Of course, I'm mad at Garran. But where was Uzziah? Sam promised to come back and get me out of that basement, but he didn't."

Adan balled his fists. *Keep it together.*

The girl clutched the metal bars. "I'm not sure about Garran. It sounds like you two will have a lot to work out, but as for the others, you don't know what happened—why they were away? Maybe it was a good excuse, and maybe it wasn't. But whatever it was, I doubt they meant you any harm." She closed her eyes. "Someone wise once told me people who hold grudges are fools who put an invisible prison around themselves. Their freedom is in forgiveness. It won't do you or your family any good for you to hold onto this anger."

Adan quirked an eyebrow. Easier said than done. "That was a pretty speech."

She laughed. "I told you he is wise."

Maybe she was right. But Uzziah had arranged for him to be marked, and then everything had happened. Adan wouldn't be able to let that go easily.

They fell into an easy silence. With no reason for the girl to stay any longer, Adan searched for something to ask to keep her here, but she beat him to it.

"A moment ago, you sat up and grabbed your chest. What did you dream?"

He shrugged. No reason not to tell her. "I was dying from a knife wound."

She gasped, her soft lashes winging up over golden eyes. "Who..." She swallowed. "Who stabbed you?"

"I can't ever tell, but the blade is gold."

Her grip tightened, turning her knuckles white. "You dream this often?"

"Yeah. For years." He forced a small laugh. "But hey. It's just a dream, right?"

"Right."

Adan stood. "I have more drawings for you." He swept them into a pile and rolled them with care. He strode to the window and started to grab the handle of the girl's carry bag. The smell of lavender met him.

The rebel stiffened. She struggled with the strap, and Adan jerked his hand back.

"I've got it."

He stood perplexed, holding the papers until she pushed the bag through the bars. He put the drawings in and stepped back.

This felt familiar. Adan would think he had a friend, but then he'd do or say something strange to drive that person away. He'd learned not to talk about his dreams, but people still saw the otherness in him. Too many had seen him wake from a dream or talk while asleep.

When she wrestled the bag back out the window, she was all business again.

She met his eyes and hesitated. "Well, I better go." She started to shuffle back the way she had come.

"Wait. Don't go. Did I—"

"There are a million things to do. I do have to go. I'll try to return tomorrow or the next day for our final prep. Even if I don't make it, carry out your side of the plan. We'll be ready."

With that, she was gone, leaving him alone on his island—population, one.

<h1 style="text-align:center">32</h1>

Evie crept back through Inevah's shadows as meager light and soft voices slipped through the cracks of shut doors and curtained windows. Laughter erupted from these points of brightness, where families gathered after a hard day's work. The smell of bread and stew drifted on the breeze. She was no more than a lonely stranger traveling in the black between these happy pockets of light.

For days, she'd been pondering another option when it came to Adan. Could she make it through the Control Room portal if she didn't kill him, but rather stole a drop of his blood?

The more she met with him, the more feasible this plan became. The Sector Six Control Room wouldn't be happy, but this time, she could explain before the supervisor did anything drastic—like summon the Death Guardians. Jesiah and Krystopher were back from their travels. She could tell them about the other gifted humans as well as the Deceiver.

And maybe, just maybe, the boys would find the missing portal home.

But Adan had been dreaming of his demise at her hand. If she was on the verge of changing her plan, shouldn't his dreams reflect that? And what if he saw her face in his dream? Would he ever speak to her again?

Did it matter? It shouldn't. She should keep her distance from him. He was clouding her thoughts.

Shunting aside the decision-making for another day, she picked up the pace. As she rounded the next bend, almost to the rebel hideout, a strange sensation played against her hip. It stopped.

She paused, looking down at her bag. Just as she was beginning to think she'd imagined it, she felt it again—a faint vibration. Light illuminated the inside of her bag. She reached inside and grabbed

Joram's communicator, then nearly dropped it in the shock of seeing the words *Connection from Travel Coordinator Five* displayed across the smooth surface.

Breath quickening and hope rising, she ducked behind a stack of crates and clicked the Accept Connection icon. Her friend's face spread across the glossy screen. Joram's relieved smile was as welcome as a life preserver thrown to a drowning man.

"Hey, Evie. Miss me?"

Laughter slipped from her lungs as tears pricked her eyes. Refusing to let them fall, she said, "Joram, you have no idea how good it is to see a familiar face."

His rich voice lifted her heart like a slow sector sunrise. "I've been trying for weeks to reach you on the slim hope you still had my communicator."

"How are you doing this? Are you in the Control Room?"

"No, I was never able to find a way to connect from there. I'm in Sector Five. I finally figured out intersector communication."

"I can't believe it. You did it."

"I expected you would be back to the Control Room by now. What's taking so long?"

Her heart clenched. "Look, I know what I'm supposed to do, but I may have found another way. Joram, an intersector portal wasn't destroyed. That's how they all got here. There are others here from Sector Five. All they have to do is find it again. I can still get blood from the boy before they do, and I'll be able to get back home and explain everything. But I can't do that yet because Adan is locked up and I have to get him out. We have a plan to make it happen in four days."

Joram's eyebrows rose. "Wait, who's we… and who's Adan?"

Evie rolled her eyes. "The boy I'm to kill. And I'm working with some humans to rescue him."

"Humans? Are you crazy?" He rubbed his face. "Look, that sounds like a huge risk. You're almost out of time. Remember what I told you. Humans are unpredictable. Their unchecked emotions will be the death of you. How do you know they won't double-cross you or become a distraction? They have to know you're different. Do any of them suspect you?"

Evie glanced away from the screen. "Maybe."

"Might these humans hinder you or slow you down or question your motives because they suspect you're different?"

"I don't know. Maybe. But everything's been fine so far. The humans trust me."

"For now. But what happens when that trust breaks or another opportunity comes along? Humans always choose what's selfish or easy. In that, they *are* predictable. Do it and come home. He doesn't belong there."

"That's another thing. Sector Six is supposed to be free of the Gifted. It's not. There are loads of them here."

"What? I don't believe it."

"It's true."

"Even if there are, your only job right now is to find the one boy. Slay him and bring his blood to the portal. I want to see you back here. Please, Evie. For me."

A tightness gripped her chest, and she shoved a lock of hair behind her ear. "It's different since I've lived among them. You don't understand because you don't know them. It's much more complicated."

"It's not complicated. You have a job to do, so do it."

Joram didn't understand. How could he?

He rubbed his face again. "Don't choose the boy, whose life is like a mist that will dry up in the blink of an eye, over your own life that could stretch on for eons. Think of all you could do as a Guardian in Five. You only have a little over four days until the portal shuts down. What if the humans detain you? Then you'll be stuck there until you grow old and die."

Evie swallowed. That was her greatest fear.

"Remember what I said. The Death Guardians will be summ—ed." His face flickered on the screen.

"Joram, are you there?"

"I'm here, but you—cutting out."

"You, too. Wait, I need to tell you something else. I think the Deceiver is here."

His brow pinched, and then his face froze on the screen.

She shook the device. "Joram, he's here, the Deceiver."

His frozen image disappeared, replaced by the words *Connection Unavailable.*

Evie slapped the communicator into her palm, then stared at the black screen.

"Joram?" she said to her sleek reflection.

She hung her head, still squatting in the dark alley. She returned the communicator to her pocket, and her fingers brushed his note. She wrapped her fingers around it and gripped the words like a lifeline. *Do what you have to do.*

33

Adan bounced his knee under the table, watching as Hattie nodded, accepting her part in a hastily formed plan. "Okay, I'll take care of it." She strode away, biting into one of her sweet plums.

"How is it possible she has access to poison?" Thomas grunted as he shoveled lamb stew into his mouth.

"Not poison, really," Grace said. "Just an herb that will make you want to puke your guts up."

James smirked at the Water Mover. "Grace, proper as always."

She smirked back and returned to freezing objects in her dinner glass.

"I can't believe the festival is only two days away," James said. "We'll be free citizens. Don't forget, if we get separated, follow through as best you can. If anyone is left behind, don't turn back. Get out, and we'll come back for them later."

Adan, Thomas, and Grace nodded. Adan had to convince the captain of the numerous ways he could make money at the festival. He'd thought persuading the man to allow his friends to participate would be difficult, but he'd been wrong.

The captain would paint himself purple and dance on the castle steps if Adan told him he'd dreamed it.

Adan even managed to find a place for the friends of the girl who tried to escape on his first morning here, though he couldn't think of a way to get many of the other special guests away. He cringed and fisted his hands.

Finding a place for Thomas had been the most difficult. Why would the captain want a Strength Wielder who needed babysitting out in the open? But Adan had convinced him. Thomas would remain in chains until his big moment. The timing had to be perfect.

But before any of that could take place, Adan needed to retrieve his book from the captain's office. Hattie had helped him come up with a plan.

He and James discarded their trays and walked up the stairs together. Adan gave James a final nod before the other boy veered into the Healing Hall. Then Adan settled at the rickety desk that had become his in a corner of Captain Curtshaw's office.

A ledger spread before the captain, and he frowned down at the scrawl of numbers. Without looking up, he said, "Any dreams last night?"

"No," Adan lied as he shifted and snagged his pant leg on a nail protruding from the underside of his desk. Great.

The captain slammed the ledger shut and tossed it onto Adan's desk.

Adan's gaze snapped to the captain, who watched him. Perhaps he should've hoped for a dream that would be helpful to the impatient captain rather than for one that would help him retrieve his book today.

"Perhaps a sleeping tonic would do the trick?"

Adan pressed his lips into a thin line. That's just what he needed—something to make him sleep through his planning time. "Um. I'm not sure." He flipped open the ledger's rough pages where handwritten numbers filled yellowed paper. "Did you have a chance to look into the discrepancies I found in your accounts?"

"No, but I'd like you to double-check the numbers before I make inquiries." Turning, the captain pulled an unfamiliar binder from the shelf behind him. "Check this one as well."

Oh, for a calculator.

Adan took it and set to work, attempting to add and subtract within his troubled mind until a soft rap brushed at the door. He stilled.

"Come in," the captain said.

Hattie shouldered through holding a tray.

"Put it on the table." Captain Curtshaw gestured and then returned to his work, dismissing her without another glance.

Hattie met Adan's eyes before she disappeared out the door.

Adan's heart began to pound, and sweat beaded on his forehead. He wiped it away, peeking over his shoulder at the food—dried bread, cheese, and the same dark plums they'd had at lunch. The captain's head was still bent over his books. The golden book still lodged high within the captain's bookcase.

Captain Curtshaw worked until lumbering to the table behind Adan.

Adan fought to keep his focus on his ledger. His muscles coiled as if he awaited his turn at one of the fighting competitions back home. He formed a picture in his mind of the captain's movements—a creak from the chair, a piece of bread ripped, a cup lifted, a slurp as juices burst from fleshy fruit.

A bead of sweat crawled down Adan's back.

Impatient, he checked the captain. The man was reading a letter and —and he looked perfectly normal. Adan returned to his calculations, though his mind was far away.

After a full fifteen minutes, the captain pushed from the table with a scrape. He strolled into view toward his desk, still perusing his note. He didn't look like someone about to be sick. Heaviness settled into Adan's gut.

What if it didn't work? What would he do?

"Aren't you done?"

Adan started at the captain's sharp voice. He glanced at the ledger. He'd scarcely worked through anything since walking in the door.

"Not quite." He set back to it, working through the simple math of balancing a book. The captain took a seat and went back to work, all calm composure and health.

Not good. Perhaps the herb took time to prove effective.

So Adan waited for any sign of displeasure.

After another hour of calculations, Adan's eyebrows rose. He found where the captain's money was disappearing. But that wasn't his concern just now.

The plan was not going to work. Afternoon training would begin soon, and this was his only chance to retrieve the book and, more importantly, the photo. Tomorrow, they'd spend all day setting up for the festival.

Perhaps he should abandon this task. So what if he lost the photo and the address scrawled across its back? It wasn't the end of the world.

When he got home, he could reacquire the information—his birth mom's last known residence—by asking his foster care caseworker. But the photograph—it was irreplaceable. It was their only photo of Ben as an infant, and it was their only link to their mother. Ben loved to look at it and make up stories about the woman they didn't know. *I can't give up.*

How could he get the captain out of this room? Even if only for a moment. Thinking fast and acting before he could talk himself out of it, Adan clamped his mouth shut and pressed his hand to the nail protruding from his desk. He yanked, releasing a pained hiss.

The captain looked up, annoyed. "What?"

"I—I cut my hand on a nail."

The other man glared at him as if he were an idiot.

Adan held his hand up, and blood dripped down his forearm. "It's my writing hand." He winced, trying to look pale. It wasn't difficult. "James could heal me."

"Fine, go to him, then come right back. We still have another quarter-hour."

Adan stood, stumbled, and then fell back into his chair. "Sorry, I feel light-headed."

The captain rolled his eyes and got to his feet. "Don't drip on the rug." He walked to the door and wrenched it open, yelling down the hall. "Vincent, call for the Healer." He closed the door and strode back to his desk.

This wasn't going according to plan B. Captain Curtshaw hadn't even left the room. What now?

A knock thumped the door.

"Come in."

James peeked in, and his brow pinched when he saw the captain, who waved him into the room. "Get in here. Adan's bleeding. Keep it off the rug and clean up the mess."

"Yes, sir." James knelt before Adan and took his wrist. Power buzzed through his throbbing hand.

"What happened?" James mouthed, nodding toward Captain Curtshaw.

Adan shook his head. "It didn't work," he hissed.

James's mouth formed a thin line.

The Healer had almost completed his task when a man barged in. "Captain. Come quick. The king's valet has summoned you."

The captain groaned. "His valet?"

"I believe it's an emergency. Something's wrong."

The two men strode for the door.

Captain Curtshaw paused on his way out. "When he's healed, clean up, and then both of you go to the Healing Hall." He strode out, leaving the door open.

James and Adan stared at each other. James grinned. Adan ran behind the desk and tried to snag the golden book. It was just out of reach. He stepped onto the bottom shelf, grabbing the volume. The shelf held, but his elbow caught a row of books, and they clattered to the stone floor. Adan and James froze. No one burst in, but dainty clicks echoed down the hall. Adan shoved the book into his pocket, and James returned the fallen ledgers to their shelf. They rounded the desk as Captain Curtshaw's wife strode into the room. James grabbed Adan's hand, inspecting his healed palm.

Mrs. Curtshaw froze, looking them over. "My husband was called away. Why are you here?"

Her eyes searched the bookcase behind the captain's desk.

"I cut my hand." Adan pointed to the bloody rag. "James healed me. We were about to leave."

The woman eyed the cloth on Adan's desk. Adan thought she was going to pick it up, but instead, she lifted the ledger under it, shaking the soiled rag to the floor. She inspected the cover but didn't open it.

"Has my husband examined this ledger?"

Her icy glare fixed Adan in place. "No, just me." As soon as he said it, he regretted it.

She scanned the room, then strode to the captain's bookcase. With a slender arm, she swiped across the row of ledgers, and they scattered to the floor.

"Guards," she shrilled. "Guards." A door banged in the distance, and footsteps thundered down the hall. Quieter, she said, "Sorry. Nothing personal."

Adan and James stood frozen. James found his voice. "What are you doing?"

But Adan knew what she was doing. "I won't tell the captain. I promise."

Mrs. Curtshaw smiled. "I know."

Two guards lumbered through the door, eyes wide and weapons drawn.

"These boys were going through my husband's things. I demand you take them to the king's prison. They could be spies."

"Th–that's not true," James sputtered. "She knocked the books from the shelf."

"See, they try to blame me now. You know I only just arrived."

The Boulder's brow creased. "Mum, I can lock them up here. Would you like to see what the captain wants to do with them before you send them to the king's hand?"

The captain would be furious if anyone found out about two of his most valued special guests. But his wife didn't care. She would suffer his wrath to keep her secrets. She'd been pilfering money from him for ages.

"But this one is his Healer, and this one keeps the books and…" The guard just waved at Adan, obviously unsure how to explain the conversations he'd witnessed.

"If you do not accompany me to escort them to the prison, I will see you in chains."

The guard swallowed. "Yes, mum." He jerked his head. "Let's go."

They descended the stairs to the main atrium.

Halfway across the atrium, the Boulder tried again. "Are you sure about this, Mrs. Curtshaw? Your husband will want to hang onto these two. He is… quite fond of them."

James snorted.

The Strength Wielder glared.

"We are going to the prison, and that's the end of it." Her dainty shoes clicked across the vast space to exit the castle.

The two guards shrugged at each other. "In that case, mum, you should know this one's a runner." The Boulder tilted his head toward Adan.

"Oh?"

"I suggest summoning another guard."

Soon, an additional Strength Wielder fell into formation. Adan's hopes plummeted. What would become of their escape plan?

The six of them strode out the door and into the courtyard where the captain nearly sold Adan. The Den was still a dark smudge on the otherwise orderly space. They walked along the side of the castle, passing through an area Adan had never seen.

Their feet shuffled along a well-manicured pebble path until the sweeping front steps came into view. Despite everything, Adan admired the castle's size and beauty. This was like being on some romanticized medieval movie set. He fancied himself watching the film of his life play out. He was an innocent victim being hauled off to the dungeon—the extra who may or may not live in the end. In similar stories, the true hero would come along, brandishing his sword, and storm the castle. He'd sneak through the courtyard, barrel up the wide sweeping steps to shove open the carved front door, save the innocents, and drive his blade into the villain. Then he'd return home a changed man, having found his true self. Oh, and of course, he'd get the girl. He always got the girl.

The Boulder shoved Adan along, and the surreal nature of where his life had gone overtook him. Not even a month ago, he'd been sitting in a room full of students falling asleep in class.

Why am I here?

He shook himself. *Focus.*

In two days, festivalgoers would crowd to the foot of the castle to celebrate. He and James had to find a way out of this mess by then.

Their entourage shuffled on and away from the courtyard to the dark prison. Moans echoed down a long corridor. The warden, a bored-looking man with graying hair and a permanent scowl, checked them in. He seemed agitated with Mrs. Curtshaw for bringing captives who'd been merely poking around, as she put it.

"They were looking through your husband's things?" He raised a brow.

The woman jutted out her chin. "They were snooping on private matters. They may be spies."

The warden scratched his head and motioned for them to follow.

They passed cell after cell of Arvad prisoners. Some plead with the warden.

"Please…"

"We've done nothing.…"

"We were taken on no charges.…"

One gaunt woman stepped forward, framing her face between the bars. "I know you." She addressed James. James's eyes widened, but when the Boulder came into view, the woman shied into the shadows. She recognized the captain's guards, too. Who were these people?

After snaking through the maze, they reached the end of a corridor, and the warden unlocked a barred door. The guard thrust James and Adan inside.

A girl sat on the lower half of one of two bunk beds in the room. She lifted wide and weary eyes as she rose to her feet, but the guards ignored her.

"You." The warden indicated Adan. "That corner." Adan moved there, and a guard clamped a shackle around his ankle. It brushed against the metal band Captain Curtshaw had given him weeks ago. A long chain protruded from the new shackle and coiled to the wall where it bolted to the stones.

After similarly restraining James in the opposite corner, the captors slammed the door and left.

Adan tugged at the shackle. When it didn't budge, he moved to where it attached to the wall, looking for weaknesses in the thick shackle and chain.

"Don't bother," the girl said. "Those chains would hold a Strength Wielder. I've seen it."

Adan kept trying.

James did, too, but with less effort now. Then the Healer sat on the other rickety bunk. His head drooped. "What just happened?"

Adan dropped the chain with a clunk. "Mrs. Curtshaw framed us."

James's head popped up. "What?"

"Or at least, she's keeping us from telling the captain she's been stealing his money. She knew I found out, and I let her know I hadn't told Captain Curtshaw yet. I handed her a reason to get rid of us."

"You mean she set us up?"

"Pretty much."

The girl, who'd been listening, rubbed her arms. "You have to watch out for that woman. She'll toss you to the wrong side of the river."

"You know her?"

"Of course."

James frowned at the girl, the gesture squinching up his freckled face. "What's your name?"

Her eyebrows rose as if she'd expected them to know. "Viviana." A regal voice caressed the word in dulcet tones as brilliant green eyes flashed from dark skin. An Inevite? Her clothes were dirty but might have been lovely a lifetime ago.

"Oh." James stammered, eyes alight. "You're Prince Hagan's… uh…"

She smirked and pulled her feet up onto her bed, dragging the chain attached to her thin ankle. "Ex-fiancé?"

"Yes. But…" James paused. "They shipped you off to Sodorrah or something."

"Well, Prince Hagan himself probably started that rumor." The girl leaned back, resting her elbows on the bed, and shifted her legs. Her chain jangled. "He wants to keep me right here so he can gloat over me, showing me which of us is more powerful." Closing her eyes, she said more softly, "As if I could ever forget."

James nodded but didn't linger on Viviana's problems. Turning to Adan, he threw his hands up. "This is just great. What now? We have to get out of here."

Adan sat next to him. What could they do, and why hadn't he dreamed about this? He hadn't, had he? James had been in his dream. He'd stood near the executioner's block and then had healed the tarnished crown. Who could make sense of it? He'd dreamed about the shackle, but nothing else.

And why wasn't the captain sick? Hattie hadn't given him any indication that the plan might fail.

A gasp slipped from his lungs. The plums. In his dream, there'd been a sack of fruit atop the executioner's block. An uneasy feeling spread through his gut. He stood. "Something's not right. Something didn't go right on Hattie's end."

But he couldn't do anything from here, and so the three unlikely companions passed the time pacing and plotting. Viviana hadn't had any companionship in a while and eagerly added her opinion.

"Perhaps someday you'll return to rescue me. If you make it out, that is."

James lifted his chin. "I'm joining the rebels. I'll tell them about you."

Viviana looked to Adan for his assurances, but he gave none. He couldn't make that promise. He needed to get home. He avoided her gaze. "James, how did that prisoner know you?"

"She was tested like you in the courtyard. It wasn't long before you came around. I didn't know her or even talk to her."

Viviana tucked dirty strands of chestnut hair away from her gleaming skin. "Rumor is most of the Arvad in this prison were sent here by Captain Curtshaw. I'm not sure what they did or where they came from."

"They were captured from their homes like me." James crossed his arms over his chest. "But unlike me, they're not Gifted. The captain doesn't know what to do with them after they fail the tests. He doesn't want them, Sodorrah doesn't want them, and he can't send them home. If he did, he couldn't keep his operation a secret."

"Operation?" Viviana cocked her head to one side, long hair slipping past her cheek.

"He's trafficking the Gifted."

As she frowned, they fell into silence. Adan worried after the people who'd still be here, wrongfully imprisoned, after he was gone. The injustice of it burned within him. But what could he do? He was just one person.

Hours later, a commotion erupted down the hallway. Boots pounded toward them. "Where are they?" a booming voice bellowed.

A red-faced Captain Curtshaw stormed closer. "Unlock this door immediately." He stood there, hands fisted, neck blotched. "I will punish them as I see fit."

James placed his hand over his heart. "Ah, Captain, I didn't know you cared so much."

"Shut up, Healer." He rounded on the warden. "Open this door."

The warden held up a hand. "Sir, I cannot. Your wife appealed to the king for judgment. They have to stay until their time before him."

"And when will that be?"

"Could be months—up to a year. You know how these petty cases go."

Now the captain's face looked like it might redden to match the color of Elias's festival clothes. He rubbed a hand over his mouth, then took a deep breath. "Listen, let's forget anything happened. They are my charges, and I'll take care of them. My wife accused them of looking through my files. That's hardly a crime worthy of the king."

"Sir, it doesn't matter. Mrs. Curtshaw appealed to the king. When their time comes, you can appear with them if you wish. There is nothing I can do. I've already filed their case."

The captain dipped his head and rubbed the bridge of his nose with two fingers. "Fine. This is not over. I need to go through more adept channels."

The warden reddened but said nothing.

"Now leave us. I want to speak to them."

The warden shuffled away.

Schooling his features, the captain ground out, "Why were you going through my ledgers?"

Adan debated telling him about Mrs. Curtshaw, but his word against hers would get him nowhere. "I was scanning some of the papers I'd already looked through. Sometimes I have more…" How to word it? He glanced at James. "Productive… uh, advice… when I jar a memory or see something of importance." It wasn't a lie. He often dreamed about the things he saw. "When your wife came in, she startled me, and I knocked some books off the shelf."

The captain scowled at Adan as if he were a child caught in a lie. "And what about him?" He jerked his thumb toward James.

"James just happened to be in the room. Remember, he was there to heal me." Adan held up his hand as proof, but the skin had already been knit back together.

As the older man rubbed his temple, another voice sounded down the hall. "Captain, the king has requested you again."

The captain gripped the bars with white knuckles and let out a slow breath. "I'm coming," he hissed. "I have other matters to attend. I'll deal with you both later." With that, he was gone.

"That was the worst lie I've ever heard." Viviana's emerald eyes glowed.

Adan scowled at her.

More silent hours passed. Adan wasn't sure whether he wanted the captain to spring him from prison early or not. What exactly did "I'll deal with you" mean?

He crawled onto the bunk above James and flopped onto his back. He replayed everything until his eyelids grew heavy.

<<<>>>

He stood alone on the path, and the strange sensation that he was preparing for something important tingled through him.

He peered through the trees in a slow circle. No one lurked in the shadows. When he'd completed his turn, a tall man with dark hair walked away from him.

"Hey," Adan called out.

The man paused, then continued without turning.

A flock of blackbirds flew into view, and rather than settling in the trees, they flew to the ground, landing on one side of the path. An eagle landed on the other, and the ram clopped around Adan's legs and stood before him. The animals began to bleat and squawk at each other. The birds hopped in agitation, the eagle flapped its wings, and the ram ducked its head, pawing at the ground.

The man rounded the corner ahead and disappeared from view.

The wooden platform loomed before him. The chopping block perched atop it, and Hattie sat upon it. The fruit from the bag scattered over the ground. She reached down, grabbed up a plum, and took a bite.

James strode around the wooden structure and picked up a tarnished crown at Adan's feet. At James's touch, it shone bright and golden.

Hattie sat motionless, clutching the half-eaten fruit. She stared ahead, unseeing, as the red juice dripped down her chin and neck where it took on a thick blood-red color. The crimson liquid circled her throat and dribbled down her chest.

The ram let out a low bleat, and the birds began to squawk, their call deafening. Sam tossed a baseball nearby—up and down, up and down.

Wake up.

<<<>>>

"Adan, wake up."

Adan jerked upright.

James and Viviana watched him with wary eyes.

"What?" Adan followed their gaze to his arm, which dangled from the high bunk. The back of his hand still glowed through his marks. He couldn't very well hide his oddity from two people with whom he shared a room.

"Adan?" James whispered. "You *are* Gifted." The glow faded, and then James's head whipped toward the barred door.

Footsteps shuffled toward them.

Adan jumped to the floor. "Listen, I can't explain now, but you're going to be summoned to heal the king. I don't know why, but Hattie's in danger. It has something to do with her fruit. You have to warn her."

James laughed. "How could you know that?" He eyed Adan's marked hand. "What Gift could you possibly have while sleeping?"

Adan tugged his sleeve lower. "I dreamed it."

James shook his head.

The footsteps drew nearer, and the warden strode into view. "Which one of you is the Healer?"

James shifted. "That's me."

The warden unlocked the door and stooped to release James's manacle. When he stood, James asked, "Where am I going?"

"The king has summoned you. His Healer has been unsuccessful."

James snapped his head to lock wide eyes with Adan.

"Warn her," was all Adan had time to say before the warden ushered James away.

34

Sam prowled along in the shadows following the perplexing, golden-eyed girl. Evaniah had been acting strangely from the moment he met her, and no doubt, she was hiding something. It had seemed, at least for a time, they'd work together. Now, however, she deliberately kept him away.

Since she became the go-between for the rebels and the prisoners, she'd become ever more elusive. Her reports were vague, and she refused to allow anyone to accompany her to the castle.

"I work alone." She glared at him after he'd pressed to come along tonight.

He relented, making plans to follow.

"Humans," she'd muttered when she thought he was out of earshot.

"Guardians," he muttered back.

Evaniah was trying to get to Adan before him. He didn't need Asher's Gift to figure that one out. But why? So many things about her didn't add up. His chest tightened. *What am I missing?*

Now, he paused behind a charred barrel as she slid around the corner of the castle. There wasn't anywhere for her to go from there. Was a door hidden from view? Sam settled in to wait, touching the corner of his eye where his bruise had faded to a disgusting yellow. The sky was inky black, and the scattered lantern light didn't allow much visibility. Evaniah didn't emerge.

Movement on the castle wall caught his eye. A black blob wriggled over the stones. When the shape rounded the corner, he sucked in a breath. Evaniah.

Was she crazy? A fall from that height would kill her.

A guard stood at a door far down the wall, but he never glanced up at the castle. Cloaked in darkness, her movement and odd shape would be invisible to anyone not looking for it.

Evaniah stopped before a dark window, but then started her descent. Sam never saw a face at the window.

When she reached the ground, she came around the corner, and he crept after her. She rounded the castle and sat to watch another, longer window only a few stories off the ground. This one was lit up and barred. Shadows moved within.

A lantern cast a faint glow over her troubled face. She took out her strange golden blade, turning it in her hands. Then she rose and walked toward the rebel base.

There wasn't anything strange about what he'd seen. Evie did say she was going to deliver a message to her informant, and now she was headed back. So why did his instincts all scream something wasn't quite right?

35

Adan woke with a shout.

Stone walls surrounded him. A bunk hovered overhead. A chain pulled at his leg. A girl watched him with narrowed green eyes.

He swallowed back memories of the previous day and yanked his sleeve over his glowing hand.

"What are you?" Viviana, the almost princess, curled her legs beneath her.

Adan put his feet on the floor and perched on the edge of James's vacated bed. "You wouldn't believe me if I told you. No one else does."

"Try me."

He met her keen eyes and saw no reason not to tell this prisoner about his greatest flaw—about the dreams that tortured his nights and the nightmares that followed his days.

Skepticism wrinkled her brow throughout his tale, but the truth had shone on his marked arm. "What did you dream this time?"

"Well, for the second time, I saw a dark-haired man, but I haven't seen his face. He walks away and out of sight. In this dream, when he leaves, a giant snake slithers toward me. It's swollen in the middle—kind of like it has already eaten—but it still swallows the other animals that have been showing up in my dream."

Huffing, he braced himself. Surely, she thought he was out of his mind. She raised a brow but nodded.

"Then the snake coils and lifts its head, staring at me like it's waiting for me to do something." He rubbed his face. "I have no idea what it means."

"What happens after that?" she asked, propping on an elbow.

"Oh, the usual." He matched her posture. "An archway appears, I see my reflection on the surface until it starts to glow, and then my assassin comes out of the light and kills me."

"You dream this often? Perhaps this part is only your fears haunting you?"

"Maybe." One could hope. "Other things I've been dreaming of for years haven't happened either. Sometimes there's this moment when my friends from back home bow to me like I'm some sort of king. It's weird."

"What do they say to this? Or did you ever tell them?"

Adan rose from the bed and stood at the barred entrance. The smell of unwashed bodies wafted down the long stone hallway. "I told them about it at first, but they got annoyed after a while. My best friend, Sam, thought it was hilarious. He never skipped an opportunity to bow to me. It became a joke between us."

"And you've dreamed of other things. Some that *have* come to pass?"

"Yeah, the more I look for meaning in a dream, the clearer it becomes."

"If what you say is true and you *can* predict the future, they'll fight to the death over you."

He was beginning to realize this was true.

"Does the captain know what you can do?"

He closed his eyes, almost afraid of the answer.

Laughing, she clamped a hand over her mouth. "No wonder he's frantic to get you back." Lowering her hand, she regarded him. "What an extraordinary Gift you have."

"I've never seen it that way. It's a curse."

"Nonsense. You are blessed."

Adan snorted. "I'm more along the lines of laughingstock."

She slid her long hair over her shoulder and fingered through the tangles, seeming more focused on them than on him. "I don't believe it."

"Believe what you like. It's true. It makes me an oddity."

"You must be worthy to be born with such a Gift."

He clenched his hands into fists, but he couldn't fight reality. "It's a mistake. My whole life is one big mistake."

"Those are harsh words." She tossed the tangles over her shoulder and sat straighter. "Why do you say such things?"

Because my mother didn't want me. Because I'm strange and different and my skin even marks me that way.

He cleared his throat and gazed down the hall, resting his forehead against two bars. "Not too long ago, kids at school made fun of my little brother for not having a family. They told him he was a mistake. We've heard similar things all our lives."

Harsh words can stick on repeat in a person's head for days, months, even years. At random times, they come to mind with perfect clarity.

You're going to be a disappointment to every person you come across.

Viviana picked at the ratty blanket she'd spread over her lap. "I would say not to listen to such nonsense, but I know it's not that easy. I don't think your Gift was a mistake." She smoothed her fingers over the blanket, ironing out the folds as though she were smoothing a regal gown. "James doesn't know, does he? I thought you were friends."

A twinge of guilt zinged him. "No, he doesn't... or didn't. My Gift makes me seem strange. This is the first time in a long time that I've been able to hide it. I felt... normal. Well, apart from the whole prisoner thing." He poked at the swirling mark on his hand, grabbing a bit of skin and pinching it. "All I've ever wanted was a normal life... to be boring."

A smile softened her hard mouth. "Perhaps that's not your destiny."

Adan paced. Like a dog on a leash, he carved a short path, moving as far as his bond allowed. The scrape of the chain was the only sound.

He'd spent the last hour reading *One's Raining Fire*, and now, to distract himself from worrying after James and Hattie, he pondered Nolan the Dreamer. Two different outcomes had been foretold for the hero. Either Nolan would send the Deceiver back to the Control Room, revealing the man's hidden identity, or the Deceiver's Immortal Warrior would kill Nolan. All this would be decided before the Maker exacted his wrath on the fallen sector. Adan wasn't yet sure where the archway fit in.

Viviana, who must have sensed his distant thoughts, asked, "What plots so darken your brow?"

"No plan. Just… thinking. Everything that's happened in the last day has been because of this book." He slid the golden volume from his pocket. "I was trying to get it back. I did get it, but at what cost?"

"Can I see it?"

He handed it over. She examined the cover and ran a finger along the vines etched onto the spine. "What do you think this is?" She pointed to where the vines swirled around a single point, forming a hollowed area.

"My friend—Asher—and I thought it used to be a keyhole. See this pale strip going all the way around. There might've been some sort of metal lock circling it."

Viviana opened the first worn page. But before she'd read even a paragraph, her head jerked up.

"Someone's coming."

Adan paused, silencing the chain.

Two voices bounced down the hall—one familiar and one not. "If this is another trick to gain my father's favor, I'll execute this one *and* the Healer."

Viviana dropped the book and cringed back onto her bed.

"A wise choice, Prince."

"My father is delusional. Why he insists on seeing these frauds is beyond me."

Adan snatched the book, returning it to his pocket. A regal young man rounded the corner. His pompous smirk complemented his regal clothing. Joromy, the Sodorran, trailed him, followed by guards.

Joromy's eyes widened when they found Adan standing in the cell among a coil of chain.

Captain Curtshaw didn't tell him I was here. He didn't know. The greedy captain had probably also failed to mention Adan's Gift. So Adan's probable kidnapper, the Sodorran steward, still didn't know what Adan could do. Interesting.

Joromy watched him, some unknown question creasing his brow. Behind him, the disgruntled warden stood silent.

The regal man stepped forward, tearing his scowl away from Viviana to examine Adan. The boredom never lifted from his gaze. "Are you the boy, Adan, friend of the Healer?"

Adan's throat bobbed. "Yes."

"The Healer believes you may be of some service to the king. I, however, am skeptical. But the king has requested your presence. Warden."

The warden shuffled forward and released Adan.

"I am Prince Hagan." Rings flashed from a soft hand as he gestured. "Follow me to my father. If I sense any treachery from you, I will have you run through. Do you understand?"

"Yes," Adan answered, mouth suddenly dry. With a nod to his cellmate, he walked forward, meeting Joromy's gaze as he passed. Adan could read nothing from the Sodorran.

The group snaked back through the prison and past the Arvad pressed together in their cells.

The guards took up positions around Adan as they led the way into the castle and up numerous flights of stairs.

A maid scrubbed the already shining floor that reflected the polished stone walls and richly ornamented drapes. An exquisitely dressed young woman passed, her shoes tapping a rhythm of elegance, and the guards stepped closer to the sculptures and paintings lining the hall to grant her ample room. But the prince stopped her before a grand library holding thousands of books on dark wood shelves.

"Have you seen my father's copy of Guardian Quest?" He leaned near her ear, breathing in deeply. "Hmm. You smell good today. The figures are made entirely of gold." When she giggled, the prince gestured into the room where the polished pieces were set out on a smooth mahogany game board. "I'll show it to you some time."

They had Guardian Quest here? Adan craned his neck to see.

"I would like that, my prince," she cooed.

Adan fought the urge to roll his eyes.

They continued to a pair of armed guards posted outside ornately carved double doors. Nothing resembled the captain's clean and functional wing of the castle.

"Wait here with the Healer. I'll see that my father is ready." Prince Hagan gestured toward James, who sat, back against the wall.

Adan slid to the floor next to the Healer. "What have you gotten me into?"

James's face was pale, and his hands shaking.

"What happened?" Adan nudged his foot with his. "Did you heal the king?"

James wiped a sleeve across his red-rimmed eyes. "That was all fine. But… I couldn't help her, and now I've failed you as well."

A sickening feeling swirled in Adan's gut. "James, where is Hattie?"

"She's gone, Adan, but listen, there's not much time. The king's talking about a crazy recurring dream he's been having. He consulted a lot of people who've tried to make sense of it, but no one has." James put his head in his hands. "I might have mentioned you could help."

"Help?" Adan said as he sucked in a shallow breath. "But what would I do?"

"I don't know. Dream or whatever." James waved a hand around Adan's head. "I thought maybe you could, like, interpret, or something."

"What? James, that's not how this works."

"I saw it as a way to get you out of prison. But…" He licked his lips, breath shallow.

Smoking Worlds. "But?"

"After I told them about you, I found out Prince Hagan's been executing those who claimed they could help the king but were unable to follow through. He says they're frauds."

Adan's body jerked, and he slammed the back of his head against the wall. After all this, would he die here?

His Gift—his *curse*—had brought him here.

"I'm sorry," James whispered.

"What made you believe what I can do, anyway? You only just learned about it this morning."

"I was called to heal the king—as you said—and something bad has happened to Hattie. Also, like you said. They executed her this morning."

The blood drained from his head. Woozy, he struggled to breathe. "No."

James nodded, eyes glassy. "The poisoned fruit meant for Captain Curtshaw went to the king. The prince found out where it came from."

"This is all my fault." Adan braced his elbows on his knees and grabbed at his dark curls.

Not Hattie. Hattie, who'd treated him like a son. Hattie, who'd taken a massive risk for him. All so he could steal back his stupid book. She was gone. The volume weighed heavy in his pocket.

James nudged him in the shoulder. "The plan was hers, and we all helped. No one person is to blame."

The doors creaked. A guard motioned them forward.

They shared a last glance and stood to follow.

Once in the room, Prince Hagan made the introductions.

"Meet his highness, King Alexander. Father, this is the boy you requested."

Adan met the king's eyes. Should he salute? Bow, maybe? No one else made a move, so Adan stayed still.

The king sat in a high-back armchair, wrapped in a blanket. In this state, he likely looked older than he was. Tired eyes peered at Adan above a graying beard. "Ah, you must be the friend of my recent Healer."

"Yes, sir."

"And what is your name?"

"Adan, sir."

"The Healer believes you may be able to help me with something that's been troubling me."

"I'm not sure, sir. James may have misspoken."

The prince threw both hands in the air. "I told you the Healer was lying to get his friend out of prison. Guards."

Two guards shoved James to his knees and held a blade to his neck.

"No, it's true." James's voice rose in a shriek. "He can read the future. I've seen it."

Prince Hagan rolled his eyes, but the king's and Joromy's gazes went to Adan. The Sodorran stiffened, his eyes wide.

"Please. Don't hurt him." Adan stepped forward. "Let me try. I don't know if I can help, but what he says is true."

"Father, this is ridiculous. These boys are taking you for a fool."

One guard adjusted his blade, awaiting the order to run James through.

"Please," Adan said. "Tell me about your dream." Perhaps he could buy time.

"Father, I beg you, don't keep up this silly quest."

The king eyed the prince. "If you continue to interrupt, you will be asked to leave this room."

Prince Hagan's eyes darkened as he clamped his mouth shut.

Joromy stood at his side.

The king leaned in, eyes finding Adan. "I have dreamt the same scene many times over in the last three weeks."

Adan frowned. That was how long he'd been here.

"What looks like a giant map is stretched under me. I stand on this castle's location facing north." The king paused, watching him, but when Adan said nothing, he went on. "There are live animals. My emblem, the ram, is present, and many blackbirds as well."

Adan's head jerked up at this.

The king's words quickened. "Do you recognize this?"

"Father, this is ridiculous. He will listen to your story and then form any interpretation of it."

"Prince Hagan, leave this room."

"But—"

"Son, do you need an escort?"

The prince launched himself from the room, slamming the door like a child.

Shaking his head, the king returned his attention to Adan.

But Adan spoke first. "Maybe it will help you to believe what I can do if I tell you the rest of the dream."

The king's eyebrows rose, and he gestured for Adan to continue.

"In my dream, there was no map, only a wooded pathway. Last night, it revealed a flock of birds, a ram, and an eagle."

"Yes, go on," the king said.

"A snake devoured them all."

Eyes brightening, the older man sat straighter. "Yes. Yes. I've seen it many times." He licked his lips. "I feel—I feel like it's trying to tell me something. And did you notice the serpent's swollen middle? It had already fed."

Adan *had* noticed the lump.

"Do you know what it means?" The king leaned to the edge of his seat.

"It seems like a warning, but I can't be sure what the threat is. The birds represent the rebels."

"The rebels?" The king sat back, his lip curled. "The group who nearly started a riot last week?"

The king rubbed his chin, his brow pinched. "Okay, go on."

"You said the ram could symbolize Inevah, right?" At the king's confirmation, Adan began to pace. "Is there a kingdom represented by an eagle?"

King Alexander faced the peaks beyond the window. "The Huldan, the mountain people, have adopted the banner of the eagle, though it's not an official symbol since they are not an official governing authority."

Adan rubbed his temple. "Maybe it could be referring to them."

"Perhaps. What about the serpent? I don't know of a kingdom with a snakelike marking."

"I don't know, either, but it did come from the north on your map, right?" Adan raised a brow, then waved toward the window. "Which kingdom is directly north?"

Joromy paled under the king's sudden scrutiny.

"Sodorrah"—the word came from the king and seemed to hang there —"and others beyond."

Transfixed, Joromy whispered, "My kingdom's emblem is a lynx."

"Perhaps Sodorrah will be swallowed up first," Adan said. "Or maybe it's already been taken."

Joromy swallowed.

Adan stopped moving and faced the king. "Here's what I think: the Inevite, the rebels, and the Huldan are so busy fighting amongst themselves they won't see the threat growing in the north. You will all be overtaken."

"That is a disturbing interpretation, indeed." The king sat back, rubbing his chin as though lost in thought.

"I can't offer more."

"Will you tell me if you have another dream?"

Adan nodded. "King Alexander, I'm not sure how it works, but some things in my dreams can be changed by changing the path you're on."

"What do you suggest?"

"It may start with uniting the three groups of people who call Inevah home. I think the rebels, the birds, represent all the Arvad—the Gifted refugees."

The king's fist clenched. "The Arvad should be thanking us for taking them in. A bunch of troublemakers, they are."

"King Alexander"—Adan chewed the inside of his cheek—"have you found out what the rebels want?"

"What they want is to cause trouble."

"I doubt that. You should find out. That would be a good place to start."

36

"Hello, dearie. Care to try one? Boar-stuffed cabbage. Excellent price for your evening meal."

Evie declined and smiled from under her hood at the green-eyed woman. But after taking in Evie's strange golden eyes, the vendor left with a suspicious scowl.

Evie grimaced, adjusting her long black wig—courtesy of Morris's disguise stash—and made an effort to blend in.

Morris's scouts were doing the same. Though the wig would do the trick, she didn't want to take any chances. She moved away, starting up another street, working ever closer to the foot of the castle. According to Morris, she wasn't supposed to be here.

After an hour of meandering, she trod her boots into the main castle courtyard. Most vendors were already set up and preparing for the following morning, but some were just arranging their stations on this eve of the Festival of Alvar. Tomorrow, from sunup to sundown, food, entertainment, and humans would fill this space. They would celebrate the Truth-Speaker and ask for his protection from poisonous lies.

Evie passed by a disorganized booth where a Huldan boy hung a sign offering the healing of ailments. A heftier boy stood behind him like some kind of bodyguard. A Huldan Healer at the castle gates— with a guard. Her heartbeat quickened. She asked the distracted Healer how much it would cost to mend a cut.

He didn't turn. "I'm not open until tomorrow. Sorry."

"Perhaps I could come by around dinner time tomorrow. Five o'clock. I hear there will be quite an explosive show."

He spun around, eyebrows raised. She peeked at the guard. "What I mean is, I hear there will be a fight among the strong arms. Are you one?"

The guard grunted.

The boy frowned. "No, I'm a Healer… Captain Curtshaw's Healer, actually."

"I'm not Gifted, sadly." She leaned against his booth. "Unless you count rock climbing. I'm good at that. I can climb a cliff face that's, say, five stories high." She glanced up the castle wall.

The boy, James, lit with understanding. "I've never tried rock climbing." He met eyes with a girl a few booths down and gave some silent signal. "It sounds fun."

A loud crash sounded where the girl stood. Her table had fallen over. The guard stalked toward her, muttering under his breath. As he bent to right the table, Evie hissed a hurried introduction.

"I'm Adan's informant. You must be James. Where's Adan?"

"Adan was in jail, but now, he's staying in the king's wing of the castle." When her eyebrows shot up, James waved her surprise and unanswered questions away. "It's a long story. He won't be in his room. He made quite an impression on the king. I think that's his room." He pointed to a smooth stone balcony jutting from the castle wall. "The rest of us are going ahead with the plan. I have no idea if they'll let Adan join the festival. He's under the king's guard now."

She stared at the stone landing above. It was even higher and better guarded than his last room. *Great.*

"Is there anything I need to know for tomorrow?" James asked.

She shook her head as a sheer curtain fluttered on the balcony. "No, I just wanted to make sure you were ready."

"We are." But his face betrayed his fear.

"Everything will be fine," she whispered, sounding almost confident as James's guard sauntered back over. Louder, she said, "Well, see you tomorrow." She waved and walked on, passing the girl who was rearranging her table with cups, honey, and an assortment of fruit. The dark-skinned Arvad watched Evie with curious light-brown eyes. Evie strolled down the line of vendors.

What now?

She continued around the courtyard pretending to take in the offerings around her, always keeping an eye on the balcony. Farther from the castle, the vendors had erected their carts in a sprawl of winding rows, creating temporary pathways through them. There were so many choices. One path would take her past a metalworker and then a booth stocked with sandals. Another would take her past an array of tapestries or a man creating blown-glass figures. Her mind wandered back to that first day in Inevah when Ben had broken the figure and then led them to the rebel base. Without these humans, she may never have found Adan.

Had it all happened for a reason? Does everything, even the bad things, happen so you might be led to the path on which you're supposed to be? After that, is it up to you to choose the right path or to continue to move astray?

Humans have choices. Every day new choices and circumstances led a person one way or the other.

Was it possible there was a purpose to all of this?

Evie lifted her watch. One day remained—a little over twenty-four hours. She never thought she'd wait to the last hours, letting her options drain away. What if she didn't make it? Had she made a terrible mistake not doing what she was tasked to do right away?

I won't be left here.

She peered again at the fluttering balcony curtains, but her eye caught on something else. A hooded figure, a man a few booths back, turned away too quickly. He grabbed a sheer pink scarf and examined it. She pressed her lips into a thin line.

She continued, passing through the row of booths to a narrow grassy strip behind it. Tall trees cast moving shadows over her body as she wandered down a row of buildings. She kept moving, changing directions, and peeking out her low hood toward the man.

Yes, he was following her. She reached the end of one building where another began. A short alley threaded between them. She dashed inside, skirting boxes, and rounded the corner. The other end spilled out onto a busy street, and she dove behind a booth selling rugs and carpets. The floor coverings hung in a splash of vivid color.

The hooded man rushed onto the street and spun in a frantic circle. His falsely green eyes passed over Evie's hiding place. Sam.

It was her turn to sneak. Now the Watcher followed the human.

She wasn't at all surprised Sam had followed her. Last night, when Morris informed Evie, Sam, and the others they would stay behind during this final sweep of the castle, Sam's eyes had shot to hers. He knew she'd go regardless.

How long had he been following her? If he knew she was in contact with Adan, he would've made it known.

Sam circled back to the courtyard and searched the faces, but eventually, he sat and put his head in his hands.

The sight softened her heart. He only wanted to find and protect his friend—protect him from her.

When two of Morris's men emerged onto the cobblestones, Sam yanked his hood lower and strode back toward the rebel base. Evie started to follow. But it was more important to scope out the balcony.

She pumped water from a fountain and then bought what looked like a Sector Five cinnamon bun. With her snack, she moved in close to the castle wall and sat on the ground as if to rest in the shade.

She planned a route, dangerous as it was, to the balcony. It would be difficult—maybe even impossible. She might be seen. Or fall. But what other option did she have? Perhaps she should find another window or door to sneak in and find him that way. Honestly, that was even more unlikely.

Attempting to appear relaxed, she slid Morris's copy of *One's Raining Fire* from her pocket. She'd almost completed the tiny volume. She meant only to seem as if she were scanning the page, but her attention snagged on the questions Nolan posed to the Maker before the final scene.

"What if I die before my escape? What if my family—my pregnant wife, my boys—go through, but I do not?"

The Maker and his Guardian, the Truth-Speaker, paused before him, their radiance in stark contrast to the crooked city sprawled around. "Your death would not be in vain," the Maker said. "It would be in defense of those you love. There's no greater love than for one to give their own life to protect someone else. Live or die, this is your destiny."

Enthralled, Evie leaned against a tree trunk as the book went on to describe the battle between Nolan and the Deceiver of Sector One. When Nolan had slain the Immortal Warrior and trapped the Deceiver upon the Control Room portal, he ran for the bronze archway. After

Nolan and his family disappeared into its rippling surface, fire began to fall from the sky like rain. The Maker wept as he burned the city and the sector to ash.

She closed the book and examined the dingy cover. Only the epilogue remained. She'd always imagined that the title referred to *someone's* raining fire. Was this an account of Sector One's destruction—Sector One's rain of fire? No one had ever told her how the Maker destroyed it, what method he'd used.

The Guardian—the Truth-Speaker—had provided a way for Nolan and his family to escape by supplying him with the plans to build the first intersector portal. It took him and his family to Sector Two.

But… the Deceiver. Something must've gone wrong.

A horn blasted from the top of the castle steps. She jolted and pocketed the book. Guards poured from the wide doorway and pounded down the steps. They fanned out over the space.

Nobles descended into the courtyard, and eager vendors fought to catch their attention and their coin. Other nobles gathered in the shade of an overhang. A finely dressed bearded man stepped out into the sun and beamed at the humans below.

"His Highness, King Alexander," another man announced. "And Prince Hagan of Inevah."

The king beckoned behind him, and two younger men followed. Most eyes were on the king, but her attention fixed on the taller of the two boys.

A sleek black jacket hugged Adan's shoulders, and his wavy dark hair, as messy as ever, stood in stark contrast to his pressed black pants and fine white tunic.

The king muttered something to Adan as he caught up, and Adan smiled, revealing his dimple. The other young man, probably the prince, rolled his eyes. The three of them strolled the courtyard perimeter while an officious man with a stack of papers prattled on. Adan's appearance wasn't out of place, but his mannerisms were. He tugged at his shirt and hung back from the others. When the group reached James's booth, the Healer did a double take, and Evie chuckled at their exchange.

When the king had moved on, Adan bent toward James, likely hiding a whisper. At something James said, Adan's head snapped up, and he scanned the courtyard. James must've told him she was here.

He was looking for her! Her heart thrilled. It beat in earnest as she watched his eyes search. What was this human reaction to being sought out?

His gaze slid past her black wig until James pointed her out. The Dreamer grinned, making the mortal organ in her chest speed even faster.

She gave a weak wave.

The king called Adan onward, and she waited as the royals continued to arc in her direction. Every few minutes, Adan's eyes found her again.

Their last encounter had come to a graceless ending. Would he treat her differently?

The king strode by first, even giving Evie a nod as he passed. He paused at the foot of the steps to converse with the talkative man as they perused his stack of papers.

When Adan approached her spot in the shade, he met her eyes and then eyed his feet. His cheeks pinked, and he glanced at Hagan, who sighed like a bored teenager.

Adan scrunched his brow. Then his eyes widened, and gesturing toward her cinnamon bun, he said, "That looks very good."

She lifted the pastry and raised an eyebrow. "It is."

"Where did you get it?"

She gestured behind her. "Over that way. Would you like me to show you?"

Prince Hagan sighed. "I don't have time for that. Let's go."

A muscle flexed in Adan's jaw. He called to the king, "Your Majesty, would you mind if I tried one of these cakes?"

"A grand idea." He gestured to the talkative man. "Phillip, buy our guest whatever he likes. And, why not, get me one as well."

Phillip frowned when the king turned away but said only, "Yes, your majesty." He tasked his assistant with the menial job.

When Prince Hagan huffed another loud sigh, the king waved an arm. "Hagan, go. We don't need you here, anyway."

The prince pressed his lips together as if warring within himself whether to be relieved or annoyed. He strode up the stairs and out of sight. While the king continued his conversation, Phillip's assistant waited patiently for Adan to lead him where he needed to go.

"After you." Adan offered her a hand up. Evie took it, and he pulled her to her feet. While she battled with a silly grin—and lost—his lips tilted into a familiar half-smile.

She led him to the baker's stand. The assistant, followed by two guards, fell in step behind, though, keeping their distance.

"I recommend the cinnamon and sugar one," she offered.

Adan nodded his assent to the woman at the booth. Neither spoke as the eager vendor passed the bun into Adan's hand. While Phillip's assistant paid and stood awkwardly to Adan's side, Adan took a bite.

"Well?" Evie rose onto her toes, cocking her head to best see his reaction, genuinely curious.

"It's good… excellent recommendation."

The awkward assistant scratched his head, gazing back toward the king and Phillip. Evie nodded her head toward him.

"Oh, you can go on. We'll be right there." The boy started to protest, but Adan cut in, "Go."

Then Adan gaped as he obeyed. They ambled toward the king. The two guards angled back as well, though still out of earshot.

"I can't believe that worked," Adan said.

"Me either."

"Nice hair." He touched a glossy black lock at her shoulder. His knuckle brushed the sensitive skin of her neck.

Her breath caught, but she steeled herself against the sensation. "It's my new look." She inched away until the curl fell from Adan's fingers. "So why don't you tell me how you got here? The short version, of course."

"I don't know if there is a short version, but I'll give it my best." He launched into his story, and his dimple and the way the light touched his dark hair distracted her. She hadn't seen him in the daylight in ages. He was slimmer and harder—as if he'd been using muscles he didn't usually use.

She wrenched herself back into the present. Joram was right. *Humans are a distraction.*

"Anyway," Adan continued, "the king liked what I said about his dream, so he moved me into this giant room down the hall from him. I don't know how I get myself into these situations."

She smiled at the gaps in his account of the last few hours. He had undoubtedly fallen into the king's favor because what he'd said to the man was spot-on. The Dreaming gift had led him here. Had it also led him to *every* crazy situation he'd found himself in?

She gave a discreet nod toward the guards, now well away. "Do you think they'd chase you if we made a run for it?"

"Probably." He kicked at the sand. "But I can't try it. Captain Curtshaw's holding my friends' lives over my head. If I don't return to him, they're all done for. I have to help them escape tomorrow."

They paused, both watching James shuffle around his booth with nervous energy.

Her hand brushed against Krystopher's golden dagger beneath her jacket. Perhaps it didn't matter that Adan refused to leave with her now. She could still do her job. She shouldn't wait another day. Taking the risk was madness. If she took this opportunity, she could be back in the Control Room before the moon reached its peak this very night. Was this the moment to which her time here had been leading?

Her hand reached toward the blade. The wind caught Adan's dark curls, and he brushed them out of his eyes.

She eyed the guards. They weren't close enough to stop her, but they might be close enough to catch her afterward. Her hand inched away from her hip.

A shout echoed through the courtyard. She jumped as if someone had grabbed her, and she and Adan whipped their heads toward the noise. Guards tackled a man to the ground before the king. A silver blade flashed in his hand. An assassination attempt?

Adan's guards sprinted toward the king to take up positions around him. And her problem was solved. The two of them—Adan and Evie— stood in the deep shade of a tree. All eyes were distracted. She swallowed and slid the blade from its sheath. Her hands trembled, and her heart raced. A bead of sweat rolled down her temple. She peeked at the beautiful boy from the corner of her eye, her breathing uneven. She looked down at the blade, now gripped at her side. The gold winked in the light falling in random bursts through the swaying tree canopy. Steeling her resolve, she faced the Dreamer.

This was the way it was supposed to be. Why else would such an opportunity present itself? *If I don't do this now, I might never have the chance before my time here is up. I can't be left here to die.*

He still faced the commotion around the king, eyebrows drawn.

He shifted, mouth open, ready to say something, and then stopped, probably noticing her distress. "Hey, are you okay? You don't look so good."

One quick thrust and then run. Easy.

He brushed a strand of hair from her face again.

Do it. The blade tilted upward, and he noticed it for the first time.

Her pulse thrummed at her throat.

He raised an eyebrow, not grasping the extent of his situation. "I could run now and get away. But how could I live with myself? I—"

He glanced at the blade again, and his eyes went wide. His hand dropped back. "The golden blade," he whispered.

They stared into each other's eyes until he took a step back. Evie's knuckles were white on the intricate handle. She bent into a fighting stance, afraid to think about her next move. His breathing grew shallow, and he started to take another step.

Something hard pelted Evie's forearm. The blade clattered onto the cobbled street and slid toward Adan. Boots pounded behind her, and Adan's two guards barreled toward them.

Adan took another step back, his face red and contorting.

Evie clutched her throbbing arm and ran.

37

A long dark alleyway swallowed the rebel girl. The girl who'd spent two weeks helping him plot his escape. The wielder of the golden blade. Adan's mind couldn't reconcile these facts.

The gleaming dagger rested on the cobblestones at his feet. He bent as if adjusting his laces and slipped it in his boot.

His guards surrounded him. "The king wants you inside. Now. There are assassins about."

Assassins. He nodded, agreeing with this statement. A guard put a hand on his shoulder, forcing him to move faster.

After only a few paces, though, something white snagged Adan's attention. The object that struck the rebel girl's arm rested at the foot of a tree.

To the guards' distress, he bent to pick it up. One guard shook his head. The other shoved him in the back. "Let's go." Neither took it from him.

His breath quickened as he held the ball at his side. He darted his gaze around but saw nothing familiar.

He ascended the stairs. It was as if he held Sector Five itself in his hand. He rubbed his thumb over the red laces. *How had a baseball come to be in Sector Six?*

38

After running, Evie sat to catch her breath. She rubbed her arm where a circular patch turned a fascinating shade of blue.

What was that?

She let out a long breath. Adan still breathed. Good. But she was also no closer to getting home. She rubbed her temple.

Now, for the first time, she contemplated the real possibility she was too cowardly to do what needed to be done. *Could* she kill Adan? This human body made her weak.

As had become her habit, she pulled Joram's crumpled note from her pocket.

Do what you have to do and come back to me.

Evie rested with the scrap of paper clutched in her fingers until she began the winding journey back to the rebel basement. When she arrived an hour later, all was quiet.

She went through the motions of entering the base. With her voice and face familiar to them now, they let her in quickly. She climbed down the hidden ladder and then sucked in a breath as hands grabbed her.

Bodies slammed her to the floor, knocking the breath from her chest. She yelled out, fighting the arms gripping her.

"She's not armed," Sam said. "She lost her blade."

She sought his eyes and gasped. Murder twisted his usually kind face.

"What are you doing?" she screamed.

Morris led the way as his rebels yanked her to her feet and forced her into a holding room down a short hallway. She kicked and fought but was no match for so many.

"Why are you doing this?" she yelled as the door slammed. She ran forward, pulling at the handle of the locked door. She shook the bars lining an eye-level window and banged her shoulder against the thick wood. Neither budged.

Evie stilled to listen when Morris's raspy voice spoke. "Sam, calm down."

"I won't calm down. I saw her with him. For weeks, she's refused to let anyone go with her to the castle. Why? And—and she was about to stab him."

She sagged against the wall. He'd never trust her now.

"I'll talk to her. Take a walk. Calm down."

Sam huffed, but his footsteps faded down the hall.

"You too, Lena," Morris said, and another set of footsteps moved away.

Evie slid to the floor and rested her head against the wall. Profound sadness over what she'd lost—their trust and friendship—washed over her.

Morris's face appeared in the window, and his calm voice echoed on the stone walls. "I don't understand you. What could your endgame be?" When she didn't speak, he asked another question. "Were you meeting with Sam's friend, Adan?"

Her tongue tasted the lie upon it, but there was no point in telling it. "Yes."

"Why didn't you tell Sam and the others? Yesterday, Ben told Lena he's afraid Adan is dead. You could've confirmed it isn't true." His voice had risen, and now he took a calming breath.

"I can't tell you. All I can say is there's a reason."

"Were you about to harm him when Sam interfered?"

Tears pooled in her eyes. "I truly don't know," she whispered.

Morris let out a heavy sigh. "As if that admission isn't enough, I told you not to go to the castle today. You disobeyed orders. Again." He faced down the hall where everyone was gathered. "You know where our base is, so what to do with you is tricky. We'll figure that out after the rescue tomorrow. For now, you stay here."

She surged to her feet. "No, Morris. Please… I have a job to do. I know you won't understand, and I can't tell you what it is. But you have to trust me." She gripped the window bars. "Please don't leave me here. I–I can't be left."

"And *I* can't trust anything you say. We'll talk tomorrow. No more distractions today." He walked away.

Another door closed at the end of the hall, shutting her off from the main room.

She yelled for Sam or Ben or anyone, but no one came.

She rested on the stone floor until, hours later, the lock clicked, and Sam shouldered through the doorway. Chase, Elias, Asher, Lena, and even Garran followed. The others stood behind Sam as he looked her over.

She straightened, still sitting against the wall, but didn't stand. She couldn't look him in the eye.

"I'll ask you one more time. Who are you, Evaniah?"

She didn't answer. Her gaze slid to the floor.

"Fine," Sam said. "If you won't tell me who you are, then help me with information. What did Adan say to you? Will he be at the festival tomorrow?"

Closing her eyes, she rubbed a shaky hand over them. They hurt. Every bit of this human body hurt. "He will if he can. You can still save him."

"But can I save him from you?"

She snorted a laugh. "It's no longer me he should be afraid of."

Sam's eyebrows drew together. "What do you mean?"

She opened her mouth, but the words didn't want to leave her lips. "If I don't do what I came to do, others will come in my place." She glanced at each of them, pleading with them to understand, though she couldn't tell them she was the assassin Sam feared her to be.

He blinked. "Evaniah, I can't figure out who or what you are. It's like you care, but you try not to." He gestured around himself. "We're a family, and we protect each other. We protect Adan. Before today, those in this room were willing to protect you, too."

Evie swallowed and ran a finger over the dusty floor. A door opened down the hall, and laughter drifted from the main room before a slam shut it out again.

"What are you hiding? Was it worth throwing that away?"

She breathed slowly, in and out. That need of this human body she could grasp, but the other needs? *Family.* That was how they'd thought of her. The liquid clinging to the base of her eye streamed down her cheek. She sucked in a ragged breath and touched her fingers to the wetness. Whispering, she said, "I'm not meant to have a family—to have friendship and love. I never was."

Ben, who'd been lurking outside the doorway, threaded through to stand beside her. He put his hand on her head and stroked her hair.

She touched his hand, just a brush of her fingers to his. Then stiffened her whole human body. "Sam, you need to get Ben home. Please. I'm not sure what will happen to you if I—"

"Just stop." Sam cut her off, leading the others out the door. "No more lies."

If I fail. Her mind finished what she dare not speak.

He put a hand out toward the boy. "Come on, Ben."

Ben knelt before her. "It'll be okay." He grabbed her hand, opened it palm up, placed a smooth object into it, and closed her fingers over it. He left, giving her a wave.

When they were gone, she opened her hand.

She'd thought there would be no more tears. The dam had broken, but surely a Watcher—one of Jesiah's Marked—would contain no more than weak drops.

She'd been wrong.

Resting on her fingers was the game piece Adan had given Ben months ago to assure him he was not alone. It was the boy's most prized possession. The only thing he had to remind him of his brother. The only thing to protect him.

Tears streamed down Evie's face as she beheld the lonely Watcher.

Part IV

He was hurled down, that serpent of old,
he which deceiveth the whole world,
was cast out unto the earth.

Revelation 12:9

39

Adan shuffled along the dusty dream path, more uneasy than usual. A warm breeze tousled his hair, and distant leaves moved like whispers within the forest, lending to a strange and unnerving quiet. Far ahead, Evie strode into view. As always, her light-colored festival dress brushed the sand at her feet, and the ribbons of her mask fluttered at her side. Snowflakes drifted between them.

She watched Adan as she fixed the mask to her face and fastened it behind her head. A strange recognition flitted through his mind and dissolved.

Calls echoed as a dark mass of birds drew nearer, forming a single black cloud in the otherwise hazy gray. When they landed, some high in the trees, others on the ground near him, they settled into an eerie silence. Some cocked their heads, and others hopped, uneasy.

They waited.

The low sun peeked through the trees. The snake slithered in the yellow grass. Distant leaves rustled within the forest. Sam, Garran, Asher, Elias, and Chase strode out of the trees and into the clearing. Ben stood near the edge of the trees, playing with a shining miniature game piece.

The birds watched with nervous energy, growing ever more agitated when the boys knelt low before Adan.

An earsplitting boom echoed within the forest. Adan's brothers rocketed into action, fighting invisible foes as the squawking birds swarmed the pathway. Their bodies almost blocked out the muted sunlight, filling the space like a fog. Sam grabbed Adan's arm, hauling him toward the others, and they bolted for the tree line. They passed a cage where Thomas reached out to him. Adan didn't stop because, if he did, he might also be captured. He moved on as an arc of crimson circled Thomas's throat.

They crashed through the trees until Adan spilled out onto another path. No, not another path, the same path. The snowy tree loomed before him, though his brothers had disappeared.

A soft swoosh caught his attention as he spun toward Evie. A thud rocked his chest. The archway's light blazed, and he looked down. His hands clutched the handle of the rebel girl's golden dagger.

"No," he yelled long and low. He didn't recognize his own voice. He crumpled to the ground, still holding onto it. A head bent over him and yanked the blade free. A tear fell from above onto his cheek. His eyes blurred, and he couldn't make out the face as it rose and walked away. A tear leaked from his eye. Ben stared in shock. Evie yelled out, and then all was deathly silent.

<<<>>>

Adan woke slowly this time. He reached to wipe the wetness from his eyes and glared at the sheer canopy overhead. All he'd ever wanted was to live a normal life, to be popular, and to be rid of these dreadful dreams. Was that so difficult? Was he meant to die?

Adan shook himself. *Don't give up.*

Ribbons of morning light rippled across the polished stone floor. He rose and opened the double doors leading to his private balcony. Sheer curtains billowed inward with the breeze, and the winding streets of Inevah spread out before him. He and his friends would escape this city today.

He returned to his bed and pulled the rebel's blade from under the mattress. He sat, turning it over in his hands. Crafted with excellence, the blade shone gold, and a subtle design carved the hilt, also gold. What looked like vines and thorns snaked along the grip, something was oddly familiar about its formation. He reached for the golden book on his bedside table to examine the spine.

His breath hitched, and he stood. The design on the hilt of the rebel's blade matched the design on the spine. The vines twisted and twirled in an identical pattern, circling together around a space near the base of each object.

What did this mean? What did it say about the rebel?

His exchange with the girl had been confusing. Was she really his assassin? Why would she spend so much time planning to rescue him, only to kill him? If she'd wanted him dead, she could have done it by now.

He caught his reflection in the blade, noting the dark circles under his eyes. Since he had the dagger for himself, how could it be the instrument of his death? His spirits rose—if only a little.

He shoved the blade back under his mattress. He needed to focus.

Finding the festival garb King Alexander had sent up, Adan dressed in a white tunic and light-gray pants. He discarded the gaudy glittering half mask. Once clothed, he paced until the sounds of a waking castle drifted in. Stomach growling, he opened his door but found the housemaid standing before him, arm raised to knock.

"Oh." She jumped. "I thought I'd have to pry you from the bed." She chuckled. "Ready for breakfast?"

"Yes." Hunger pains gnawed at his stomach.

"Okay then, I'm sure this fellow will show you the way while I tidy up in here." She gestured to the guard behind her and then, without invitation, moved inside to begin her chores. The sour-faced guard, who must've stood outside his door all night, shuffled down the hall. Was the man there to protect Adan or to keep him from leaving?

After the best breakfast he'd had in weeks—eggs, bacon, sweet bread, and freshly squeezed juice—a page fetched Adan to join the king. The festival was underway, and the king was to do his duty of addressing the crowd.

When Adan approached, the king beckoned. "Dreamer, come. Look what I've decided to do."

Stacked bags of grain, rice, and other food items cluttered the castle entrance.

"Every year during the festival, we give away food to the registered Inevites. This tradition dates back to my great-grandfather. The harvest was plentiful this year. Our stores are overflowing. I shall give to all who wish it. I've already sent runners across the river to spread the word to the Arvad." He clapped Adan on the shoulder. "What do you think? Will I unite them? Will we stand together against the threat in the north?"

Attendants were already carrying the stores out into the castle courtyard.

The corner of Adan's mouth turned up. "King Alexander, this is an excellent start."

"Dreamer, what more should I do? Please tell me. Did you have any more visions during the night?"

"No, nothing helpful."

Loud, uncaring voices filled the space. Prince Hagan approached with a beautiful young woman on his arm. Many others followed, including Joromy and Captain Curtshaw.

Adan lowered his voice. "Things are happening under your watch that will keep the rebels from trusting you. You have to take care of it."

"What do you mean?"

But the prince had arrived, demanding the attention. "Let's get started!" Arms upstretched, he turned in a circle, then flashed his perfect white teeth to the giggling girl.

The chatty man with the clipboard ushered them forward.

Adan straightened his clothes, pulled up his hood, and checked that his sleeves covered his marks. The king's entourage marched to the front door and into the brilliant sunlight.

The crowd cheered as the king addressed the people. The early birds had already formed a line and jostled for front positions. Most had bright-green Inevite eyes, but some brown, gold, and gray hues mixed among them. These people seemed unsure—as if they waited for someone to tell them this was some sort of joke. But their fears dissolved when the king assured them their stores allowed food for everyone.

Adan stood by, observing. The festival attire was not so different from the festival costumes back home—light-colored shirts, dresses, jackets, as well as white feathered masks. But in Sector Five, the costumes were almost too perfect. Here each had been made a little different. Probably handmade rather than purchased at a shop.

The smell of food wafted about, and a band out of an old-time movie set up near the castle steps. As their lively music played, white-clad youths danced in the crisp morning air. A circular fighting cage perched to the side near the foot of the stairs, empty for the moment.

Eager vendors were open for business. There were games to play, food and goods to buy, performances to watch, and even healing to be had.

James gave Adan a nod.

Grace, positioned two booths down from James, was concocting frozen drinks made from fruit juice. Her hands were at work freezing the liquid and then topping it off with a fan of decorative ice. Adan had suggested these smoothies to make the captain money.

"Smoothie?" Grace had said with a blank expression. They had all looked at him as if he were crazy. A freezer in the home was technology beyond their imaginations.

"That's why it's a brilliant idea. No one else will be selling anything like it." Adan had not been wrong. A line had formed at her station already.

Thomas wouldn't arrive until his appointed time, and Hattie… Adan's throat went dry. He'd been looking for the woman's sweet treat stand before he realized what he was doing. Hattie was dead. She wouldn't escape today. She would never return to her family. Her children might never know what became of her.

The king drifted forward in his stark-white festival garb, and the crowd cheered as he signaled the handout to begin. Each family moved forward, bowed to the king, and then was given the correct number of bags according to their family's size. A scribe marked each in a ledger.

Adan helped move sacks from inside the castle to the tables as the king greeted each family who passed. So many people trickled into the courtyard.

Two hours passed before the king retreated for lunch, bringing his party with him. It might have been pleasant, but for Hagan's shouts and grumbles. The prince had been intent on showing off his father's priceless game set only to find an essential piece was missing. This golden version of Guardian Quest had been handed down for generations, and Hagan was on the warpath to find out who'd swiped the Deceiver.

When Adan returned to the courtyard, the line was still moving, and he did what he could to help. Something in him relaxed. Handing out food to families who needed it was rewarding in a way he'd never thought about before. Uzziah had always told the boys that, rather than sitting around bored when their lessons and training were done, they should find someone to help. Volunteering or doing something random for someone else was a two-sided coin—you do something for humanity, but you also spark something within yourself. Adan had always thought Uzziah said this just to get them off the couch, but… maybe his Guardian had been right all along.

Captain Curtshaw strolled by, giving Adan a disapproving scowl. Last night, in a rage, the man had pulled him aside.

"Remember all those lunch buddies you left in my wing? If you as much as whisper a word about my business dealings, my use for each one of them might come to an abrupt end. Make it your priority to find a way back to me when your time here is done. Your friends' lives depend on it."

Now, as the captain passed, his sharp-nosed training master grumbled that some of his Strength Wielder guards weren't at their posts. Adan grinned beneath his hood. He knew where those guards were. Grace had frozen them into the baths this morning.

The back of his neck tingled. Joromy leaned against a wall near the top of the steps. The green-eyed Sodorran watched Adan with unchecked curiosity. His hands fidgeted in his coat pocket. Though his posture was casual, his face was anything but. Uneasy under the young man's greedy gaze, Adan turned away.

Dinnertime approached, and the sun had long since reached its peak. Gray clouds gathered.

Adan locked eyes with James and then Grace. When he looked to the fighting arena, Thomas glowered back. Captain Curtshaw was walking away from the cage, keys jingling from his belt. Thomas grinned. Almost time.

Adan grabbed a few bags of flour and moved them to the table beside the king. The king gestured Adan to his side. Adan obliged and adjusted his sleeves as the next family moved forward into the open space before the food stores.

"We thank you, our king. We appreciated your generous hospitality."

Adan jerked his head up at the familiar voice. He sucked in a breath and took in each of the white-clad boys before him. Chase flipped his hair and winked, Elias shuffled his horrid red shoes, Garran stared back, emotionless, Asher might burst with the desire to say something, and Sam… Sam smiled at Adan with profound relief.

All words left Adan, and he stood swaying at the impossibility. He closed his eyes. Was this a dream? When he opened them, his brothers were still standing there waiting, backs straight, attempting to look regal. They were here—here, in Sector Six. Somehow, they'd found a way to come for him. He'd been so mad at Sam for breaking his promise to come back. But that feeling melted away as he watched his best friend fidget with nervous energy—energy he usually spent tossing a baseball.

The king motioned them forward, and they drew near.

Adan's gaze snapped to the king and then back to his brothers. A small gasp entered his lungs. He'd seen this moment. As he gave the boys a friendly but smug I-told-you-so smirk, Sam rolled his eyes. Then together, as one, his brothers took a knee and bowed low before Adan and the king.

40

Sleep eluded Evie during the long and lonely night. In the early evening, she paced, occasionally testing the locked door. Then she'd given up, sagging against the wall beneath the flicker of a solar-powered bulb. With a finger, she traced the shape of flowers, trees, and mountains onto the sandy floor. There she'd stayed until noises from the main room signaled morning had arrived. Too soon, though, the sounds died away. Most everyone had gone to the castle to carry out the mission.

Lena delivered bread and water, and now, hours later, Evie still leaned against the wall doing nothing, trying to think of a way out.

She was a Watcher from the Control Room—a would-be immortal. How could this one door in the least advanced of Jesiah's sectors hold her?

She was weak. Humanly weak. That's how. She could be held easily, could be killed easily, and could fail easily.

Just as the humans left her behind in this room, so the Control Room would leave her alone in this sector. All hope fled as she shed every bottled tear she'd stored away over the last weeks.

Her watch switched away from marking the days sometime during the night and now hours, minutes, and seconds slid away with unrelenting persistence. She could almost feel her immortality slipping away like sand from an hourglass. Six hours, forty-two minutes, and eight seconds remained.

She hung her head until, sometime later, the stiffness in her body forced her to move. She paced and pulled *One's Raining Fire* from her pocket to read the epilogue. When she finished, she closed the book, threw it across the room, and sank to the floor. This wasn't the prophetic book she'd thought it to be. Nolan the Dreamer had escaped the destruction of Sector One only to later be hunted and killed. The Deceiver had escaped the trap Nolan set for him. He'd then evaded the Maker's eternal fiery rain by passing through the portal Nolan built. Believing history could one day repeat itself through Nolan's descendant—one marked by Krystopher—the Deceiver had hunted and killed Nolan's entire family, thus ending his line. It had all been for nothing.

As for her, the last weeks had all been for nothing.

A click sounded at the end of the hall, and her head jerked up. Soft footsteps shuffled near. They quieted in front of the locked door, but when she stood and peeked out the window, she saw no one in the dim hallway.

"Hello?"

"Shhh," a timid voice hissed from below. She crept back as the lock began to grind. It squealed, and the stranger let out a gasp. The lock turned again and gave with a sharp snap. The door creaked open, and a figure with soft dark curls and wide sapphire eyes stepped over the threshold.

"Ben," Evie hissed, "you scared me. What are you doing?" She eyed the open door and the hallway behind. Was he alone?

"I came to give you a message."

"They sent *you* with a message?"

Ben glanced behind him and lowered his voice. "She told me to help you and then tell you something."

"Who told you to help me?" Evie glanced out the door. She saw no one.

"Alizah."

Her head whipped back to Ben. "Who did you say?"

A smile tugged up his lips, revealing a dimple nothing like Adan's. "She said this would freak you out."

"Did you say Alizah? Alizah gave you a message?"

"Yes."

"How?"

"In my dreams, silly. From the fancy computer room, like always."

"Like always?" Evie whispered, mostly to herself. "Um. Okay. What's the message?"

"She says time is running out, and you need to do what you came to do. Use Krystopher's blade."

Evie's heart plummeted. Even Alizah knew she was failing. Evie had failed as a Watcher. She'd failed as a mortal. She'd even failed to keep Krystopher's golden weapon. And, most of all, she'd failed to do her job.

But perhaps there was still enough time. She could find Adan. She could kill him.

But was she strong enough?

Either way, she could acquire a drop of the Dreamer's blood and make a run for her portal in the mountains. If she killed Adan, her safe passage was guaranteed. But if she spared him and stole some of his blood, the blood portal might reject her. Was it worth the risk? She wasn't sure which she would choose, but she would accomplish nothing by staying in this room.

"Ben, I need to go. I need a weapon and a disguise. Is anyone else here?"

"A few of the rebels stayed behind. I can get you a dagger and maybe one of those masks everyone's wearing."

Oh, right, the Alvar Festival. She nodded. "Go see if anyone's outside the hallway. If not, I'll sneak to the ladder. Meet me there."

"Why did they lock you up?"

She lifted a shoulder, not wanting to tell him about Adan if he didn't already know. "I didn't follow orders."

Ben rolled his eyes and disappeared down the hall. Long minutes later, he emerged near the ladder with a blade, a mask, and a clean shirt.

Evie examined the silver blade. There was no shine to this one, so unlike her missing golden dagger. Even the edge was dull. The mask, however, was perfect.

Noticing her distaste for the blade, Ben said, "There wasn't much in the weapon's room. The rebels took it all."

"Don't worry about it. I bet I can sharpen it on a rock along the way."

As she stowed the blade in her boot, she asked, "Ben, why did you decide to help me? Sam's the one who locked me in there."

He waved both hands, palms up. "Because Alizah trusts you."

Evie ruffled his hair.

"Evaniah, can I come with you?" He cast her a look that she was sure won others over. It didn't win her. Not today, not in this.

"It's too dangerous. I need you to stay here. I'll get the others, and we'll come back for you if everything goes well. I want you to stay safe."

"That's what everyone says." His head drooped. He didn't protest any further but stepped back to watch her go.

She put a hand on his shoulder. "Ben, you can call me Evie. That's what my friends call me. That means we're friends."

He stared at her eyes and cocked his head. His brow pinched. "Evie?"

Before he could voice the questions in his mind, she pulled him into a hug, burying her face in his hair. He returned her embrace, and tears welled under her eyelids again.

No. No more. No human emotions.

She let go. "You're an amazing kid, Ben." Then, remembering his track record, she added, "And don't follow me."

His too-compliant nod was unconvincing, but she tried not to dwell on it.

He forced a smile. "Will I see you again?"

Remembering a day in Sector Five when he'd asked her this same question, she gave him the same answer with a smile and a shrug. "Who knows."

41

That was the moment Adan had dreamed of so many times? It was a bit anticlimactic. Smiling, Sam shook his head.

He and the others now stood to the side, waiting, pretending to sort through their bags of grain.

Sam, trying to appear relaxed, sank onto the grass, and his brothers followed his lead. Onlookers might think they were listening to the music. They wouldn't realize they waited for something.

Something big.

Adan's worried face sneaked glances their way, and Sam signaled for him to wait. He did.

"I've got the one on the left." Garran sneered, indicating a Strength Wielder stationed near the fighting cage. The man leaned against the bars as he snacked on a melon. Every few seconds, he turned toward the cage and spat his seeds onto the ash-haired Strength Wielder locked within.

Sam nodded. "I'll get Adan and then help with the other one."

Chase sat in the grass at Sam's feet and busied himself by sharpening his blade on a rock. "Look at all these weapons." He tipped the blade to the light. "Imagine if we were at the park back home, and I was just sitting there sharpening a knife this size."

"You'd be arrested for sure," Elias said.

Sam found a rock and tossed it, a poor replacement for his baseball. "Some soccer mom would call it in. You'd be on the news."

They laughed, and he scanned the courtyard, noting the other rebels and looking for signs of trouble. He continually returned his focus to Adan, afraid his friend would somehow disappear.

His gaze caught a man staring back from across the courtyard. His pointed beard and lanky frame were familiar somehow.

Why? He held his breath. Then it whooshed out. This man tried to nab Ben after the blown-glass incident—the one he and Evaniah had allowed to leave after killing his comrades. His unyielding gaze disquieted Sam, but at least, Ben was safe at the rebel base.

The would-be kidnapper walked toward the castle. Sam followed his movements until the man climbed a few steps and leaned toward another tall, well-dressed noble. A few words were exchanged, and the regal man paused, stilling his hand, which had been turning an object that glinted gold in the sunlight. His head snapped up, and he peered at Sam.

Caught staring, Sam studied his feet. But, when he raised his head, the man passed the object to the kidnapper, who then strode down the steps and out of sight.

The dark-haired noble continued to watch Sam until a mighty blast echoed off the castle walls. Sam and his brothers shot to their feet, drawing weapons. It was time.

A cloud of smoke crawled over the courtyard.

Sam and his brothers barreled toward the guards they'd targeted. The rebels, this time wearing festival clothes and white feathered masks, swarmed the area. They yelled and struck, spreading chaos and fear like a plague. Smoke billowing from a well-placed food cart snaked through the crowd and blotted out the golden sun. Onlookers scattered. Soldiers took up arms. And the rebels flew.

Sam sprinted for Adan, and as he did, he glanced up the stairs only to find the well-dressed man watching him. All others on the steps spirited away, but still, he stood. He smiled at Sam until he was no longer visible in the smoke.

42

Adan ducked, covering his ears. He'd known the blast was coming, but the sound was startling all the same.

Guards darted for the king, gathering him up and not sparing a glance for Adan. Captain Curtshaw's guards sprinted up the steps, away from the noise, and to the captain. James and Grace made for Thomas and his cage.

Someone grabbed Adan from behind, and he spun to find the sour-faced guard who'd stood outside his room all night.

"Come on." The man tugged at Adan.

Adan spun and maneuvered out of his grip.

The guard raised a brow but didn't relent. "Come inside now."

Smoke cast the area into a deep shadow. Sam and the others ran toward Adan as the king's soldiers poured past him from the castle.

"If you don't come willingly, I'll knock you out and drag you."

"You can try," Adan replied as the man reached for him again.

With years of training, Adan deflected the man's weak attempt. Luckily, this man was not a Strength Wielder. After a shuffle and an exchange of blows, the frustrated soldier reached for his sword. While he occupied his hands, Adan put his elbow to the man's temple, dropping him.

Turning his back on the man, Adan started for his brothers who'd stalled on the other side of a sea of soldiers. Adan paused as Sam—*Sam*—threw a guard away from him, tossing the fully armed soldier like a rag doll. Adan's mouth fell open. Glowing Guardian marks leaked from his friend's sleeve.

The others darted about, striking and retreating. More soldiers filed forward and formed a wall protecting the castle doors, Adan on one side and his brothers on the other. Sam beckoned him forward. It would be easier for Adan to pass the distracted guards and get to them rather than for them to come to him.

The Healer and Grace bent over Thomas's lock. They were to freeze it until it broke by force. Thomas, arms aglow, smashed his fists onto it, using all his considerable power.

When James saw Adan watching, he shook his head. It wasn't going to work. The lock was meant to hold Strength Wielders, and it was working perfectly. Thomas yelled at them to go, but they didn't stop trying.

A shout resounded behind him. The captain and four of his guards, including two enraged and dripping females, reached the top of the stairs. The ice had thawed.

Adan's brain willed himself to look away. He should go to his brothers and disappear into the smoke, leaving the castle behind. Sam yelled to Adan again, begging him to move—to come to them. This could very well be Adan's only chance at escape, his only chance of going home.

But his heart forced him to look back one more time. James's face had gone ashen as the captain charged down the stairs. Adan saw the moment the boy knew they weren't going to succeed. He and Grace froze with indecision, still, even now, unwilling to leave their friend to follow a beckoning group of rebels. Thomas yelled again, and the two of them sprinted away to be led to safety.

With a yell of frustration, Adan rushed toward the cage. Sam followed his movements, tossing soldiers aside. Adan ran sidelong into the captain, grabbing the keys dangling from the man's belt. He tossed them into the cage with Thomas and, with the same momentum, threw a punch into an unprepared guard's nose before Sam slammed into him, flattening him onto the stone steps.

How easily Sam took down the Strength Wielder! But already another guard came at Adan swinging. Vincent the Boulder was out for blood. Adan, faster, dodged his blows, avoiding snapped bones.

Thomas, now free of his cage, grunted beside Adan as he traded blows with one of the female guards. Adan hardly recognized the friendly giant, whose face reflected a quiet rage. Thomas delivered a blow to the woman's head, causing her to stumble and sway.

Adan dodged another swing and spun behind his lumbering opponent. "Run, Thomas."

Thomas smirked and continued to fight.

Tiring, Adan knew the Boulder would make contact. A hand gripped the back of this jacket and towed him backward. He slammed against the fighting cage as a hulking figure stepped in front of him, taking up his fight.

Garran?

Garran, the boy who'd sold him to a stranger. Garran, who'd threatened him countless times. Garran, who hated Adan. Garran, who was now standing in front of him, defending him.

Adan froze, watching the other boy deliver blow after blow to Vincent, whose face betrayed fear.

Adan jumped as a zing of cold metal wrapped his wrist. He yanked his arm on instinct, but it didn't budge. A silver cuff encircled his wrist. Captain Curtshaw smirked as Adan jerked it again. A short chain attached him to a bar of the cage.

Energy drained from his body as he faced the smug face he'd come to hate. Not even Sam or Garran could save him now.

Garran returned to Adan, having flattened Vincent, unconscious, onto the steps. Garran avoided Adan's gaze, but his eyes went wide as Adan heaved at the chain. Captain Curtshaw slunk away as Garran yanked at it. It's didn't as much as groan.

"Sam!" he yelled. "We have a problem. See if you can break it."

Had the worlds flipped on end? Garran, always eager to prove he was the strongest among them, was calling Sam over for help?

Bodies slumped around the cage, and Sam jogged over, his latest opponent sprawled upon the steps. He grabbed the chain, twisting it around his hand.

"Hey, brother," Adan said.

Sam smiled. "Hey, brother." He pulled, and his arm glowed brightly.

The metal whined, but it didn't give.

Adan's last shred of hope fell away. He tried to smile but failed. He gazed at his brothers as Sam still worked. They'd come for him. He'd thought he was all alone in this world. He'd been wrong.

Chase, Asher, and Elias stood by, swords raised, watching for more trouble. Garran offered whispered suggestions to Sam, who was growing increasingly panicked.

Adan shielded his eyes from the light radiating from Sam's blackened marks. Adan cleared his throat. "Since when can you throw grown men around?"

"A lot's changed since you left." Sam switched tactics and strained against the bar of the cage.

"Left? You mean when I was sold?"

To his credit, Garran didn't make some excuse or spout some snide remark.

Bodies began to materialize on the cobbled ground as the smoke wafted away. Soon all would be visible in the courtyard. The rebels had scattered, leaving only the king's guards gripping their weapons before the castle doors.

Adan put a hand on Sam's shoulder. "You have to run. It's no use. I dreamed of this part too."

Sam froze, as did the others. Shock etched their faces, but disbelief did not. No skepticism creased their brow. No mocking words flowed from their mouths. They believed him. They believed he was the Dreamer.

Sam's jaw twitched. Voice breaking, he ground out, "But we have to try."

"It's no use..." Adan's protest trailed off when he heard the most wonderful and terrifying sound.

"Adan?" the childish voice yelled. Adan's head snapped up as a slight figure slammed into him, clutching tight to his waist. Adan pried the boy to arm's length and drank in his brother's face, his innocent blue eyes, and messy shock of dark curls.

"Ben." Adan choked on the word as tears stung his eyes. He made no attempt to keep them from falling. He hugged his brother close. "Why? Why are you here?"

"I wanted to help find you."

Adan scowled. "You brought my nine-year-old brother with you?"

"Nah," Sam said. "He followed on his own."

Ben tugged on Adan's shirt. "Come on, Adan. Let's go home."

Adan suppressed a sob. He'd accepted that he couldn't leave. He'd made his choice, but now, here was Ben in Sector Six. Ben needed him now, needed his protection, and he couldn't give it. "I can't, buddy." He lifted his cuffed wrist, and Ben jerked at the chain.

"Sam, you have to protect him."

"I know." Sam nodded. "He was supposed to stay at the rebel base." He gripped Ben's shoulder. "How did you find your way?"

"Oh, I followed Evie. But I lost her in the smoke."

"Evie?" Adan whispered.

A shout broke their reunion. The fight around them had quieted, but the remaining guards were now zeroing in on their group.

"Go," Adan whispered. "There are too many of them, and they have longswords."

Sam rattled the chain again as the rest hesitated, fearful. Adan tried again, desperate for them to leave. "Look, they won't kill me. They know what I can do. Get Ben out of here."

Soldiers approached under the captain's orders.

Sam dropped the chain. "We'll be back."

Garran pried Ben from Adan, carrying the sobbing boy over his shoulder like a sack of grain. He disappeared into the smoke, followed by Chase, Asher, Elias, and Thomas.

When Sam remained, Adan clutched his arm. "Go home. Take Ben back." He hesitated. "I'm—I'm to die here."

Sam started to protest, but Adan cut him off.

"Nothing I do changes my dream. It will happen."

The guards were closing in.

Sam yanked his glove off, then shoved something into Adan's hand. "I don't accept that," he yelled as he ran after the others.

Soldiers followed at a sprint.

"I'm trying not to either," Adan whispered as he peered at the enhancement ring on his palm. Alone, he once again awaited his fate.

43

I failed. I failed him again.

Sam caught up to his friends as hopelessness settled on his shoulders. Not only had they failed to rescue Adan, but also a new problem had developed.

They waited in a line at the city gates where soldiers searched every traveler before allowing them to exit the city. More soldiers stood at wide increments along the wall as far as Sam could see.

"How did they shut it down so quickly?" Chase stared ahead where Adan's friends—Thomas, Grace, and James—and two more dark-eyed rebels approached the checkpoint.

"I don't know, but we have to get out and across the river," Sam said. "We have nowhere to stay, and there are too many of us."

"They're at the gates." Chase hissed.

With held breath, Sam fidgeted as Adan's friends' bags were searched. When the soldiers allowed the group to exit the city, he hissed out a breath he hadn't known he was holding. "Okay, it's going to be fine. Asher, is this the way we should go?"

The boy shrugged. "I don't feel anything that tells me otherwise."

Not that helpful, but okay.

The wide space before the gates filled as those who lived outside the city walls poured onto the street, eager to escape the chaos inside.

"Ben, keep your hood low and look down. Let them check your bag, but try not to talk to anyone." Soldiers generally ignored the children who traveled with adults.

Ben held Sam's hand in a death grip.

Horses clopped into the space, and pedestrians scrambled out of the way. Regal soldiers sat atop them, looking down at the weary travelers with their green-eyed gazes. Each carried a strange silver weapon in their gloved fingers. The crowd quieted, but when the soldiers made no move other than to watch the proceedings, the muttering began again.

"Check every bag until we find the thief. A month's wages to the one who does," a man said to the soldiers at the gates.

"Thief?" Elias muttered.

"Should we come back another time?" Garran asked, eyeing their silver weapons.

With new intensity, the eager soldiers tore open the bags belonging to the family ahead of Sam and his group. With uncaring hands, they dug to the bottom of each, even spilling precious grain onto the ground.

They're looking for something.

"No, we stay. We'll look guilty if we leave now. Besides, they're looking for a thief. That's not us."

When the family in front of them shuffled through the gates, Sam moved ahead, keeping Ben behind him.

"How many are in your party?" a soldier asked.

"Six."

"All of you. Step forward. Bags on the table."

Sam pulled Ben along, and they tossed their packs and food bags onto the rickety structure.

"What's your purpose for being in the city today?"

Sam cleared his throat and indicated the bags of grain and rice. "For the king's handout."

The man peered at Sam's green eyes. "You don't live in the city?"

"No, we live just outside. Our fathers are farmers."

The man nodded, and his search was hurried and incomplete. To this man, Sam's green eyes lent him innocence. He shrugged at Sam as if to say, "Sorry about this."

Other soldiers searched his friends' bags, and Sam's interrogator waved him through.

He let out another breath. That wasn't so bad.

"Sam," Garran hissed.

When Sam turned back, the other boy's face had gone ashen. His eyes were wide. Another man approached on horseback.

"Here. I've found it. This boy has it," one of the soldiers yelled.

But Sam's eyes were on Garran. "Garran, what is it?"

"It's him," he whispered, and for the first time, raw fear passed over the overgrown boy's features.

"Who—?" He stopped when he heard Ben's squeak of fear.

"It wasn't me. I didn't even know it was there." Ben looked to Sam, blue eyes wide and bright. "Sam, I swear I didn't take anything."

The area quieted, and Sam's mouth went bone dry as a solder lifted something shining from the bag of rice Ben had been carrying.

A smooth, polished figure—a game piece—a golden Deceiver.

The guard yanked Ben by the arm.

Chase, Asher, and Elias unsheathed their weapons, and Garran stepped forward. "Get your hands off of him or—"

A round disk shot over Sam's shoulder and suctioned to Garran's bicep. He lurched and fell to the ground.

Sam shoved Ben's captor away and tugged the boy to himself. He spun to find a well-dressed man striding toward them, polished black boots crunching on the cobblestones. He clutched a silver StrengthShock before him. This regal man was no soldier.

This was the noble who'd watched Sam from high on the castle steps —the one who'd spoken with Ben's almost-captor.

The man smiled pleasantly. He was tall—as tall as Adan perhaps. "It seems this boy stole from me."

"You're mistaken," Sam ground out as he shoved Ben behind his back.

"The proof is before us." He gestured to the golden Deceiver. "Guards, take the boy."

"No." Sam's marks flared bright but were extinguished when a disk flattened itself onto his neck. He fell to his knees, not losing consciousness but feeling like a sluggish prisoner in his own body. His muscles spasmed, and he toppled onto his side.

The man stood over Ben. "Hey there, what's your name?"

Ben stared at the ground. "Ben." A pause. "I didn't take your toy."

The man chuckled and whispered so only those closest could hear. "Oh, I know."

He knelt before Ben and pushed his hood back. Ben met his gaze, blue eyes shining in the evening sunlight.

"So it's true. There are two blue-eyed boys." No shock registered on his face only delighted satisfaction. "These boys are not what they seem. Bring them all."

44

Evie pressed her back against a jagged wall, facing the looming castle. An overhang jutted above her head, casting a shadow across her light tunic. A white feathered half mask dangled from her fingers. For once, she didn't wear a hood to cover her hair. She'd left her pack behind. Her festival costume, Joram's communicator, and the borrowed dagger were her only possessions.

The castle and the surrounding courtyard were deserted now. Only the king's soldiers remained. The festivalgoers had fled, taking their merriment with them. They left a gray evening that smelled of smoke and fear.

The wind whipped at her reddish-gold hair. She shoved it behind her ear, chin tilted upward, her attention drawn to the wide balcony. The sheer curtain billowed out, beckoning her. *It is time*, it seemed to say.

I can't, her mortal heart answered.

The traitorous heart thundered in her chest as a fork of lightning struck, lighting the clouds above the jagged mountains. Its answering crack echoed across the courtyard like the tick of a giant clock—her final day almost spent.

She'd arrived in time to watch Sam sprint away with a few prisoners. Rebels had spirited away other Arvad. But not the Dreamer. Not the beautiful blue-eyed boy whose blood determined her future.

Guards had ushered Adan inside, and now her watch showed just enough time to do what needed to be done and sprint for the mountains. The other Sector Five boys were on their own. They'd find the portal in time. They'd go home. But she'd never return home if she didn't finish her job now.

So why couldn't she move?

I'm not strong enough. Her head sagged forward.

A familiar vibration arrested her hip. She sucked in a breath and fumbled into her pocket, almost ripping it open, until she held Joram's communicator. She sought the Accept Connection icon, instead, a notification for a day-old digital message flashed on the screen.

<<<>>>

Evie, I've tried to reconnect our video feed. I'm attempting to write you a final warning. A plea, really. Do it. You have no choice if you want to go back to the Control Room. If that doesn't convince you, then maybe this will: They are rallying the Death Guardians and will send them. They will not bring you back with them. As of right now, the powers that be don't know others from Sector Five crossed over, bringing their Gifts with them. I didn't tell them. The Death Guardians, however, might be able to sense them and eliminate all with a Gift. If you doubt me, then remember what Alizah and I told you about Sector One. It was destroyed with fire and still burns to this day. The Death Guardians spared no one. Do it for yourself and your future, but also do it for me. I miss you. You're my only true friend. Remember who you are and what you want to be. Don't let that dream die along with your aging human body. Come home.

Joram

PS I'm still trying to find the portal in Sector Five so I can come to your aid.

<<<>>>

She tilted her head back against the rock. A tear drifted down her cheek. The curtain billowed.

So that's it. There are no more options. Only death. Adan's death or everyone else's—including hers, in time.

She shook herself. There was no more time for mortal weakness. Shoving her humanity away, she willed herself to be unfeeling—inhuman. It shouldn't be so hard to be indifferent. She refused to think about Adan until she was before him. She thought of Ben and his bright, innocent eyes. Her act would protect him.

Numb, she tied the white mask to her face and crept behind a tree near the castle wall.

When a guard had passed and there seemed no better opportunity would present itself, she began to climb, hoping the lingering fog would shield her from the distracted soldiers.

Step after step, reach after reach, she made her way. Her heart grew heavier with every inch until, surely, the ache alone would cause her to fall, to weigh her down until she lost her grip. Too soon, she found herself level with Adan's balcony. She slid over the edge and crouched out of sight next to the stone railing.

Quick breaths passed over her lips. Distant lightning lit the gray sky. The answering thunder boomed.

Please be here. Please don't be here.

Evie shut down. She had to protect the others. She wanted nothing more than to go home—to be a Guardian.

Closing her eyes, she held tight to Ben's Watcher in her pocket.

Maker, help me.

She took a deep breath and moved.

45

Adan stood transfixed on the now-worn path of his mind. Things—a blur before—now presented themselves in sharp focus. The snowy tree wasn't snowy at all. A full bloom of delicate white flowers covered it. Its fuzzy cotton drifted on the breeze.

The sandy path held deep rivets as if narrow-wheeled contraptions traveled it often. The snake did not slither in yellow grass lining either side but, rather, on a bed of bright petals. Tiny yellow flowers littered the green, running ahead like rivers of gold.

Light caught his eye, and he peered at his arm. The pale marks swirling over his skin were glowing. The light moved and pulsed, leading his eye along the luminescent swirls that met to circle his pinky finger where the mysterious enhancement ring rested. It, no doubt, was responsible for this crystalline dreamscape. The ring, however, appeared brighter and more colorful than it did in his waking hours. He tilted his hand. The tiny prisms positioned in a circular pattern around its round face caught the fading sun in a riot of reflected light.

He raised his other hand and found the golden dagger in his grip. It glowed in his palm as crimson blood dripped from its edge.

Trees loomed on each side of the path, and he felt the eyes on him. A snake slithered nearer, and a girl with reddish hair spoke frantically in his direction from within the dense foliage. He'd seen this girl in his dreams before. She'd been deep within the shadowy forest. Today, she stood in a ray of golden light. Her skin shone as Evie's did in his dreams. Her mouth moved, but no sound came forth. A warning?

His heart thrummed in his chest.

Something was coming.

He rotated in a slow circle, the gleaming dagger held before him in trembling fingers.

A single bird flew past in an ash-and-golden blur. It disappeared into a blinding light flaring ahead. Adan shielded his face until the blaze faded. Before him, Evie waited, watching. She wore a flowing, white floor-length dress that swayed in the breeze. She glowed with an otherworldly light as she fixed him with bright golden eyes shining behind a white feathered mask. Tendrils of dark hair haloed her head.

Adan waited, but she did nothing.

The red-haired girl also watched Evie. "Adan," she mouthed.

"Adan," Evie said in a voice not quite her own. Adan glanced between the two of them. The girl's lips moved again, and Evie said, "You have the key."

He locked eyes with the redhead. She started to turn and walk away but stopped, facing him one more time.

She spoke, and Evie said, "Being human is not a weakness." The redhead turned away, and Evie shook herself.

Blinking, she said, "Wake up, Adan. It's time."

≪◇≫

Adan's eyes flew open. He surged into a sitting position, a death grip on his ivory bedsheets. He took in his cavernous room with wide eyes. It was empty, save the usual items. All was quiet.

He let out a breath and swung his legs off the side of the bed. He'd only meant to rest his eyes. Shaking his head, he walked to the basin next to the empty wardrobe and splashed water over his face. He hung his dripping curls over the bowl, arms resting on the edge.

He was so very tired. The ring Sam had shoved into his hand, sparkled with wetness on his pinky finger, but its appearance was normal—utterly unremarkable.

"Worthless ring," he muttered, tilting his hand in the dim light, trying to steady his racing heart.

He lifted his head to the oval mirror. It was almost as if a stranger stared back.

"Who are you?" he whispered. The boy with the dull brown eyes only frowned. Adan grabbed a white box resting next to the basin and plucked the tinted contacts from his eyes.

He looked in the mirror again, and this time his blue-eyed reflection gazed back. Better.

"Why are you here?"

No answer was forthcoming, so he swiped his book from the bedside table and slipped it into his pocket. He then moved about the room, preparing for the inevitable shadows that would crawl across the stone floor as the clouds moved closer.

When the space danced with candlelight, the translucent curtain billowed outward in a gust. The distant sky lit with a flash of electricity. A dark shape shifted in the momentary brightness, and a soft scrape drifted on the wind.

Adan froze.

A girl with long flowing hair stood in the open air of the balcony just beyond the curtain. She watched him.

The muted light behind her cast an eerie glow on the fabric, throwing the shape of her into silhouette. The wind moved, and between the two strips, he was granted an unimpeded peek before they fell again.

Evie?

His mouth went dry. His lips parted as a ragged breath passed through them.

She moved forward, pushing the curtain aside, and crossed the threshold.

No, not Evie. Her hair was too light. It was his rebel friend. He'd never seen her with her hair down. A feathered half mask—the style from back home—covered her face. Long white ribbons flowed behind her in the wind, and a white tunic hung low over black pants.

The curtains billowed about her. She didn't smile but watched him watching her. Again, a strange sense of dual recognition struck him.

The girl wasn't surprised to see his natural blue eyes. She blinked, and her bright golden gaze caught the candlelight behind her white feathered mask.

Could it be?

"Evie?" he whispered.

She continued to watch him—no denial on her lips. But no confirmation either. He was no longer sure who she was, but one thing was certain. She was here to kill him.

He took a step back. "You found me."

She let out a desperate, humorless laugh. "Yes."

Then she removed her mask and dropped her hands, holding it at her side. The ribbons flowed out from it, catching a sudden breeze. Raindrops sprinkled onto the stone floor, staining a dark irregular pattern.

He shifted toward his bed. "I wasn't expecting you."

She took one step forward. "Are you sure?"

He wasn't. He took another sidestep. "You're here to kill me."

Resigned, and as if on cue, she slipped a silver blade from a sheath at her waist. The slow ring of metal broke the silence. She held it at her side, body rigid. Dropping the mask onto the wet floor, she said nothing.

He continued his path with another shuffle. "But you don't want to."

Surprise passed over her face. She masked it. "What makes you say that?"

"You've had plenty of opportunities. You didn't take them." He paused, taking another step. "You cry when it's done."

"How could you know that?"

He smirked. "You already know."

She didn't deny it. Her knuckles were white around her blade. Was her hand shaking? A fork of lightning slashed the sky behind her. The sun still peeked from below the cloud bank.

Adan took another step, and she glanced at the bed. She must've guessed what he was doing because she sprang forward, slashing with her blade, and he dove, throwing a hand under the mattress. He kicked out with his booted foot and knocked her attack away, smacking the side of her hand. She didn't drop the blade but stumbled to the side. He groped for the hidden weapon, hoping not to cut his fingers. Mercifully, he felt the hilt and drew the golden blade free. It winked in the candlelight.

Her eyes went wide. Perhaps he should've left it hidden away.

The girl lunged again, and he, with speed on his side, deflected her swing. She came again, face tight. He dodged and parried attack after attack. He was good, but she was better. Twice, she drew blood from his arm, and he only narrowly avoided a skewer to his midsection. He had thought only to incapacitate her. Even now, he didn't want to kill her, but she moved with lethal grace and with death in her eyes. She would end him. *Kill or be killed.*

Her face pinched, though he wasn't sure the anger was toward him. A tear rolled down her cheek. She swiped it away.

"Why?" he rasped around labored breath. "Why are you doing this?"

"I have to." She drew a silver arc across the space in front of his stomach, only just missing him as he threw himself backward.

He followed her momentum to the side, grabbing her wrist and swinging it over her head. In the same movement, she grabbed his weaponed wrist, and they stumbled backward until the girl's back hit the wall, their arms and blades pinned above their heads.

He had the advantage. His body pressed against hers, holding her in place. She struggled but couldn't break free. Neither released their blades.

She stilled, breathing hard, and they stood locked together. His breath rustled the hair at her forehead. Tears streamed down her face.

He swallowed and, voice low, said, "Who sent you to kill me? At least tell me that."

She was quiet, and he thought she might not answer. Finally, she said, "It doesn't matter. If I don't, they'll send others to kill Sam and your friends. Even Ben."

He stiffened. "What?"

She leaned her head against the wall to look up at him. Lavender filled his senses. They breathed the same air now. She stared into his eyes before she shook herself. "You were never meant to come here, Adan. Sector Six is to remain free of the Gifted. You tripped an alarm when you arrived."

"But I'm not the only Gifted person here."

She closed her eyes. "I know… it's… puzzling."

"Puzzling? You're trying to stab me with a knife, and you say it's puzzling?" She was infuriating. "You didn't answer my question. Who sent you?"

"The Control Room. The Maker sent me." She was yelling now. New tears streamed down her freckle-dusted cheeks.

"Sent you? But you're Huldan." His mind rebelled against what he knew.

"Can't you see? I'm no Huldan. I'm not even human. I take on the appearance of the sector I'm in."

"You look human." He felt her rapid pulse under his fingers where their hands were still tangled overhead. "You *feel* human."

It struck him then. This girl had been in Sector Five. "You *are* Evie. The same Evie I met that day by the pond in Sector Five."

She nodded.

"That was the day I was captured. Why were you there? Did you help the man who brought me here?"

She jerked her head up. "No, of course not."

Did he believe her? He still wasn't sure.

"What about my brothers? Did they trip an alarm?"

"Not that I know of, but another from the Control Room told me only hours ago that the Death Guardians are on standby. If I fail, they will come."

"Death Guardians?"

"The Guardians who annihilated Sector One. Like in your book. But they won't kill only you. They'll kill everyone in Sector Six with a Gift. That's why I'm here. I can't procrastinate any longer. I kill you now, or someone else kills you all later."

Adan loosened his grip, but she didn't move. This is why he always lost, why he always perished in his dreams, and why nothing ever changed. Even if he did best his opponent, he'd still die. He would die to protect his family. But he had to know one more thing.

"Evie, why were you there that day? It's too much of a coincidence."

"Maybe someone—the Deceiver, perhaps—used my mistakes as a cover for your capture."

Mistakes? "But why you? Why were you in that park? *You* came and sat by *me*." Her timid smile and how she'd quoted a line from *One's Raining Fire*...

"I—" She stopped as if unable to force the words past her lips.

His jaw clenched. "Why. Were. *You*. There?"

She swallowed, and something in her face softened. She ducked her head. Was she embarrassed? "I sneaked to the ground with another Watcher, a Traveler Coordinator. I... I had to see the Dreamer for myself."

His eyebrows lifted. "Why?" he whispered.

Her cheeks pink, she released his wrist. He didn't dare do the same with her other hand. They stayed pinned to the wall as she slid that hand down to his face. She traced around the outside of his jaw, her eyes following the movement. She touched the place where his dimple appeared when he smiled and then touched the corner of his lip. In a whisper so low he almost didn't hear her, she said, "I don't know."

Her pulse raced under his fingers. His heartbeat had quickened. She fixed him with her golden stare and dropped her hand to her side. Was she playing a game with him? Was she trying to lower his defenses? It no longer mattered.

"I don't have the luxury of trying to figure out what that's supposed to mean. If what you say is true and my friends"—his voice broke—"and my brother are in danger, then I won't try to stop you." He released her and stepped back.

She gripped the silver dagger, eyes wide.

He took a deep breath, steeling himself. "If you're sure it's the only way to protect them, then do it."

<h1 style="text-align:center">46</h1>

Back still pressed against the wall, Evie gaped at Adan. What was he doing? This wasn't how it was supposed to go.

When she didn't say anything, he ordered, "Do it."

The color had drained from his face, and his balled fists hung at his sides. He shifted from foot to foot.

She raised her silver dagger. His eyes, now saucer-sized sapphires, trailed it. He looked back at her, his face vulnerable and desperate. She lowered the blade. Raised it again. Lowered it. With her free hand, she pulled Joram's crumpled note from her pocket and fisted it at her side.

Adan's eyes followed her movements, and the golden blade, still clutched at his side, winked in the candlelight.

"Ugh!" She threw her hands up. What was wrong with her? She stepped around him, and he turned, still facing her, brow drawn. She took up a fighting stance, her frustration spilling over. "I can't kill you like this. Fight me."

Her only relief had been in knowing he'd defend himself. Fight her. Try to kill her.

When he made no move to raise the golden blade, she clenched her teeth. "Fight me."

He backed into the wall and leaned into it as if he needed the support. He dropped her dagger, and it clanged onto the stone floor. "No."

"Why not?" Now she was the desperate one, almost pleading.

"I've dreamed of this for years. A big chunk of my life has led to this day, possibly this moment. Something's happening, and I don't think it has much to do with me. You have to do this. It's part of some grand plan. You're doing what you have to do." He dipped his chin, then found her eyes again. "Also, how could I choose myself over Ben, Sam, Asher, Elias, Chase"—he chuckled—"even Garran?"

His dimple winked.

He was making it impossible. He was… good. A good person. How could she kill him? She thought about how it would feel to plunge her dagger into him, watch his life drain away. His spirit would go to the Waiting Place, and she would go to the Control Room. She would never see him again. Not in person. And not even on her vidfeed. The thought caused her physical pain. She'd never felt like this in the Control Room. Never had friends like Lena, Sam, or Ben. Before, she thought she'd been pretending with everyone. But not everything had been an act. The friendships she'd made were real. And she'd never met someone who made her feel like Adan did.

But perhaps more than her selfish human desires was the fact that he was willing to die for the people he loved.

There is no greater love a person can demonstrate than to give their own life to protect someone else—the Maker's own words. Surely, someone who held that much love and willing sacrifice didn't deserve to die by *her* hand.

"Stop making me wait," he rasped. "Please. It's torture."

She lifted the silver dagger but made no move toward him.

He gave her a nervous half-smile. "There's no hesitation like this in my dream."

"You saw me kill you?"

"Yes." His lips turned down. "Well… no, not really. It was never clear. But you were always there. And more recently, someone else was there too—a dark-haired man. And always the blade." He glanced down at the golden dagger at his feet.

Evie did, too. What had Krystopher said when he'd handed it over? *There may be a time that you will need it. I don't know when or where or why.*

She paced in front of Adan. "I've known for weeks what I have to do. I never expected to feel so human. It's… confusing. No one else in the Control Room would hesitate." She stopped pacing. "There *is* something wrong with me. Maybe I don't belong there."

"Human," Adan whispered, face pinched.

"What?"

"Something you said in my dream before I woke up and found you here." He stood taller, lifting his weight from the wall. "Only it didn't sound like you. Someone was speaking through you. You said being human is not a weakness."

Evie froze. Jesiah—the Maker—had said those words to her mere hours before she came to Sector Six. A flash of lightning reflected from the golden blade lying on the stone floor. But after that, Krystopher had given her the mysterious blade. Had they been trying to tell her something—perhaps telling her to follow her human instincts? How was she supposed to figure this out?

"Evie?" Adan prodded.

She shook her head. "I don't know."

Over the balcony, the sun was sinking toward the mountains on the horizon, just visible below the cloud bank before gray mist swallowed it up. The room fell into deeper shadow. One of Adan's many candles, the one closest to the window, winked out. "I don't know what I'm supposed to do."

There was a pound on Adan's door.

"Evie," a familiar voice shouted from the other side. Her eyes went wide.

He made it to this sector.

"Evie, are you there?"

A weary smile crossed her face. At last. Someone to help her solve this problem.

Something like suspicion slid onto Adan's face as they moved toward the door.

But as she started forward, still gripping the scrap of paper, she slowed. *He will try to help me. He will kill Adan.* She put her hand out, and Adan stopped beside her. They both jumped as another more powerful blow shook the frame.

"Don't open it," she whispered.

Another splintering pound shook its hinges.

She nodded toward the balcony. "We need to—"

The doorframe gave way, and the door swung open. She and Adan jumped back, avoiding the spray of splintered wood as a hulking Strength Wielder stumbled into the room and lumbered aside. A handsome golden-eyed man followed him.

"Joram," Evie whispered.

Adan shot her a confused look as the tall, dark-haired Travel Coordinator approached.

The corners of Joram's lips turned up. "Evie, you're okay. Thank goodness." He let out a breath. "But I see you're not quite done here."

He drew his blade but held it pointed toward the floor.

Adan glanced between them. "Joram?"

Her eyes stayed locked on her friend. "You did it. How did you get here?"

"I found the portal in Sector Five, of course."

She eyed the blade. "What are you going to do?"

"I came to help you. I thought you might not be able to do it on your own—you might be overcome in battle. You *are* a mortal." Then his lip quirked up. "But maybe I should've worried about you being overcome in a different way."

Adan leaned closer. "Evie—"

"Not now, Adan," Joram cut him off. "You don't want to get in the middle of this. Evie, finish your job. Go to your portal. Go home. Your time is almost out."

He was right. It was now or never.

"Everything can go back as it was. Don't let these weak humans stand in your way. There will be other promotions, and you'll make Guardian. Everything you've ever wanted."

He wasn't entirely wrong. That was what she had wanted—had dreamed of for eons. But Joram was wrong about one thing. It wasn't *everything* she'd ever wanted. After visiting Sector Five and then coming here and having human friends, she'd come to realize being a Guardian alone wasn't what would make her happy. She thought of Ben and Sam and Lena and all the other rebels who'd taken her in and laughed with her and fought with her. They'd made mistakes together—cried together. They were human, and they'd been her family. At least until she betrayed their trust. They were not weak.

Adan opened his mouth like he wanted to say something, but he did not.

"If you don't finish it, you'll never be accepted back to the Control Room." Joram spread out his hands, blade glinting. "You have a choice right now to get your life back. Put all this nonsense behind you."

When Evie still made no move, Joram lowered his arms, his shoulders curling in. "You're smitten with a mortal. They'll never understand it. They don't understand humans like you and I do."

Adan's head tilted her way, and her cheeks grew hot.

Perhaps Joram did understand humans better than most immortals since he walked among them often. And maybe she and Joram weren't so different. But another also seemed to understand humans. Jesiah. *Being human is not a weakness.* Friendship was not a weakness. Krystopher had given her the blade, but he'd never been one for violence. Was it for another purpose?

"What of the Deceiver?"

"Go back and tell them what you know. That's your only move right now. You can't defeat him on your own."

He was right, but she didn't move.

"Fine." Joram huffed. "We'll do it. Vincent."

The Strength Wielder stomped forward.

Moving with conviction, Evie positioned herself in front of Adan. "No, I won't let you."

"You can't be serious. Do you have any idea what you're doing? I'm trying to help you."

"Maybe I don't. But it's the right thing."

"It will be easy. His brothers were brought in by the king's soldiers only moments ago. They're in the holding cell downstairs."

Adan and Evie both froze.

"What did you say?" Adan asked in a deadly whisper.

"I'll take care of this messy business. Evie, you can still make it to your portal. Then I'll lead the others to the intersector portal I arrived through. It's not far from here. The Death Guardians won't be summoned."

Her muscles tightened. "They all go to the intersector portal. Including Adan." She raised her chin. "Joram, where is it? Someone moved it. You have to tell us where it is."

The Travel Coordinator rolled his eyes. "You're acting like a child."

She lifted her blade, and Adan stepped to her side. He must've picked up the golden dagger when she'd turned her back. He now held it before him.

Joram's eyebrows shot up. A whisper passed his lips—"Krystopher's blade."

His throat bobbed, and Adan shifted his grip on the gleaming weapon.

"Evie," Joram started as if scolding a child. He watched the blade. "You're making a terrible mistake."

"I won't let you hurt him."

"You're willing to give up everything?"

She let the crumpled note slip to the floor. "Yes," she seethed. "Where is it? Where is the portal?"

"Your judgment's clouded. I won't let you make this mistake." He gestured with his dagger to the Strength Wielder still standing by the door. "Kill the boy."

The boy, though unarmed, crept forward.

She and Adan raised their blades.

"Vincent, you're not even armed. What are you doing?" Adan asked.

Vincent rushed them with a yell, and she spun like a dancer to slice a deep rivet into the flesh of his shoulder. He screamed out as Adan did the same to his thigh, though with much less finesse. But Vincent didn't stop. He charged toward Adan, who slid out of reach. Evie whirled on Joram, her blade outstretched.

Joram matched her stance, though, for the first time, an ugly fear twisted his handsome face. "Evie, I only want to help you."

"Then let us go."

Adan slashed at Vincent. The Strength Wielder stumbled and crashed over a porcelain washbasin, sprawling onto the floor. He struggled to stand, bleeding. The drops splattered onto the rain-peppered floor and fanned out in the water. Adan clearly didn't want to deliver a finishing blow.

Joram lifted a palm, his ancient eyes sad. "Do as you wish."

She gripped Adan's arm. "Let's go." They burst through the splintered door and vaulted over a crumpled body. Adan gaped at his fallen guard but didn't slow.

"Ben," Adan panted as they rounded a corner.

She nodded.

"I know where the holding cells are." He sprinted down a hall until they slowed, listening.

Voices echoed ahead as footsteps drew near.

"Come on." Tugging her along, he slid into an inset of the wall where a tapestry hung over the opening. They waited, impatient for the people to pass. Evie feared they'd hear her heavy breathing, but boisterous laughs drowned the sound. Adan's wary blue eyes tracked her all the while.

Eyes never leaving his, she wrapped her fingers around his wrist. She put the silver dagger into his hand and took the golden blade from the other. He didn't protest, but his throat bobbed as if he half-expected her to run him through.

He'd never trust her.

She lowered her gaze and the blade.

He let out a pent breath. "You okay?"

Not trusting herself to speak *and* hold in the human emotions, she lifted a shoulder.

When the passage cleared, they continued on quiet feet to the holding cells. Evie crept behind the only guard on duty and knocked him in the temple with the hilt of her blade like her trainer in the Control Room had taught her. He sank to the stone floor.

"Evie!" Ben yelled. His was the only face she could see, and her lips curled up. She put a finger to her lips.

Then, seeing Adan behind her, the boy called out to his big brother in an excited but poorly executed whisper. "Adan." Ben reached through the bars of his cell, and Adan ran to grab his hand.

"Shhh."

Hands moved forward to grasp the bars of other cells lining the hall. Sam, Asher, Elias, Chase, and Garran—all with wide, relieved, and distrustful green eyes.

"We have to hurry," Adan said. "Where are the keys?"

Sam pointed to a desk in the corner. "There. They're in the desk."

She and Adan rummaged through the drawers. Her hands fumbled in her haste until she released the lock for Garran and Asher. Adan retrieved Ben and was opening the door for Sam when Sam's half-whisper floated out. "I don't trust her. She's not who she says she is."

Adan only shook his head, letting out a frantic laugh. "Believe me, I know."

47

The eight companions escaped the castle with surprising ease. Most guards remained at the front gates, and an air of chaos clung to the courtyard and surrounding areas. As guards turned pedestrians away, no one paid much attention to a group leaving the vicinity. It seemed almost as if no one had known there were people in the holding cells.

Once clear, they took off at a run, winding through Inevah until well away from the looming castle.

Evie's feet pounded beside the others. She peeked over her shoulder for any sign of Joram or soldiers or worse.

What were they to do now? How would they escape the Death Guardians?

Adan slowed. "Wait."

They stopped on the open street, and the Dreamer eyed her. "You really don't know where the portal is?"

"No." She panted. "It was gone when Sam returned to it to send Ben back home."

Sam's jaw dropped. "You followed us? Even then?"

She ignored him. "The portal didn't just disappear. Someone must've moved it."

Adan pulled at his hair and spun in a circle. "Where's Asher?"

"There he is." Chase pointed back the way they'd come.

Asher stood in the street, his face glazed over, eyebrows pinched. The few pedestrians who still wandered about stayed well away from him.

"His mark. It's glowing."

"Come on," Sam yelled, and they ran back to the boy with wide, bright eyes.

"This way. We need to hurry."

Asher sprinted into an alley, and they followed. He wound an intricate path through the cobbled streets and dark alleyways. He didn't stop or pause.

"Asher, Ben needs to slow down." Elias huffed as he hobbled along, holding a stitch in his side.

Asher stopped.

"No, I—" Ben started.

"Shhh." Elias nudged the boy.

Evie put her hands on her head and shook her legs out. Her mouth was dry, and sweat trickled down her back. Above her, the gray sky withheld the moisture her body desperately wanted. Distant thunder rumbled.

Asher moved on, pacing them at a brisk walk.

She lagged, keeping an eye on the path behind, and Adan slowed, matching her strides. "This isn't over. Is it?"

"I think not." She met his blue stare, then ducked her chin. "But if I can get you all through the portal in time, you might make it."

"Won't you come through with us?"

"I don't know if I can."

"You'll go back to the Control Room?"

"No." She glared at her watch. Fifteen minutes. "There's no time. I—I am exiled."

"Exiled?" He halted, grabbing her arm. "You're exiled? Because of us?"

She opened her mouth to blame Jesiah, to blame Krystopher or Gavrie or the supervisor of Control Room Six—or Joram—but the words wouldn't come. "I made my own mistakes. I did this."

His brow pinched. "What will you do?"

"I don't know."

"Is this it?" Asher stopped outside a low stone wall. A rickety wooden fence rested on rusted hinges. The marks on his arm faded along with the determined tilt to his features. He frowned as Adan parted through his friends and pushed the gate open. Asher shrugged. "It's a garden."

Adan entered, and the others followed.

A riot of color spread over the space. Yellow and red flowers crawled along the grass, over tree trunks, and around ragged rock formations.

"'In a river of blood and gold, the Deceiver waited.'" Asher turned wide eyes to Evie. "Like the game. Like the book."

"This is it," Adan whispered as they crept through the garden's open entrance and entered a narrow dirt path lined by tall trees. Yellow flowers spread over the grass along its edge.

Adan's breaths were quick and labored. The Dreamer tilted his face to the gray sky, perhaps noting the position of the hidden sun. A tall tree covered in white flowers snagged his focus. A breath of wind sent its cottony pollen to flight. The puffs swirled around them in a summer snow.

She splayed a hand, and one drifted into her palm.

The corner of her mouth quirked up, but it fell again when she caught Adan's flushed face. He eyed her, his features contorting. His gaze slid down to the golden blade sheathed at her side.

"This is where it happens. This is where I die," he whispered so only she could hear. "Are you going to kill me?"

She fisted her hands. "No. I gain nothing from your death. I have nothing left to lose."

Adan swallowed. "Why does the Maker want me dead?"

"I think it's the Deceiver who wants you dead."

"Why?"

"He thinks you're Krystopher's Marked—like in the prophecy. But that's impossible. Uzziah marked you."

Adan closed his eyes as their feet flattened rivets in the fine sand. Puffs drifted from the earth with each footstep. "Actually, he didn't. Uzziah made everyone think he did it. But it was done in secret... by another."

"What?"

"It was done by another. A man with golden eyes like yours. Younger than Uzziah with darker skin."

"Krystopher," Evie breathed, taking in the pale marks on Adan's golden skin. "So it's true. *One's Raining Fire* is true. You *are* the one. You're Nolan's descendant." She pressed a hand to her mouth. "Nolan failed, so the prophecy is playing out again through you. We have to go. He'll never let you leave."

They picked up the pace, searching for the bronze archway.

How had Nolan's line survived if the Deceiver killed them all? Evie sucked in a breath. Nolan's wife had only recently found out she was pregnant. The Deceiver didn't know. They must have hidden the baby.

"Evie, there's another thing," Adan said. "Your friend back there… the one who tried to help you. He's from the Control Room, too?"

She nodded. "He's going to be so mad at me."

"And you know him as Joram?"

"Yes. That's his name."

"I met him almost as soon as I arrived in Inevah weeks ago. He was interested in what my Gift might be. I never told him, but he found out."

"That's impossible. He only arrived today."

"No, he was here. Not only that, but everyone seems to know him. They *have* known him. He's been working for the steward of Sodorrah for years."

Evie nearly stumbled, couldn't move.

Adan stopped, turning to look at her.

No. It couldn't be. It was too unfathomable. "Sodorrah?"

"He goes by Joromy."

Her heart lurched. "No."

"There it is," Sam called over his shoulder.

Evie recalled a particular passage from *One's Raining Fire*. She hadn't thought about it much at the time, but now, she knew. She'd been a part of this plan all along. *The Deceiver's only hope was to kill the Marked One. He and his Immortal Warrior, one trained in combat, might send him to his early grave.*

Evie touched the smooth watch at her wrist. "*I* am the Immortal Warrior." She earned those marks in the Control Room months ago.

"And a lousy one at that," a voice rang from the trees.

The Deceiver sauntered onto the path, blocking the way to the portal. Two of the captain's Strength Wielders followed.

"It's him," Garran whispered beside Evie. "He arrested us at the city gates. And he's the whisperer who came to me in Sector Five. He wanted Adan."

Garran's words confirmed what Evie already suspected. Adan was wrong. This immortal wasn't *working* for the steward of Sodorrah. He *was* the steward. A man skilled at making people believe what he wanted—and at making them forget.

One of her oldest friends stepped into the dying light. The Deceiver revealed at long last.

<<<<>>>>

Evie slipped the golden blade from its sheath.

"Evaniah, you should have listened to me." Joram shook his head. "I tried to help you."

"Help me? You've been using me." Her voice broke. "I thought we were friends."

As Adan's gaze slid her way, she shook with pent-up anger.

Joram lifted a hand into the air as if waving these concerns aside. "You *are* my friend. You're the immortal who's most like me. I would've asked you to join me in my endeavors for the worlds. I did want to see you back home. I wanted you to make Guardian—be my partner." He frowned with what appeared genuine sadness. "I gave you every opportunity, but you failed me. You became distracted." His eyes slithered over Adan. "Now… now you know too much. You must know I can't let any of you leave."

Evie's wrist vibrated, and a persistent beeping filled the silence. She glanced at her watch.

Joram smiled. "Time's up."

She gripped her dagger and scanned the garden, expecting a Death Guardian to materialize.

"Oh, Evie." Joram flashed his palms. "They're not coming. It's only you… and me."

"What?"

"And it's probably a bad time to tell you that you could've returned to the Control Room portal and gone home at any time. Blood portals only activate with the blood of Jesiah's Marked. You could have activated it at any time using your blood."

"Everything—*everything*—has been a lie." Numbness weighed down her limbs, slowed her heart. "All this time."

"Nothing personal, of course." With a wave, he paced in front of them. "My plans have been in motion long before Jesiah formed you."

Lies. All lies. Carefully crafted plans to deceive an immortal fighter into killing Krystopher's Marked. How could she have been so stupid?

"Not to worry, Evaniah. You can remain here in Sector Six. I've always enjoyed your company. I will no doubt have to tell the Control Room you're dead, though." Wincing, he ducked his head and shook it.

Keep him talking. Think of something. "When you spoke to me on your communicator, were you in Sector Five?"

"Oh no, I was here. I was waiting for you. I came because I thought you needed some prodding. You did, did you not?"

"If not through Five, then how did you get here?"

He spread both arms, moving in a slow circle as if to encompass all the sectors. "Sectors Five, Two, Six—I can go to them all. I have many secrets. A network of restored portals is my greatest. I've used this portal many times over the last weeks. I never even missed a shift in the Control Room while keeping an eye on our friend." He paced, his golden eyes blazing with fiery pride. "By the time Jesiah finishes Sector Seven, I'll have created a path to it."

A flurry of pollen drifted around them.

Joram brushed his shoulder where one of the puffs landed. "But this has not been my greatest power. No, my most treasured asset is in my ability to make the weakest mortals forget. I can make them forget my face, my voice, or even their own lives."

Evie shook her head, still battling what she knew to be true and what she wanted to be true. "It's been you all along. For eons. In all the sectors." Her chin jutted upward. "Why?"

"Why not?" He raised his arms and took in his surroundings. "When I discovered my Gift, my Gift of persuasive words, the worlds were mine for the taking."

"That's not good enough. There must be more. Jesiah was a father to you and Krystopher, a brother. I've heard many say you and Krystopher are so much alike."

Joram's face darkened. "I am not like Krystopher!" Lunging forward, he spat out the words. "I wish only to thwart his plans. He annihilated all of mine. Sector One was mine. He should've left it long before he did. Everything I'd worked for evaporated in an instant—burned to ash by Jesiah and his Death Guardians. All because the humans followed me instead of Krystopher."

He shook a finger at Adan. "It's why I took the Dreamer. I was working to take Uzziah's Strength Wielder, but Krystopher sent a message to Uzziah to mark this one on the holiday. If Krystopher wanted it done, I'd be there to ruin it. It wasn't until yesterday that I knew he was the Dreamer. Krystopher marked you in secret, didn't he?"

Adan didn't answer.

"But you *are* like Krystopher." Evie plunged on. "I've seen it. You both have great passions. Much more than the others."

Joram huffed. "Much like you, Evaniah. Have you not wondered why you are different? Why did Jesiah create you, a lone Watcher, ages after he'd made all the others?" He cocked his head, smirking, apparently enjoying the havoc he wreaked in her mind.

She stumbled back a step. He'd put to voice the fears she held closest.

He circled her now, his words gliding over her. "Do you even know what plans Jesiah had for *you*?"

When she didn't answer, he said, "I thought not."

Let it go. Just keep him talking.

Garran took a slow step back.

Joram's attention drifted to Adan as a flash of lightning lit the sky. "You were a mystery. Marked by Uzziah—but not a Strength Wielder. Yesterday with the king, I learned your true Gift. You can see the future. I thought I'd taken care of that little problem when I wiped out Nolan's line. But here you are. Both of you."

He stopped circling Evie, cocked his head toward Ben, who held Asher's hand.

Sam blocked Ben from view.

"It's a problem, you see." Joram waved a hand. "I don't know which of you Krystopher thought would be my undoing. So, you both have to die."

The guards lumbered forward. A gust of wind tunneled through the trees. The cotton drifted, weapons rose, and a flock of blackbirds raced overhead. Squawking drowned the constant rumble from the clouds.

The Strength Wielder, Vincent, glared at Adan. Blood still oozed from his wounds and stained his clothes crimson.

"Vincent," Adan said, "we've never been friends. But you would murder my family? My little brother? Even the captain would want you to take us alive."

Vincent opened his mouth to say something but closed it again. His brow pinched.

"Vin, remember what I told you." Joram prowled around the Strength Wielder. "They deserve to die for the trouble they've caused. Adan has made a fool of you. Remember that? You will help me kill them. They'll only cause more trouble."

Vincent's face hardened.

"That's better." Joram's golden eyes gleamed. "Some are more easily manipulated than others. Now"—he rubbed his hands together—"Garran, why don't you join us."

Garran, who'd backed away several paces, stopped.

"Garran, fight it," Adan yelled.

Garran met Adan's eyes, but Evie could see his rational self leaving him. It must be easier for Joram to manipulate one he'd already overcome many times.

"Come, Garran." Joram flicked his wrist. "We'll make quick work of this."

Garran's face went slack when he'd been overcome.

"Kill that one." Smiling, Joram pointed at Sam. "The Strength Wielder."

Without hesitation, Garran barreled into Sam. They brawled with their fists as the others scattered. It was unclear who would best the other since Sam no longer wore the enhancement ring.

But all Joram had needed was a distraction for Sam. Joram set his two guards on the rest of them.

"Asher, Elias, get Ben to the portal," Adan commanded. Asher grabbed Ben's hand, and the three of them moved away from the fight. They'd wait for a clear path. Chase, with his bow, took cover behind a tree, nocking an arrow as he went. Evie turned, standing by Adan, and met the force of two giants as they barreled forward.

She ducked, avoiding the fist of one while Adan whirled, evading Vincent. She clutched her dagger and sliced the air in front of her, but the Strength Wielder's momentum carried him out of range. From the corner of her eye, she saw Adan ducking around Vincent. Vincent was fast, but Adan faster. Her opponent rounded on her, picking up a rock as he did. He launched it, but she dodged the throw. When he rushed forward, swinging a beefy fist, she hit the ground, slicing out with her blade in a golden arc toward his calf. Blood blossomed from the shallow wound. She launched to her feet, and the Strength Wielder reached out to grab her. A soft whirl sounded at Evie's ear, and the shaft of an arrow sprouted from the Strength Wielder's shoulder. He stumbled back with a yell.

She didn't dare turn toward the forest to thank Chase. Instead, her grip tightened on her weapon, and she glanced to where Sam and Garran's fight had grown quiet.

Sam staggered forward, his lip bloody. Garran lay in a heap behind him, but the boy's chest still rose and fell.

Sam met her eyes and then shifted his attention to Joram, who lurked near the edge of the trees. Paling, Joram produced a short dagger from within his jacket. It trembled in his fingers.

"To the Strength Wielder!" Joram shouted.

Vincent abandoned Adan, and though the other guard still carried an arrow in his shoulder, he also obeyed. They lurched like robots toward Sam.

Joram relaxed and laughed, having not yet entered the fight. He twirled his blade and watched Adan and Evie. They both breathed heavily, sweat dripping from their bodies.

She cocked her head. Joram stayed back, remaining at the edge of the fight, always just out of reach. She glanced at the three Strength Wielders, their marks glowing brightly, and then back to the Deceiver.

He waits for them because he is afraid.

"Adan, he's afraid of you. He knows you're meant to be his end. He won't engage you in combat."

"Should we take the fight to him?"

She nodded, and they moved.

His smile faltering, Joram took a step back.

From the corner of her eye, Evie caught movement from the trees. Elias and Ben raced past, toward the unguarded portal as Sam had led the guards away. Asher must've circled around because he was already there attempting the activation sequence.

"No!" Joram shouted, still holding tight to his dagger. "To the portal!" he screamed to his Strength Wielders.

Sam had Vincent pinned, but the other guard barreled toward the archway. He'd get there first. Adan and Evie sprinted to intercept him, and Adan ducked under his outstretched arm, twisting the arrow shaft still protruding from his flesh. The Strength Wielder howled, but Evie cut his scream short as her golden blade buried to the hilt in his neck. He fell sideways, on top of Adan, who struggled to free himself.

Ben and Elias were almost to the portal when Elias tripped and sprawled onto the ground. "Go," he yelled to Ben, who had paused.

A glint of silver caught Evie's eye. Joram had lifted his blade, aiming for the boy. Ben froze openmouthed. There was no time to think, only to act as the Deceiver let it fly. The dagger flew end over end toward Ben's small chest. Evie flung herself in front of him, and with a sickening thud, Joram's blade buried deep into her stomach. Agony followed, and she loosed a scream as she fell onto her side.

"No!" Ben yelled as she landed and rolled onto her back. "Evie."

Adan dropped to his knees beside her, Ben at his side. His face ashen, Adan took in her wound. "No, no, no," he whispered to no one.

She touched the hilt protruding from her stomach. On a day, not so long ago, she'd wondered what it would be like to watch the blood drain from this body. It was more awful than she could have imagined.

The commotion seemed to pause as she lay bleeding onto the ground, surrounded by the golden flowers.

A river of blood and gold.

She met Joram's eyes, and even the almighty Deceiver froze, his eyes blinking rapidly.

"No. No, this is not how it was supposed to be." His hands hung at his side. "You sacrificed yourself for a mortal. Why would you do that?" He grabbed at his hair. "You will die.… You will die and be forgotten."

Ben took Evie's hand and whispered through his tears so only Evie and Adan could hear. "You can't die. You're not finished yet. Use the golden blade like Alizah said." He was pleading. "You have to."

Adan watched the boy, confused.

Evie's fingers twitched, and she was unable to speak around her pain. It was no use. All was lost. The Deceiver would win.

Ben tried again. He whispered, "His blood on the blade." Evie snapped her eyes to him. She tried to clear the fog from her brain.

Krystopher had said, "There may be a time that you will need it." What had he been speaking of before that? "I'm working on a new kind of portable blood portal."

Adan snatched up the blade and held it out to her.

Her knees curled in. "I can't. Adan, you have to do it. I–I think it's a blood portal. Activate it, then pierce him. The blood of Jesiah's Marked. It will send him back."

As, beside her, Adan fumbled with the golden blade, she reached trembling fingers into her pocket and then tucked Ben's wooden game piece—the Watcher—into the boy's open palm.

He held her hand as she let out a low moan and then tipped her head toward Joram. But a delicate yellow flower protruded from the ground in front of her face. It stood beautiful, unmarred even on this battle scene. Something lovely to focus on, throwing the one who'd deceived her into a dull blur in the background of this nightmare.

The flower was so beautiful, its dark center forming an intricate circular pattern. The same pattern on her back—the Maker's Mark. The same pattern on the flower the boy had given her in Sector Five, millions of light-years from here. The reason flowers always seemed so familiar to her. The Maker's hand did span the breadth of the universe.

Her eyelids fluttered and drifted together until all was dark and her agony complete.

48

Adan peered at the golden blade. He clutched the vine-etched hilt in a white-knuckled grip.

What do I do?

The black clouds thundered, and the breeze picked up, shaking the sand at his feet.

Behind him, the portal began to ripple and glow. Asher beckoned, but neither Ben nor Adan moved.

Joromy—no, Joram—ordered his guards to the portal.

Adan stood, positioned between the Deceiver and the archway. He faced Joram putting the otherworldly light at his back. Joram, now weaponless, squinted at the Dreamer and raised a hand to his brow, shading his face from the brilliance. To the Deceiver, Adan would be but a black shadow—a dark silhouette.

Joram's injured Strength Wielders limped toward the portal.

"Come on," Asher bellowed over the wind that cut around Adan.

Adan stroked this thumb over the golden vines gripped in his palm. In one place on the gleaming dagger, they met and swirled into a perfect circle. On *One's Raining Fire,* whose spine mimicked this dagger's hilt, the circle had once been a keyhole. Adan pressed a finger into it, testing. Nothing happened. As he tilted the blade, prisms within the space caught the brilliant light. He froze. The pinky finger of his marked hand twitched.

You have the key.

Adan fitted the dagger to the back of his hand, inserting the round face of the ring into the circle. The blade burst with light.

Joram ripped his attention from the portal as Adan took aim and loosed the gleaming blade. It cut through the brilliant light, flying end over end. With a revolting thud, it sank deep into the Deceiver's chest, near his shoulder.

Clutching at the hilt, Joram hit his knees with an earsplitting scream. His Strength Wielders slowed, blinking as his hold on them faltered.

Joram gripped the blade with both hands.

Adan sucked in a ragged breath, caught in a profound déjà vu. All this time, he'd dreamed of this. Sometime over the last three weeks, the dream had changed. It had been right all along. His interpretation of it, however, had been wrong. He was not the victim in this scene. The dream had begun to show it to him through the victim's eyes. Adan—a teenager from Sector Five, descendant of Nolan the Dreamer, foster kid, brother, friend, fighter—he was the wielder of the blade. He was the tall, dark-haired man who stood before the portal, lost in its ethereal light.

With another yell, Joram pulled the glowing blade from his body and dropped it to the ground. Light and blood poured from the wound.

The Deceiver laughed as blood dripped from his lips. "Your aim wasn't true, Dreamer. I only need a… Healer." But as he spoke, he lifted his hands, looking at them with incredulous fear.

"What have you done?" he whispered.

He glared at Adan with the kind of hate that reaches back to an unfathomable time. Louder, he bellowed, "What have you done?"

As the glow protruding from his side grew to a blinding light, Adan covered his eyes. Ben grabbed him around the waist and buried his face in Adan's side.

As quickly as it had surged, the light vanished. Darkness enveloped Adan, and his eyes fought to adjust. Only the portal's rippling light illuminated the sandy path.

When he could see again, he walked to where the Deceiver's body had been. He was gone. Not even a drop of blood evidenced his death. Only the golden dagger remained, spotless, reflecting the moonlight.

A moan broke the silence. Evie's body shook on the fine sand. On her side, she'd curled around the blade.

Adan rushed to her, eyeing Vincent, who gaped at the spot where Joram had been. Sparing only a glance at Adan, he melted into the twilight without a word.

Adan knelt beside Evie and clasped her bloody hand in his. "Evie," he whispered, his breath ragged. She was lost to her pain. He wiped tears from her cheeks and pushed damp hair from her face. With so much blood on the ground, she would pass from the sector soon. He should be glad to be rid of this beautiful liar, but the feeling didn't come. A tear raced down his cheek.

She'd come here—Jesiah's Marked, come down a mortal—to kill him, and now here they were.

He froze, breath hitching.

Jesiah's Marked.

Adan stared at Evie as her breath labored in shallow and erratic pants. He released her hand and sprinted toward the golden blade. Grabbing it up, he returned to her side.

"What are you doing?" Sam asked.

"I–I know she's not an immortal right now, but she *is* one of the Marked. She's dying anyway. If she goes back to the Control Room, maybe they can help her." Determined not to think too much about what he was doing, Adan again pressed the dagger's hilt to the enhancement ring. Light flared, and as a tear fell from his cheek onto hers, he drove the blade into Evie's side. She moaned and shuddered and then went deathly still.

Her eyes turned glassy. Her face an awful gray.

Adan checked for a heartbeat as her new wound blazed with dazzling light. Finding no movement, he shifted his fingers. Then he stepped back and shielded his eyes. Again, Ben buried his face in Adan's shirt.

When the light had vanished, Adan peeked between his dirty fingers. Fluffy pollen blew over the yellow flowers at the trail's edge and disappeared into the shadowy forest. All traces of Evie had vanished— whisked away by the blinding light.

Joram's and Evie's blades lay side by side at Adan's feet—not a drop of blood on them. Joram's weapon reflected a dull bronze color that might have once been gold. But those days had long since passed. Evie's dagger, however, caught the portal's golden light and shone like a beacon in the darkness, guiding its wielder home.

<<<<>>>>

"Is Evie dead?"

Adan glanced down at Ben, who dragged his feet on the damp asphalt. The boy held Adan's hand in a death grip, and dark circles curved under his eyes. How much sleep had he missed over these last weeks in Sector Six?

"I don't know," Adan said. "I–I may have killed her before she disappeared."

Ben scowled at the pavement as they trudged along the familiar streets to their apartment building. Moments ago, they passed through the portal into a parking garage, of which Adan had no memory.

His friends followed along in the early morning light. Sam took in the city like a long-lost friend. Chase, Asher, and Elias were quiet for once, limping through their bumps and bruises. And Garran—Garran was unreadable, his head bent and hands buried in pockets. But for the first time in ages, the lines of anger didn't mar the Strength Wielder's bruised face.

After all this time, the city's abruptness shocked Adan—the lights, the sounds, the cars. He jumped when a taxi whizzed in front of them with the blast of a horn. Pedestrians eyed their strange and bloodied clothing until Asher talked Sam into removing his ridiculous weapons belt.

What would become of James, Thomas, and Grace? A pang pierced Adan's gut, and he sucked in a sharp breath. He hadn't said goodbye. Would they join the rebels? Would they ever know he'd escaped? And now that the Deceiver was gone, would they remember the things he'd made them forget? Perhaps they'd help free those still in the castle and the jail. But Adan would never know.

When Uzziah's apartment building came into view, Adan released a long sigh and squeezed Ben's shoulder. The group took the elevator up, the soft music out of place among their dirty and bloody bodies. Adan grinned when Chase muttered, "I hate this song."

They trudged into the grand foyer, and Adan's mind wandered to the humble homes of Inevah. Even the castle wasn't as grand as this one building in downtown Shura.

"They're back," someone yelled from the training room door. "And they have Ben!"

Adan laughed as the trainees—and even Uzziah—barreled down the hallway, colliding with them.

Uzziah, with tears in his eyes, gripped Adan into a fierce embrace. Another wave of guilt blossomed. How many times had Adan suspected Uzziah of purposely setting him on this path?

The Guardian bent to hug Ben and then pushed him to arm's length. "I'm so happy you're okay. But you and I have things to talk about when everything's settled down. We've been looking everywhere for you."

Ben's eyes went wide as Uzziah moved on to greet the others.

Adan nudged his little brother. "What? All you did was sneak off through a secret portal to another world. No big deal."

Ben huffed a sigh.

Sam clapped Adan on the shoulder, smiling. "Good to be home. And glad to have you back… Dreamer."

Adan rolled his eyes. "If you're testing out a new nickname, forget it. Don't call me that."

Laughter shook Sam's chest. "We'll see."

"What now?" Adan asked.

"I'm going to go call my parents."

"I thought you were eternally mad at them."

His friend shrugged. "I may have gained a little perspective."

"Hey, the Dreamer's back." Todd moved to ruffle Adan's hair, and Adan bent to dodge his hand. "Guess you were okay after all. Any nightmares lately?" Todd snickered, waiting for Garran's reaction.

The Strength Wielder only gave Adan an apologetic shrug.

Adan sighed. How was it he'd been through so much and his dreams had even been helpful over the last weeks, but nothing had changed here?

Garran nudged him in the shoulder. "Hey, don't worry about him."

Adan nodded, his gaze locked on the floor. Garran didn't move away. "Look, I know you'll never forgive me for what I did, but for what it's worth, I'm sorry."

Adan's muscles froze.

"I won't try to say I wasn't jealous of your relationship with Uzziah, but that doesn't make it okay."

Garran, jealous of me?

Adan was the strange boy who had weird dreams and no money. The Dreamer lifted his gaze to this boy who'd sold him—sold him for a few bills to be taken to another world. It was no small thing.

But if Adan refused to forgive him, it would not only fester resentment within Garran but also open himself up for heartache. Adan had felt for himself the power of Joram's words. Any one of them could have succumbed to his whispers. Perhaps the presence of jealousy in Garran's heart made it that much easier for Joram to get Garran to do what he wanted.

"I do forgive you, Garran. I forgive you for everything. I'm not saying what you did was okay. But I am saying you and I are fine and I'm going to let it go. It does neither of us any good not to." Adan clapped Garran on the shoulder.

Garran smiled, and the tension left him, his big muscles loosening up. Adan felt it, too—felt the walls of a foolish, invisible prison fall away, and he breathed in the sweet air of freedom.

Later, Adan walked out of another apartment, in another neighborhood, on another side of town. This morning, he'd thought he couldn't wait another day to visit this address, but now, he wished he had.

Sam leaned against an iron fence across the street. When Adan approached, he said, "Well? How'd it go?"

Adan shook his head, and they pointed their feet toward home, leaving the rundown street behind. "Everything I had in my mind was wrong. She didn't have this perfect house with this perfect life. I always thought she'd get it together and decide to be a mom. She'd look for us and bring us home and make us dinner and marry someone great." Adan paused, choking on the words. "But that's not reality. She said she thinks about us a lot, but she never got clean, and she wasn't looking for us."

Sam clapped him on the back. "I don't know what to say."

"There's nothing to say. I'm just glad I didn't bring Ben."

"He'll want to come someday."

"I know." Closing his eyes, Adan exhaled. "And we will."

"Will you come back before then?"

"I don't know." Adan shoved his hands in his pockets. "Maybe."

They took the subway back to their neighborhood in silence.

When they emerged from underground and blinked into the afternoon sunlight, Sam reached into his jacket pocket. "I'm going to head back. Uzziah wanted me to give this to you after your visit." He pulled a folded paper and held it out to Adan. "I'll wait for you at home."

Adan took it, brow pinched, as Sam sauntered down the street.

Adan walked another block to his favorite park and found a seat beneath the statue of the outstretched hands holding the five perfect spheres. He carefully unfolded the fine paper and held it open before his eyes. An unfamiliar hand had scrawled across the parchment in black ink.

<<<>>>

Adan,

A family is made up of the people who love you and take care of you. I put you where you are. I picked them for you and you for them. You don't have to be related by blood for that to be true. You were not a mistake because you were made by the Maker, just like everyone and everything else.

You have fulfilled one purpose. Now go and find another. Your purpose in life can be found in many places. Sometimes purpose will be handed to you, and sometimes you have to seek it out. A purpose will change and stretch and grow as you move through life. You don't have to go far to find it, though you can. It may be big, or it may be small. All you need to do is look around you. Seek, and you will find.

I'm sorry your birth mother was not what you had hoped or imagined, but your purpose is not wrapped up in her, though through her you are related to Nolan the Dreamer. She never knew this truth. Forgive her and perhaps even get to know her, but remember, you are separate—set apart from her mistakes. Nobody's lineage is perfect, after all.

Krystopher

<<<>>>

That night, Adan sat on his bunk, surrounded by the snores of his brothers—his family. Ben tossed and turned in the bunk above him. Then the bed groaned, and the boy climbed down the ladder and crawled onto Adan's mattress. He sprawled out on top of the blanket next to him. He seemed almost asleep as he mumbled something that sounded a bit like *Alizah*. Adan chuckled. Ben rested a hand on Adan's arm, and almost immediately, the boy fell into a deep, peaceful sleep.

Turning away from Ben, Adan took up Evie's blade, which he'd hidden between his mattress and the wall.

Krystopher had made this. Its craftsmanship was perfect, though since it left Krystopher's hands, it had been in the care of imperfect people. With a finger, Adan traced the vines etched on the hilt. Its purpose was fulfilled—for now—until a new one came along.

He put the blade away and rested a hand under his head.

What dreams will come now? He could only imagine.

With a ready heart, he fell asleep thinking about golden eyes set in a pale face.

49

"What's wrong with her?" a familiar voice cut through the nothingness.

Evie shuddered, and a hard surface bit into her hip.

"Why's she lying like that?"

As the feeling returned to her extremities, she became aware of huddling on her side atop an unforgiving surface. Her arms curled over her middle.

Afraid of what she might see, she cracked her eyelids open.

No blade protruded from her belly.

No blood pooled beneath her.

Not a drop of crimson or a speck of dust marred her crisp white tunic. It had all left her in that mysterious space between worlds.

Only, a thin slash in the fabric remained where Joram's blade had found her. And another on her side. She touched her fingers to it.

"Evie?" came the voice again. She raised her head and lifted herself to sitting. There was no pain. Her body was in sync with her surroundings, but her brain struggled to catch up. *What happened?*

"Evie!" the voice said louder.

Her head snapped up to meet golden eyes set in a familiar face surrounded by strawberry-blonde curls.

"Al–li–zah?" Evie's voice cracked. When her friend smiled, Evie reached for her. As Alizah pulled her into a fierce hug, tears pricked Evie's immortal eyes.

Krystopher and several Sector Five employees stood nearby. Most smiled, but Krystopher frowned under a pinched brow.

"I can't believe you're here." Alizah laughed. "Joram said you were dead."

The grin slid from Evie's face.

Alizah's smile faltered. "What's wrong?"

"Joram is here?" Evie fisted her hands, her body tightening, coiling.

"Gavrie took him to get the debriefing paperwork."

Evie met Krystopher's golden stare. He watched her, a question in his eyes. The truth washed over her like the light from an opening portal. Krystopher had known all along—or suspected. He'd known when he sent her off with that golden blade.

A voice—a terrible voice—echoed along the pale-gold floor and into the Sector Five Travel Center. Evie couldn't make out the words.

Then Gavrie's booming voice answered, "You were not sanctioned to travel to Sector Six. The protocol for travel to that sector is particularly strict. What were you thinking?"

The room fell into silence as the others took in Evie's and Krystopher's grim expressions.

She rose to her feet atop the portal, standing taller than the others.

"I shouldn't have gone," the Deceiver lied. "I worried about Evie. I wanted to help her get those boys back home. If only I could have gotten to her before they killed her."

Her nails bit into her palms.

The door swung open, and Gavrie and Joram walked in.

Joram flipped through a stack of papers as he continued his poisonous speech. "It's lucky Krystopher sent that blood portal with her, or I may not have gotten away."

Gavrie stopped, noticing Evie. His eyes widened, and a brilliant smile cracked his lips. But it fell as he observed the tense room.

"Gavrie, aren't you coming?" Joram lowered the papers, his head tipping at the supervisor. When the Deceiver saw the man's face, he swung around to see what held his attention, noting Krystopher and each employee until his gaze landed on Evie. His golden eyes went wide.

She glared back, her breaths labored. Her fingers searched for her blade, but it wasn't there.

Joram cleared his throat. "Evie, you're okay," he said, falsely upbeat.

Her nostrils flared.

Gavrie's eyes narrowed. "What's going on?"

"Evie returned." Krystopher stepped forward.

"Evie, you suffered a lot on the ground." Joram rubbed the back of his neck. "Are you okay? You might have been hallucinating before you passed out." He looked around the room. "Anything she's said may have been fabrications of her mind."

Alizah, blinking as though still confused, moved to stand by Evie. "She hasn't said anything yet."

"Well, I—"

"Just stop," Evie cut Joram off. "Stop your lies. Stop your… deceit. It's over."

Alizah and the others gaped at the accusations.

Tsking, Joram spread out his hands. "See, I told you. Delusions."

Krystopher took another step forward, eyes never leaving Joram. "Three weeks ago, I sent a letter to a Guardian. I asked him to mark a boy on a particular day. No other person knew of the letter. It would only pass through one hand before it reached Guardian Uzziah, whom I trust implicitly. I trusted him so much I placed Nolan's descendant, along with my enhancement ring, with him five years ago. My premonitions led me to know the Deceiver's secret was nearing its end, and the boy—the one I marked—would be the one to reveal it. I sent the letter, I marked him in secret, and then I waited."

Joram paled, but he backed toward the doorway. "I don't know what you're talking about."

But another blocked it.

Jesiah stood, arms crossed, a profound sadness in his eyes. Power emanated from the Maker.

Joram swallowed and moved away as if he couldn't stand to be near such radiance.

"Please, Krystopher, continue," Jesiah prompted.

"Most believed the Deceiver to be a Gifted human who somehow acquired unnatural immortality. But I never believed it. I've long suspected the Deceiver to be an immortal with free access to the Control Room—even someone I trusted, perhaps. Someone who knew where Nolan and his family had settled in Sector Two. As you all know, they were killed. All but one, that is. And I never let anyone know she existed. And so Nolan's line remained. Though hundreds of years have passed since that time, the day was drawing near when I would trap the Deceiver."

Joram edged a step back.

Krystopher crossed his arms. "If my suspicions were correct, the Deceiver wouldn't be able to resist trying to obtain the boy to interrupt my plans. Our rivalry goes back to the beginning of time. I postponed the promotions and placed the letter into my suspect's hands, and then I sent him on his way. I had hoped it would not be you, brother. But you did as I expected, didn't you?"

Whispers swept the room as others discovered what Evie already knew.

"You went for the boy." Krystopher dropped his arms as Joram backed toward the control panel. "I intended to trap you as you did. But I didn't foresee outside interference."

Krystopher's hand swept toward Evie. "But this was what needed to happen. The Dreamer's visions told him what to do. The boy who would bring about your downfall stood before you, and you didn't even know... not until the end. It probably drove you mad trying to figure out what he was and why I had done what I did."

Krystopher rubbed a hand over his face. "You even sent Evie to Sector Six to retrieve him and take him home."

"That's not true," Evie blurted. All eyes snapped to her. "He didn't ask me to take him home. He ordered me to kill him."

A muscle twitched in Joram's jaw. Then he laughed, and resignation echoed in the hollow sound. "Ah, Krystopher, I knew this day must come." Hatred contorted the Deceiver's handsome face. "It's sad it took you this long."

Krystopher swallowed, not appearing smug in the least. If anything, he depicted heartbreak.

The hatred eased its grip on those handsome features as Joram reached as if to touch Evie before dropping his hand. "I wanted him dead, but I wanted to see what his purpose to Krystopher was first. So I sent you to the ground far away from him so I could have some time before you, the immortal warrior, took care of the problem. And later— after you made Guardian—I had hoped you'd work with me. We would've been great together."

Never! The word pulsed through her blood before exiting her lips. She stepped down from the portal. "I would never work with you."

His eyes darkened.

"So this is your confession?" Jesiah finally spoke up, his voice soft. "It was you? The Deceiver of the worlds."

Joram only backed another step into the room, away from the Maker.

"I will forgive you, Joram." Jesiah lifted his palms. "We can be as we were. Hurts can be mended. You need only ask, and it will be given."

"Never." Joram backed another step. "I will never ask your forgiveness. And I will certainly never give it."

His body jerked, and he yelled out. He reached over his shoulder to grab at the space below his neck. A burning stench filled the room.

His golden eyes blazing, Jesiah lowered his hands. "You no longer bear my mark."

Joram's jaw clenched, and a low, angry growl reverberated through the room. "So be it." He spun and typed a quick sequence in the control dock and rushed onto the portal.

The room exploded into movement, but it was too late. The portal rippled and shone.

Evie shielded her eyes as Joram faded to nothing.

<h1 style="text-align:center">50</h1>

Evie spent hours with Gavrie, Krystopher, and Jesiah, while they debriefed her of her time on the ground. They wanted to know everything Joram had said or done. They'd also debriefed Alizah.

When the Maker's Mark vanished from Joram's skin, Alizah and many others—including most Sector Six employees—had remembered things they'd forgotten. Joram had been using his mind-altering Gift on many in the Control Room. As with humans, his Gift didn't work well on everyone, and he'd aligned himself near those most susceptible. Krystopher didn't believe Joram's Gift was wiped entirely away when Jesiah destroyed the mark. But with it weaker, the Deceiver would work harder to persuade humans to his side.

During their debriefing, Alizah began to remember that Joram had assigned Evie the task of killing Adan. She'd witnessed it all. The Deceiver had then coerced Alizah to forget this.

"How were you able to talk to Ben from here?" Evie asked Alizah after Jesiah dismissed them to make the trek to their private quarters.

Alizah explained how Ben's extraordinary Gift allowed him to step into the Control Room's archive center whenever he slept. However, he had little control over his coming and going. If Alizah happened to be there when Ben arrived, they could talk as if they occupied the same space.

"Unfortunately, Ben didn't know much," Alizah said as their soft footsteps echoed down the quiet hall.

"But how did you know to tell me to use the blade?"

"A cryptic message with no explanation? Who do you think it came from?"

"Krystopher," they said simultaneously.

Alizah grinned and then shook her head. "Joram was thorough. The Sector Six Team found evidence he'd tampered with their detection system, so no other gifted people in Sector Six tripped an alarm."

"But then why did it detect Adan?"

"Jesiah thinks Krystopher's Dreaming Gift was too strong. It first detected Adan when he was dreaming. There must've been a surge of power. Joram didn't count on that. But he remedied the problem later because Adan never tripped the alarm again."

They arced to the side as three other Watchers passed by, making their way toward the Control Room.

Evie let out a slow breath and decided not to comment on their open stares. "I can't believe intersector portals are still out there—at least two. And based on what Joram said, I bet there are more."

Frowning, Alizah rubbed at her forehead. "Joram found the old plans for building a portal in the archives room. The ones Krystopher gave Nolan in Sector One. We can assume he has a copy."

"Krystopher the Truth-Speaker. I should've known. Of course, he gave Nolan the plans to build the first portal. It's Krystopher they celebrate during the festival." Evie laughed, but her smile fell. "Joram may have had the plans for the portals for a while."

"You're probably right." Alizah grimaced. "Ben has dreamed of the archives room many times. He may have heard Joram watching footage from Sector One's destruction."

Evie nodded, remembering the time in Sector Five when Ben had told her about his nightmare. No wonder the boy had been frightened. He'd witnessed the Deceiver's rage and vengeful plots.

The two friends parted, each intending to return to their own room. Evie tried to find some semblance of normal, but as the shock wore away and after an hour of pacing, she couldn't bear the perfect, stark space.

She approached the screen built into her mirror. "Is anyone in the training room?"

The silvery light flashed. "No, Evaniah, the training room is empty."

Perfect.

She made her way there and found comfort in practicing the defensive moves Morris and his people taught her.

What about Morris and Lena? What were they doing now? Were they already on another new adventure?

Sam, Ben, Adan, and the others had arrived safely in Sector Six. Would they be back at school tomorrow? Would life go back to how it had been before?

They'd all returned to their rightful place. Even Evie was in the Control Room as she'd wanted.

So why did she feel so rotten? So lonely? She shoved the humans from her mind by rocketing her fists into a punching bag. She kicked and jabbed, but her thoughts returned to Joram.

How had she been so wrong? He was one of her precious few friends here in the Control Room. He'd pushed her out the door to become a murderer. Or to be exiled.

After Joram's abrupt exit from the travel center, Jesiah declared the Deceiver forevermore banished from the Control Room. He'd tasked engineers with blocking Joram from all Control Room portals.

They'd attempted to discover his whereabouts—to no avail. Joram had tampered with the Sector Six portal and could very well be in any of the inhabited sectors. He knew the portal system better than anyone.

And he'd gone to the ground as an immortal. Their hunt could last eons.

She pummeled her punching bags. The emotions she'd been trying to keep buried bubbled to the surface as she worked her arms into a blur of motion.

Why am I not overjoyed? Why, when she was back in her immortal body, could she still remember how it felt when Ben rested a head on her shoulder? Or how Sam and Lena protected her, how Lena laughed at her terrible jokes, and how they'd called her family. And how it felt when Adan had brushed a strand of hair away from her face or smiled at something she said?

Tears began to stream down her face, and she yelled out. She steadied the bag and rested her forehead on it, then sank to her knees as great sobs erupted. She had never seen any Control Room worker cry. They probably thought it wasn't possible. They were wrong.

The door slid open, and she lowered herself to a sitting position with her back to the entrance. Hopefully, whoever it was wouldn't stay. She put her forearms on her knees, letting her head droop. She tried to catch her breath as she swiped at her tears.

Soft footsteps drew near until a lean figure settled in front of her. She raised her head and beheld Jesiah, the Maker himself, watching her with his steady gaze. She wiped her eyes again, trying to make herself presentable but couldn't hide that she'd been crying—certainly not from him.

He took in her red eyes but made no comment about her emotions. He watched her, his own golden eyes wide and bright.

Then he rested a warm hand on her shoulder. "Your tears are nothing to be ashamed of. They tell me you are not uncaring. You feel deeply." His smile seemed to glow, hover over her, and pour into her heart. "And that's precisely what I intended."

"What do you mean?" she whispered.

"When I created you, long after I created the other Watchers, I was hoping to find myself with a brave and caring soul who could sympathize with and care for the humans as I do. As Krystopher does." Pain etched on his face. "As I once thought Joram did. I do love the other Watchers, but something is missing in many of them. A human empathy—a capacity for forgiveness and redemption. The most human among us are the ones who go to the ground as Guardians. Did you know that's how we choose recipients of promotions?"

She sucked in a breath. "No."

"It is."

"Is that why you have asked Alizah?"

"Yes. But she refuses for her own reasons."

"Why?"

"If she's not told you, then you should ask her."

He pushed the rolled sleeves of his button-up shirt up his strong forearms. "You died for that boy… for all those human children. Or you would have if Adan hadn't sent you here. I've said it before, and I'll say it again: There's no greater love than to give your life to protect others. Evie, you have far exceeded my expectations."

Love? Was that why she did it? Was that what this was—this feeling lingering even in her immortal body? The slightest smile twitched her lips as she ducked her head. "Thank you, Jesiah."

If she were still in a human shell, she would feel a blush spreading over her cheeks.

But questions still needled her. "Joram said, when you created me, it was to mimic him and Krystopher, but something went wrong." She kept her head tucked down. "That I was a mistake and that you now have other plans for me."

Jesiah brought one knee up and draped an elbow over it. "I do have a job in mind for you if you would like it when the time comes."

Her head jerked up. "What's the job?"

"I'll tell you in good time." Again, his smile settled inside her. "But since Joram is free in the sectors, I have a different task for you."

He stood and offered a hand to help her up. "Come. I'll show you."

As they walked together toward the door, he returned to her other question. "And as for Joram's other admission, I assure you, you were no mistake. I didn't create you to be like Joram or Krystopher." He stopped her then, clasping her shoulders to look her in the eyes. "I created you to be like me."

Two days later, Evie stood, armed, upon the portal in the Sector Six travel center. Jesiah, Krystopher, Alizah, Gavrie, and a handful of others were there to see her off. The entire Control Room was in a buzz. They'd not seen so much occurrence in a millennium. For the first time since Jesiah closed the intersector portals, they were sending a Guardian to Sector Six.

Evie, however, would not be a typical Guardian.

She was to return to the ground and search for Joram and his resurrected portals. She wouldn't be bound to one sector as most Guardians were. Jesiah had given her leave to travel between them should she discover the pathway to do so.

Krystopher wrapped her in his warm embrace. He tucked something into her hand. A ring. "Once again, my visions aren't clear. This ring is not for you, though you may have occasion to use it. Another may need it. You'll know when."

Smiling at Krystopher—cryptic as ever—she tucked it into her pocket. "Thank you."

He backed away.

Alizah thrust a handheld communicator into her palm. "Don't forget to keep in touch." She squeezed Evie's hand. The two of them were to test Krystopher's latest invention—a beta communicator allowing Evie to talk to the Control Room as she traveled from sector to sector.

"Of course, I will." Evie pulled Alizah into a hug. "I'll miss you, friend."

Alizah backed away as Jesiah approached.

Anticipation thrummed in Evie's chest.

He took her offered hand and traced a swirling design over the back of her fingers and up her arm. His finger moved over her shoulder, above her sleeveless top, and around the Maker's Mark. Then, taking her other hand, he performed its mirror on her other arm and shoulder, completing the symbol to mark her as a Guardian. On her immortal body, there was no blister left to heal. When Jesiah had finished, the marks shone white against her skin.

"A Guardian's Gift is decided at the time I create them. Yours was suggested to me by Krystopher all those years ago. You may have noticed it in small ways on the ground. Do you know what it is?"

Her eyes went wide. "No," she breathed.

"You are a Healer, Evaniah."

Sam had told her he'd seen her glowing mark. One of Ben's assailants had nicked her with their blade. Later, she had no mark to show for it.

"This doesn't mean you cannot be killed or injured when you're in mortal form or you can bring a human back from the brink of death. Your Gift wouldn't have saved you from Joram's mortal wound."

Her throat bobbed, and she touched the silver blade at her hip.

"Remember, there are multiple ways to heal and more hurts than only the physical. Words and actions can heal a great many things."

The Maker moved away, and she stepped to the center of the circular portal. She'd programmed her human form to be the same as it was while she was in Sector Six. She wanted to look like herself and feel like herself as she had during her time there. She wanted to retain both her good qualities as well as her flaws—all the things that had made her, well, her. With an adjustment to her pack, she nodded to Krystopher, who activated the control panel.

She gave a final wave as her hands began to tingle.
She took a deep breath and smiled.
And then she was gone.

Dear Reader,

Thank you so much for reading *This Dreamer*! It means so much that you gave it a chance.

Are you looking for more clean books like this one? Me too! I'm always searching for books for my teenagers and for readers like you. Sign up for my newsletter, and I'll send **clean YA book recommendations** as I find them. (I'll also let you know when I have bonus material for This Dreamer!) Join here: sarawatterson.com.

And **don't forget to let booksellers know we would like to see more clean and wholesome teen fiction** by giving it a few stars and letting them know what you think—not just for this book, but for any clean book you or your kids read.

If you have questions about *This Dreamer*, the next book in the series, or writing, please email via the contact form on my website. I look forward to hearing from you!

Thanks,
Sara

Author's Note

This Dreamer is a Christian youth fantasy novel inspired by the Biblical story of Joseph found in Genesis chapters 37 & 39-47. Adan's path follows this arc. But, as you may know after reading this novel, I took many creative liberties. Evie's story is entirely fictional. She's a character born of some questions that popped into my mind as I read Joseph's story in Genesis. What if someone outside the story was to blame for Joseph's capture? What would their role have been? What if he or she was a guardian angel of sorts?

This led to other fantastical questions like, what if I wrote a book using only supernatural powers found in the Bible (healing, strength, wisdom, moving water, etc.), and what if God created more than one earth? I love the thought of a universe containing other planets with other people, all created by the one God, of course. I believe in the sanctity of scripture but also think exploring fictional stories with Biblical tie-ins is interesting.

I wrote pages and pages of backstory for my characters and this book's setting, the entirety of which could never possibly be included in my novels. Sign up for my newsletter at sarawatterson.com, and I'll let you know when I publish snippets of that information on my blog.

I've read other fantasy retellings where the author wove several fairy tale characters into one story, each book building on the next while also following one specific storyline. I thought, why can't I do that with a few favorite Bible characters? The events of this novel left the Joseph storyline somewhere around chapter 43. Adan and Evie will continue into Book Two of this series (I have much more to tell!), while I also layer a few new storylines into the plot. It will read as a retelling of Queen Esther mashed up with a portion of Samson's story.

I've already set these characters up for you. Can you guess who? Esther was an orphan living in a foreign land, raised by her uncle. If you guessed Estalena (Lena), you're on the right track! Read the book of Esther at bible.com if you're unfamiliar with the story. While you're there, read Samson's story found in the book of Judges, chapters 14-16.

Oh, and did you pick up that Nolan the Dreamer from Adan's golden-spined book represents Noah and his ark (Genesis chapters 6-9)?

Join my mailing list at sarawatterson.com, and I'll keep you updated on the next book and my other writing projects.

Acknowledgements

I want to thank my wonderful family for supporting me during this fun but very long process. Thanks to my husband Preston for being my biggest encourager. You're the one who consistently asked me, "what's your next goal?" or "did you meet your goal today?" Thanks for keeping me accountable (even if it occasionally got on my nerves). We both know you're the inspiration for Adan's piercing blue eyes and that oh-so-cute single dimple. xoxox

Thank you also to my kids for encouraging me and putting up with writing weekends and holiday editing. I love that I could incorporate all your names into this book. I love you so much and can't wait to see what God has in store for you!

A special thanks to my editor, Deirdre Lockhart. I'm sure you had no idea what you were getting yourself into with me! Thanks for teaching me so much, and sorry about all the clichés. You slashed them like a ninja!

Thank you so so much to my early readers: my mom, Dianne, my sister, Leah, and my bestie, Lori. Your feedback helped shape this novel into what it eventually became. (And thank you to my other sister, Amy, who was appropriately offended when I didn't ask her to be a beta reader. Though, we all know fantasy fiction is not your thing.) Love you all!

And a very special thank you to Stacy (another bestie) for being the very first to read This Dreamer. In fact, I think you read it twice before anyone else did. Your extensive notes, questions, and edits were invaluable to me, and your encouragement and accountability kept me going when I wasn't sure I could or would finish even a first draft. I absolutely could not have done this without you!

And thank you, Jesus, for equipping me with the time, the words, and the right people at the right time to get this thing done. These, among many other requests, were among my prayers during the long hours of writing, and you followed through. Every. Single. Time.

Sara Watterson is a fiction writer, author of young adult science fiction and fantasy.

Sara holds a BS from the journalism and mass communication department of Abilene Christian University. She teaches digital art to high school students while also managing her growing website, bookseriesrecaps.com.

When not writing, teaching, or enjoying her kids' myriad activities, Sara likes reading on the back porch, drinking coffee, and hanging out with her super-cute hubby. She lives in central Oklahoma with her husband and three children.

Stay up to date by joining Sara's mailing list here:

https://www.sarawatterson.com/

@sarawattersonwrites

Facebook.com/SaraWattersonWrites

Instagram.com/SaraWattersonWrites